THE TIGER'S PREY

Wilbur Smith was born in Central Africa in 1933. He was educated at Michaelhouse and Rhodes University. He became a full-time writer in 1964 after the successful publication of *When the Lion Feeds*, and has since written over thirty novels, all meticulously researched on his numerous expeditions worldwide. His books are now translated into twenty-six languages.

For all the latest information on Wilbur visit his author website, www.wilbursmithbooks.com. To learn about the work of the Wilbur and Niso Smith Foundation visit www.wilbur-niso-smithfoundation.org

🅕 WilburSmith
🅣 @thewilbursmith

Tom Harper is the author of thirteen thrillers and historical adventures including *The Orpheus Descent*, *Black River* and *Lost Temple*. Research for his novels has taken him all over the world, from the high Arctic to the heart of the Amazon jungle. He lives with his family in York. For more information about Tom's books, visit www.tom-harper.co.uk.

ALSO BY WILBUR SMITH

THE EGYPTIAN SERIES

River God
The Seventh Scroll
Warlock
The Quest
Desert God
Pharaoh

THE COURTNEY SERIES

When the Lion Feeds
The Sound of Thunder
A Sparrow Falls
The Burning Shore
Power of the Sword
Rage
A Time to Die
Golden Fox
Birds of Prey
Monsoon
Blue Horizon
The Triumph of the Sun
Assegai
Golden Lion
War Cry

THE BALLANTYNE SERIES

A Falcon Flies
Men of Men
The Angels Weep
The Leopard Hunts in Darkness

THRILLERS

The Dark of the Sun
Shout at the Devil
Gold Mine
The Diamond Hunters
The Sunbird
Eagle in the Sky
The Eye of the Tiger
Cry Wolf
Hungry as the Sea
Wild Justice (UK); The Delta Decision (US)
Elephant Song
Those in Peril
Vicious Circle
Predator

THE TIGER'S PREY

WILBUR SMITH

WITH
TOM HARPER

HarperCollins*Publishers*

HarperCollins*Publishers*
1 London Bridge Street
London SE1 9GF

www.harpercollins.co.uk

This paperback edition 2018
2

First published in Great Britain by HarperCollins*Publishers* 2017

Copyright © Orion Mintaka (UK) Ltd. 2017

Wilbur Smith asserts the moral right to
be identified as the author of this work

A catalogue record for this book
is available from the British Library

ISBN B-format: 978-0-00-753594-1
ISBN A-format: 978-0-00-823006-7

Set in Minion by Palimpsest Book Production Ltd, Falkirk, Stirlingshire

Printed and bound in Great Britain by
CPI Group (UK) Ltd, Croydon, CR0 4YY

MIX
Paper from
responsible sources
FSC™ C007454
www.fsc.org

This book is produced from independently certified FSC™ paper
to ensure responsible forest management.

Find out more about HarperCollins and the environment at
www.harpercollins.co.uk/green

I dedicate this book to my wife Niso,
who illuminates my life day and night.

I love you more than words can wield the matter.

The *Dowager* was carrying too much canvas. A warm monsoon breeze whipped the ocean into white peaks that glittered in the sun that shone from a sapphire sky. Her sails bulged, topsails and topgallants straining fit to snap their sheets. Her hull, heavy-laden, wallowed in the high waves rolling across the Indian Ocean. She was running for her life.

Her master, Josiah Inchbird, stood on the quarterdeck and looked astern at the ship following them. She'd appeared at dawn, long and low and sleek as a ravenous wolf. Red-painted gun ports chequered her black hull. She was gaining on them.

He checked the clouds of canvas flying overhead. The wind had stiffened; and the sails were straining at their seams. He dared not fly much more without risking disaster. On the other hand, disaster was certain if he did not take that risk.

'Mr Evans,' he hailed his mate. 'All hands to set staysails.'

Evans, a hollow-eyed Welshman in his late thirties, glanced

up at the sails and frowned. 'In this breeze, sir? She can't take much more.'

'Damn you, Mr Evans, but you'll get those sails bent on *now*. I'll hang our laundry from the yards if it'll get us another half a knot.'

Inchbird had spent twenty years sailing these oceans, working his way gradually up to command while lesser men with better connections had overhauled him at every turn. He'd survived voyages when half the crew had been buried over the side in their hammocks, in the pestilential ports of India and the Spice Islands. He wasn't going to jeopardize his ship now.

'What are you doing?'

A woman's voice, calm and authoritative, cut across the quarterdeck. Some of the crew paused, halfway up the ratlines. After three weeks at sea, the sight of a woman on the quarterdeck was still a spectacle they enjoyed.

Inchbird bit back the curse that rose naturally to his lips. 'Senhora Duarte. This doesn't concern you. It is better if you remain below decks.'

She glanced up at the sails. Her long dark hair blew out in the wind, framing a smooth olive-skinned face. Her body was so slim that it seemed a strong gust might have whipped her overboard. Yet Inchbird knew from bitter experience that she was not so frail.

'Of course it concerns me,' she said. 'If you lose this ship, we all will die.'

The men were still watching from the rigging. Evans, the mate, lashed out with his starter. 'Get on with it, lads, or you'll feel the bite of my rope end.'

Reluctantly, they began to move again. Inchbird felt his authority ebbing away as the woman stared him down.

'Get below,' he ordered. 'Do I have to tell you what pirates will do to ladies they capture?'

'*Deck there*,' called the lookout in the crosstrees. 'She's

2

running up her colours.' Then, so loud they all heard it on deck, 'Sweet Jesus.'

He didn't have to say any more. They could all see it: the black flag snapping from their enemy's mainmast and, a second later, the red flag at her fore.

'No quarter!' was the warning it gave them.

On the *Fighting Cock*, Captain Jack Legrange watched the flags snap taut in the breeze and grinned hungrily. They'd been shadowing the merchantman for three days, ever since they sighted her off Madagascar. She'd sailed late in the season, missing the convoys that most ships used as protection against the pirates who infested the Indian Ocean. The breeze had backed in the night and he'd crowded on more sail, betting that his ship could sail closer to the wind than the fat merchantman. The wager had paid off: they were now only a league or so back, and closing fast.

He looked down the length of his ship. She had started life as a Bristol slaver, plying the route from East Africa to the colonies in America and the Caribbean. Legrange had been first mate – until, one day, the master discovered him stealing and had him flogged. Next night, with the blood still soaking through his bandages, he'd led a gang from the forecastle and hanged the captain from his own yardarm. Then they'd sailed the ship to a deserted cove, where they'd cut down her forecastle and quarterdeck, stripped out all her partitions and bulkheads, and pierced a dozen new gun ports on either side. They'd sold the healthy slaves for a profit, saving a few of the prettiest for their own amusement; the unhealthy ones had gone over the side weighted with a length of chain – together with the ship's officers, and all the crew who refused to join them. Now she was a man-of-war in all but name, a hunter that could prey on anything except the largest Indiamen.

'Run out the bow chasers,' he ordered. 'See if she goes faster with a slap on the arse.'

'If she crowds on any more sail, she'll lose her topmasts,' said the mate beside him.

Legrange smiled. 'Exactly!'

His men started loading the bow chasers; long thirty-two pounders mounted either side of the ship's prow. The gunner fetched an iron brazier from below and lit the coals to heat shot. They wanted the prize and her cargo intact – but if she threatened to outrun them, Legrange would rather see her burned to the waterline than escape.

'What about that one, Cap'n?' asked the mate.

Far off on the starboard quarter, another sail danced against the horizon. Legrange found her with his spyglass and she leaped into focus. She was a sloop; a lean, flush-decked vessel flying along under topsails and jibs. He could see her crew gathered at the rail, watching and pointing. One man was holding a telescope trained on the *Fighting Cock*. Probably shitting his breeches, thought Legrange, and thanking God the pirate had a richer prize to prey on; for the moment at least.

He chuckled, and lowered the telescope. 'We'll finish our business with the Indiaman first. Then we'll catch up with that sloop and see what trade she has on board for us. But she won't trouble us for now.'

Tom Courtney lowered his telescope. The pirate ship, with her black and red flags billowing from her mastheads, receded to a diminutive shape on the horizon.

'The merchantman is piling on more sail,' he observed. 'She might outrun them yet.'

Light flashed from the pirate's bow. A second later, they heard the dull clap of cannon-fire roll across the water.

'Still out of range,' said the man standing beside Tom, as a plume of water rose a few cables back from the merchantman's stern. He was taller than Tom, his shoulders bunched with muscle as he moved. A pattern of scars covered his black face

4

with raised whorls and ridges, the ritual marks of the African tribe into which he had been born. He had known Tom since he was a small boy – and his father, Hal, before that. Yet his ebony skin betrayed not a wrinkle, and not a single grey hair showed on his shaved cranium.

'Not for long, Aboli. She has at least a couple of knots on that fat sow.'

'The merchant would have been wiser to surrender. We know what pirates do to those who resist them.'

Tom glanced behind him. Two women sat under the awning on the foredeck, making no attempt to hide the fact they were listening to every word the men said.

'I suppose we ought to leave the merchant to her fate,' he said dubiously.

Aboli knew what he was thinking. 'Forty guns to our twelve,' he warned. 'And at least twice as many more men.'

'It would be foolhardy to get involved.'

One of the women on the foredeck stood and put her hands on her hips, her blue eyes glinting. She was not conventionally beautiful: her mouth was too wide, her chin too strong and her flawless skin had been tanned a golden brown by the tropical sun. But there was a vivid, living quality to her, a lithe energy in her body and intelligence in her face that had smitten Tom the first moment he laid eyes on her.

'Don't be a ninny, Tom Courtney,' she declared. 'You really aren't going to leave those poor blighters to be murdered by pirates?' She snatched the spyglass from Tom and put it to her eye. 'I do believe there's a woman on board. You know what will happen to her if the pirates take the ship.'

Tom shared a glance with the man at the helm. 'What do you think, Dorry?'

Dorian Courtney frowned. The two men were brothers, though few would have guessed it. His skin had been tanned deep brown by years spent in the Arabian deserts. He wore a green turban wound about his red hair, and a pair of loose sailor's trousers with a curved dagger stuck in the belt.

'It doesn't sit well with me either.' He said it lightly, but they all knew the bitter experience that lay beneath his words. At the age of eleven, he had been captured by Arab pirates and sold into slavery. It had taken Tom ten years to find him again, ten years in which he had believed him dead. Meanwhile, Dorian had been adopted by a benevolent prince of Muscat, and become a warrior in his household. When Tom and Dorian finally met again, in the wilderness of East Africa, Tom had not even recognized him. They had come within inches of killing each other.

'It will not be easy, Klebe,' warned Aboli. Klebe was his nickname for Tom; it meant *hawk* in the language of his tribe. Aboli had his own reasons for hating slavers. Some years earlier, he had taken two wives from the Lozi tribe, Zete and Falla, who had born him six children. While Aboli was away on a trading expedition, Arab slavers had fallen on the village and captured its people. They had taken as slaves Zete and Falla and his two eldest sons, and killed all the infants. Four of Aboli's baby sons and daughters had had their brains dashed out against a tree trunk, for they were too young to be worth taking on the forced march to the slave-trading ports on the East Coast.

Aboli and Tom had hunted them across Africa, following the trail beyond exhaustion. When they overtook them, they freed Zete and Falla, with their two surviving sons, and took savage vengeance on the slave traders. The boys, Zama and Tula, were now grown almost to manhood, as imposing as their father though as yet without his ritual facial scarring. Tom knew they were desperate to earn the right to wear them.

'That merchantman's heavy laden,' said Dorian, as if it had only just occurred to him. 'That's a good cargo to collect a salvage fee on.'

Aboli was already priming his pistol. 'You know what your father would have said.'

'Do good to all men, but at the end remember to collect your fee.' Tom laughed. 'Nonetheless, I do not like going into battle with the ladies aboard.'

Sarah had disappeared below decks. Now she reappeared, carrying a gold-hilted sword, with a blue sapphire sparkling in the pommel.

'Are you going to wear this Tom Courtney, or must I do so myself?' she demanded.

The crash of another shot rolled across the ocean. This time, they saw the ball tear a piece of carving off the merchantman's stern.

'Good God, Mrs Courtney, I think the pirates would rather abandon all the gold of the Great Mughal's treasure fleet than defy your wishes. What do you say, Yasmini?' He addressed this to the lovely sloe-eyed Arabian girl standing behind Sarah. She was Dorian's wife, dressed in a simple full length dress and white headscarf.

'A good wife obeys her husband in all things,' she said demurely. 'I shall prepare my medicine chest, for no doubt it will be needed before you are finished.'

Tom buckled on the blue sword – the Neptune sword. It had been his father's, and his grandfather's before that. But it had originally been presented to his great grandfather Charles Courtney by Sir Francis Drake after the sack of Rancheria on the Spanish Main. With that sword, Tom had been dubbed a Knight Nautonnier of the Temple of the Order of the Holy Grail, like his ancestors before him – and he had used it to send countless men to the deaths they so well deserved. It was made from the finest Toledo steel, and the supple weight of the blade was perfectly balanced by the star sapphire in the pommel.

Tom drew the blade from its scabbard, and rejoiced in the way the sunlight danced off the gold inlay.

'Load the guns, Aboli. Double-shot them with partridge.' The small lead balls would spread out in a cloud to wreak havoc on all that stood in their way. 'Mr Wilson, bring her down three points to windward.'

The pirate's bow chasers roared again. One ball went wide; the other tore off a piece of the stern carvings, throwing up a cloud of splinters. Warm blood rolled down Inchbird's cheek from where one of them had pricked him.

'They're aiming for the masts.' The pirate had altered course fractionally, angling herself so that the *Dowager*'s masts presented themselves all in a row, like ninepins.

'That's a difficult target from this distance,' the mate demurred.

As if to give him the lie, a crack sounded from above. All eyes turned upwards – just in time to see a tangle of wood and canvas plummeting towards them. Men threw themselves aside. Some were too slow. The mizzen topmast struck the helmsman and shattered his skull. The ship started paying off to leeward. The topsail settled over the man's body like a shroud.

'Cut it away,' Inchbird shouted. 'We must free the steering.' Men ran with axes and started chopping at the shattered spars.

Another shot drowned his words, and Inchbird staggered in the disrupted air as the cannon ball flew over the deck, a foot in front of his face. He could feel his ship slowing as she came off the wind, slewing around. Her hull shivered; sails cracked and ropes snapped.

By the wheel, the crew had cut the sail free and were hauling it away. The canvas came away bright with the helmsman's blood. Beneath it, the wheel lay in splinters where the spar had struck it. It would take hours to rig a replacement, and they did not have that time.

Off the port beam, the pirate was closing fast, bearing off to come alongside. So close now, he could see the men gathered

8

on her deck. Some brandished their cutlasses aloft; others carried long, wicked pikes.

Inchbird gritted his teeth. 'Stand by to repel boarders.'

The *Fighting Cock*'s helmsman brought her alongside the *Dowager*. The men aloft reefed her sails, while the rest of the pirates massed at her side, balanced on her gunwale and clinging to her stays and shrouds. The ships knocked and rocked as their yardarms touched. Only a few feet of open water separated them now.

Legrange leaped up onto the rail. This was almost too easy, he thought complacently. Looking down onto the merchant's deck, he could see it was deserted. Her crew must be below, frantically trying to hide their valuables. A wasted effort: he'd soon have them screaming, begging to tell him where they'd hidden every last dollar.

He raised the speaking trumpet. 'Strike your colours and prepare to receive boarders.'

His men jeered. Legrange ran his eye along the row of the merchant's guns, and saw that all of them had been abandoned. They'd make a useful addition to the *Cock*'s arsenal. Or, more likely, he could refit the *Dowager* and add her to his flotilla. With two ships, all the oceans would be his. He grinned wolfishly at the thought.

A flash of colour caught his eye: an orange glow, like sunlight gleaming on metal near the breech of one of the guns. He peered at it. It wasn't sunlight. It was the flame of a burning slow-match worming its way into the touchhole. Quickly he scanned the row of cannons and his blood froze. Every gun was loaded and shotted, and aimed at him.

'Get down,' he bellowed. The unmanned guns crashed out a point-blank broadside, grape shot laced with carpenter's nails that pulverized the bulwarks and cut down the front rank of his men in a chaos of blood and pulped human flesh. A cloud of splinters tore through the line of men standing close behind and threw them to the deck. The awful silence that followed was immediately shattered as the *Dowager*'s crew poured out of her hatches and companionway armed with muskets and pistols, clambering up on her quarterdeck to fire down on the survivors of the carnage. As quickly as the pirates clambered to their feet, musket balls knocked them down again. The *Dowager*'s crew cheered as the ships began to drift apart.

Legrange's prize was slipping away. But the *Fighting Cock* had carried over two hundred men; the *Dowager*, even at full strength, had fewer than a hundred. For all the losses the pirates had suffered, they still outnumbered their prey. All they needed was courage.

With a howl of pure fury, Legrange grabbed the dangling end of a rope that had come loose in the broadside. Wrapping it around his wrist, pistol in his free hand, he clambered back onto the rail.

'No quarter,' he roared. He swung across the open water, through the smoke that still hung in the air, and landed on the *Dowager*'s deck. One of the sailors, seeing him coming, dropped his spent musket and reached for a sword. Legrange shot him point-blank in the face, discarded the pistol and drew another from his belt. Another sailor stumbled towards him. Legrange shot him too, then drew his sword.

All along the *Dowager*'s side, grappling irons and bare feet thudded onto the deck as Legrange's men followed him aboard. Splashed with the blood and guts of their shipmates, they swung out of the smoke that choked the air. The *Dowager*'s crew was almost immediately overwhelmed. Even after the broadside, the pirates still heavily outnumbered them – and they were in a savage mood for what had just overtaken the rest of their crew. One by one, the *Dowager*'s crew were cut down, until only a small knot remained herded below on the poop deck. Some of the pirates, seeing the battle won, ran below to begin the looting. The rest surrounded the *Dowager*'s men at the stern, prodding them with their cutlasses but making no effort to kill them. They knew their captain would want to take his time, to exact slow revenge for the defiance they had showed in resisting.

Legrange strode across the bloody deck, stepping over the corpses of the fallen. 'Which of you is the captain?' he demanded.

Inchbird shuffled forward. Blood soaked his shirt from a cut on his arm. 'Josiah Inchbird. I am the master.'

Grabbing his shoulder, Legrange pulled him forward and threw him to the deck. 'You should have surrendered,' he hissed. 'You made us work for it. You should not have done that.'

He pulled the knife from his belt and pressed the blade against Inchbird's cheek. 'I'm going to skin you alive, and then I'll feed your guts to the sharks while you watch them eat.'

The men around him laughed. Inchbird squirmed and pleaded.

'We've spices and calicos from Madras in the hold, and pepper in the ballast. Take it all.'

Legrange leaned closer. 'Oh, I will, you can be sure of that. I'll pull your ship apart, every plank and bulkhead, and find every last dollar you've hidden. But I'm not going to punish you for that, but for your defiance and for what you did to my men.'

A commotion from the companionway distracted him. He turned around, as two of his men emerged from below decks dragging a prisoner between them. The men at the stern hooted and whistled as they saw it was a woman, clutching the neck of her dress where it had been torn open. They dropped her on her knees in front of Legrange.

'We found her in the captain's cabin, trying to hide these.' One of the pirates opened his palm and let a handful of gold coins spill over the deck. The others whistled and cheered.

Legrange cupped her chin in his hands and lifted her face

to force her to look at him. Dark eyes stared back at him, brimming with hatred and defiance. He'd soon change that, and he grinned happily at the thought.

'Fetch me the brazier,' he ordered. He pulled her up by her hair so she was forced to stand, then gave her a hefty shove. She stumbled backwards, tripped on a rope and sprawled on her back. Before she could move, four of the pirates pounced, spread-eagling her arms and legs and holding them down.

Legrange stepped over her. He slit open her skirts with the blade of his sword and his men spread them apart. The woman twisted and writhed, but the men had her pinned tight. Legrange pulled the skirts further apart, exposing her creamy thighs, and the dark tuft of hair where they met. The men whooped and cheered.

He glanced at Inchbird. 'Is she your wife? Your doxy?'

'A passenger,' grunted Inchbird. 'Let her go, please sir.'

'That will depend on the ride she gives me.'

Two men came with a brazier on an iron tripod. The coals glowed dully. He stirred them with the point of his sword until the steel glowed red. He lifted out the smoking blade and held it over her. He looked into her deep brown eyes. Now there was no defiance – only terror.

A thin smile curled his lips. He lowered the blade towards the junction of thighs, letting it hover inches from her woman-hood. She'd gone very still, not daring to struggle for fear of touching the sword. Smoke rose from the glowing steel.

He darted it at her and she screamed, but it was a feint. He'd stopped the blade a hair's breadth from her parted genital lips. He laughed. He hadn't had this much fun since the last of the slave girls had died from his attentions.

'Take it,' she pleaded. 'Take the cargo, the gold, anything you want.'

'I will,' Legrange promised her. 'But first, I'll take my pleasure.' The tip of his sword had cooled. He plunged it back into the brazier until it glowed hotter than ever, then held it in front of her eyes. Sweat beaded on her forehead. 'You see this? It won't kill you, but it'll make you hurt more than you ever thought was possible.'

'Go to hell where you belong,' she hissed at him.

Her defiance only whetted Legrange's appetite. He liked a woman with spirit – so much more satisfying when she finally broke down. He licked his lips and tasted blood. From below decks, he heard shouts and the clash of arms, but he was too caught up in his sport to pay it any heed. Probably his men quarrelling over the loot. He would deal with them later.

He wiped his mouth with the back of his free hand and said softly, 'I'm going to burn you, woman. I'm going to burn you, and then I'll have you, and then I'll give you to my men to finish any way they like.'

'Ship your oars,' Tom ordered quietly. All eight dripping oars slithered inboard, as the *Centaurus*' jolly boat came under the pirate ship's black hull. Tom eased off the tiller. He didn't look up: all his concentration was fixed on bringing the boat alongside as silently as possible. In the bows, Aboli and Dorian trained their muskets up at the *Fighting Cock*'s deck, where a swivel cannon was clamped ominously on the gunwale. If any of the pirates had stayed aboard the pirate ship and had not crossed over to the prize, he could churn them to mincemeat with that weapon.

Tom looked back at the *Centaurus*, standing off about half a mile away. The pirates hadn't noticed her – or were too busy with their pillage to bother with her yet. He'd left only two men aboard with Sarah and Yasmini. If they failed here then the women were doomed. He put the thought out of his mind.

The bows of the jolly boat touched the pirate ship with barely a whisper. Aboli grabbed on to her steps and gestured upwards. Tom shook his head. Near the waterline, a row of hatches studded the pirate's hull: too low to be gun ports. He realized that they were probably ventilation hatches, a remnant from her days as a slaver.

Tom took the knife from his belt and worked it into the seam of the nearest hatch. When the slaves were aboard, it would have been padlocked from the inside, but the pirates would not bother with niceties such as that. His blade touched the latch inside. He jimmied upwards.

The latch gave. He swung the hatch open and peered in at the gloom of the lower deck. No one challenged him. With Aboli holding the boat steady, he wriggled through. The others followed him, passing their weapons ahead of them. Aboli, with his broad shoulders and powerful body, struggled to squeeze through.

The lower deck was cramped and close. Tom crouched, and still nearly hit his head on a beam. He moved among the piles of stores and plunder the pirates had stored here, working his way towards the light coming in through the gratings from the main deck. Dorian and Aboli followed close behind with the rest of the crew men from the *Centaurus*. Among them was Alf Wilson, who had sailed with Tom's father; and Aboli's two sons, Zama and Tula. Their eyes shone white in the darkness, hardened to fury by the evidence they saw of the ship's slaving past. All of them knew too well that in other circumstances they might have found themselves chained to the iron rings that still protruded from the wooden walls, carried across the ocean to be sold like animals to the colonists in the Caribbean and America; always supposing that they survived the voyage. They fancied they could still smell the residue of suffering and human misery leaching from the planks.

Tom shinned up the aft ladder and cautiously put his head through the hatch. He'd come up under the quarterdeck, near the mizzen mast. Out in the burning sun, only dead men lay sprawled across the main deck. All the living had gone across to *Dowager* to plunder her.

Tom beckoned for his men to follow him up onto gun deck. He pointed to one of the long guns, its muzzle protruding out through the open port and pressing right up against the other ship's hull.

He snapped an order. 'Run that in.'

Zama and Tula leaped to the tackles that held the gun to the ship's frame. Alf Wilson and the other men joined them, and together they hauled it back. It rumbled in on its trucks, leaving the gun port an open square of light. Tom stuck his head through. The two ships moved together, their hulls knocking when they touched. A thin strip of clear water sparkled between them.

He unbuckled his sword belt. 'Anchor me, Aboli.'

With Aboli grasping his legs, he wriggled out through the gun port until he could touch the other ship's side. This far back, she had no gun ports: he found himself opposite her stern windows, looking into the captain's cabin. He could see figures moving around inside behind the glass, ransacking the interior to carry off anything valuable. He froze, but they were too intent on their work to notice him in the deep shadow between the vessels.

'Give me a hand with this,' one of them called. 'It's bloody heavy.'

His voice came clear through a broken window. As Tom watched, another man joined him. Together, they lifted a strong box and carried it out the door.

The cabin was empty. Tom stretched as far as he could, glad of Aboli's powerful arms belaying him. He reached through the jagged hole in the glass, careful not to cut his wrist, and undid the latch. He pushed the window open.

'Let go,' he whispered to Aboli. He grasped the window sill and hauled himself through. A pile of cushions broke his fall,

15

their covers slit open and their stuffing ripped out in the pirates' search for valuables.

Aboli passed Tom's blue sword through the window. Tom buckled it on and checked the priming of his pistols as the others crawled through one by one. By the time they were all in, the cabin was so crowded they could barely move.

A roar of laughter sounded from the quarterdeck above. Tom wondered what was happening.

The door swung open. A pirate stood there. He must have been looting the wardroom, for he carried a fistful of silver spoons in one hand, and a candlestick in the other.

'What are you doing? This is mine.' And then, as he took in the strange group assembled there, 'Who the bloody hell are you?'

There was no room to swing a sword in the cabin. Aboli extended his arm, blade in hand, and ran the pirate through the neck. He dropped to the floor clutching his throat. Blood gurgled through the wound. The spoons and candlestick clattered to the deck.

'On me, *Centaurus*!' Tom ducked through the door out onto the lower deck. It was a scene of utter carnage: men hauling bales of cloth from the hold, tipping out seamen's chests, spilling precious spices across the planking. Further forward, some had broken open a cask of rum and they were drinking from the bunghole.

None had their weapons in hand. Most didn't see the men emerging from the cabin, or didn't realize who they were.

The *Centaurus*' boarding party rushed at them. Dorian and Aboli were experienced warriors, veterans of countless fights. Zama and Tula, who had grown up with tales of their father's wars, fought with the ferocity of young men given their first taste of battle. Alf Wilson and the rest of the crew had followed the Courtneys into more contests than they cared to remember. They knew precisely what they had to do.

16

The pirates barely realized what was happening to them, before most were felled without a fight. A few tried to protect themselves with whatever came to hand – navigation books, tankards or bales of cloth – but they were cut down swiftly. From the corner of his eye, Tom saw Dorian pressing forward with sharp, precise movements. One of the pirates had a knife in his hand. Dorian disarmed him with a flick of his sword, turned the blade and slid it between his ribs and through the pirate's heart. With a twist of his wrist, the sword came out cleanly, in time to punch the steel guard into the next man's face. The man reeled back, and Dorian stepped forward and ran him through.

But a few of the pirates had managed to escape up the forward ladder. 'Up on deck,' shouted Tom. Some of the pirates above must have worked out what was happening. If the pirates battened down the hatches, Tom and all his men would be trapped between decks.

Tom shot up the companionway, taking the blood-slicked steps three at a time. A man appeared at the top; Tom drew one of his pistols and shot him left-handed. At that range, he couldn't miss. The man toppled towards him. Tom sidestepped him, took the last steps in a single bound and landed on the main deck.

With his senses heightened by the rush of battle, he took in the scene at once: the knot of prisoners corralled at the back, surrounded by armed pirates; the captain on his knees, bleeding from his face and arms; and the woman pinned down on her back, skirts spread, with a bearded pirate holding his sword between her thighs.

Tom raised his second pistol and fired. Too quick: the ball went wide of the mark and hit one of the men behind. The pirate captain jerked up. With a snarl of rage, he raised his sword to stab it through the woman beneath him.

Another shot rang out. Dorian had come up beside Tom.

Smoke blew from the pistol in his hands; the pirate captain dropped his sword and stumbled back, bleeding from his wrist.

Tom grinned at his brother. 'Good shot, Dorry.'

'I was aiming for his heart.' Dorian jammed the spent pistol in his belt, and swapped his sword back to his right hand. A pirate lunged at him with a pike. Dorian sidestepped the blow, caught the man off balance and lunged with his sword. It took him in the centre of his chest and the blood-smeared point appeared a hand's length from between his shoulder blades.

Aboli had already cut his way back onto the quarterdeck. Tom followed him up the ladder. Another fierce melee boiled across the ship's stern. With cries of 'huzzah' and '*Dowager*', the merchant's crew had turned on their captors. They were unarmed, but the pirates were off-guard. Some had gone to join the looting; others had been too busy watching Legrange toying with the woman. Some of them had put down their weapons, and now they were caught from both sides. Sailors wrestled swords from the pirates, or grappled them so closely they couldn't bring their weapons into play. Tom moved through the melee, searching eagerly for the pirate captain.

His foot caught on something. His eyes flicked down. It was the woman he'd seen earlier, curled into a ball, holding her torn skirts around her. Nearby, he saw a smouldering brazier sitting on the deck, utterly forgotten as the fighting raged around it.

Even in the heat of battle, Tom felt a spike of alarm. Fire was every sailor's worst fear – the one thing that could reduce a ship to black ash in minutes.

Aboli had seen it too. He picked up the brazier by one leg and hurled it over the side, onto the pirate ship. Hot coals skittered across her deck. One came to rest against a pile of rope, but with all the uproar aboard the *Dowager*, no one noticed it.

Tom stood over the woman, threatening off anyone who

came near, still scanning the throng for the enemy captain. The men from *Centaurus*, the crew from the *Dowager* and the remaining pirates were all locked in mortal combat. More pirates emerged from below deck like rats: they kept coming, fighting with a ferocity he'd rarely seen equalled. Men who had everything to lose.

And then, like a shift in the wind, the pirates started to give way. Space opened in front of Tom, space to lunge and strike. He advanced, cutting down men as they ran from him. For a moment, he didn't realize why they were running. Then he smelled it. It was not the acrid tang of gunpowder that had stampeded them, but the powerful choking scent of burning wood and tar.

Caught between determined foes and a burning ship, the pirates raced to get back to put out the fire that was sweeping through their own ship. Tom skewered one just as he made to leap from the *Dowager*'s side. He toppled into the gap between the ships and was crushed between their hulls. Tom looked across. Black smoke billowed out of the *Fighting Cock*; flames licked over her gunwale and started running up her stays.

'Cut her loose!' Tom yelled. If the fire jumped across to the *Dowager*, they'd all burn and drown. Zama started cutting away the grappling ropes with his boarding axe. Two of the *Dowager*'s men grabbed cutlasses that had fallen on the deck and joined him.

The flames ran higher. Still the ships remained locked together. Looking up, Tom saw the *Dowager*'s yardarms caught in the pirate's rigging, forming a high bridge between the two ships.

'Give me that axe.' He grabbed it from Zama and ran up the ratlines. Dorian followed him.

He swung himself around the futtock shrouds and out onto the yard. As master of his own ship, he rarely went aloft any longer, but he had not lost the knack. He ran to the end of the

19

yard and started hacking away at the tangle of lines and shrouds that had snagged it. The fire burned beneath him, jumping so high it looked as if the flames were licking the soles of his boots. Smoke made his eyes water. Dorian joined him, kneeling on the yard to cut away a block that had jammed on the clew-lines.

Still the ships stayed fast in their mutual embrace.

'Why won't she go?'

Dorian pointed to a piece of tackle that had wrapped itself in the braces. He took the boarding axe from Tom and moved towards it.

Something struck the yard. Tom felt the vibration even before he saw the hole gouged in the side of the spar, just by Dorian's foot. Down through the smoke, Tom saw the pirate captain lowering the musket he had just fired.

He means to kill us both, he thought. Without hesitating, he ran to the very end of the yard and leaped across into the *Fighting Cock*'s shrouds, swung around and grabbed for a stay. He slid down so fast he burned the skin of his palms, bracing himself as he landed hard on deck. In the smoke and chaos, no one noticed him. Her crew rushed about with buckets, trying to put out the blaze; others were trying to lower her long boat, which hung cockeye on its moorings.

Legrange was reloading the musket. Tom hurled himself at him. They both went down, the musket trapped under Legrange's body. Legrange bucked and tried to throw him off, but Tom's weight pinned the pirate down, while he reached for the knife in his stocking.

Under him Legrange reached out blindly, scraped his finger-nails across the deck, trying to find a weapon. They closed around a handspike lying forgotten under the carriage of one of the cannons. With all his strength, he swung his arm back and slammed the iron spike at Tom's head. Tom saw the move-ment just in time. He rocked back, so that the spike glanced off his shoulder – but that gave Legrange all the space he needed to free himself. He rolled out from under Tom and came to his feet. He snatched up the fallen musket and aimed it at Tom. He pulled the trigger.

The flint struck sparks from the steel. Tom flinched – but the musket had misfired. With a howl of fury, Legrange reversed the musket and came at Tom again, swinging the weapon by its barrel.

Wind whipped the smoke away. Behind Legrange, Tom saw that the two ships were drifting apart. Dorian had cut the *Dowager* free. He had to get across to her – but Legrange was blocking his way, brandishing the musket like a club. Tom edged backwards, ducking to avoid the pirate's furious blows. The fire was taking hold; most men had abandoned any attempt to fight it and were instead trying to save themselves. Still Legrange came on, too quickly to allow Tom any chance to pick up a weapon from the littered deck.

Tom took another step back – and came up short against the ship's side. He vaulted up onto the gunwale, just avoiding another wild swing of the musket.

Balanced on the narrow ledge, he darted a glance at the water below him. The ship was drifting down wind. If he fell he realized that he would be pushed under her hull and cut to ribbons by the razor-sharp barnacles that coated her bottom. That was if the sharks did not get to him before that happened.

Legrange knew it too. He paused a moment to savour the situation. He didn't know who Tom was, where he had come from or how he had got aboard, but he knew he had cost him his prize – and probably his ship also. Snarling with fury, he lunged at Tom with the musket to force him overboard.

Tom anticipated the blow, and jumped backwards off the gunwale. To Legrange's astonishment, he did not drop into the waves below but he swung out into space, flying out from the ship's side as if he had sprouted wings.

Legrange had not noticed the taut halyard attached to the ship's yardarm high above, that Tom had seized hold of. Tom reached the limit of his arc and started swinging back, gathering speed as the ship's hull rolled and gave him impetus. He pulled his knees up onto his chest and then shot them out as he swooped back at Legrange. Both his booted heels slammed into the pirate's forehead, driving his head back so hard that clearly Tom heard his vertebrae snap. Legrange staggered backwards with his legs giving way under him. He fell into the leaping flames that were sweeping across the deck towards him. They engulfed him instantly. For a second, Tom had a hellish vision of Legrange wreathed in fire. His beard, hair and clothes alight and the skin of his face blistering and shrivelling.

Tom swung out over the water on the halyard, and when he reached the limit of its arc he released his grip and dropped into the water. With powerful overarm strokes he covered the distance to the *Dowager* easily, before the sharks could scent the blood on him. Dorian was waiting on the bottom rung to give him a boost aboard.

'Where are Sarah and Yasmini?' Tom gasped, before he had fully recovered his breath. Desperately he scanned the waters around the *Dowager* and then exhaled with a great sigh of relief as he saw her well clear of the burning hulk of the *Fighting Cock*.

Tom switched his attention back to the pirate ship. Pillars of fire engulfed her masts and ran along her yards, devouring the canvas and outlining her in flame. Men hurled themselves into the water, flames leaping from their backs. The pirates who had been trapped aboard the *Dowager* fared no better. The crew were in a savage mood: they'd been given no quarter, and they offered none now.

'We should lower a boat,' said Dorian, pointing to the pirates floundering in the ocean. Screams rang out across the water as the sharks closed in on them.

'It would be no mercy, rescuing them so they could be hanged in Cape Town,' Tom pointed out.

Just then an enormous explosion sucked the air out of their lungs, then blew it back in an angry breath. A huge wave rocked the ship and sent the men staggering across the deck. Burning debris rained down on the roiling waters. But the *Fighting Cock* had vanished. All that remained were charred timbers settling on the water.

Tom pulled himself upright. There was no point searching for survivors now. Any men in the water would have been knocked unconscious and drowned by the force of the blast.

'Her powder magazine must have caught.' A weather-beaten man joined them at the ship's side. He'd lost his coat; and he was bleeding from his arm and an open wound on his cheek. Even so, Tom recognized the air of command that was imprinted on his face.

'Are you the master of the *Dowager*?'

'Josiah Inchbird.' The man nodded at the remnants of the *Fighting Cock*, the wide field of flotsam spreading across the water. 'Good riddance to her and the thieves that sailed in her.'

Tom waited for him to pass comment on the battle, to acknowledge the help he'd received. But Inchbird said nothing further.

'It was lucky we were in sight when you were boarded,' he said pointedly. 'We saved your ship.'

Inchbird took his meaning at once. 'You'll get no salvage,' he warned sharply.

'Your ship was overrun by pirates. You'd surrendered,' observed Dorian.

'I never surrendered.'

'Then you gave a convincing impression of doing so.'

'If you want to press the matter, you can take it to the Admiralty court in London.'

Tom swallowed. He had left England fifteen years earlier as

23

a fugitive from justice, wanted for the killing of his eldest brother, Billy. A black-hearted man, quick to fury, Billy had tried to kill Tom in a midnight ambush on the Thames docks. Tom had killed him in self-defence, not recognizing him in the dark, but that would count for little in an English court. If he went back, all he'd face would be the hangman's noose.

Inchbird couldn't have known that, but he sensed Tom's weakness. 'If you wish to pursue the case, I will gladly give you passage to London aboard my ship.'

'I risked my life to save your ship.' An excited chatter arose from the sailors on deck. The *Centaurus* had come alongside, and Aboli was helping Sarah and Yasmini aboard. 'I risked my crew, my ship, and my family,' Tom insisted.

Inchbird softened his tone. 'You must understand, sir, my hands are tied. If I concede anything now, without consulting my owners, I will never see another command. For myself, I would gladly give you everything aboard for what you did. But for that, you will have to ask the supercargo.'

Tom nodded. The master was responsible for the ship, but the contents of her hold belonged to the supercargo. 'Then I had best speak to him.'

Sarah and Yasmini climbed the ladder to the quarterdeck. Sarah put her hands on her hips and looked around the carnage on deck.

'The trouble with men,' she declared to Yasmini, 'is that they always leave things in such a mess.' She turned to Inchbird. 'I apologize if my husband has caused your ship any distress.'

Inchbird gave an awkward bow. 'We were just discussing that very matter.'

'Your husband saved us all,' said another voice. The woman Tom had earlier rescued from Legrange came up the companion-way. Her voice was low and husky, tinged with an accent Tom couldn't place. She'd changed into a new dress from the one Legrange had sliced open with his sword. It was a

simple blue calico that mirrored the sea a̶̶̶̶̶̶̶ᷛ
just below her full breasts. Her hair was tied back in a ribb̶̶̶̶̶
with a stray wisp floating just above her neck. She couldn't be
much past twenty, but there was strength and wisdom in her
face beyond her age. Every man on deck stared at her. An hour
ago, they'd seen her most private parts exposed, but she bore
their attention now with unflinching equanimity.

'I hope, Captain Inchbird, you have not forgotten your
manners,' she said. 'These men saved our lives, and I do not
even know their names.'

Tom gave a little bow. 'My name is Tom,' he said. 'My brother,
Dorian; his wife, Yasmini; and my wife, Sarah. I am glad we
could have been of service.'

'I am Ana Duarte. And those pirates would have robbed us
of everything.' A small shudder rippled through her body. 'I
understand why Captain Inchbird cannot offer you salvage for
his ship. But I do not want you to think we are ungrateful.
Whatever the pirates left of our goods, please take what you
feel is fair recompense.'

Tom waited for Inchbird to protest. However the captain
had gone curiously silent.

'I'm glad of your concern, ma'am, but I fear the supercargo
may not like you being so free and easy with his goods.
Especially if he is of the same mind as Captain Inchbird here.'

She tilted her head. 'They are my goods.'

'Yours?'

'I am the supercargo.'

'You?' Tom could not hide his astonishment.

Sarah jabbed him in the ribs with her elbow. 'Tom Courtney,
you great booby. You've traded up and down the coast of Africa
with every chieftain, brigand and cannibal you could find to
take your goods. And now you are flummoxed to find a woman
who can trade?'

Ana and Sarah shared a glance – some intuitive under-

25

standing that made Tom feel dull and dumb. Caught between them, he didn't notice the strange look Captain Inchbird shot him when Sarah spoke his name.

Sarah looped her arm through his elbow and tugged him away. 'Come,' she said sweetly. 'Miss Duarte has suffered enough for today without having you gawping at her. Let us choose a couple of bales of cloth, to pay for our powder and shot, and then leave these good people to continue their voyage in peace.'

In fact, it took the rest of the day and the next before they parted. Sarah and Yasmini tended the wounded, while Tom, Dorian and Aboli helped Inchbird's men repair damage to the *Dowager* and jury-rig a fresh topmast. She had lost almost half her crew, and *Centaurus'* men were needed to help splice her rigging and splint her masts before she could get underway again.

'But we can make Cape Town, if the weather holds fair,' said Inchbird. 'And there I can find a replacement crew to get me home to London.' Much remained to be done, but Tom could feel Inchbird's eagerness to be left alone with his ship, and he respected that. They said their farewells and cast off. The wind freshened. As night fell, Sarah and Tom stood at *Centaurus'* taffrail and watched the sun sink towards the hidden African continent in the west.

'You're thinking about that Duarte woman,' said Sarah.

Tom started. 'I am not.'

'If only we had a son, she's the sort of woman I would want for his wife.'

Tom hugged her to him. Ever since they had married, he and Sarah had tried desperately to conceive. A few years ago, she had become pregnant while they were trading on the Lunga river; Tom had felt their life was about to become complete. But she had miscarried, and since then, despite all their efforts, her womb had remained barren.

26

'Do you ever wish you'd stayed in England?' she asked. 'Married a nice Devon girl and settled down at High Weald with a dozen children?'

He stroked her cheek. 'Never. Anyway, High Weald belonged to Black Billy.' Under the laws of primogeniture, the entire fortune passed to the eldest son. Billy, already married to the wealthiest heiress in Devon, had hastened their father to his grave to get his hands on the inheritance, though he had not lived to enjoy it.

'The estate will have passed to Billy's son Francis.' Tom paused, remembering a red-faced baby cradled in his mother's arms. 'I suppose he must be fully grown now, and lord of High Weald.'

Sarah smoothed her skirts against the stiffening breeze. 'Time deals unkindly with us all, Tom Courtney.'

He stared at the horizon, where the last tongue of sunlight licked the sea. Waves hissed along *Centaurus'* hull as it carved through the water, south-west to Cape Town at the southern tip of Africa. The town which was the closest thing he had to a home since he had been driven from High Weald. In Cape Town they would refit and re-provision, sell their goods and buy more – and then many months later another voyage would begin.

He sighed. He grudged nothing in his life, but he had not forgotten how it had felt growing up: the big old house, the chapel with so many Courtneys buried in its crypt, the servants who had nursed his grandfather and whose children would one day serve generations of Courtneys yet unborn. The sense of belonging, that however far the family tree might spread, it remained rooted strong and deep in that place. He had cut himself off from it, and not yet found new soil in which to replant himself.

He put his arm around Sarah and kissed the top of her head.

'I wonder whatever became of baby Francis,' he mused.

* * *

27

Rain lashed the big house. A high wind howled around its turrets and gables, slamming the loose shutters on their hinges. All the windows were dark, except for the last room on the upper floor.

There, in the master bedroom, a single candle guttered and flickered on the mantelpiece, casting monstrous shadows around the vast room. Wind howled down the chimney, rattling the dead embers in the grate. Two figures sat in chairs drawn up beside the fireplace, though the fire had died hours ago, when the last of the coal ran out. A woman stitched her embroidery, while a young man pretended to read a book by the meagre light. It had been opened on the same page for the last fifteen minutes.

The woman gave a little cry. Her son looked up.

'Are you all right, Mother?'

She sucked blood from her finger. 'It's so hard to see in this light, Francis.'

Alice Leighton – once Alice Grenville, later Alice Courtney – looked at her son, touched by the concern on his face. Not yet eighteen, his body was fully grown, big and strong. But there was a softness in his heart that made her worry for his future out there in the wide and wicked world. His jet-black hair framed a handsome face with smooth amber skin and lustrous dark eyes. A rebellious black forelock curled over his forehead, almost touching his left eyelid. She'd seen the way the girls in the village looked at him. It was the same way she'd looked at his father, once upon a time.

The shutters flapped and banged, like the devil himself hammering on the door. Francis closed his book, and rummaged in the grate with the poker. All he stirred was ashes.

'Do you know where Father is?'

His father – his stepfather, technically, though the only one he'd known – had spent most of the last week locked in the library, going through papers he would not let them see. The

28

one time Francis had tried to go in to him, Sir Walter had cursed him and slammed the door.

Alice put down her embroidery. Her dark hair was streaked with premature grey, her eyes sunken, her grey skin drawn tight across her cheeks. Francis still remembered when she'd been beautiful and gay. His earliest memories were like that: his mother returning from some ball or party, coming into his nursery to kiss him goodnight, her skin radiant and her eyes sparkling. He could almost smell the scent of her perfume as she leaned over his bed, her peach-soft skin against his cheek and the diamonds glittering at her throat in the candlelight. The diamonds had been the first to go.

A bang echoed through the empty house, shivering the floorboards and making the coals rattle in the grate. Francis leaped to his feet.

'Was that thunder?' said Alice uncertainly.

He shook his head. 'Nor the shutters, either. It came from downstairs.'

He went down the long gallery and descended the great staircase. Wax dribbled from the candle and scalded his fingers: there were no silver candlesticks in High Weald any longer. He paused at the foot of the stairs and sniffed the air. He knew the smell of gun smoke well enough from game shooting, and watching the local militia at drill, but he'd never smelled it in the house before.

Dread rose in his chest, and his heart began to pound. He hurried crossed the hall to the library door. 'Father?' he called. 'Father is all well with you?'

The only answer was the rattle of rain on the windows. He tried the door handle, but it was locked. He knelt, and put his eye to the keyhole. The stub of a key in the lock blocked any view inside.

'Father?' he tried again, louder this time. His father had been drinking almost without pause these last two weeks. Perhaps he'd lost consciousness.

29

Putting the candle aside, he reached in his pocket for his penknife and opened the blade. Then he pushed it gently into the key hole and fiddled the key, until he heard it drop on the floor inside. The old door had a good inch gap beneath it. He found a riding crop hanging on the hat rack in the corner of the hallway. Reaching with the tip of it under the door he was able to slide out the key.

He unlocked the door and opened it. The candle pushed back the shadows as he advanced across the long room. As a child, he could remember sliding across the polished floorboards. Now they were rough and splintered; they hadn't been polished in many years. Empty bookcases lined the walls; the books had been sold like nearly everything else. He could see shadows on the plaster where shields and swords had once displayed the proud crest of arms and armorials of the Courtneys. Like the silver and cut glass, all of it had been sold.

At the far end of the room stood an old oak table, covered with papers and an open bottle of wine. No glasses or decanter. His father lay slumped in the chair behind it, as if he'd fallen asleep. A dark red pool spread across the papers.

Francis paused. Then, all in a rush, he ran to the figure and threw him back in the chair. Stronger than he'd intended: the chair tipped over and fell. His father sprawled backwards and crashed onto the floor, one arm outstretched towards the pistol that lay nearby.

Francis fought back the nausea that rose in his throat. 'Father?'

Sir Walter Leighton had been handsome, once, before his addictions ruined him. Even in death, his face still bore a trace of that irresistible energy Francis remembered so well; the man who would fling him into the air as a boy and catch him, who would bet him a guinea to jump a fence on his horse, or propose a sudden trip to London. Now his lifeless blue eyes stared up at Francis, as if pleading for forgiveness. From the front, he looked completely untouched. Only further back could you see the edges of the jagged, bloody wound where the pistol ball had blown his brain out through the back of his head.

A short, shrill scream sounded behind him. He spun around to face it. Alice was standing there, her hands raised to her mouth, staring at the body on the floor.

'I told you to wait upstairs,' said Francis, horrified that she should have to see this. He ran and wrapped his arms around her, holding her face to his shoulder to block the sight.

She sobbed into his shirt. 'Why did he do it?'

Francis steered her to one of the leather wingback chairs and made her sit down, where the desk top hid the body from her. She pulled her shawl tight around her, and didn't try to follow when he went back to the table.

Francis grabbed the topmost paper from the pile and held it up to the light. It was a letter from a solicitor, a firm in London he'd never heard of. He read through the orotund legal phrases, struggling to understand. One paragraph leaped out at him.

If you fail to discharge these debts by midnight on the nineteenth of October, I shall have no alternative but to send bailiffs to seize the said property, including all fixtures and furnishings, in satisfaction of the same.

'They are speaking about High Weald,' Francis realized. 'That's tonight.' He looked at the clock on the mantelpiece. It was later than he'd thought. The steeple bell in the little chapel on the hill would already have struck eleven, though he hadn't heard it over the storm. Horror dawned on him. 'They'll be here within the hour.'

He looked down again at his father's corpse. Anger rose inside him, driving out the sorrow he'd felt. It had been so long, he couldn't remember when he first realized his father was a compulsive gambler. The way silver disappeared from the chest without explanation, only to reappear equally mysteriously some

31

months later. The card parties in the drawing room he was never allowed to enter, that went on so late he could hear them still going when he woke the next morning. His stepfather's swings of mood: drawn and silent for weeks at a time, then bright and merry and bringing presents into the house for Francis and Alice. The strange men who arrived on the doorstep at all hours, watched by Francis from behind the banisters on the upstairs landing. The rows afterwards, Alice screaming at him behind the closed bedroom door.

But he'd never realized it was this bad. A frantic banging erupted from outside, and for a moment he thought the bailiffs had already arrived. But it was only the shutters again. A glance at the clock said he had fifteen minutes left.

'We have to go,' he cried. He pulled his mother to her feet and led her upstairs again, locking the front door as they passed. Her face was pale, her hand cold as glass. 'Get your things together, whatever we can carry.'

Listlessly, she went to her wardrobe and pulled out some dresses and petticoats. Francis went to his room and filled a bag with his few possessions. He could almost hear the seconds ticking past.

He ran back to his mother's room and found her sitting on the four-poster bed surrounded by her clothes.

'Come on,' he said fiercely. 'They'll be here any minute.' He started stuffing her clothes into a bag. 'If only my father—'

'Don't call him that,' she whispered. 'Sir Walter was not your father.'

'I know that. But you always said I should call him—'

'I was wrong. I married him because I was a widow and you needed a father. After William died, my family disowned me; they didn't even attend his funeral. My father hated me for marrying a commoner, even from a family as rich as the Courtneys. Then the circumstances of William's death, the scandal that attached to it . . . He never forgave me.'

32

'You never told me.'

'You were an innocent child who had already suffered too much. Sir Walter Leighton was loving and charming and he made me laugh. I didn't recognize his true character. Just as I didn't know your father, until it was too late.'

'But you always said my father – my true father, William Courtney – was a good man. A kind, noble man.'

Her face crumpled. 'Oh Francis, those were all lies. I could not bear for you to carry the sorrow of knowing what sort of man William Courtney was. A black-hearted brute who almost danced a jig when his own father died; who beat me black and blue, and would have beaten you too if he'd lived. He almost killed his own brother, Thomas.'

Francis' legs felt weak under him. He sat down hard on the bed. Angry tears pricked his eyes. 'No. It was Thomas who killed *him*. You told me, Mother. *You told me.*'

'Yes, that was true. Tom did kill William,' she admitted. 'But it was self-defence.'

'Were you there?' Francis demanded. 'Did you see it?'

'William went to London and never came back. The story went about that Tom had killed him, but I knew if that was true, he must have been provoked. Tom couldn't have killed his brother in cold blood.'

Francis struggled to breathe. 'He must have.'

A sudden, clamorous hammering sounded from downstairs, and this time there was no mistaking it: the sound of a heavy fist on a heavy door. Francis heard muffled shouts, and the rattle of someone trying to turn the handle.

Alice clasped him to her. 'You are nearly of age, now. It is time you learned the truth of things.'

'You're lying.' He shook her off and grabbed the bag. Another furious bout of knocking came from downstairs. 'I have already lost one father tonight. Now you are trying to destroy the memory of the other.'

33

'Open up,' called a voice, loud enough to impose itself over the storm. 'Open in the name of the law.'

Francis moved to the bedroom doorway. 'We have to go. If they find us here, they will take everything.'

'I will stay.' Alice wrapped her shawl tightly around her. 'They will not leave a poor, grieving widow without any succour or shelter. And with Walter dead, they cannot pursue his debts so easily. As for this house, let them have it. Excepting you, my darling, it has brought me nothing but misery and loss.'

He stared at her. Emotion choked his thoughts; he wanted to speak, but no words would come.

'Open up,' shouted the voice below once more.

Francis ran. He slipped down the back stairs, through the silent kitchens and into the stable yard. The grooms and stable boys had all been dismissed; the thoroughbreds he had ridden as a boy had long since been sold to new owners. Only one horse remained, Hyperion, the chestnut gelding his stepfather had given him on his thirteenth birthday. Alone in his stall, he whinnied as he heard Francis approach.

Francis lit a lamp and saddled him, working quickly. It wouldn't be long before the bailiff's men worked their way around to the back of the house, looking for a way in. He grabbed an oilskin cape from a hook on the wall and led Hyperion out into the yard.

A figure stood there, waiting for him.

'Mother?' His anger melted away at the sight of her, a grey apparition in the stable yard. Her soaking dress clung to her slender frame, like a little girl lost in the rain. She held a small velvet bag.

'I couldn't part from you without saying goodbye.'

He hugged her. 'Goodbye, Mother.'

'Where will you go?' She had to shout in his ear to make herself heard over the rain.

He hadn't thought about it until that moment – but the moment he did, he knew the answer.

'The only family I have left in the world is my uncle Guy, in Bombay. I will go to the East India Company in London, and ask them for a position, and passage in one of their ships.' He glanced back at the great house, so pregnant with memories. 'Perhaps I will make my fortune, and return one day to reclaim High Weald.'

She twisted the drawstring of the little velvet bag in her fingers, trying to hide the pain in her heart at the thought of her only son going so far away.

'It is a good plan. But be careful with your uncle Guy. Strange to say, when you were two years old you were the largest shareholder in the East India Company outside its Court of Directors. Your grandfather Hal had amassed more than twenty thousand shares, and when William died so soon after his father, they all came to you. They were to be held in trust, but Guy advised us to sell them. I followed his advice, but since then I have always wondered if he dealt honestly with us. If we had kept those shares in a trust, Walter could never have touched them. Once we converted them to cash . . .'

She sighed. Whatever William's faults, he had left her one of the richest widows in England. In the fifteen years since, her second husband had turned that inheritance into nothing but debt and regret. How could she ask Francis to stay? There was nothing for him here. Sir Walter had seen to that.

'Take this.' She handed him the velvet bag. Rain had soaked the fabric, but he felt something hard and heavy inside. He opened it.

After the poverty of the past months, it was like a vision of heaven. By the light of the stable lamp, he saw that it was a large golden medal depicting a lion with a shaggy mane. It was holding in its paws the globe of the world, with diamond stars shining in the blue enamel heaven above.

'What is this?'

'The order of St George and the Holy Grail. The Courtneys have worn it for more generations than I can count. Now it belongs to you.'

'But . . .' He struggled to take it in, like a starving man confronted with a banquet. 'This must be worth a fortune. The diamonds alone . . . If we sold it, we could keep High Weald.'

'No.' She held his gaze. 'This is the honour of the Courtneys. Wherever you go, whatever you do, never lose it.'

Shouts sounded nearer, around the side of the house. She folded his hands around the bag and kissed him.

'Go. The man to see in London is Sir Nicholas Childs. He was a friend of your grandfather's, and he is still a powerful man in the East India Company. If there is any man alive who can help you, it is he.'

Francis had been to London many times as a boy, but always with his parents, travelling in a well-sprung carriage with a coachman to clear their way with a crack of his whip, and footmen to fetch and carry at every stop. Now, the journey took almost a week, long slow days struggling against boggy roads and relentless autumn weather. He slept in ditches, tethering Hyperion out of sight behind hedgerows, terrified lest anyone should come across him and find the red velvet bag under his shirt. One morning, near Salisbury, he was woken by a gang of Sheriff's men, who called him a vagabond and a horse-stealer, and chased him across several fields until he finally escaped. At Richmond, he spent his last few coins on a bag of oats for Hyperion, and a mug of small beer for himself. By the time they reached London, the horse was almost lame and Francis was caked with mud.

The city terrified the horse: the crowds and noise, the carts and carriages rattling over the stones. He had to dismount and lead Hyperion by his bridle, whispering comfort in his ears. In the busy streets, most people ignored him, but he saw the way others looked at him, a shabby boy with such a fine horse. His cheeks flushed as he read the suspicion on their faces; he had never felt so alone.

At last he found a livery stable. The ostler gave Francis one look and declared he must pay in advance. The fee would be five shillings.

Francis patted his pockets. 'I have nothing.'

'Then I've got nothing for you.'

'Please.' Night was falling, and the thought of trudging around this hostile city any longer was too much to bear. 'I can find the money tomorrow.'

A sly look came over the ostler's face as he took the measure of Francis' desperation. 'You could sell the horse.'

Francis started in horror. He opened his mouth to reject the offer, but the words wouldn't come. What had he expected? If he were going to make a new life in India, he would never be able to take Hyperion with him.

Tears pricked his eyes, but he refused to cry.

'How much?'

'Not for myself. I'll find a buyer. He can stay here, until I do.'

Francis wrapped his arms around the horse's neck, and pressed his face against its mane. Hyperion whinnied, glad to have the familiar smells and sounds of the stable yard around him again.

'Can I at least have a bed for the night?'

The ostler looked him up and down. 'You can sleep in the stables.'

Francis slept badly and woke early. He washed himself as well as he could in water from the trough, and brushed the mud off his clothes with a horse brush. It didn't help much. Walking down Cheapside, he caught his reflection in the shop windows and grimaced. His dark hair stuck out at all angles, his eyes were rimmed with purple bags like bruises, and he had a week's adolescent stubble darkening his cheeks. His clothes were tattered, and though the horse brush had taken off the worst of the muck, the mud had left deep stains all over the fabric. His big toe poked through a hole in his right shoe.

He was going to call on one of the richest men in London. Sir Nicholas Childs was the man who had built the East India Company from a small company of merchant adventurers into a behemoth that governed half the world's trade. Francis had known the name for as long as he could remember – though if ever he or his stepfather mentioned it, his mother always changed the subject.

It seemed half of London knew the house on Leadenhall Street, and he obtained directions to it readily. At ground level, there was nothing very remarkable about it. Wooden shutters and a pair of heavy, studded doors hid the interior from casual passers-by; the only ornament was a pair of ornately carved oriental columns flanking the doorway, and a liveried porter. But if you raised your eyes, you would begin to notice details that suggested something grander. On the first floor, a wooden balcony fronted the street, with glass galleries behind; above it, a royal crest stood large and proud on the second-storey wood-work. Above that, so far up you had to crane your neck, the cornice had been painted with a gaudy mural, ships under full sail on a bright wave-flecked sea, flanked by dolphins and crowned with the statue of an honest Elizabethan sailor, scanning the spires and chimney pots of London.

Anyone who didn't know might have mistaken it for a chandler's yard that had misplaced itself in the city. In fact, it was the headquarters of some of the most powerful men on earth.

Francis hesitated, screwing up his courage. He approached the porter.

'Please inform Sir Nicholas Childs that Francis Courtney

wishes to see him on urgent business.' Anxiety made the words come out higher than usual. He wished he didn't sound so childish.

The porter stared down his nose at him. 'Sir Nicholas Childs is busy today. And Sir Francis Courtney died in the reign of good King Charles.'

'I am his great-grandson. And please, I must speak with Sir Nicholas.' He tried to push past, through the great studded door. A stout arm blocked his way and pushed him back into the street.

'Sir Nicholas is not receiving visitors.' The porter emphasised every syllable with a jab of his finger on Francis' chest. 'And if you keep obstructing this door, I will have you charged with vagrancy.'

Francis retreated across the street, into the shadow of a coffee house. Through the windows, he could see men sat around tables in earnest debate, studying newspapers and sipping steaming cups of coffee. Nothing but glass between them, but it felt like another world.

A wave of powerless rage rushed through him, shaking him to his bones. There had been times, in the past few years, where he had felt as if he had nothing. He had never realized how much he had. Now he saw, with the bitter clarity of despair, how hopeless he had become. Nothing was possible without money. Lack of it had killed his stepfather, parted him from his mother, and cost him his home, his horse – everything except the clothes on his back and the emblem around his neck.

He looked at the men inside the coffee house again and imagined himself among them, regaling his fellow merchants with tales of investments recouped, profits taken and vast fortunes made in the Indies. Whatever was required to join their company, he would do it. He would sail to the far side of the world, suffer any hardship and risk any hazard. Even kill a man or many men, if he had to do that to succeed, though the thought made him tremble. He swore that he would win his fortune, or die in the attempt.

He settled down to wait. Every time the door to the coffee shop opened, the smells from inside made his mouth water. As the morning wore on, people began to walk past carrying steaming meat pies and hot pastries. He felt faint. The bag around his neck weighed heavier and heavier: so valuable, but he could not think of selling it. He thought about returning to the inn, to see if the ostler had sold Hyperion, but he didn't want to miss a possible meeting with Sir Nicholas.

He had no idea how he would recognize him. His mother had said Childs was a friend of his grandfather Hal, so he must be of a great age by now. He watched the comings and goings at the house on Leadenhall Street. Older men in immaculate wigs, younger men stooped under the weight of bulging satchels of books and documents. Each time the door opened, the porter stepped out and glared at him, but he didn't cross the street. Once, Francis thought he saw a man studying him from the shadows of the first floor balcony, but he retreated inside before Francis could get a good look at him.

The October day wore on. Shadows lengthened; the coffee house emptied. The church bells started chiming for evening prayer. Francis began to wonder where he would go that evening, and where he could eat. He had forgotten his noonday dreams of fortune and trade. All he wanted was a meal. He touched the velvet bag that bulged slightly under his shirt. He'd seen a pawnbroker's near the inn: surely he could get a good price there. Only for a few days, until he had the money from Hyperion. The thought made him feel ashamed of his weakness.

Lost in thought, Francis didn't see the porter hurrying towards him until he was halfway across the street. He was carrying a hotcake wrapped in a napkin.

'I've been watching you all day. You haven't eaten a thing.'

Francis almost snatched the cake out of his hands. He buried his face in it, too hungry to taste the sweet flavours of sugar and almonds filling his mouth.

He was so busy eating, he didn't notice the two men who had accompanied the porter across the street. The first he knew was stout hands seizing his arms, another hand over his mouth and the porter holding a stick across his throat. He choked. The cake fell half-eaten to the ground and was trampled under hobnailed boots.

He struggled, but he had no chance. The porter and his men bundled him across the road and inside the building; he couldn't even cry out. If any of the passers-by noticed, they knew well enough to keep on walking.

The house was much larger inside than it had seemed from the street. The men dragged Francis down a long corridor, thick with the smells of cloves and pepper, then up many stairs. Francis heard laughter and conversations, but all the doors were closed and no one looked out.

The men brought him to a great door on the top floor, with a brass handle shaped like a snarling lion. The porter knocked respectfully. Even he seemed to hesitate before opening the door, as if approaching the lair of a fearsome beast.

It was dark inside, the air hot and damp like a greenhouse. A small fire burned in the grate, and a candle burned on the vast desk by the back wall, but they cast little light on the curtained room. The walls seemed to lean in, huge paintings of ships and battles hanging floor-to-ceiling in ornate gilt frames. The air smelled rotten, as if a slab of meat had been left too long and forgotten. Francis searched the gloom but didn't see anyone: only a large mound behind the desk, like a heap of discarded laundry.

His captors let him go and doffed their caps. Caught off balance, Francis stumbled forward and almost fell. He rubbed his throat.

A wet, rasping cough sounded behind the desk. The heap began to move. It was a man, Francis realized, as his eyes adapted to the gloom. It was an enormous, great-bellied man with a blanket over his knees and a silk dressing gown wrapped around his shoulders. His neck had disappeared beneath a cascade of wobbling chins. His head was shaved, but badly, so that white hairs sprouted out like the spikes on a thistle. Broken veins mottled his sagging cheeks. Only his eyes, sunk deep in folds of flesh, remained bright and alive.

'Who are you?' he demanded. He did not rise. In fact, Francis thought, he was probably not able to do so. Later he learned that the iron rings hanging from the arms of his chair, were there to enable him to be carried on the rare occasions when he left this office. They said that when he was at stool, it took three men to lift him onto the privy, and wipe his backside when he was finished.

One of the guards stepped up and slammed his fist into Francis' stomach. 'Answer when Sir Nicholas speaks to you,' he barked.

Francis tried to speak, but the blow had winded him badly and no words would come.

'Who sent you? Was it Norris and his Dowgate men?'

'Who?' Francis gasped. 'I know nobody with that name.'

'Do not play the fool with me, boy.' Sir Nicholas twitched his head and another blow struck Francis hard in the guts, doubling him over. 'You have been watching this house all day. Who were you spying on?'

'I'm not—'

'Was it those damned interlopers? They know the consequences if they attempt to steal my trade. I will burn their ships and see them rot in an Indian prison if I catch them.'

'Please,' said Francis, as another blow jabbed into his kidneys. 'I am Francis Courtney. My mother sent me.'

Sir Nicholas' face was crimson with rage. 'What impudence is this? Sir Francis Courtney died near fifty years ago.'

'My great-grandfather.' Francis fumbled for the velvet bag inside his shirt. The guard saw him and though he was reaching for a weapon. He kicked Francis' legs from under him, dropping him to the floor, and aimed a kick at his ribs.

Francis pulled out the bag. The guard snatched it from him. He jerked the drawstring stretched open, and the golden medal of the lion holding the globe in its paws fell out onto the floor.

The guard had raised his fist again.

'Stop,' called Sir Nicholas. 'Give me that.'

Two of the men held Francis, while the porter retrieved the golden lion and laid it on the desk. Sir Nicholas held it up, letting the candlelight sparkle on the inset rubies and diamonds.

'Where did you get this?' he demanded of Francis

'It belongs to my family. My father left it to me.'

Sir Nicholas turned the emblem in his fingers. He waved his men to let Francis go.

'Who are you?' Sir Nicholas said again, but more thoughtfully this time.

Francis drew himself up, determined to ignore the pain that shot through his body when he moved. He'd rehearsed the words all day, though he'd never imagined delivering them in such circumstances.

'I am Francis Courtney, son of William Courtney and grandson of Hal Courtney, Baron Dartmouth and Nautonnier Knight of the Order of St George and the Holy Grail. Twenty years ago, my grandfather gave his life defending your company's shipping from pirates. Now, all I ask is some preferment, an opportunity to join the Company's service and prove my worth.'

Childs stared at him as if he were a ghost.

'Leave us,' he ordered his men.

They withdrew. Childs studied the boy. For decades, now, he had governed the East India Company as his personal

43

domain, stretching out his tentacles from this office in Leadenhall Street to the furthest corners of the globe. Kings and Parliaments had come and gone, some of them claiming the Company was too powerful, that its monopoly should be withdrawn. He had seen them off, broken his competitors and outlived them all.

Courtneys, too, had come and gone. For a time, they had been useful servants and helped him build up the Company fortune. When that ceased to be the case, he had dispatched them as easily as he had done his enemies, with never a prick of conscience. From his home at Bombay House, he had sent Tom Courtney to be murdered by his brother William. To his surprise, Tom had sprung the trap and turned the tables on William, but that had not troubled Childs. Tom had fled, a wanted murderer, and William's seven per cent holding in the East India Company had passed to his infant son. Childs had had little difficulty persuading the widow to sell it to him on the most advantageous terms, cementing his control still further. He had all but forgotten young Francis Courtney.

Now the boy stood before him, grown almost to manhood. A livid welt coloured his neck where the men had choked him; his face was pale, but firm with the unyielding pride Childs had seen twenty years ago in his grandfather Hal. He thought that this was a lad who could be useful, or dangerous.

'My boy,' he adopted a more kindly and avuncular tone, 'come closer where I can see you better.'

It was an act: his body might be failing, but his blue eyes remained as clear and sharp as his mind.

Francis took a few hesitant steps forward.

'I am sorry you were so roughly handled,' Childs said. 'My enemies have many spies, and will stop at nothing to thwart me and this noble company. I trust you were not seriously hurt?'

Francis rubbed his side. He could already feel the skin tightening as the bruises formed.

'I am a little hungry, your lordship.'

'Of course, of course.' Childs rang a hand bell that stood on the corner of his desk, and bellowed for the servant to bring food. 'Now, my boy, take a chair and tell me everything. How do you come to be here? If you had written, I could have given you a kinder reception.'

Francis lowered himself painfully into the chair. 'My stepfather died last week. He left me nothing but the golden lion.'

Childs mopped his brow with a handkerchief. 'I am sorry to hear it. Your mother probably never told you, but I always took a keen interest in your upbringing. The way your father died – I am afraid I feel some guilt for it. You see, I was the last man to see your uncle Tom before he committed the murderous deed. I have always asked myself, was there something I could have said or done to change his course? Could I have discerned what he intended, and taken steps to prevent it?'

He broke off in a fit of coughing, dabbing his mouth with the handkerchief. It came away dabbled with specks of fresh blood.

'I'm sure you are beyond reproach, sir,' Francis protested.

A troubling thought nagged him as he remembered those last frantic moments with his mother.

'May I confide in you, sir?'

'Of course, my boy. As your own father.'

'Before I left home my mother made a most outlandish suggestion. She said – she believed – that my uncle Tom may be innocent of the crime. She said he only killed William in self-defence.'

Childs shook his head so hard, all his chins wobbled. 'She is mistaken. Grief has addled her wits, poor woman. I saw William Courtney in the House of Lords the day he died. The concern he expressed for his brother, the love and affection he bore him

– no man could doubt it. That very day, he told me, he intended to advance Tom ten thousand pounds to fit out an expedition to rescue their brother Dorian, who had been seized by pirates – though it later transpired that the boy was dead. But that was not enough for Tom Courtney. He ambushed William on the Thames path late at night, demanding a greater share of their father's inheritance, and when William refused Tom cut him down without mercy.'

Francis shuddered as he imagined the scene. 'You are sure of it?'

'I had a full report from a boatman who witnessed the entire tragedy. Even after so many years, I remember every detail.'

A servant knocked and entered with a silver tray. He set out the dishes on Childs' desk, mounded platters of roast meats, and poured two glasses of claret from a crystal decanter. It was all Francis could do to wait until the servant retired before he fell upon the food.

Childs ate almost as ravenously as Francis did. Gravy dribbled down his chins and dripped onto his shirtfront.

'Do you wish to avenge your father?' Pieces of food sprayed from his mouth as Childs asked the question. He went on without waiting for a reply. 'Of course you do. You are a Courtney, and I know well what blood runs in those veins of yours.'

Francis took a gulp of wine. 'Yes, sir. But I do not under-stand—'

'Your presence here today is most auspicious; it is almost as if fate guided your footsteps. You see, a week ago a ship from the Indies docked at Deptford. The *Dowager*, under Captain Inchbird. He brought a most remarkable tale. Twenty-two days out from Bombay, near the coast of Madagascar, he was attacked by a pirate and nearly taken. It was a fierce fight by all accounts, but while he was gallantly fending off the enemy a small sloop joined the fray. Her captain was none other than Tom Courtney.'

Francis felt the room spin around him. The pictures on the wall seemed to press in on him, and the wine throbbed in his head. 'That cannot be, sir. Tom Courtney died in Africa while I was a child. My uncle Guy confirmed it.'

'Your uncle was wrong. Tom Courtney is alive and well, trading along the coast of Africa. Inchbird believes he resides in Cape Town, when he is not at sea.'

Childs put down his knife and fork. 'You asked me for a position in the Company. For the love I bore your grandfather, and our long association with your family, I will gladly give you a clerkship with your uncle Guy in Bombay, and free passage on one of our ships. But I can give you more. The vessel will call at the Cape en route to Bombay. It may be there some weeks, provisioning and watering. If you wish, you will have time to disembark. You could find your uncle, if he is there.'

Francis chewed a piece of pork, struggling to take in this latest intelligence. Childs leaned forward. Wine stained his lips the colour of blood.

'When Tom Courtney fled England, we offered five thousand pounds for his capture. I, personally, guaranteed the reward. It still stands. Five thousand pounds,' Childs repeated. 'A princely sum for any man, let alone a youth of your age just starting to make his way in the world. And if you invest it wisely in Bombay, you could double or triple the sum by the time you return.'

Francis tried to imagine that much money. He imagined returning to High Weald in a coach and four and taking possession of the house. Establishing his mother in her own apartments, scrubbing off the years to make it the bright, happy place he remembered from his youth.

The wine was hot inside him. He knew he should not drink so fast on a famished stomach, but he couldn't resist. He felt sure there was more he should ask, important questions about Guy and Tom and his inheritance, but Childs' tone brooked no discussion. When he poured more wine, Francis drained it gratefully.

'This is the revenge you have waited for your whole life,' said Childs. 'A chance to settle unfinished business for both of us.'

The St George medallion still lay on the desk, half hidden under a sheaf of papers. Francis lifted it up, missing the flash of disappointment that crossed Child's face. He stood, unsteady on his feet after so much wine.

'Upon my father's honour, Sir Nicholas, I will find Tom Courtney and bring him to justice.'

Tom and Dorian sat outside the tavern, nursing their drinks and looking down at the ships anchored in Table Bay. Tom was drinking a sweet muscadel wine, but Dorian was true to his adopted religion and eschewed all alcohol. He was drinking diluted orange juice. Behind them, the top of Table Mountain ruled a flat line across the sky, while the lesser summits of Devil's Peak and Lion's Peak reached out to enclose the bay in a natural amphitheatre. Below the forests on the lower slopes, a hundred or so stone-built, white-washed houses dotted the landscape, running down to the sea where warehouses and taverns lined the shore. At the northern end, the Dutch tricolour blew over the five-pointed fort that left no doubt as to where the power in the colony lay.

An Indiaman was beating in to the harbour. From her colours, and the state of her rigging, Tom saw she must be fresh from England. He made a quick calculation of what her arrival would mean. Ivory prices would rise, as the English merchants sought supplies to take to India; in return, they would want to trade knives and steel goods from England. The ship was late in the season, and most of the ivory stocks had been sold, but Tom had kept back a few good tusks from their last voyage for just such an eventuality. He smiled as he thought of the profits to be made.

Soon, he and Dorian would return to the boarding house where they lodged during their interludes in Cape Town. He had some ten thousand pounds deposited at the offices of an Amsterdam bank here, though he had never used it to buy his own home. The Dutch authorities laid ferocious restrictions on foreigners owning property in the colony, but a few rix-dollars in the right palms might smooth the way around that. He had never tried. Year after year, he waited out the monsoon in the boarding house, impatient for the next season to begin.

'Are you bored, Tom?' Dorian asked. In reply Tom swept his arm in a full circle, taking in the mountains and the sea, the cotton-fluff clouds and the sun sinking towards the horizon. 'How could I ever be bored with all this to enjoy?'

'I know you too well, brother,' Dorian chuckled. 'You haven't fired a gun in anger since the day we rescued the *Dowager* from that pirate Legrange. And that was almost a year ago.'

The past ivory-hunting season in the African interior had been a quiet one. Tom and Dorian had taken an expedition almost two hundred leagues up the Zambesi River, but found none of the slavers he had warred with in the past. Even the hunting had been less bountiful than past years. *Centaurus* had returned with her hold only half full of ivory.

'Fighting is bad for business,' Tom said, without conviction.

Then he blinked with astonishment as he saw out on the far horizon, where the last rim of the sun was slipping away, a sudden flash of the most brilliant green he could ever imagine. It startled him; although he had heard of the phenomenon before, this was the first time he had actually witnessed it.

'Did you also see that?' Tom demanded as both of them jumped to their feet in amazement, staring at the distant horizon.

'Yes, indeed!' Dorian was as excited as he was. 'Neptune's Wink.' It was one of those mysteries, like St Elmo's fire, that you would seldom see unless you lived your life on the wild oceans of the globe.

'I have heard tell that the man who sees it acquires special wisdom,' Tom enthused as they resumed their seats.

'Bully for you,' Dorian teased him. 'You can certainly use all the wisdom you are able to lay your hands on.'

In retaliation Tom grinned and poured the dregs of his wine over Dorian's head. 'For such impertinence you can buy me another glass of wine,' Tom told him.

When Dorian returned from the bar with Tom's glass topped up they settled down again in companionable silence to enjoy the last of the sunset, and to watch the Indiaman drop anchor in the bay.

As its anchor splashed into the darkening waters the bum boats from the beach swarmed about the ship, as eager as lambs for the teat.

'They won't bring their cargo ashore until morning,' Tom decided. 'We can wait until then to see what we can sell them.'

He left a coin for the drinks, and together they went back up to the slopes of the mountain, following *Die Heerengracht*, the 'Gentlemen's Walk' that ran between the parade ground and the Company gardens. Deep in conversation, they didn't notice the woman in the blue dress coming down the path towards them until she was almost abreast.

'Tom Courtney?' she said, and he looked up in surprise.

'Ana Duarte?' he responded, and her face flushed with pleasure.

'You remember me!'

'How could I ever forget you? In fact, my brother and I were just this instant recollecting the day we met. But I did not know you were here in Cape Town.'

'My ship arrived two days ago from Madras.'

'I hope you had an easier crossing than the last time.'

She touched a silver cross that hung at her throat. 'Thankfully, yes!'

Suddenly Tom thought of the *green flash*. Though he was

50

not superstitious, he wondered if perhaps it had portended this unexpected meeting.

'You must dine with us,' put in Dorian. 'Sarah and Yasmini would be delighted to see you again.'

'I would like that very much.' She smiled. 'In fact, I was hoping for it. I have a proposal for you.'

The Courtneys' boarding house was at the far end of town, just under the walls of the Dutch East India Company's garden. The Malay housekeeper, Mrs Lai, kept it spotless. The food she cooked was simple yet delicious, a unique blend of spices from the Indies with the flavours of the English recipes Tom insisted on.

Tom poured wine from a decanter. Dorian, as usual, drank only fresh fruit juice.

'No wine for you?' Ana noticed.

'I am a Muslim.'

'Are there many Muslims in England?'

'It is a long story.'

'But a good one,' put in Tom.

'Then I would be glad to hear it,' said Ana.

So Dorian explained how he had been captured by Arab pirates as a boy of eleven, enslaved, bought by a Prince of Oman because of the red colour of his hair, the same as the prophet Mohammed, and raised in his household as an adopted son. Ana urged him to tell her more, so he told her how he had grown to manhood as a warrior of Islam, and how finally he had embraced that faith.

Ana listened in total absorption to the story of his life. When he was done she asked quietly, 'Is there a man around this table who does not have a price on his head?'

Tom started. 'How do you know?'

'I have many contacts with the East India Company factors in Madras. From them I learned that the Governor of Bombay

51

was a man named Guy Courtney. So I followed up and learned that you are related.'

Tom and Dorian exchanged a look that was fraught with meaning.

'Guy is our brother,' Tom admitted. 'So far as he knows, Dorian died in Oman, and I disappeared somewhere in the African wilderness.'

'You have not informed him that you are both very much alive?'

'That news would give Guy no great pleasure. Frankly, he would prefer us both dead.'

Ana sipped her wine, as if this news was the most natural thing in the world. 'I will not ask what came between you,' she murmured.

'It was a woman,' Dorian said flatly.

'And the woman was my sister,' said Sarah, speaking up for the first time. 'We were passengers on that fateful voyage, when Dorian was captured by pirates. I was still a child but my elder sister, Caroline, was in full flower. Silly thing; she was much too free with her charms. She went to Tom's bed only too willingly.'

'I believe it was actually the powder magazine,' said Dorian with a grin. 'It was the only place on the ship they could find privacy.'

'It was my fault,' said Tom, embarrassed to have this history raised in front of Ana. 'I should have realized that Guy was in love with her.'

'Guy was not in love with Caroline,' said Sarah flatly. 'Guy wanted only to possess her, like he would a horse or a cargo or a chest of gold. As soon as he had married her, she no longer was of any value to Guy. You forget, I lived with them as Guy's ward for years after they were husband and wife. I saw the way he treated her.' She closed her eyes. 'He did not love her, God knows.'

'Yet even though he married her, he could not forgive you?' Ana asked Tom.

'It was more than that. There was . . .' Tom broke off. There were some things he could not discuss with Ana.

What have I done? he asked himself. *One brother I killed, and another wants me dead. The two greatest mistakes of my life, and there is nothing I can do to atone for them.*

He thought again of the green flash on the horizon the night before. *God grant me wisdom.*

Ana nodded gravely. 'All families have their secrets.'

'I think you are very brave,' Sarah told her, lightening the mood with her bright voice, 'coming to dine with these two wanted scallywags.'

'You saved my life, all of you!' said Ana, addressing the whole table. 'You were in no danger. Your ship could have sailed on and left us to our fate. Ninety-nine men out of a hundred would have done that.'

'Ninety-nine men out of a hundred do not have Yasmini and Sarah telling them what they must do,' grinned Dorian. 'The choice was not ours.'

The conversation moved on. After supper, they retired to the parlour, where Sarah entertained them on her harpsichord, playing arias from William Babell's *Book of Lady's Entertainment.* Tom had ordered the new harpsichord shipped all the way from England.

'Tom threw the first one I had into a river,' Sarah confided to Ana, in between pieces.

'In fairness, you should mention we were stuck on a sandbank in an overloaded ship, pursued by an army of Arab swordsmen who wanted to murder us, and I was near to death,' said Dorian, sitting on the floor on an ornately embroidered cushion.

'I am sure Miss Duarte could not conceive it could have been otherwise,' said Yasmini.

Sarah played some more, ending with a flourish. The others applauded. Sarah took a seat next to Tom.

'Miss Duarte,' Tom began. 'When we met yesterday you said you had a proposal for us.'

She smoothed her skirts. She was the youngest person in the room by at least a dozen years, but she carried herself with calm assurance.

'What do you know of India?' she asked Tom.

Tom swirled wine in his glass, staring at the dregs. 'What I hear on the waterfront. The traders say it is a dangerous country since the old emperor died.'

'Since old Aurangzeb died two years ago, India has become a battlefield,' Ana agreed. 'His three sons are contesting the succession, and while they fight each other, every other prince and nabob makes war on his neighbour. In the west, the Marathas have been fighting the Mughals from their mountain fortresses for thirty years. On the Malabar Coast, the pirate Angria has established his own kingdom, ruled from the impregnable fortress of Tiracola. In the south, the Nawabs are in open revolt. The Mughal Empire is tearing itself apart.'

'Bad for trade,' said Dorian.

Tom waited while Ana hesitated, as if unsure how to proceed.

'Before I explain my proposal, I must tell you something of myself and my family. My father was a Portuguese merchant from a family that had settled in Goa; my mother was Indian, the daughter of a local *Mansabdar*. Neither family approved their marriage, so they fled together to the British settlement at Fort St George – Madras. They began with nothing, but they worked hard. Soon, they had a thriving business in the cloth trade. They bought calicoes from the weavers around Madras, and shipped them to Europe. At first, they sold them to the East India Company, but the Company was greedy: they cheated us on the price. So my father resolved to find another way. He contracted with a Danish sea captain to carry his cargo.

'Guy Courtney, the president of East India Company, learned of this. You know what they call these men, private traders who threaten their monopoly? *Interlopers.* She almost spat the word out. 'The East India Company believe these private traders are nothing more than snakes in the walled garden of Eden which they imagine they have built. So the president informed the pirates when our ship would be sailing. They fell upon her near Cape Cormorin. There were no survivors.

'My father had put everything he owned into that voyage. Even so, he knew the risks. If it had been an act of God, he would have borne the hardship. But President Courtney wanted to gloat. He summoned us to his house and told us to our faces what he had done, as a warning to ourselves and to others. There was nothing we could do, no hope of justice. The president is the judge and the jury.

'My father died a few months later, brokenhearted and ruined.' A tremor shook her voice; Sarah laid a hand on her arm. 'I took on his affairs. That is why I was aboard the *Dowager*. The captain charged me a terrible fee to take my cargo, but I thought I would be safe on an Indiaman.'

'Do you think the pirates we met had been alerted to your coming?'

'No. That was just a stroke of bad luck.'

She pressed her fingertips together. 'This is my proposal. I am a merchant, like you. I want to transport my goods to the market at the least cost, to sell for the best price. To pass safely from Madras to Cape Town, you need a pass from the British, a pass from the Dutch, a pass from the pirates and a pass from the Mughal emperor. Even if I bought my own ship, I could not afford to defend her. The crew to man the guns, the protection money I would have to pay . . . It is impossible.'

'You want us to carry your trade?'

'This is not just for myself. The Indian Ocean is crawling with pirates. The East India companies, the Dutch and the English, they can afford the ships to see them off – but they make their suppliers pay for the protection they give them. But there are other merchants, syndicates and traders in London, Amsterdam, Ostend, a dozen cities I have never seen, who could finance the trade and offer better terms, if only they could manage the shipping.'

'The East India Company has a monopoly on the India trade,' Tom pointed out. 'Lord Childs has threatened to hang any man he finds breaking it.'

'It has a monopoly on the "out and back" trade – from England to the Indies. The country trade, between the ports of the Indian Ocean, is open to all. Divide the journey in two, by trans-shipping the cargoes in Cape Town, and the monopoly does not apply. That is how I persuaded Captain Inchbird to carry my cargo. The European merchants would pay you handsomely to bear the risks of the Indian Ocean, while the factors in India would sell their best wares to you because you would pay more than the Company, and still make a handsome profit.'

'The VOC, the Dutch East India Company, controls all the trade in Cape Town.'

'And they will smile on any venture that weakens their hated English rivals.'

'That would still mean *we* had to contend with the pirates,' mused Tom.

'I have seen how you deal with pirates. And why just India?' She turned to Dorian. 'You said your adopted father was the Caliph of Oman. There must be men in the Arab ports – at Lamu, Muscat, Mocha and Gombroon – who trust you. You speak their language and you pray to their God.'

'The *old* Caliph was my adopted father. The *new* Caliph is my adopted brother, and he hates me every bit as much as Guy hates Tom.' Dorian stroked his red beard. 'But . . . there are other men I know.'

'If you go about it in the right way, you could own the trade of a whole ocean.'

The proposition hung there, dangling between them.

'We will think on it,' Tom said. 'Tomorrow, I will give you our answer.'

Dorian walked with Ana to escort her back to her lodgings. From the veranda of the boarding house Tom watched them descend the hill. He had eaten and drunk his fill, but it had not dulled his mind. He needed air, and space to think.

'I am going to take a turn in the gardens,' he told Sarah.

'Don't let the lions gobble you up. Take your sword.'

'I don't need it,' he retorted. 'I kill lions with my teeth, didn't you know?'

Leaving the house, Tom didn't notice the single figure lurking in the shadows of the cottage across the road. He walked briskly, whistling 'Spanish Ladies' softly to himself, and reached the nearest gate into the botanical gardens of the VOC. The gate was purely ornamental. On the other three sides, the gardens were open, with only a low ditch to keep wild animals out as the ground rose towards the slopes of Devil's Peak. Sarah's quip about the lions had not really been a joke.

The VOC had built the gardens for the pleasure of the residents of Cape Town. They had spent heavily when laying them out but recently they had been neglected. The further Tom went, the more derelict they became. Hedges soared twenty feet high, blocking the moonlight and overhanging the paths, which were overgrown with weeds. The sunken ponds had fallen in, becoming slimy holes filled with mud and rubble. The few flowers that had survived grew in sparse, sporadic clusters.

But Tom ignored his surroundings. Ana's proposal had set his mind on fire. Twenty years ago, he would have agreed to it right there in the parlour. Now, older and wiser, he knew enough of himself to pause before leaping in.

But why not? The Courtneys were a restless family: it was their nature to move on to new lands, new adventures. *We have been ploughing the same old furrow much too long*, he thought. *This is the opportunity I have been waiting for. Why not?*

Out in the night, he heard the crazed giggling of a pack of hyenas, scavenging in the colony's rubbish heaps.

Because of Guy, the more cautious part of his mind answered him. *Because if you do this, you will be tweaking the East India Company's tail, and sooner or later Guy will get to hear of it. Because the last two times you met, he tried to kill you, and if you meet a third time you know one of you will probably die.*

Gravel crunched on the path behind him. Tom spun around. A figure stood behind him. Shadows from the wild hedges hid his face, but enough light seeped through to gleam on the naked sword in his hand. Tom was unarmed.

'Are you Thomas Courtney?' said an English voice.

'I am he.' Tom began to relax. He stepped forward, but the man lunged at him with sword in his right hand.

The morning after the *Prophet* anchored in Cape Town bay, Francis Courtney took a bumboat ashore. He stood in the bows and gazed at the high peaks cradling the bay, the rolling surf and the few houses clinging to the fringe of this great continent. As a child, he used to pull out the old charts in the library and pore over the strange names and distant shores. In his schoolbooks, he would draw his own maps and imagine exploring those undiscovered countries. And, at last, now he was here.

He went to the harbourmaster's office to register his arrival.

'Name?' asked the clerk. Ink dripped from his pen.

He reached into his coat pocket and produced the false papers that Childs had given him. 'My name is Frank Leighton.'

From the harbourmaster's office, he walked along the shore to the fort. It stood about a musket shot from the town, commanding the harbour and the landing areas. Francis stared at it, trying to imagine his great-grandfather labouring in the heat. Growing up in High Weald, Francis had been surrounded by the memories of his ancestors: their effigies in the chapel crypt, their coats of arms in the stained glass, their portraits lining the walls. One by one, those portraits had disappeared: he remembered the first time he'd run down the long gallery and seen a gap on the wall, and the ache each time another painting disappeared to cover Sir Walter's debts.

Yet here he was. His great-grandfather, the man in the portrait with the stern face and great mane of black hair, had stood on this very ground. So, according to the stories his mother told him, had his grandfather Hal. He imagined them now as they must have been: no longer flat on oil and canvas, but as living, breathing men.

A tremor went through him. He felt the presence of his ancestors, as if all the portraits in the long gallery had come alive, stepped out of their frames and crowded around him, impressing upon him the full weight and expectation of the Courtney name.

If he killed Thomas, would he be any better than the man he killed? A man who murdered his own family.

'I owe it to my father,' he told himself, trying not to think of the reward of five thousand pounds Sir Nicholas Childs had promised him. It seemed a mean motive for an act of such enormity.

He realized the sentry at the castle gate had started to take an interest in him. Francis turned, and hurried back to the waterfront where he found a tavern. This early in the morning it was almost deserted, but he needed a drink.

The beer was deep red in colour, flat and sour. Francis took one sip, and thought of the mornings he had come downstairs to find his stepfather already halfway through a bottle of wine.

A woman came over and sat on a stool at his table. She had bright red lips, and almost enough powder on her cheeks to smooth out the wrinkles that lined them.

'Looking for something, dearie?' She played with the ribbon that laced the neck of her blouse. 'I can help you with whatever you want.'

Francis blushed furiously as he realized what she was offering. For a moment, he could hardly speak. Growing up in High Weald, rarely venturing far, he had never encountered such a person, though he had occasionally heard of them in whispered speculation with other boys.

'I'm looking for Thomas Courtney,' he mumbled. And then, seeing the recognition light her eyes, 'Do you know him?'

He put a coin on the table. The woman snatched it up. She polished it on her skirts, and then slipped it into a pouch which she tucked inside her bodice.

Francis waited. 'Well?'

'Aren't you going to buy me a drink?' she wheedled. 'A proper gentleman always buys a lady a drink.'

Awkwardly, Francis called the barmaid, who fetched the woman another glass of beer. She gave Francis a pitying look as she put it on the table.

'First time, dearie?' said the prostitute, slurping her beer. 'A big, handsome lad like you? I don't believe it.'

'I'm looking for Thomas Courtney,' Francis insisted.

'He won't do the things I can do for you.' Under the table, her foot rubbed against his calf. Francis hastily pulled it away.

She grinned at his discomfort. 'Got any more of those silver coins in your purse? For another one of those, I'll not just tell you where to find him. I'll show him to you.'

Francis realized he had been foolish to give her money without getting anything in advance. He took out another coin, but kept it firmly pressed under his thumb.

'This is yours. When you've taken me to him.'

The prostitute looked disappointed. 'You're a quick learner. I could teach you a few other things you'd never forget. For another coin that is.'

'Take me to him,' Francis insisted.

'I don't have to. I can see him from here.'

She pointed out the tavern's window, smeared with lamp soot and salt spray. Beyond it was the harbour front, and the wooden jetty extending out into the bay. The *Prophet*'s boats had moored alongside, and a gang of black stevedores was unloading her cargo. In the midst of the bustle, three men stood talking, studying a bill of goods. Francis recognized the first two, the *Prophet*'s captain and the harbourmaster. The third was the tallest, standing over six feet with shoulders as broad as any of the porters working around him. He wore his thick black hair pulled back in a sailor's queue. He was smiling as he talked, but his hard features said this was a man who would yield to no one.

'The tall one is Tom Courtney,' said the prostitute, with more than a little admiration in her voice.

Francis felt as though the blood was freezing in his veins. For so long, Tom Courtney had been an almost mythic figure, the demon who stalked his nightmares. Now he stood a few yards away, talking and joking with the other men. Utterly unaware of the vengeance that awaited him.

The prostitute read the look on Francis' face.

'You hate him,' she mused. 'You want to kill him. Yes?' she asked, then as Francis started to protest, 'Do not argue. I have seen the look that is in your eyes before, though mostly on men who had drunk a good deal more than you.'

Francis couldn't take his eyes off Tom. 'What of it?'

'Tom Courtney is no stumbling sailor still on his sea legs. He's the most dangerous man in the colony. The stories they tell of him . . .' She shook her head.

His stepfather had failed in many things, but he had made sure Francis knew how to fight with sword and fists. More than once, Sir Walter's debts had led him to the duelling field at dawn; he knew how to account for himself. Sir Walter had been a ferocious instructor, drilling Francis until his knuckles bled and his numbed fingers could hardly close around the hilt of his sword.

One day, this will save your life, he had insisted.

'I can defend myself,' Francis assured the woman stiffly.

'Of course you can, luvvy,' she leered. 'But why take the risk? Do you even have a sword? You are not the only enemy Tom Courtney has in Cape Town. There are others I know who would be only too willing to help you.'

Reluctantly, Francis dragged his gaze away from the window and looked at her. 'What are you offering?'

'Buy me another drink, and I'll tell you.'

As darkness fell, Francis climbed the hill. The sword in his belt slapped against his thigh, and he put his hand on the hilt to steady it. Its solid presence reassured him. This was how he would kill Tom Courtney: not the distant, anonymous death of a musket or pistol ball, but the intimate end of a blade through the heart. The same way Tom had killed William.

He cast a nervous eye at the men around him. They were dark figures, their skin grey in the moonlight. Long, straight-bladed cane knives swung easily in their fists.

Behind Francis, Jacob de Vries strode up the hill, swatting at the flowers by the roadside with his cane knife. The knives – heavy blades, more like swords – had been destined for the sugar plantations of Barbados, but the vagaries of trade had brought them to Cape Town, where Jacob had found more than one use for them.

He studied Francis, wondering about this raw English boy. When the prostitute introduced them, he'd half suspected a trap. The boy was so scrawny, his new beard barely hiding his callow cheeks, he looked as if a stiff drink could knock him down. But Jacob had put him through his paces with the blade he had found for him, and discovered he was a more than adequate swordsman: quick with youth, always aware, and with a few moves that had surprised even Jacob. And the fire in his eyes, when he spoke of Tom Courtney, could not be feigned.

Jacob knew that feeling well. Two years ago, he had been bringing a cargo of slaves down from Mozambique when his ship grounded on a sandbar. Tom Courtney had salvaged him – but as his fee he had forced Jacob to free all his slaves. He had lost a fortune, and one beautiful slave girl in particular he had wanted for himself. The bitch Sarah Courtney had taken her, teaching her manners and giving her a passage to England where she could live as a freedwoman.

Desire stirred in his loins as Jacob thought of the girl. She'd been completely naked when she came aboard, high breasted and hair plucked after the fashion of her tribe, leaving nothing to the imagination. He thought of what he would have done to her, and what he would do to Sarah Courtney once Tom was out of the way and could no longer protect her.

They reached the top of the hill. There were a few houses here, but one was empty: the owner had gone to Amsterdam, and wouldn't return for months. Jacob and his men hid in the shadows of the garden wall, watching the boarding house opposite. Harpsichord music drifted out; lamps burned brightly inside. Through the windows, Jacob saw Tom and his brother and their wives sitting in the parlour. The brother wore a turban wound round his head, no better than a Kaffir. Jacob wondered if the turban would stay in place when he'd separated the head from its neck.

He tapped Francis on the shoulder. The boy jumped as if he'd pissed himself. Not a good sign, thought Jacob.

'Do we go in now?'

Francis shook his head. Jacob wondered if he was having second thoughts. If it came to it, he could get rid of the boy with one stroke of his cane knife. Jacob knew places where bodies could be left, so that by the time anyone found them the jackals and vultures had picked them bare.

But there was no harm in waiting. And, in fact, a few minutes later, the door opened and Dorian Courtney came out, escorting a woman Jacob didn't recognize. A half-caste, by the look of her. Perhaps he could find her later, once he was through with Sarah.

For now, Jacob couldn't believe his luck. Though he wouldn't admit it, the prospect of fighting both Courtney brothers – even with his strength of numbers – had worried him. Now he could pick them off one at a time.

He waited until Dorian and the woman were out of sight, then he grabbed Francis' arm.

'Now,' he hissed.

But just as he was about to move, light flooded onto the lane again. Tom stepped out the door. Jacob ducked down hurriedly, but Tom was too lost in his own thoughts to notice the movement. When Jacob risked another glance, he saw him walking towards the high wall of the Company garden. He was unarmed.

Jacob chuckled happily. He looked at Francis again. *Whoever you are*, he thought, *you have the Devil's own luck.*

'Is that him?' Francis asked. Sweat beaded on his face and his eyes were wide. Jacob wondered if he had the balls to see this through. It wouldn't matter. Whoever wielded the blade, Tom Courtney would die that night anyway.

They followed Tom, keeping a safe distance behind. Again, luck was with them. Tom headed deeper into the garden, away from the town and anyone who might hear. He walked quickly, but he never looked back.

Scavenging hyenas giggled in the night. Francis drew his sword, trying to envision the look in Tom's eyes as he suffered the killing blow. Francis had dreamed of this moment so long, but now it was upon him he felt more fear than anger. He had never killed a man before. The sword weighed his arm down, and his legs were as soft as wax.

Do it, he told himself. *Do it for your father's memory.*

And five thousand pounds' reward, added Sir Nicholas Childs' voice in his head.

Jacob sensed his hesitation and started to move forward, the cane knife at the ready. Francis waved him back. 'He's mine,' he mouthed.

Jacob shrugged and nodded. The boy had paid him: let him have his chance. If he failed, Jacob was ready to finish it.

Francis drew back his arm. He had imagined this moment a thousand times on the long voyage from England. Yet now he was actually here, it was not like he had thought it would be. In his mind, he had called Tom's name, and watched the surprise in Tom's eyes turn to horror as Francis told him who he was, and the reason he must die. He had savoured the terror as Tom finally understood that justice would be done; had allowed Tom to fall to his knees and beg for his life, before finally ending it.

But now that he was here, all he wanted was for it to be over. His mouth was dry; he could not issue the challenge.

It did not matter, he told himself: the deed was all that mattered. He aimed the sword at the middle of Tom's shoulders, holding the blade flat, the way his stepfather had taught him, so it would slide between the ribs. The blood sang in his ears. He stepped forward.

He trod too heavily. Gravel crunched under his foot. Tom spun around. For the first time in his life, Francis came face to face with the man who had killed his father.

'Thomas Courtney,' he asked, trying not to let his voice waver. He looked surprised. 'I am he.'

Francis lunged. Tom leaped back, just in time. The tip of the sword sliced open his shirt front; cold steel stung his skin, but it was only a scratch. The movement brought Francis too far forward, off balance. Tom could have knocked the sword from his hand, but already another figure was coming up beside the first, his heavy straight blade poised for a blow at Tom's head. Tom retreated, out into a patch of moonlight that shone through a gap in the hedge.

In the moonlight he saw that there were five of them. He knew Jacob de Vries, and three of the others were familiar faces, rough men who he had seen before in Jacob's company. The fifth was the youth who had attacked him with the sword. He had never laid eyes on him before. However, his features were hauntingly familiar.

He had no time to think about it. The boy came at him again, a flurry of quick, well-trained strikes that almost took his arm off. The other ruffians fanned out in a loose cordon, cutting off his escape and slowly tightening the net around him.

The boy was clearly the ringleader. The skill and ferocity of his attack marked him as the danger man.

'Who in the Devil's name are you?' he challenged him. 'Don't I know you?'

The only answer he got was another lunge with the sword. Tom jumped back. Too late, he saw triumph light up his assailant's face. The ground gave way beneath Tom. He tumbled down a muddy embankment into one of the empty sunken ponds. The youth stood at the top of the bank, breathing hard, looking down on his unarmed adversary.

Behind him, Jacob turned to one of his men. 'Stay here with the boy, make sure he finishes the job.' He would have liked to watch Tom die, but he had to get back to the house before Dorian returned. Dorian would be helpless if Jacob was holding a knife to his wife's throat. Perhaps he'd make him watch what he did to her, before he turned his attention to Sarah.

He leered down at Tom. 'It's high time I paid a call on your pretty little wife. I'll leave the boy to finish with you.'

With a last glance of triumph at Tom Courtney, he headed back to the boarding house. Two of his men followed; the third stayed with Francis.

In the bottom of the empty pond Tom was trying to recover his footing in the treacherous mud. He had killed so many men, perhaps it was inevitable that one day the angel of good fortune would desert him. His father had died before his time; so had his grandfather. But he still had no idea who this implacable enemy might be.

And while he breathed, he would not let Jacob de Vries lay a finger on Sarah. He pressed his hands into the mud to push himself up and there, half buried, he felt something hard and sharp. He wrapped his fingers around it, and pulled it out of the mud. It was a length of heavy three-inch pipe that had once carried water to feed the pond.

Francis came sliding down the muddy bank of the pond balancing like a dancer, with the sword poised to split Tom's skull. Tom came to his knees and raised the metal pipe and blocked the blow. Metal rang on metal; but Tom was able to stop the blade inches from his own face.

Tom pushed back, throwing Francis off balance. Francis' feet shot out from under him and he went down in the black mud. Tom pushed himself to his feet and ran at him with the metal pipe poised. But before he could reach him one of the other men charged down the bank brandishing a cane knife. Tom turned to meet him and ducked under the swinging blade. Then he grabbed the wrist of the man's knife hand and used the impetus of his blow to keep him turning off balance, twisting his arm up behind his back until his shoulder joint popped out of its socket. The man screamed with the pain and dropped to his knees. Tom swung the water pipe in his right hand into his temple and he toppled face down in the mud.

Tom snatched up the cane knife from where it had fallen from the man's hand and turned back to face Francis. But

Francis was plastered with mud, and he had lost his sword as he fell. Now he refused to meet Tom again, and he staggered back up the bank, sobbing with terror and shame. Tom hurled the water pipe after him and it caught him in the middle of his back with a hefty thump. Francis screamed with pain but kept running. He disappeared into the darkness, and Tom let him go. His only concern now was for Sarah.

Jacob de Vries' threat echoed in his ears as he started to run: 'It's high time I paid a call on your pretty little wife.'

Tom raced out of the gates of the garden and down the path that led to Mrs Lai's boarding house. Two of de Vries' henchmen stood on guard at the open door to the boarding house. They saw Tom coming but in the darkness they did not recognize him, and with the cane knife in his hand they took him for one of their gang.

'You took your time, Hendrick,' greeted one of them. 'Jacob's already getting started on the Courtney bitch.'

A high-pitched feminine scream echoed from the house and the two guards laughed and turned to peer back through the door. One of them died without seeing the stroke of the cane knife that killed him. The second guard heard the blow and the sound of the falling body and began to turn. But he was too slow. Tom's cane knife chopped into the side of his neck, cutting through his vertebrae so that his head, still partially attached to his shoulders, flopped forward onto his chest.

As Tom jumped over their bodies and ran through the doorway with his heart pumping wildly, a pistol shot rang out ahead of him. He did not pause, but burst into the sitting room. Sarah stood across the room facing him, veiled in a thin cloud of gun smoke. Behind her crouched Mrs Lai, sobbing with terror and clinging to Sarah's skirts.

In her right hand Sarah held her tiny flint-lock Derringer pistol still fully extended at arm's length. On the floor at her feet was the spread-eagled body of Jacob de Vries. He lay face down. The back of his skull had been blown away by the exit of the bullet. His buttery yellow brains were splattered over Mrs Lai's colourful Chinese carpets.

Sarah and Tom stared at each other for the hundredth part of a second then Sarah dropped the empty pistol and ran into his arms.

'Tom Courtney!' she cried, and her voice was half a sob and the other half hysterical laughter. 'You promised to love honour and protect me. But where were you when the chips were on the table?'

'Oh, my darling, my beloved darling.' He dropped the cane knife and hugged her to his chest. 'I shall never leave you again. Never! Never!' Now they were both talking at the same time.

Then there was a fresh hubbub at the front door and Dorian came through it, shoving a dishevelled and mud-soaked figure ahead of him.

'Sarah! Tom!' Dorian shouted with relief. 'Thanks be to Allah, you are safe. I heard a pistol shot and then I saw this creature running down the hill.' He gave his captive a kick in the back of his knees which dropped him to the floor. 'I thought he was up to no good so I grabbed him.'

Tom saw that it was the youthful swordsman who had attacked him in the Botanical Gardens.

'Yes! He is one of the gang, if not the ringleader,' Tom said grimly. Still with one arm around Sarah protectively he came to stand over the man on the floor.

'Who are you?' he demanded in a murderous tone. 'Give me a good reason why we should not kill you the way we have done with your henchmen.'

The man on the floor looked up at him. Then with an obvious effort managed to control his terror, and scowled, 'Yes, Thomas Courtney. You are a natural born killer. You murdered my father – why not do the same to me, his son?'

Tom flinched at the accusation and the ferocity of his expression faded into uncertainty. It was a few seconds before he could gather his wits.

'Tell me then, who was this person that you accuse me of murdering?' he demanded.

'My father was William Courtney, your half-brother and my father.'

'William . . .' Tom gaped at him, 'You cannot mean that Billy, Black Billy was your father?'

'Yes, sir. William was my father.'

'Then that must make you Francis; Francis Courtney.'

Again, Tom remembered the green flash of the Mermaid's Wink. *A soul returning from the dead.*

He stooped and took Francis by the wrist and pulled him to his feet. 'It seems that you and I have much to discuss.' His tone was mild, but tinged with remorse, 'At the very least I owe you an explanation.'

When Francis awoke, he was lying in a feather bed. After months at sea, cramped in a narrow cot, it felt like heaven. For a moment, he thought he was back in High Weald, waiting for the servants to bring his breakfast.

He rolled over. A spasm of pain went through his side, and he remembered everything. He wasn't at High Weald. He hurt all over, he realized.

He opened his eyes. A coffee-skinned woman sat beside him, a shawl drawn over her hair. Behind her, a huge black man with a scarred face guarded the door.

'Where am I?'

'In the house of Tom and Dorian Courtney,' said the black man.

Francis jerked upright – too quick. Another bolt of pain shot through his head. He tried to get out of bed, but the agony was too great.

70

'Tom Courtney will kill me if he finds me here,' he gasped.

'Tom Courtney has spared your life. Who do you think had us bind your wounds and treat you like the gentleman I doubt you are?'

'Drink,' said the woman. She pressed a cup of some foul-tasting concoction to his lips. Francis tasted it, gagged and pushed the cup aside. The scar-faced black man stepped to the bed. He pinched Francis' nostrils to force him to open his mouth.

'Miss Yasmini says you drink, so you drink!' The woman tilted the cup between his lips, and Francis took the easy option, he drank. The effect was swift. The pain of his injuries abated miraculously, and was replaced by drowsiness. The bed was so soft. He closed his eyes.

Yasmini had cleaned his wounds; they were superficial. She had dressed them with ointment that she had prepared from wild herbs she collected with her own delicate hands. With Allah's grace, they would heal cleanly.

'Is he really Dorian and Tom's nephew, I wonder?' Yasmini asked.

'If he is not then he has come a long way for a lie.' Aboli shook his great shaven head. 'I knew William Courtney from the day he was born. This boy is his spitting image. Also, there is this.'

He showed her the decoration that sat on a dresser: a golden lion with ruby eyes, holding the world between diamond-spangled heavens. 'This belonged to Klebe's father. The boy was wearing it beneath his shirt. It proves beyond a doubt that he is who he says.

'But they say that Tom killed William, his brother. That is why he can never return to England. Tom never forgave himself for what happened with William. He will not make the same mistake with the son,' said Aboli.

A knock sounded at the door. Tom peered in. 'How is the patient?'

71

'You did not manage to kill him,' said Yasmini tartly. 'If you can keep yourself from assaulting him again, he will live.'

Tom went to the bed and looked down at Francis who was sound asleep. He had his father Billy's dense and coarse black hair, but his features were soft, almost girlishly pretty. Not at all like his father's had been. Tom hoped that his nature was also different. Black Billy had been hard, domineering and cruel.

Tom counted back the years since he had last seen the squalling baby Francis on the stairs at High Weald. The boy must be seventeen by now – the same age Tom had been when he left home.

Or rather when he had been forced to leave home, and never return to High Weald or to England. A wanted man with his brother's blood on his hands and on his conscience. He would never forget the dreadful moment when he had lifted the brim of the hat from the face of the man who had attacked him murderously in a dark alley in the dock area of the Thames, and whom he had been forced to kill in self-defence . . . and found that it was his own half-brother.

He picked up the decoration of the Order of St George, the gilded Lion cupping the world in his paws, and felt the weight of its magnificence. Though Tom had been dubbed a Nautonnier knight, he had never worn the decoration. William had seen to that.

'Call me when he wakes,' he told Aboli and Yasmini as he turned back to the door.

I could not save the father. Perhaps I can redeem myself with the son.

When Francis woke again, the woman had gone but the black man still guarded the door. He did not seem to have moved; Francis almost wondered if he might be carved from wood.

He sat up, tentatively, and found that if he moved slowly the pain was tolerable. He swung his legs out of the bed and stood, leaning on the wall for balance. Aboli did not try to stop him.

'Yasmini's medicine is working,' he observed.

Francis stared at him, then at the small window. Was it big enough? He wore nothing but a borrowed nightshirt. He would look like a lunatic, running through Cape Town. Would he be arrested?

Aboli indicated the corner of the room, where a shirt and a pair of breeches sat folded over a chair.

'If you wish to go, you had better get dressed.'

'You will not stop me?'

Aboli stepped aside from the door. 'You are safe, here. But if you are determined to leave. . .'

'Safe?' Francis echoed. 'Tom Courtney killed my father.' He had meant it to shock, but Aboli merely nodded. 'You do not deny it?'

'I knew your father from the day he was born,' said Aboli in measured tones. 'I can tell you from my heart, he was an evil man. A week before William died, Tom went to High Weald seeking help for their brother, and William attacked him. He would have killed Tom, but Tom was the better swordsman, and in the end it was he who had his sword at William's throat. Yet when Tom tried to make the final blow, he could not do it. His hand would not obey him. A week later, in London, William ambushed Tom on the docks without provocation; he watched other men do his work, and when they failed he drew his pistol to shoot Tom dead himself. I was there. Tom would have died that instant if he had not put his sword through your father's chest.'

He went on, making no allowances for the impact his words had on the boy. 'And even then, I think if your father had shown his face – if Tom had known who he really was – Tom would not have been able to strike the blow.'

'Why are you saying this?' Francis demanded. 'To turn me against my father?'

'It is the truth,' said Aboli. 'You may accept it, or not: it is your choice. But if you cling to a lie, eventually it will destroy you.' He gave a small bow. 'I will leave you to dress.'

After he had gone, Francis sat a long time on the edge of the bed. The storms that had raged inside him had blown themselves out; he hardly knew who he was any more. He looked at the clothes on the chair, and was not sure he had the strength to put them on. Aboli's words chased themselves around inside his head until he thought it would split open.

There were some things he could not remember from the night before, but one fact was branded in memory. Tom could have killed him, but he had not done so.

And that one fact had upended everything Francis believed in. He remembered what his mother had told him: *Tom couldn't have killed his brother in cold blood.* He had not believed her. Now that he had been at Tom Courtney's mercy, and lived, he had to consider that she could have been telling the truth.

Sitting there, he saw himself with new eyes. Consorting with thieves and prostitutes, trying to murder a member of his own family: what had he become? And in return, Tom Courtney had repaid him with mercy and kindness.

If you cling to a lie, eventually it will destroy you.

But did he have the strength to let it go?

When Francis came down, Tom was in the parlour sitting in his chair and staring at the Order of St George in his hands. Francis had dressed in a pair of Dorian's breeches and a shirt of Tom's which hung off him like a mainsail. He paused on the stairs; Tom thought he might flee at the very sight of him. But Francis knew he could not put this off. He swallowed his fear and continued down.

74

He reached the bottom of the stairs. The two men stared at each other, uncertain of what to say.

Tom broke the silence. 'Sometimes it's easier meeting a man with a sword in your hand,' he said gruffly. 'You don't have to think what to say.'

Francis nodded. Then, all of a sudden, words burst out of him, 'I am grateful to you for your care. I . . . You would have been within your rights to send me to the authorities. Or worse.'

'I am glad we can meet on more tranquil terms,' said Tom. He stared at the boy as if he might disappear into thin air. 'Are you really Billy's son?'

Francis straightened. 'I am.'

'Then how did you come to be in the Company gardens with scum like Jacob de Vries?'

'We met in a tavern. A . . . a whore introduced us.' Francis looked shamefaced. 'Perhaps I should tell you the whole story.'

Tom called Dorian and Aboli to join them. Francis stared in wonder at the two men, Aboli with his scarified face and Dorian in his turban and Arab dress. His real shock came when he learned who Dorian was.

'Is everything I was told a lie? I always believed you were dead.'

'It is a long tale,' said Dorian. 'Which you shall hear in its turn. But first, I think you were about to tell my brother how you came to find us here.'

Sitting on the torn cushions, Francis told them everything. Tom paced; he cursed audibly when he heard how Sir Walter had ruined High Weald.

'Poor Alice. Everything stems from the day I killed Billy.'

'She would have been no happier with William,' said Aboli. 'You saw how he treated her. The way he beat her, he might have killed both her and Francis. No,' he added, seeing Tom's protest, 'the boy must know the full truth about his father.'

'I knew it already,' said Francis. 'Before I left, my mother told me about my father and the way he treated her. She said you acted to defend yourself.' He shook his head, embarrassed. 'I did not believe her.'

'Aye,' said Tom, remembering that infernal night. 'But it was not all Billy's fault. I am certain he would not have known where to find us, had Lord Childs not arranged it.'

Francis' face paled with shock. 'Sir Nicholas Childs? Then I am doubly forsaken. It was he who sent me, who told me where I might find you. He promised me five thousand pounds if I killed you.'

'For five thousand pounds, even I might have considered it,' said Dorian, turning it into a little joke, but Tom continued seriously.

'You would never have seen the money. Childs is a spider, spinning webs that reach to the furthest corners of the globe. He sits in his lair, his office in Leadenhall Street, and devours any man who threatens so much as a penny of his fortune. I had helped earn him twenty thousand pounds in prize money, yet he ordered me killed because I refused him a share of a tiny sloop. He is a monster.'

'I see that now.'

'Wiser men than you have been snared by his schemes. Even your father Billy, I think, did not realize he was but a pawn in Childs' machinations. Billy wanted to kill me, but it was Childs who gave him the means. No doubt, had Billy succeeded, Childs would have found ways to use his guilt against him.'

Francis frowned. 'Then what shall I do? Lord Childs gave me letters of introduction to my uncle Guy at the Company factory in Bombay, but—' He broke off as he registered Tom's reaction. 'What is it?'

'Guy is another story entirely.'

'But Francis is a Courtney, and he should know the truth of our family,' said Dorian gently. 'It is these secrets and half-truths that drive us apart, and give men like Lord Childs the leverage to use us against each other.'

Before Tom could answer, there was a knock at the door. Ana Duarte came in.

'Am I interrupting? I thought we had agreed to meet this morning to discuss my proposal further.' And then, taking in the presence of Francis, she asked, 'Who is this?'

A curious expression had come over her face. Her lips parted; she stared at Francis as if he were the only man in the room. Unconsciously, her hand moved to adjust the neckline of her dress.

Tom gathered his thoughts, and introduced them. 'This is our nephew, Francis. He arrived from England, er, somewhat unexpectedly last night. Francis, this is Ana Duarte. She is a business partner of ours, or perhaps I am being premature.'

Francis nodded, as if in a dream – the most lucid dream he had ever experienced. Everything about Ana seemed to leap out at him with minute clarity. A lock of hair curling from behind her ear; the playful curve of her lips; the depths of her honey-brown eyes, locked on his.

The silence stretched out. Everyone waited for him to say something, but he did not trust his voice.

'Francis took a blow to the head last night. Perhaps he has not quite recovered,' said Tom.

Worry clouded Ana's eyes. 'Is he hurt? What happened?'

'Tom had to knock him out to stop him trying to murder us,' said Dorian.

Ana looked between the two brothers. She took in the cuts and contusions on their faces and arms. She had been aware of the smell of burned gunpowder in the air and the spot of blood on the carpet that all Mrs Lai's exertions had not managed to remove.

'I trust you have persuaded him to reconsider?'

Dorian peered at Francis. 'I believe so. I think he was under a misapprehension.'

Francis stood carefully, not sure his legs would oblige. His mouth had gone dry. 'I was poorly advised.'

No, he realized, that was not right. He felt the others watching him, Ana most of all. It was time for him to take responsibility.

'I listened to other men's lies, and not to those I should have trusted. I am sorry for the danger I brought on your family, and if there is anything I can do to make amends I will do it gladly. I have learned my lesson.'

Tom put his arm around his shoulders. 'Come,' he said. 'Before you arrived last night, Miss Duarte had just suggested we become partners in business. You left England to seek your fortune: perhaps we can help you find it.'

Francis nodded, and followed the others to the dining room, holding the door for Ana.

He had entirely forgotten the conversation that had been interrupted by her arrival. Only much later did he think to wonder: why had Tom acted so strangely when he mentioned his uncle Guy?

In the brilliant sunshine the surface of the sea seemed so smooth and bright that it might have been carved from solid rock. Even where the wavelets met the land, they undulated but did not break. Just off the beach two East Indiamen swung lazily on their anchors.

In the estuary, a ring of low-lying islets clustered around a marshy basin. Stone built forts crowned every hilltop. The tiered towers and multiple eaves of a great pagoda rose from a grove of ancient twisted Banyan trees. Across a narrow channel, barely wider than a musket shot, lay the shores of the great Indian subcontinent.

Christopher Courtney heard the fort gun boom out the noon hour. He wiped his face, sweating in his best coat and heavy breeches. All the merchants in Bombay concluded their business in the early morning before retreating to the relative cool of their houses. At this hour, he was the only man abroad.

'Two monsoons are the age of a man,' said an old Bombay

proverb – to reach it Christopher had only to survive two years. For some men, that was optimistic. The foetid air rising off the salt marsh, coupled with the noxious stink of the rotted fish the natives used to manure their coconut palms, claimed some arrivals even before they got off their ships. The rest stayed indoors as much as they could, counting their profits and the days until they could escape to England.

Christopher had now survived fifteen monsoons – his whole life, leaving aside three years spent in Zanzibar. Indeed, while other men wilted and died, he had flourished: tall and lean, with a firm jaw and deep brown eyes – not a bit like his father, men said approvingly, though never in his father's presence.

Despite the heat, he was shivering. A slouching sentry let him through the gate, and across the courtyard to the Governor's house. It was a relic from the time when the Portuguese had owned the islands: an imposing three-storey building with a Portuguese crest still carved above the door. It towered over the walls of the fort, which had been built around it when the English took over the island.

Even though it was his home, Christopher's breath quickened with anxiety as he entered. He climbed the stairs, and knocked timidly on the stout teak doors that guarded the Governor's office.

'Enter,' barked the familiar voice.

Guy Courtney sat at his desk, in front of three tall windows from which he could look down on every ship anchored in the harbour. Papers were stacked neatly on his desk: letter books and consultation books, manifests and loading bills, all the ink and paper that drove the Company's trade no less than the winds that sped her ships. On the wall to his left, Guy's father Hal looked down from an oil painting, his hand resting on the hilt of a great golden sword. A huge sapphire bulged from its pommel, painted with such lustre it seemed to glow off the canvas.

A black servant stood beside Guy, wafting him with a silver-handled peacock feather. Guy didn't look up.

'What is it?' he snapped.

Christopher clutched the brim of his hat. He took another deep breath. 'I have come to ask your permission to marry, Father.'

Guy went still. '*Marry?*' He repeated the word as if it stank of dung. 'What in the world possessed you of this notion?'

'I am of age.'

'That hardly signifies. Who is the girl who has caught your foolish fancy?'

'Ruth Reedy.'

'Who?'

'Corporal Reedy's daughter. From the garrison.'

'That wench? She's little more than a punch-house doxy!' Guy's expression changed. He tipped back his head and laughed. 'For a moment, I thought you were serious. I had heard reports you were seen together, but I assumed you were merely tupping her behind the stables, like a dozen other youngsters of your age are doing to her. Perhaps I gave you too much credit.'

'I love her.'

Guy studied his son through half-closed eyes. The boy had always been headstrong – like his father. Quick witted and strong willed, he had all the makings of a fine merchant. So much potential: Guy had taken great pains in his education. He had beaten him blue, trying to thrash out the contrary elements in the boy's nature, to make him fit for the future he alone could give him. And still the boy had not learned.

Perhaps kindness could succeed where force had failed. He softened his tone.

'I know how it is to be young. When I was your age, and foolish, I loved a girl so hard I almost gave my life for her honour. It was only later I found she was a common whore, a bitch who'd give herself to anyone who had a few rupees.'

80

Even after so many years, the memory made him hot with anger. He forced himself to be calm. He had made her pay many times over, once she became his wife.

'Your mistakes are not my concern, Father.'

'But yours are mine. You will not marry this girl. I forbid it, as your father and as Governor of the Bombay Presidency. You know that any marriage contracted in this colony must be approved by me in order to be valid.'

'You would deny your own son?'

'When he is out of his mind, yes.' Guy pushed himself back in his chair. 'You wish to marry? I will see to it. You are of age now, and it is right you should take a wife. I have been remiss: if I had acted sooner, perhaps we would have avoided this foolishness altogether. After the monsoon, we will sail to England together, and I will find you a suitable bride. Sir Nicholas Childs has a niece who is eligible, or perhaps the Earl of Godolphin's grand-daughter. We will make a match that secures your prospects admirably.'

And mine, he thought, though it hardly needed to be said. What use was a son if not to advance his father's interests? Already, in his mind, he was counting the extra shares he might acquire with a well-contracted marriage. Perhaps a seat on the Court of Directors, even a royal appointment as Ambassador Plenipotentiary.

Christopher just stared at him. He had always been a sullen boy, Guy thought, despite all his paternal efforts. An ingrate, who could not conceive how much Guy had sacrificed for him.

'I hear from London that Sir Nicholas Childs is not a well man,' Guy went on. 'One day, perhaps you may find yourself sitting in the great office in Leadenhall Street.'

Even this optimistic prospect drew no reaction from the lad. It occurred to Guy that perhaps Christopher had not even been rogering the corporal's daughter. Perhaps he had been saving himself, out of some misguided ideal of marriage. When Guy was his age, after all, he had believed in a pure, chaste love. Before his brother Tom had snatched his illusions from him.

'I know you have needs. I am guilty of neglecting them.' He pulled a golden pagoda from the locked drawer in his desk and tossed it to Christopher. 'A down payment on your future bride's dowry. Take yourself to the brothel by the customs house – the clean one, where the officers go – and find a girl who can service you.' He chuckled. 'Just don't fall in love with her, for God's sake.'

Christopher stared at the coin as if he had never seen one before. He held it up, so that the golden light played across his face.

'You would do all this? For me?'

Guy felt a rare spark of paternal pride. 'All I have ever wanted is a great future for you.'

The coin slipped through Christopher's fingers and fell onto the desk. It landed on its edge, spinning round and round making a glittering orb.

'You are a monster, Father. A cruel, calculating ogre with nothing but a strongbox where your heart should be. You would sacrifice your only son's happiness to make me a pawn to your ambitions. I will not play that game.'

The coin fell flat as Guy stood, pushing the desk away from him in fury.

'How dare you defy me?'

Christopher stood his ground. 'I am not a little boy any longer, whom you can beat to your will. I will make my life how I choose, not how you design it. I will go where I please and marry whom I please.'

The veins in Guy's neck throbbed. 'Be careful, Christopher. There is nowhere on either side of this ocean that my power does not reach.'

'I do not fear you.'

'You should,' said Guy dangerously. 'I could destroy you.'

Christopher stared at him. 'Can you hear yourself? What sort of a man would say such a thing to his son? Sometimes I think you cannot be my father.'

His words struck a nerve he had never touched before. With an incoherent howl of rage, Guy grabbed a silver paper knife from his letter basket and hurled it at Christopher. It flew past his ear and stuck, quivering, in the doorframe.

Christopher didn't flinch. He stared down at his father, his body rigid with controlled fury. It occurred to Guy that he had never noticed how tall his son had become.

'Farewell, Father. We shall not meet again.'

'Wait,' Guy called. But Christopher had gone.

The sunlight struck him like a bolt of lightning before his eyes. Dazed, reeling from the enormousness of what he had done, he stumbled across the square. Ruth met him by the shore, where rusting anchors and cast-off lengths of rope littered the strand. Though it was less than an hour since she had seen him last, she flung her arms around him and clung to him as if they had been parted for years.

She had arrived with her father nine months earlier. Christopher had watched the arrival of the Indiaman that brought her. From the castle walls, he had glimpsed her in the boat that rowed her ashore: just sixteen, with alabaster skin and rich red hair, colours he'd never seen on a girl before. As her boat passed the castle, she had looked up – doubtless wondering about her new home – and caught Christopher's eye. At that moment, he had felt a stir in his loins such as he had never felt before; he could hardly breathe with desire.

Of course, an English girl arriving in Bombay was like a rose in the desert, and there was no shortage of men wanting to pluck her for themselves. But they all retreated when they learned Guy Courtney's son was interested.

Even then, it took time. Christopher was awkward; he did

not know how to speak to a girl who was not a servant. Many nights he lay awake, abusing himself, imagining the taste of Ruth's lips, furious at his lack of courage.

But Ruth was patient. She understood how Christopher felt, in a way his mother and father never did. She saw the love in his heart, and coaxed it out. At an assembly in the Governor's house, where soldiers' families were admitted because there were so few other women, she sought him out for a dance. The first time he touched her hand, his whole body convulsed. He had danced the whole night almost bulging out his breeches, certain that everyone must be laughing at him. But Ruth did not laugh. She helped him around the dance floor, and when they moved towards each other she overstepped just a little, so that she pressed against him and he felt every curve of her body through her thin cotton dress.

After that, he saw her almost every day: snatched moments behind the warehouses, or on the beach at Back Bay, beyond the coconut plantations. They held hands and walked across the sand while she told him about England, the country he came from but had never seen. She had seen so much, things he had only ever read in books or heard discussed among his father's Company colleagues. She spoke to him with respect, talking easily while he stood tongue-tied by her beauty.

They kissed, and he thought life could not get any sweeter. Later, she had allowed him to unlace her bodice and touch her breasts, while she slipped her hand inside his breeches and teased his throbbing manhood. But she would not let him go further. 'I cannot, until I am married,' she insisted; and he buried his face between her breasts and promised, 'I will marry you.'

Now, she saw Christopher's desolate expression and cupped his face in her hands. 'What did he say? Dear heart, are you ill? Did he give his permission?'

'He forbade it.' Christopher sat down hard on the hull of a

rotting boat drawn up above the tideline. A cloud of flies rose off it in protest.

Tears clouded her innocent blue eyes. 'Whatever will we do? I cannot live without you, my love. I would rather die.'

Christopher closed his eyes. The blinding light made it impossible to think. He rubbed his temples, replaying the conversation with his father. His love for Ruth was so pure, so true, how could his father deny it? How *dare* he? For a moment, the futility was so bleak he contemplated tying one of those rusting anchors to his leg and throwing himself into the harbour. He would end it all, escape the suffocating weight of his thwarted love and *make* his father understand.

But that would be no victory.

'I will leave Bombay,' he said suddenly.

'Let me come with you!'

He shook his head. 'My father has left me with nothing. I must earn my fortune the hard way, and it will be no place for a woman. Stay here, stay with your family, and wait for me to return.'

'I cannot.'

'You must. I know it will be hard, but you must for both our sakes.' He stood and hugged her tight to him, breathing in the perfume of her hair. He was alive with desire for her, but even more than that he longed to prove his father wrong. 'Stay here, and let him think he has won. When I return, my victory will be complete – and so will our happiness.'

She kissed him on the lips. 'Promise me, Christopher. Promise me we shall be happy.'

'I promise, my love. If you wait for me, I will make such a fortune that even my father cannot touch us.'

'I will wait. I swear it, even if you are gone twenty years I will wait for you. I will sit every day in this place and watch the sea for your return.'

'Like Odysseus and Penelope,' said Christopher, stroking her hand.

She wrinkled her brow. 'Who?'

'It doesn't matter.' He shrugged off the coat that was now heavy with his sweat. Now that he had decided, he was suddenly impatient to be away. Shading his eyes, he stared out into the harbour. The East Indiamen still slumbered at their moorings, but there was movement on the deck of a small coastal trader as her crew made ready for sea.

'That ship will be sailing on the tide. I will take passage with her, and go wherever she takes me.' He kissed her again, and she thrilled at the feel of his strong arms around her.

'Wait for me, my love.'

'I promise I will.'

He had no baggage to take with him. All his possessions were in his room in the Governor's house, and he could not go back there. Christopher went to the landing place and hailed one of the small bumboats to take him out to the trader. He read her name *Joseph*, carved on her transom as the boatmen rowed him out to the trader.

He went aboard. Most of the crew were Indians, dark-skinned men working almost naked to stow the cargo. The only white man on deck seemed to be the master, a large man with close-cropped hair and a mermaid tattoo on his bulging forearm. He broke off from supervising the loading and came over.

'Well?' he barked.

'I want to join your ship.'

The master looked him up and down. His face soured. 'I know you. You're Christopher Courtney, the Governor's son.'

Christopher nodded.

'He's a sorry twat.'

He was so close that his spittle sprayed Christopher's face. Christopher didn't flinch.

'Well?' said the master. 'Are you going to let me insult your father and just stand there? What sort of a man would do that?'

'If I cared what my father thought, I wouldn't be here.'

The master gave him a stinging slap across his cheek. 'That's enough impertinence. You respect your betters on this ship, or else.'

He bared his teeth, daring Christopher to strike back. Christopher fought the urge and forced himself to stay still. If he had learned one thing from his father, it was how to take a beating.

The master spat on the deck. A gob of phlegm landed next to Christopher's toe.

'Have you ever worked a ship?'

'No, sir.'

'Ever been to sea before?'

'No, sir.'

'Then why should I take you on my crew? This isn't one of your father's gold-plated Indiamen with a crew of layabouts. Every man here earns his keep, or by God I'll have him off this ship so fast you won't even hear the splash.'

'I'm a hard worker, sir.'

'You don't know the meaning of hard work.' He snatched Christopher's hand and turned it palm up. 'Look at that lily-white skin. The only thing you've ever used these hands for is jerking your own cock.' He turned his back. 'Get off my ship, before I throw you in.'

'Wait,' said Christopher. He grabbed one of the bales of cloth sitting on the deck. 'What is this? *Culbeleys*? Silk mixed with carmania wool? And this is *jurries*, the longest-lasting cotton cloth. This one—'

'Get your hands off my cargo.' The master grabbed Christopher by his shirtfront, lifted him off the deck and carried him to the side. He pushed him out over the gunwale.

'Eight rupees,' gasped Christopher. 'Eight rupees the yard. That is what the East India Company will pay for *culbeleys*. Six rupees for *jurries*.'

He teetered on the gunwale. The master's face loomed above him, framed by a matrix of rigging and the blue sky behind.

'How do you know this?'

'I clerked for my father. I wrote the entries in his ledger books. I know what the Company will pay for every cargo in every port on this coast.' Big hands choked his neck; he could hardly breathe. 'That knowledge could be useful to you.'

The master let him go. He slumped onto the deck, rubbing his neck.

A heavy boot kicked him in the ribs.

'Get up.'

Ignoring the pain and the nausea in his stomach, Christopher stood. The master studied him like a hungry shark.

'I'll take you as my apprentice. Your pay is four rupees a month, less deductions for rations and slops.' He saw the look on Christopher's face and laughed. 'You think you're worth more than that, you lily-fingered bum boy? Find another ship.'

Christopher clenched his fists. *You knew it wouldn't be easy*, he told himself. *You must learn a trade before you can hope to make your fortune.*

'I accept.'

The master almost looked disappointed. *He wants to hit me again*, Christopher realized. The thought didn't frighten him. Growing up with Guy, he took it almost for granted.

The master fetched the muster book and Christopher signed his name. His neatly printed English letters were like genteel islands against the sea of marks, crosses and Indian characters the other sailors had left on the page.

In the heat, the ink dried almost faster than he could put it on the page. The master slammed the book shut.

'You belong to me now, and God help you if I catch you shirking your duty. Aboard my ship, your father's name counts for nothing. You may have white skin and pretty writing, but

I'll flog you as hard as any of these darkies if you cross me. You understand?'

'Yes, sir.'

The master glared at him. Christopher dropped his head meekly, stooping his shoulders in a submissive attitude he had often adopted during his father's tirades. The master grunted.

'Now get to work.'

In less than ten minutes, Christopher discovered the hardship he had let himself in for. Stripped to his waist, still wearing his best wool britches, he joined the other seamen on the capstan to haul up the anchor. The sun flayed his naked back; the capstan bars rubbed his hands raw. He glanced up, staring at the horizon to take his mind off the pain. Ashore, he saw a commotion on the waterfront: a group of men in Company uniforms gesticulating at the *Joseph*. Was it his father? Perhaps he had reconsidered.

A heavy blow fell across his back. He jerked around, and was almost knocked down by the capstan bar swinging into him from behind. He resumed his position at the capstan bar. From the corner of his eye he saw the master watching from the sidelines, dangling the short length of rope he'd used to strike him.

'No second thoughts, Lilyhands. Desert, and I'll see you keelhauled.'

'Don't let him goad you,' whispered a voice behind him. He spoke Portuguese, the *lingua franca* of the Malabar coast. Christopher craned back, still trudging at the capstan, and saw a slim youth with dark skin and bright eyes, pushing at the near spoke. He must have been younger than Christopher, but his hands were calloused and his young body rippled with muscles.

'Captain Crawford's a devil,' he whispered again, barely audible over the creak of the capstan. 'But there are ways to avoid him. The more you fight him, the more he'll try to break you.'

The anchor came up and was catted and fished. The sails were loosed, and slowly they filled with the afternoon breeze coming off the sea. Christopher hauled on the ropes as he was ordered, always with a lick of Crawford's starter rope to encourage him. He refused to look back.

That night, he made his bed on deck, near the bow. He lay on the hard planking, feeling the aches racking his body, and stared at the stars. That morning, he'd woken in his feather bed at the Governor's house, servants jumping to his every need. Now he didn't even have a blanket to lie on.

A dark figure came and sat beside him. White teeth gleamed in the darkness. It was the youth who'd spoken to him on the capstan.

'My name is Danesh,' he introduced himself.

'Christopher.'

'Is your father really the Governor of Bombay?'

'Yes.'

'You must hate him very much.'

Christopher remembered the look in Guy's eyes. 'Yes. I do.'

Danesh handed him a blanket. 'Before we are finished, you will hate Crawford even more.'

The next three weeks were the hardest Christopher had known in his life. On the second day, Crawford sent him aloft to reef a sail. It was only when he was halfway up the shrouds that he looked down and realized no one had followed. The other men waited on deck, watching him, making wagers among themselves.

A gust of wind made the ship heel over. Only gently, but to Christopher it felt like a hurricane. He tipped back; the waves seemed to race towards him. The men on deck catcalled and jeered, Crawford shouted something, but he could hardly make out the words above the blood pounding in his ears. His grip started to slip.

The ship rolled back. His stomach lurched again. His gaze began to drift down, but he knew that if he looked at the sea again he would let go and fall. He wrenched his gaze upwards, fixing his sight on the main top and forcing himself to move, one hand at a time, hauling himself up. Each step was pure terror; each time his hands closed on the ropes again, he gripped them like a baby clutching his mother's finger.

At last, he reached the top. It was misnamed, for it was only the top of the main mast – the topmast and topgallant mast rose higher still – but to him it felt as if he'd conquered the highest mountain.

Down on deck, no one cheered him. With a shock, he realized they were not impressed with what he had achieved. Rather, they had wanted to see him fall. That was all his life was worth: entertainment to liven up the watch.

They might yet get it. His ordeal wasn't over. Now he was up, he had to edge out along the main yard, with nothing under his feet except the thin foot rope. Reluctantly, the other sailors joined him. They ran along the yard, balancing like monkeys and immune to the roll of the ship. Some jostled Christopher intentionally, treading on his fingers or knocking his shoulders as they passed.

They want me to die.

His fingers slipped and fumbled as he struggled to undo the gaskets that bound the sail. The foot rope swung under him, the thinnest thread that felt like standing on thin air. Then there was the descent, the terror every time he lowered a foot, finding each foothold by touch because he didn't dare look down.

When he finally reached the deck he clung to the shrouds, not trusting his legs to keep him upright. He nearly vomited over the side. But deep down, a small ember of satisfaction glowed inside him. *He'd done it.* From across the deck, Danesh mouthed, 'Well done.'

91

The slap of the starter rope across his shoulders scattered his thoughts. He spun around, raw and vulnerable, to see Crawford leering at him.

'I didn't order you to come down.'

Christopher bit back the retort that came to his lips. Automatically, he lowered his head and waited for Crawford's temper to pass.

'I want you keeping lookout. There are pirates in these waters. If one of them gets within a mile of us, I'll skin you alive.'

Christopher flinched as if he'd been hit again. He looked up at the main top, impossibly high. Could he really go there again?

Crawford followed his gaze, and an evil smile spread across his lips.

'You won't see anything from there. I want you on the cross-trees.'

High above the main top, the crosstrees were little more than a wooden grating sticking from the top of the topmast. So small, Christopher could hardly see it from the deck. Even looking up at it made him dizzy.

He didn't move. Crawford licked his lips and coiled the rope. He flexed it, testing its strength.

'Are you disobeying an order?'

Christopher fought back the tears that were pricking his eyes. He would not give Crawford the satisfaction.

'No, sir.'

'Then get your lily white arse aloft before I have to order you again. And you'll stay there,' he added, 'until I give you permission to come down.'

Christopher began to climb.

He had hated before, but he hated this more than anything in his life. Even more than his father. Indeed, he rarely thought of Guy any longer. The constant work of handling a

92

ship, forever fumbling, always the last to finish his tasks, left no time for idle thoughts. When he stumbled off watch, he would curl up in the forecastle, nursing his aches and rubbing oil on the blisters that formed as big as pagoda coins on his hands.

The rest of the crew shunned him. As a white man, he was alien; as a sailor, they despised him. Only Danesh showed him any kindness, and even he seemed cautious about being seen with Christopher too often. He had never been so lonely. In time, he began to look forward to being sent up to the cross-trees, though he could never look down. Sitting among the sails, he felt like a god in the clouds, far above mortal men and their petty fears and hatreds. In those moments, he tried to imagine his future with Ruth, the house they would live in and the fine presents he would buy her. But all too often, those thoughts turned dark, as he began to dream of how he would get even with Crawford, his father, and every man who had ever done him wrong.

One afternoon, during the dogwatch, he went below to fetch water. He liked going into the hold. The smells of baling yarn and freshly packed cloth reminded him of the Company ware-houses where he'd played as a child.

'Chris,' Danesh hissed from the gloom. 'See this.'

Something gleamed in the palm of his hand. A brass key.

'What's that for?'

'The forward locker,' whispered Danesh. 'I stole it from Crawford's cabin while he was inspecting the rigging.'

The forward locker was where they kept the spirits. It was supposed to be for the use of the crew, but it was widely rumoured that Crawford kept most of it for sale on his own account.

Christopher glanced anxiously over his shoulder. 'What if he finds us?'

'He won't miss a few bottles. We can sell them in port. Hurry.'

Danesh slipped the key in the padlock and sprang it. The sharp tang of spirits wafted out through the open door.

'You stay here and keep lookout. If he catches us, he will flay us alive.'

Danesh handed Christopher the key and ducked into the store. Christopher stood there, staring. He knew he should run, leave Danesh to his fate and disclaim all knowledge if he was caught. It wasn't his idea. But Danesh was the closest thing he had to a friend on the ship. If he lost him, he'd have nothing.

Feet thudded on the deck above; the ship's movements made shadows flit across the square of light that came through the hatchway.

'Be quick,' Christopher called. 'I think someone's coming.'

Danesh reappeared, with four bottles of brandy cradled in his arms. He laid them on the floor.

'Crawford keeps enough to make an elephant drunk,' he whispered. 'One more load will be enough for both of us.'

'No,' hissed Christopher. 'Let's go now. We—'

The ladder creaked under the weight of a heavy tread. A pair of shoes appeared, giving way to a pair of fat legs in white stockings, then a pair of breeches, then a corpulent torso straining the buttons of its shirt.

Quick as thought, Danesh dived behind the anchor cable, whose huge coils made a nest big enough for a man. Christopher, petrified, stayed rooted to his spot.

Crawford ducked his head under the hatchway and stepped off the ladder. Deliberately, he took in the open locker, the bottles at Christopher's feet and the key in his hand.

'I thought I might find someone here when I noticed my key was missing.'

Christopher said nothing.

'How did you get it? Who helped you?'

Christopher stared straight at Crawford, fixing his gaze so

he wouldn't betray Danesh with a stray glance. Crawford took it as arrogance.

'Do you think you're better than me because your father's Governor of Bombay? Do you think that gives you the right to steal from me?'

Crawford's face was dark with rage, like clouds threatening thunder. Christopher knew that look. He braced himself.

'Boatswain,' Crawford bellowed. 'Bring Mr Courtney on deck, and summon all hands to witness punishment.'

Rough hands dragged him up the ladder. By the time he reached the top, all the crew had gathered around a small barrel that had been set out behind the mainmast. Crawford went to his cabin and returned with a length of rope, thinner and suppler than the starter rope which he usually used. He ran it through his fingers, then tied two knots in the end.

'Prepare the prisoner,' he ordered.

They bent Christopher over the barrel. The iron hoops, which had been sitting in the sun, seared welts across his naked chest, but he knew that was just a taste of the pain to come. The boatswain held his hands, while one of the sailors pinned his feet, so he was stretched over the barrel like a piece of laundry.

Behind him, Crawford rolled back his shirtsleeve. Methodically, he uncoiled the rope. He cracked it on the deck, twice, limbering himself up. He planted his feet firmly, reached back his arm and the first blow hit Christopher with a sound like a musket shot. The pain was excruciating. He bit down on the rag between his teeth, determined not to cry out. Before he could even draw breath, a second blow hit him between the shoulder blades. Then a third, then—

He almost lost count. Pain came in waves, one after another so fast they blurred together into a single moment of agony. Crawford had abandoned all pretence of discipline: this was a thrashing, savage and uncontrolled, as if he wanted to crush every bone in Christopher's body.

But Christopher forced himself to keep counting. Through the agony, he counted every stroke. It was how he had survived his father's beatings, and it was how he survived this one, drawing strength from the number he had endured. Totting up the blows in some imaginary ledger, to be repaid with interest one day. As long as he could number them, he would survive them.

The blows became weaker. Crawford swung his arm with undimmed fury, but he was tiring. He dropped the rope, its end frayed and matted with Christopher's blood and skin. The crew drifted back to their tasks. The men who had pinned him let Christopher go: they were spattered with his blood. He rolled off the barrel into a heap on the deck. He closed his eyes, soaking up the pain.

Someone put a mug of rum to his lips and he drank thirstily. Danesh. It didn't make the pain go away, but it did dull it a little.

Danesh cleaned his back. Crawford refused him fresh water: he had to use a bucket dipped over the side. The salt water hurt almost more than the whip. A black haze covered Christopher's sight; he wanted to move, but his limbs wouldn't obey.

'Forty-nine,' he croaked.

'What do you mean?'

'Forty-nine lashes.' Christopher grinned, his lips cracking with the effort. 'He couldn't even get to fifty. Weakling,' he said, and fainted.

A week later, the *Joseph* anchored in the port of Trivandrum. The crew were merry: it was their first opportunity to go ashore since Bombay, and they planned to enjoy themselves to the full. Crawford brought out a table and stool onto the main deck, and the men queued to receive their pay.

Christopher waited until all the others had finished, scrawling their marks in the book and walking away with a few coins in their fists. At last, when it was his turn, he stepped forward and put out his hand. Crawford leered at him.

'What do you want?'

'My wages.'

'Of course.' Crawford made a great play of counting out the coins. He pushed them across the table, but as Christopher reached to take them, he grabbed his wrist and bent it back until the coins spilled out.

'What do you think you're doing?'

Tears of pain blinked in Christopher's eyes. He thought his wrist would snap.

'Taking my wages.'

'Are you thieving from me again? Those belong to me.'

'You said four rupees a week.'

'You signed on as my apprentice. That means all your wages go to me.' Crawford let go of Christopher's wrist, so that he stumbled backwards into the group of watching sailors. No one caught him; he landed hard on the deck. Crawford swept the coins off the table and put them back in the box. He snapped it shut and stood, hand twitching at the knife in his belt.

'Have I made myself clear?'

Christopher lay on the deck, clutching his wrist. Hatred consumed him: all he wanted was to stick the knife in Crawford's guts and see him bleed out on the deck. He felt the eyes of the whole crew watching him, enjoying his humiliation, and he hated them too.

He pushed himself upright, ignoring the pain that shot through his wrist, and faced down Crawford. The master looked surprised to see him standing.

'I understand,' said Christopher thickly. He didn't trust himself to say more.

Crawford was about to provoke him again, but something made him pause. Even in the few weeks of their voyage,

Christopher had changed from the callow youth who had come aboard in Bombay. His shoulders had broadened out, and his arms had become thicker. He no longer stooped as much. But it was in his face that the difference was most obvious. Harder and firmer, with black eyes that unsettled with the intensity of their gaze. Though Crawford would never admit it, they frightened him.

He turned away. 'Lower the boats,' he ordered. 'We're going ashore. Not you,' he barked at Christopher. 'You stay aboard to keep anchor watch. Anything happens to my ship while I'm away, I'll nail you to the topmast and let the crows have you. Understand?'

Christopher saw Danesh giving him a sympathetic glance. None of the others even glanced in his direction. All Christopher could do was watch as they clambered into the longboat and rowed ashore. Danesh went too. A group of women waited on the beach to welcome them, dragging each man towards the nearest punch house. Whatever pay they'd had, it would be gone by morning. That was no consolation to Christopher.

He settled down in the shade of the awning, whittling a piece of wood with his knife. He had the ship to himself, and he revelled in the solitude. All his life he had been kept on his own, an only child forbidden to mix with the other children in the settlement, because his father deemed them inferior. Of the few he had befriended, most had died or gone back to England. His mother kept to her chamber, for fear of rousing his father's temper. He was used to being alone.

But he now realized that he would never make his fortune this way. Even if he survived Crawford's bullying, it would be years before he had enough money even to buy himself a new suit of cheap clothes. He could not ask Ruth to wait so long.

There was another lesson he had learned from his father. Sitting in the Governor's house, quiet and unnoticed, he had watched men come and go from his father's office. In the silent house, conversations carried. He had heard men abuse his father in terms he could not have imagined, and walk out of the office with their heads high, convinced they had won a victory. And he had seen those same men weeks or month later, boarding ships to England in poverty or disgrace, broken men who had lost everything. One had even been taken aboard in irons, all for having been discovered in a unnatural act with a sepoy drummer boy.

Never forget. Never forgive. And take your vengeance when it will most hurt your enemy. He had discovered a new axiom.

He brooded on this, until the sun went down and the land disappeared. The lights in the harbour burned bright against the darkness.

He lit the ship's lamps fore and aft, and checked her anchor cable. He went to the galley, and helped himself to stew from the pot the cook had left. Rummaging through the stores, he found a bottle of arak, the local liquor. He gulped down three or four mouthfuls, delighting in the fiery taste. It gave him courage.

'I didn't escape my father to serve another tyrant,' he muttered to himself. He slipped through the hatch to the lower deck. Much of the *Joseph*'s cargo was bulk goods, bales of cloth and sacks of rice too large for his purposes. He scrabbled around until he felt the smooth sheen of a parcel of silk. That would do.

This close to the waterline, he could hear the water lapping against her timbers. Every creak of the ship echoed down through the mast. Something knocked against the hull – probably just a wave, or a piece of driftwood, but it set him on edge. Sweat prickled his hands; the liquor rose like bile in his throat.

He stuffed his pockets with betel nuts from a sack, hoisted the silk bale over his shoulder and stole up the companionway. The longboat was still ashore, but there was a small jolly boat he could row single-handed. He took out his knife and started sawing through the ropes that held it.

'Where do you think you're going?' growled Crawford. He stood silhouetted against the stern lantern, casting a long shadow across the deck. 'Are you stealing from me again? Didn't I beat it out of you last time?'

He had come aboard without Christopher hearing. Whether because he did not trust Christopher, or because he had come back to finish the boy without witnesses, Christopher never found out. The captain stepped forward and punched Christopher in the face so hard he flew backwards into the rigging.

'You'll have to hit me harder than that,' Christopher told him. A dangerous wildness had come over him. 'You hit like a small girl or an old woman.'

With a grunt, Crawford charged. Christopher stood his ground. He put up his hands, forgetting for a moment he was still holding his knife. In the dark, rushing like an enraged bull, Crawford didn't see it either.

Instinct took over. Christopher swayed out of the way of Crawford's lunging fist, and as the big man grappled him he thrust forward.

The knife slid into Crawford's belly almost before Christopher realized it. Hot blood gushed out. Crawford screamed and writhed; he tried to pull away, but only succeeded in opening the wound further. His guts spilled out over Christopher's hand.

Christopher jerked away, pulling the knife free. Crawford clutched his stomach to hold in his entrails, bellowing like a wounded bull.

The sound must have carried far over the water. Surely, someone on shore or aboard one of the other boats would soon hear and come to investigate – and find Christopher with a knife in his hands, covered in blood. He had to end it.

He had no choice. Christopher tightened his grip, lifted the

100

knife, and plunged it between Crawford's ribs straight into his heart.

Crawford dropped – dead. Christopher stared down in disbelief at the corpse that lay at his feet. The knife fell from his hand; he was shaking all over.

'*You are a murderer,*' a cold voice like Guy's whispered in his head.

He couldn't take his eyes off the body. The thing that had been a man, now simply a butchered piece of meat.

'*You did this,*' insisted the voice.

But the longer he looked, the more he forgot his guilt. Warmth returned to his veins; he stopped shivering. The man who had flogged him, beaten him, taunted and cheated him was dead. He could not hurt Christopher ever again.

'I did this,' he told himself. His whole body tingled, like taking a hot bath on a cold day. 'How did I live so long, cowering, and never realize my own power?'

He wiped his bloody hands on Crawford's breeches, then rolled the body over and rummaged until he found the man's purse. Coins clinked inside – *his* coins. He took the purse and stuffed it in his breeches.

Something else caught his eye. A key, tied to a leather cord around Crawford's neck. Too small to fit the lock on the spirit locker, but he had seen it before that day. It was the key to the money chest, bright with the blood that had spilled from the hole in his heart. Christopher took it, snapping the cord in his haste. He wound it around his wrist, and hurried to the cabin. The money chest lay stowed under Crawford's cot. Even with the crew's wages taken out, it still took all his strength to carry it out on deck. A good sign.

He ran down to the stores and found a bottle of lamp oil. He splashed it over the bales of cloth in the hold, and added powder from the small keg they kept for the swivel guns. He moved quickly, driven by a freedom and an energy he had never known. He told himself it was a sensible precaution, to hide Crawford's body and so that none of the crew ashore would think to look for him. The truth was he did it from sheer devilish abandon.

Halfway up the ladder, he turned and tossed the lamp back into the darkness. The glass shattered; fire caught the oil-soaked cloth and flared up. Flames licked through the hold.

Christopher stared, hypnotised by his own handiwork. *I did this*, he thought again. The destruction he had unleashed coursed through his veins like a shot of opium.

A blast of hot air from the hold below blew into his face, and he knew it was time to go. He climbed the ladder, crossed the deck and sent one last kick into Crawford's corpse for spite. No time to launch the jolly boat, but there was the hollowed-out tree trunk that Crawford had come in, tied up near the bow. He lowered the chest on a rope, clambered down into the small boat and grabbed the oars. He rowed with all his strength, keeping ahead of the orb of light that spread behind him as fire engulfed the ship.

His boat grounded on sand. He splashed out, carrying the chest on his shoulder, and ran up the beach. When he reached the safety of the treeline, he looked back. The *Joseph* burned like a bonfire on Gunpowder Treason day, lighting up the dark and turning the night sea golden. Down on the waterfront, townsfolk came running half naked from their beds and gawped at the sight. Several of the *Joseph*'s crew were among them, some with their women still clinging to them. He wondered how they would get home, how long it would take them to find another ship.

He stumbled inland until he came to a track winding through the trees. He didn't dare go to the harbour, not with the *Joseph*'s crew still there, but he had been watching the coast and he knew there were many towns and villages in the interior where he could seek refuge.

He was about to turn north, when he saw a light approaching through the trees. He dragged the chest back off the path and crouched in the bushes.

The figure grew nearer, carrying a lamp made from a hollowed-out gourd. He stopped just in front of Christopher's hiding place, examining the footprints and the drag marks Christopher had left in the dusty track.

'Chris?' he called.

It was Danesh. With a wave of relief, Christopher floundered out from the undergrowth. Danesh recoiled in horror, not recognizing him: all he saw was a half-naked demon smeared in blood and dust.

'Chris?' He stared. 'I saw you come ashore.' He took in the blood, and the wild look in his eyes. 'What have you done?'

'I killed him.' Saying it aloud was not as easy as saying it to himself. But then he looked at Danesh, and fancied he saw new respect in his friend's eyes.

'And the ship?' said Danesh.

'Gone. I burned it to the waterline.'

Danesh looked grim. 'That ship was our work. Our pay.'

'*Your* pay. Crawford gave me nothing, remember?' He went back to the bushes and hauled out the chest. 'But I made *him* pay. With this, we can buy our own cargo. We'll charter a ship. No more hauling ropes and feeling the bite of his rope end: we'll give the orders, now. A few good voyages, and we can buy a bigger vessel. Then two.' Already, he could see himself sailing into Bombay harbour on a fine merchantman, her gunports picked out in dazzling gold leaf. He saw Ruth waiting for him on the waterfront, swooning in his arms as he stepped ashore, and the impotent rage on his father's face as he realized he was beaten.

Danesh's expression had changed. 'What about the key? Did you bring that?'

Christopher unwrapped the cord from his wrist and slotted

in the key. The lock sprang, the lid tipped back. Gold and silver gleamed within.

'With this . . .' Danesh scooped up a handful of coins and let them trickle through his fingers. 'A man could live like a king.'

'Careful,' Christopher laughed. 'We must not spend it all at once. If we invest it, we will soon have a fortune ten times larger.'

The punch hit him without warning. A clean hit to the jaw that sent him reeling back. Danesh was a slighter build, but he had been working ships since he was ten years old. He had a lean, wiry strength – and Christopher was exhausted. He stumbled, tripped on a root and fell. Before he could even raise his fists, another blow knocked him momentarily unconscious.

Danesh took the rope belt from Christopher's trousers and ran it through the handles of the chest to make a crude strap. In taking the belt, he found both the knife and Crawford's purse tucked into his trousers. He took that as well.

Christopher was coming round. He spat a gob of blood and raised himself on one arm. A threatening motion from Danesh made him think better of it.

'I thought you were my friend,' he pleaded.

The look he got back showed nothing but contempt. 'You are a child,' Danesh said. 'Gold has got no friends.'

He hoisted the chest onto his shoulder and set off down the road. Christopher didn't try to follow. He lay there, watching the light fade, until he was left in darkness.

A re you going to attack me?'

Christopher opened his eyes. On the far side of the road, a man leaned on a wooden staff, watching him. His body was lean and hard, the stubble on his cheeks was grey.

'Are you going to attack me?' he said again. He spoke Portuguese, though his face and dress were Indian.

Christopher rubbed his temples. His jaw had swollen, and every movement brought a flare of pain racing up his neck into his head.

'Do I look so dangerous?' he groaned

'There are many bandits on these roads. Some lie in wait, pretending to have been robbed or waylaid, and when the good traveller stops to help him, he himself is attacked.'

'I don't think I can even stand up.'

The man didn't move any closer. 'Where did you come from?'

'My ship caught fire. I swam ashore.'

The man nodded thoughtfully. He took in the dried blood cracking and flaking off Christopher's chest, and the bruises darkening his face.

'I can take you to Trivandrum to rejoin your crew. Surely they will be concerned for you.'

Christopher shook his head. He pointed to his left, away from Trivandrum. 'I'm going that way.'

'Ah.' The corners of the man's mouth lifted in a dry smile. 'So am I.'

'Will you take me with you?'

He considered it, for about three seconds. Then he moved. So fast, Christopher saw it as only a blur: two bounding steps, and the staff thrusting towards his head. He put up his hands, though they were little protection. The point of the staff stopped, an inch from his eyes. The old man stood over him, just out of reach of his feet. He wasn't even breathing hard.

'If you are lying – if you try to do me violence – I will kill you,' he warned.

Christopher stared at him. 'Who are you?'

'A man who can defend himself.' He touched the bruise on Christopher's chin with the tip of his staff. 'You, it seems, are a man who cannot.'

Christopher patted his belt. 'I don't even have a knife.'

'There is more than one way to kill a man, and not all are

so crude. We have bandits in this country who will strangle a man with nothing more than a loincloth.'

He said it so casually, Christopher suddenly realized with perfect certainty that he spoke from personal knowledge.

'Are you a bandit?'

'Now you insult me?' He said it good-naturedly. He extended the tip of his staff so Christopher could haul himself up.

'What is your name?' he asked.

Christopher opened his mouth. *Christopher Courtney*, he was about to say. But Christopher Courtney had robbed and killed a man. Christopher Courtney was a fugitive. Worst of all, Christopher Courtney was Guy Courtney's son.

He remembered long, sweltering Sunday mornings in church in Bombay, killing flies and listening to the minister drone on. He thought of one of the few Bible lessons that had captured his imagination: the story of King David's son, who overthrew his father and drove him out of his kingdom.

'My name is Absalom,' he said.

The old man looked keenly into his eyes, as if he could read the lies and the guilt behind them.

Nonsense, Christopher told himself. *They're only my eyes; a body part no different from my feet or my elbows.*

'I am Ranjan.' The old man looked away, and Christopher felt a great weight lift from his soul. 'I will take you to the next village.'

They walked in silence. The sun rose higher; the road grew busier. At the side of the track, toddy tappers hung off the palm trees like giant spiders, draining the sweet liquor inside. The old man didn't say a word, while Christopher brooded on everything that had happened. Again and again, he replayed those moments with Crawford, and the savage exultation as the knife ripped open his stomach. He wished he was back on the ship, just so he could do it again.

The village was a humble place, a few mud-walled huts

thatched with palm leaves. Gaunt cows wandered between the dwellings. On the beach, fishermen rolled out their nets, while drying fish flapped from lines strung between trees.

'What will you do here?' the old man asked.

Christopher shook his head. He hadn't considered it. He could try the fishermen, though the largest craft on the beach was no bigger than the *Joseph*'s longboat. But the thought of going back to sea appalled him.

'Do you have food? Money? Friends?' enquired the old man.

'None,' he answered.

'Then come with me.'

They walked on, many miles more, past fishing villages and pagodas and long, sandy beaches. Close to sunset, they reached their destination. This was a sizeable town, a little inland, far bigger than the villages they had passed through. There was a large market, and many fine temples.

Ranjan led Christopher to a compound on the far edge of the town. From the outside, he thought it must be a temple. Ranjan had such an ascetic air about him he could easily be a monk.

A young man wearing only a simple loincloth opened the gate. Christopher stepped through – and stared about him in wonder. Everywhere, bare-chested young men were fighting. In one corner, they clashed with long wooden staves very similar to the old man's staff. In another, they wielded sickle-curved swords, whose blades rasped and rang as they twisted together, as though in some intimate mating ritual. A few of the men fought with nothing but their hands and feet, moving so gracefully that the jarring force of their kicks and punches were not readily apparent.

'What is this place?' Christopher asked in amazement.

'This is the *kalari* – a school for warriors. We teach *Kalaripayattu*, an ancient martial art. Some say the most ancient in the world.'

'You know this art?'

107

'I am the *aasaan*, the teacher.'

The movements, quicker than thought; the clash of arms; the smells of sawdust, sweat and blood astonished him. He thought of all the beatings he had suffered in his life: His own father, Crawford and even Danesh. He had learned to accept them, because he could not defend himself.

These men in this arena could defend themselves.

'Can you teach me this art?'

'Some of these men have been training since they were boys,' Ranjan warned him.

'I can learn.'

Ranjan looked into his eyes. Again, Christopher had the feeling that he saw things Christopher didn't even know existed.

'Yes,' he nodded thoughtfully. 'Yes, I think you can.'

L ife on the ship had been hard; life in the *kalari* was even harder. On the ship, the beatings were incidental: here, they were the whole purpose. Christopher stopped counting the bruises, the sore muscles and the cracked ribs that made it hard to breathe. He never complained, and he never missed a day's training.

His body changed. The muscles that had started to develop at sea grew stronger, honed to a new level. His stomach tightened. He walked taller and straighter. He was no longer the round-shouldered adolescent who had run away from Bombay, or the bandy-legged sailor who had stumbled ashore. Tall by any standards, he towered over most of the native Indians training alongside him. Some complained to the *aasaan* that it gave him an unfair advantage, but he sent them away saying, 'Only the gods can choose your opponent.'

Christopher learned quickly. He learned the eight steps and the eight stances. He learned the one hundred and eight *mamras*, the vital parts of the body; the *vaikalyakara* points that would paralyse an opponent, and the *bindu* points where a single blow could kill him. He learned to chant the mantras to unlock his powers, and the way to read a man's face and posture to anticipate his next move. He learned to fight with a staff and a sword, and the sickle-shaped *thotti*.

Then, at the end of each day, he learned how to heal himself: how to rub his body down with oil, how to massage the vital places to tease out the hurts and bruises, so that he could fight again the next day.

Once a week, all the students gathered in the exercise yard around the raised platform at its centre. The best students would fight on the dais, a whirlwind of strikes and lunges that moved so fast Christopher could hardly follow them. Later, as he learned the strokes himself, he began to recognize them. Now when he watched the fights, his body twitched, copying the moves in his mind, desperate to master them.

The other students mostly ignored Christopher, but Ranjan kept a close eye on him. One day, he took Christopher to a wood-carver's workshop. The smell of oil and wood-shavings was rich in the air. On the benches, half-finished animal gods stared from their blocks, their faces merging with the raw wood.

Christopher stood watching, waiting for the *aasaan* to explain why they had come. The carver tapped with his chisel, each stroke taking off a minuscule sliver of the hard wood.

Without looking up, the carver spoke – in a local dialect Christopher couldn't understand.

'What did he say?'

'He says the figures already exist in the wood. His job is merely to peel away the outer layers and reveal what is within. With every blow of the chisel, it becomes more like itself.' He looked at Christopher. 'Do you think the wood has feelings?'

'No.'

'According to our Hindu faith, every living thing has consciousness. Even the plants can feel. If that is so, do you think the wood enjoys being carved?'

The carver tapped the hammer. The sharp blade bit into the wood.

'It must be agony.'

'And yet each blow helps it to become itself. The path is hard, Absalom – but the destination . . .' He stroked the face of Ganesh, the elephant god, carved so lifelike Christopher thought its trunk might unfurl and wrap around his neck.

'The destination is the truth of who we are.'

When he was not training, Christopher earned his keep through labour. At first, this involved cutting trees for firewood, or tending the gardens where they grew food for the *kalari*. Sometimes, when they had too much of one thing and not enough of another, Ranjan sent him to the market to barter. Apart from when he was fighting, these were Christopher's favourite times. He took pains to learn the local language, and picked it up quickly, chatting with the merchants who soon came to recognize him. They never smiled when he came to their stalls. They knew he would bargain ferociously, not content until he had squeezed the last possible *dam* off the price.

One day, in the market, an Indian approached him. Jewelled rings crusted his fingers; servants fanned away the flies around him. Christopher moved to get out of his way, but a glance from the Indian made him pause. One of the servants stepped forward. Well-dressed, with an emerald-tipped pin in his turban and gold thread embroidering his robe, he was clearly a steward in the rich man's household. His fat lips were rendered even more conspicuous by the red betel-juice stains around them.

'This is my lord Parashurama,' he announced. He kept a clear distance, as all high-caste Indians did, fearful of defiling himself through contact with the foreigner. 'He is the wealthiest merchant in this town.'

Parashurama smiled at him. 'I have heard of you. They say you are a fearsome fighter in the *kalari*.'

Christopher bowed.

'Other men say you drive such bargains to make merchants weep.'

'My father taught me there is always a better price to be had.'

'Indeed – but not all men know how to get it. I could use a man like you.'

'My master has a cargo that must be brought to the town of Neyoor,' said the steward. 'The roads are not safe, and when it arrives he expects the best price. Perhaps you are the man to do it.'

'What is the cargo?'

'Salt.'

'In return,' said Parashurama, 'I will give you five per cent of whatever you sell it for.'

'Twenty per cent,' said Christopher.

The steward scowled. Parashurama laughed. 'Truly, your reputation is deserved. Let us agree on ten per cent. And,' he added, as he saw the argument rising to Christopher's lips, 'if you serve me well in this, I may have further work for you. I trade in many goods, and there are more valuable cargoes than salt.'

'I must ask my master,' said Christopher. But when he spoke to Ranjan, the old man simply opened his palms in blessing.

'I am not your master, and you are not my slave. As long as you choose to stay with me, I will teach you. When you choose otherwise, you may go.'

'Am I ready?'

The old man studied his palms. 'What is the first precept?'

'Never choose a battle; only fight if you cannot walk away.'

'If you remember that, you will come to little harm.'

In fact, the trip passed without incident. Christopher was almost disappointed when they arrived at the house in Neyoor he'd been directed to. He haggled hard; at one point, he ordered the servants to reload the mules and was halfway out the gate

111

before the merchant called him back to continue the negotiations.

The next day, he returned home and presented himself at Parashurama's house. He handed over the purse he had brought back.

'How much did you get for the salt?'

'Twenty rupees,' Christopher replied.

The steward counted out the coins suspiciously, biting each one to check its validity and weighing them in a little scale.

'It is correct,' he said at last, grudgingly.

Parashurama smiled at Christopher. 'My steward, Jayanthan, did not trust you. The first sack of salt contained a letter to the merchant in Neyoor. I asked him to send his fastest runner with a reply to me, informing me the price he had paid you for the salt.'

Christopher's cheeks burned. 'You didn't trust me to give a fair account?'

'Now I know I can.' He counted out two coins and handed them to Christopher. 'This is your fee – for now. I will find you again soon: I always have work for men I trust.'

Over the next few months, he was as good as his word. Different cargoes and different towns; sometimes other men went with Christopher, sometimes he went alone. Once or twice, groups of men made threatening moves, but at the sight of Christopher's sword they invariably backed off. Each time, Christopher felt nothing but disappointment. He could feel the power growing inside him, tensed like a bowstring; he needed a release. In the bouts on the dais, he fought with such ferocity that one week he almost blinded a man.

'What is the second precept I taught you?' asked Ranjan.

'*Channiga*,' said Christopher, sullenly.

'And what is *channiga*?'

'Patience.'

*   *   *

One day, the rich man's steward Jayanthan came to the *kalari*. 'My master has another errand for you.'

At Parashurama's home, the merchant tipped out the bag onto his hand. Rubies glinted in the soft light that came through the carved wooden shutters.

'I need you to take these to a Tamil trader in Madura, on the other side of the mountains. The journey will take many days, and the roads through the mountains are infested with bandits.'

Christopher barely heard him. He was staring at the rubies. They winked at him like a whore in the doorway of a brothel. A wicked thought bloomed in his mind: that he could kill these two men here and now, and escape with the gems. Then he would have sufficient rupees to marry Ruth. His whole body ached with the temptation, with the awareness of his own capability.

What is the third precept? Ranjan's voice resounded in his head.

Self control. His own inner voice responded.

He forced his face into a passive mask to hide his thoughts.

'Jayanthan will go with you,' said Parashurama, unaware how close to death he had come. 'Only the two of you. I could send a caravan of many men – but that would attract attention, and every chieftain between here and Delhi would be drawn to the scent. Two men may hope to slip through where twenty could not.'

Christopher bowed. 'I will honour your trust.'

They set out the next day, heading inland. The road was nothing more than a track through the wilderness, churned by the last monsoon rains and the few carts that had attempted it. Tamarind trees shaded the way, and the sounds of birds and insects were punctuated by the clack-clack of looms, where the weavers set up their workshops by the roadside.

Christopher had lived almost his whole life in India, but this

113

was the first time he had ventured more than a few miles from the coast. Even working for Parashurama, his journeys had always been to the settlements along the coastal strip. Soon, the villages grew fewer and meaner. The clack of looms was replaced by the chatter and piping of birds he had never heard before.

They slept that night in the courtyard of a roadside temple. Next day, the road began to climb towards the Ghats, the great range of mountains that ran like a rampart down the west coast of India. The air grew cooler, the landscape ever more savage. They walked through an untouched forest of great timber trees and bamboo, giant creepers and orchids. Mosses grew luxuriantly, while the red flowers of the silk-cotton trees spattered the roadside like drops of blood.

They weren't alone on the road. A few peasants joined them, struggling under heavy burdens: bundles of coir mats, baskets of fruit. Each time they approached, Jayanthan would grab Christopher's shoulder and whisper loudly, 'Be on your guard.'

However the moment the peasants realized Jayanthan's high caste, they dropped to the ground and pressed their faces to the bare earth until he and Christopher had passed.

'At least *she* can't be a bandit,' said Christopher, pointing to a woman leading a donkey laden with mangoes. She wore a demure white sari and white bodice, with a row of copper bangles on her arm.

As if she'd heard him, she turned back to look. Unlike the other peasants, she did not bow her head or flinch away the moment she gauged their status. She met Christopher's gaze full on, her eyes frank and wide open. Her lips parted in a shy little smile that seemed to promise possibilities Christopher could only begin to imagine. Desire throbbed through his loins.

'Brazen bitch,' said Jayanthan. 'She should be whipped for her insolence.'

Without hurrying, the woman led her donkey to the edge

of the road and let them pass. Christopher tried to catch her eye again, but she was fiddling with the girth on her donkey's panniers and did not look up at him again.

They passed a small shrine at the side of the road, in which sat the statue of Ganesh the elephant god, draped with garlands of faded flowers.

Jayanthan looked at the sword in Christopher's belt. 'I hope you are ready to use that weapon. That shrine marks the spot where a traveller was killed by bandits.'

As if on cue, a shrill scream broke the silence behind them. A moment later, a braying pack-mule bolted around the corner of the pathway. Christopher drew his sword and started back at a run.

'Wait,' shouted Jayanthan. 'Your duty is to protect me.'

Christopher ignored him. He ran back, feet drumming up clouds of dust. Around the bend in the road, he found the woman he'd seen earlier. She lay on the ground, her skirts pushed up around her hips, the bodice torn from her pert young breasts. A muscular dark-skinned man held her down with his one hand, as he knelt between her knees and with his other hand opened the cloth that revealed his erect and burgeoning genitalia.

Bellowing the war-cry he had learned in the *kalari*, Christopher charged at him. But the rapist was not so overcome with lust that he had lost all sense of caution. He saw Christopher coming; and he leaped to his feet. With one quick glance he took in the sword in Christopher's right hand, and he ran.

Christopher was fast, but the man was even faster. After a dozen paces pursuing him, Christopher realized he could not catch him in a straight chase. He came to a halt and dropped his sword to the ground. With both hands free Christopher lifted his tunic.

Wound around his waist, hidden from casual view, he wore an *urumi*. This was a thin ribbon of double-edged, razor sharp steel ten feet long and as flexible as the lash of a whip.

It was the last weapon he had learned how to use at the *kalari*, and the hardest to master. Used incorrectly, it could decapitate the man who wielded it.

The ivory handle fitted into his hand with perfection. With a flick of his wrist he unleashed the blade. It seemed possessed of its own life. It reached out, uncurling as it snaked through the air. The rapist was at the extreme range of the *urumi*; however the supple steel tip wound around his bare ankle like a serpent and tightened into a noose. It sliced through skin and flesh and tendons, and then it crushed the bones of his ankle. With a cry of agony the man fell and sprawled full length.

Christopher walked up to where he lay whimpering. He did not hurry but took his time, letting the blade of the *urumi* come back to his hand; slithering through the dust of the path and recoiling itself like a live cobra.

He stood over the man's body and smiled down at him. 'My friend, I think you know that your time has come. You can bid this world farewell.' He spoke in English which the man did not understand, but the tone and sense of the words was obvious. He whimpered and bleated for mercy, but still smiling Christopher flicked his wrist, and the *urumi* uncoiled itself and licked across the man's throat. His flesh opened like a second mouth. The breath from his lungs erupted from his severed wind pipe. Almost immediately after it the blood jetted from his carotid artery, pumping to the rhythm of his heart. It splashed across Christopher's feet, but he made no move to avoid it. He waited until the bleeding shrivelled and then stopped completely before he squatted down beside the corpse and rifled through his clothing. On a belt beneath his tunic he found a leather purse. He loosened the drawstring and poured the contents of the purse into his open hand. The coins were mostly copper but with sufficient silver to make him smile again.

The woman who the rapist had assaulted came up to where

he squatted and leaned over Christopher to see what he had found. She was adjusting her clothing and straightening her skirts. Christopher looked up at her. This close she was very pretty. Her hair was thick and glossy with the oil with which she had combed into its tresses. One of her breasts was still protruding from her torn blouse. She saw Christopher looking at it and she smiled as she tucked it away unhurriedly.

'Thank you, Sahib. May all the Gods smile upon you. I will be eternally grateful to you for saving me from this animal.' Her voice was low and sweet toned. She placed her hand upon his shoulder and squeezed it. And Christopher wanted her.

But she seemed unaware of the effect she was having on him.

'Where is your companion?' she asked him.

'Oh, sweet Christ!' Christopher swore. He had forgotten about Jayanthan. He jumped up and ran back around the bend in the path, and almost collided with Jayanthan who was puffing towards him.

'How dare you abandon me?' he raged. 'When my master hears of this—'

'That woman was about to be raped by a bandit,' Christopher reminded him coldly. 'What would you have had me do?'

'What if it had been a trap? If the bandit had friends waiting to pounce on me the moment your back was turned? You do not forget your duty because some low-caste peasant bitch is getting a tupping.'

It took all Christopher's self-control not to retaliate. The dead man's blood was warm on his shins, and the joy of the kill was fierce inside him. He might have taken out Jayanthan's tongue with the *urumi*, just for speaking so crudely.

Instead he turned away and went back to where the woman was gathering the mangoes that had spilled from her basket and was reloading them onto the donkey. Now she offered one to Christopher.

117

'Take it,' she encouraged him. 'It is all I can give you, for now.'

He thanked her warmly and quartered the fruit with his knife. Then he popped one of the quarters into his mouth and chewed with gusto.

'Sweet,' he told her. 'As sweet as the girl who gave it to me.'

She smiled coyly, and dropped her eyes to her feet. 'My name is Tamaana,' she told him.

'Chris . . .' he started and then caught himself and switched to, 'Absalom.' Bemused by her beauty, he had almost given his real name. He glanced at Jayanthan, but the steward didn't seem to have noticed.

She looked at the empty jungle around them and shivered. 'Will you walk with me today to protect me, please Absalom?'

'No,' said Jayanthan.

'Yes,' said Christopher.

'No,' repeated Jayanthan. His voice rose to a petulant high pitch. 'You are being paid to escort me and obey my orders.'

Christopher spread his legs wider and folded his arms across his chest. 'If you wish to continue by yourself, then of course you may do so. However, I will walk with the lady.'

'When our master hears of this . . .' Jayanthan spluttered, touching the place on his chest where the bag with the rubies hung.

Tamaana stepped between them. 'I do not wish to cause trouble with your friend.'

'He is not my friend and he is not my master.' Christopher took the donkey's bridle and started walking. 'I am going where I was ordered to go.'

'What about him?' she grimaced at the dead body in its pool of blood. Already, flies had started to settle.

Christopher shrugged. 'Leave him there as a warning to others.'

* * *

They walked together for the rest of the day: Jayanthan striding silently ahead, Christopher and Tamaana following behind him. Jayanthan did not as much as glance at Tamaana: she was lower caste, and therefore virtually invisible. Christopher could hardly keep from staring at her. He could not stop thinking of what he had seen, the ripe swelling of her breast poking through her torn bodice, and the shadowy curls clustered between her thighs when the rapist had pulled her skirts up around her waist.

Think of Ruth, he told himself. *Think how much sweeter it will be when you are finally together as man and wife.*

But it was hard to think of Ruth when he had Tamaana by his side. Thinking of Ruth made him sullen, knotted up inside, but Tamaana brought him out of it with her chatter and her smiles. She was not much older than he was, but she was precocious and lively, with a friendliness and openness that stemmed from her humble upbringing. Her father was a farmer, in a small village near the coast, she told him. He had heard from a traveller that there were food shortages across the mountains, where the Nizam of Hyderabad had been waging war, and so his daughter had suggested taking a load of mangoes to see if they could get a better price.

'You travelled alone?' Christopher marvelled.

'My brothers are all needed to work on the farm.'

'What about your husband?'

He couldn't help looking at her as he said it. He blushed as she caught him. She gave a smile that was not entirely shy.

'I have no husband. My father could not afford a dowry. And, in truth, he needs me to help work the farm.'

Christopher stared at her. 'I cannot believe anyone so beautiful as you could not find a husband.'

She lowered her eyes. 'I must do as my father commands.'

As dusk fell, they came to a temple, at a lonely place not far below the mountain peaks. A walled enclosure surrounded a small pagoda, though the courtyard was overgrown with weeds and brambles. Blackened fire circles showed that other travellers had camped here before them.

Jayanthan laid out his blanket inside the pagoda. Christopher cut down a patch of weeds near the door and made his bed there.

'I prefer to sleep outside,' he told Tamaana. 'Inside, the vermin and insects prey on you.'

They did not light a fire, in case it drew unwanted attention. They ate a simple supper of rice and daal, and one of Tamaana's mangoes. Christopher insisted on paying her for it – 'Otherwise, you will have none left and nothing to show for it by the time we have crossed the mountains.'

It took Christopher a long time to get to sleep. He lay on the grass, listening to the sounds of the night. Beyond the walls, the jungle creatures were vociferous. There would certainly be tigers in these mountains, and only the Lord knew what else. The forests hid a thousand places where unseen lookouts could have monitored their progress, waiting for their moment to strike.

Something rustled. Not in the forest, but inside the walls. He reached for his sword, his pulse racing. He felt no fear: his body longed for the chance to fight again.

'Absalom?'

Tamaana came wading through the waist-high grass, holding up the skirts of her sari to avoid the brambles. She sat down beside Christopher, so close their shoulders almost touched.

'I could not sleep. I kept seeing . . .' She shuddered. 'You cannot imagine.'

'You're safe now,' Christopher reassured her.

She leaned against him, nestling her head in the crook of his arm. He held himself rigid, confused. He felt a raw and overwhelming urge to kiss her.

He gritted his teeth. *Ruth*, he told himself. *Be strong for Ruth.*

'The way you dealt with that monster who attacked me! I have never seen anything like it. It is a terrible weapon you wield. Wherever did you learn to use it so skilfully?'

'I learned it in the *kalari*.'

She shifted her weight, twisting slightly. Her hand slipped onto his knee for balance.

'You must have studied there many years.'

'Not so long. I grew up far from here, in Bombay.'

She looked intrigued. 'Are you not an Indian, then?'

'No.' The question didn't surprise him. With his dark hair and dark eyes, he really had the look of a native. The long hours in the sun in the *kalari* had completed the transformation, turning his skin a deep nut brown. Only his size marked him out from other men.

'My father is English, but I have lived almost my whole life in this country.'

Her hand slid up from his knee onto his thigh. Her fingers settled naturally into the crevice between his legs.

'Is England a hot country?'

'No. My father says it is cold and it rains all the time.'

'Like here in the time of the monsoon?'

'Maybe.'

Her hand had moved again. Now it rested squarely between his legs. Her fingers worked dextrously through the thin cotton, rubbing and teasing. *Make her stop*, his mind ordered; but his body betrayed him. His manhood rose eagerly, stiffening to her touch.

'This is not right,' he gasped. 'There is . . . someone else.'

'I understand,' she said, though she didn't move her hand. 'You are married?'

'No.'

'Then how can this be wrong?' She started moving her hand faster, massaging him until Christopher thought he would explode with desire.

'Have you ever been with a woman before?'

'No,' he admitted.

She unlaced her bodice. The two halves fell open, revealing her breasts, full and perfectly shaped.

She took Christopher's hand, opened his fingers and laid it on one of them. In the cool night air, the nipple was firm and proud. He squeezed it between finger and thumb, and she gasped.

'Gently,' she whispered. Straddling him, she untied his waist cloth and parted the folds. Her long hair brushed his chest; her lips covered his face with kisses. She rubbed herself against him.

Ruth, a small corner of his mind pleaded, but he ignored it. His desire was compelling, a raging fire that would burn through his skin rather than be held in check.

With a soft cry of longing, he rolled over on top of her. She lay back and opened her thighs, then she clamped them around him. She crossed her ankles over his buttocks, and hunted for his manhood with her lower body. She found it standing out hard and hot to meet her. She gasped as she engulfed it with the lubricious lips of her vagina, and he met her thrust for thrust. It seemed to last for an instant and forever, and then she felt his body convulse above her and his penis throbbing as it pumped his generative essence into her womb. She drove her heels into his buttocks, forcing him deeper still into herself, determined to suck in every drop he had to offer her.

Christopher woke late. In the *kalari*, he always rose before dawn, performing his chores before the day's training began. He could not remember the last time he had slept past sunrise.

He savoured the luxury. Memories of the night raced back, so vividly he felt himself beginning to stiffen again. Had it really happened, or was it a dream? No. He could smell her scent on his skin, the smells of coconut and musk and sweat.

A smile spread across his face. His body glowed from the night before, and the sun was warm on his skin. He put out an arm, but Tamaana was no longer with him. Maybe she didn't want Jayanthan to find them together. With a pang of residual lust, he sat up and looked around.

Her blanket was there, spread over the crushed grass. Her donkey still stood tethered to the same tree, munching on weeds. But she was gone.

A crow flew across the courtyard and glided into the pagoda. He wondered why Jayanthan had not come to wake him. Normally, he never missed a chance to point out Christopher's failings.

Reluctantly, he went to find Jayanthan. Climbing the steps to the pagoda, he saw the crow just inside the door, pecking at something on the ground, but from where he stood he couldn't make out what it was. A cloud of flies buzzed around the crow. Rats scuttled into the gloom as he stepped into the building, and he remembered the warning he'd given Jayanthan. *These buildings are nests of vermin.*

After the bright sun outside, it took a moment for his eyes to adjust to the gloom. Then another moment to understand what he was looking at.

Jayanthan lay on his back, but he wasn't asleep. His throat had been cut in a long vertical slit from the point of his chin to his sternum. The gash was opened so wide that Christopher could see the vertebrae poking through. The bag with the rubies was gone. A puddle of drying blood surrounded him, crawling with flies. At its edge, a small bare footprint lay stamped in blood on the stone floor. The same size as the feet that had been clenched against his buttocks the night before.

With a snarl of fury, Christopher ran outside. He strapped on his sword, grabbed the *urumi* and ran out to the road.

Morning mist had damped down the dust, and there was

no one else abroad that early. He could read Tamaana's naked footprints plainly. He followed them towards the mountain, every step fired by his hatred. The *urumi* hissed at his side, and he imagined the things he would do to her when he caught her.

Not far up the road, her footprints veered off towards a goat track that led out along a spur of the mountain. Christopher paused. The path was stony, too hard for Tamaana's light feet to have made any impression. Had she gone this way? Or was it merely a feint to throw him off her scent?

She had tricked him all along. The mango farm, the poor old father who couldn't afford her dowry: all lies. The rape had been staged. Jayanthan had been right about that, though Christopher was too angry to feel guilt. The rapist must have been Tamaana's accomplice. No doubt he was meant to escape as soon as Christopher appeared, perhaps return to Tamaana in the night. At least that part of the plan had failed.

He wondered why she hadn't killed him when she had the chance. Sentiment? He remembered the feel of her body around him, the touch of her skin, and clenched his fists in rage at her betrayal. He would make her suffer when he caught up with her.

He checked further up the road, but there were no more footprints. She must have taken the goat track. He followed it, winding across the steep face of the mountain. He was not an expert tracker, but in a small depression where the earth was still damp he saw a bare footmark, freshly printed. He hurried on, flexing the *urumi*.

The path rounded a bulge in the mountain, and came out suddenly in a small ravine. And there she was. Alone, standing on a boulder unarmed. She must have heard him coming, but she had made no attempt to escape from him. She had lost her sari, wearing only her bodice and a pair of short deerskin trousers he had not seen before.

'You followed me,' she said. She sounded amused.

In his fury, he almost rushed her at once. But something in her pose stopped him. There was a power within her – a sense of self satisfaction with what she had achieved – that penetrated his anger and made him wary.

'Where are the rubies?' he demanded.

'In a safe place. Your friend Jayanthan was a loyal servant. When he saw me coming, he tried to swallow his master's gems to keep them from me. I had to cut them out of his gullet to retrieve them.'

'I will make you pay for that.'

'You would have done the same thing. I saw the way you looked at him yesterday. I know what was in your heart.'

Christopher didn't deny it. 'But now I have you trapped.'

'Do you?' She clicked her tongue. Five men rose from behind the rocks that had hidden them: rough, unshaven men in ragged clothes. All of them carried sharp blades.

'I think I have *you* trapped.'

'You will need more men than that,' said Christopher. As he spoke, he scanned the faces of the men around her, judging who would be the fastest, the first to move, the hardest to kill. He saw nothing that gave him pause.

'The first man who comes near will lose his head,' Christopher warned. Tamaana was about ten paces away, just out of range of the *urumi*. He edged forward. Almost close enough. He readied his muscles to strike.

Tamaana reached behind her and pulled a long, brass-muzzled pistol from the waist of her trousers. In a single gesture, she levelled it at Christopher and pulled the hammer back to full cock.

He stopped dead. She saw the impotence in his face and laughed. 'Even the greatest *kalari* warrior cannot fight a bullet.'

'Then why did you bring me here? Why not just murder me in my sleep the way you did Jayanthan?'

'Because I do not want to kill you.' Christopher edged a fraction closer. 'But I will if you come any closer.'

'Why?'

'Is it really your ambition to be an errand boy for the rest of your life? To serve fat men you could kill with a single blow, letting them lord themselves over you merely because they have money? I saw how you wielded that *urumi*. A fighter like you could be the most feared man on the Malabar coast.'

'And become what? A brigand?'

'Become free.'

Tamaana stared down the barrel of the gun. Her arm was slender, but the pistol never wavered.

'What do you wish to choose?'

A re you sure we're doing the right thing?' Tom wondered aloud.

He and Dorian sat in the stern of the pinnace, Tom resting one arm on the tiller to steer through the fleet of merchantmen anchored in Table Bay. Sarah, Yasmini and Ana sat facing them on the thwart, while behind them Alf Wilson had the crew pulling on their oars in perfect unison. Alf's father had been a Bristolian, but his dark complexion came from his mother, a high born Mughal woman. Tom could guess how excited Alf was to be returning to the country of his birth.

'If we were ever truly certain of what we were doing, then it would certainly be the wrong thing,' laughed Dorian. 'It is doubt that gives the adventure substance.'

Sarah cocked an eyebrow at Tom. 'It is unlike you to have doubts, husband dear.'

'I was merely thinking aloud.' In truth, he had had no time for doubts since that extraordinary night when Francis had appeared unbidden and unknown at their boarding house intent on killing him, and Ana had proposed their joint venture. Since then, life had been ceaseless activity: acquiring a ship and outfitting her, filling her hold with a cargo that would turn a handsome profit in India, and taking on a crew to man her. Tom had overseen almost every aspect of it, rising before dawn and staying late at the harbour, trudging up the hill in the dark to pore over his accounts by lantern light.

'Some women are widowed when their husbands go to sea,' Sarah had said. 'I must look forward to him sailing so I can get him back.'

Tom had taken her in his arms. 'When we are at sea, I will have eyes only for you.'

'You will have eyes for the horizon, and the weather, and the set of the sails and the well-being of your crew,' she retorted. 'But at least you will not be able to wander too far from me.'

'There will be many hours to while away before we reach India,' he promised with a gleam in his eye.

Now, he nudged the tiller to guide the boat past a deeply laden Indiaman. Her golden gun ports gleamed in the midday sun, reminding him of the *Seraph*, the ship that had first brought him to Africa when he sailed with his father Hal, hunting the pirate Jangiri. He wondered how much all the Indiaman's gilding had cost the East India Company, and what infinitesimal fraction of their profits it represented.

'It is a lot of money,' said Yasmini.

He knew she wasn't talking about the Indiaman. She was talking about what they'd spent these last few weeks. The ship had cost them dear: there were few to be had in Cape Town, and her owner had pushed Tom so hard he had nearly given up. They had emptied their account in the bank on the Heerengracht, and found they still needed more. The War of Spanish Succession, which had dragged on in Europe for nearly ten years, had inflated the prices of cordage, powder, shot and a hundred other sundries.

'But look what we have got for the money.' He straightened

course. The longboat came out from under the Indiaman's stern, and there she was dead ahead: a three-masted ship in the Dutch style which they called *schoeners*, meaning 'beautiful'. In English, the word had become 'schooners'. It was an apt name. Longer and leaner than the great Indiamen, she was graced with elegant lines, from her raked bowsprit to the fine carvings around her stern cabin. From the moment she had arrived in Cape Town, Tom knew he had to have her. He had named her the *Kestrel*, after the birds he had hunted with in his youth in Devon. Like her namesake, she would fly in the slightest of breezes.

She lay at anchor beyond the rest of the fleet, with only the Courtneys' faithful sloop *Centaurus* for company. She was out of range of the fort's battery: a wise precaution that Tom had learned from his father.

He brought the pinnace alongside the *Kestrel* and they climbed the ladder. Aboli was already aboard, supervising the last preparations. Francis was beside him, listening carefully and writing everything down in the ledger.

He ran to the side as he saw Tom's head appear through the sally port.

'Welcome aboard, Uncle. All is ready and the wind is fair. Aboli says we only await your order to weigh anchor.'

Tom smiled at the boy's eagerness. He had sent him to live aboard the *Kestrel* as soon as the ink was dry on the purchase, lest anyone ask questions about Jacob de Vries and the other men who had gone missing the day Francis arrived. From Aboli, he had heard nothing but good reports: the boy was an eager student, a quick learner and an able pupil. Though he had never set foot on a ship before the voyage to Africa, Tom could see he had the makings of a formidable mariner.

'He has Black Billy's mind for business,' Aboli told Tom one night. 'But his heart comes entirely from his mother.'

Tom realized that Francis was no longer looking at him. He

was staring over his shoulder, the ship and her cargo forgotten. His face lit up with undisguised joy. Ana had come aboard.

I must watch those two, he thought. Aboli's report on Francis had touched on more than the boy's nautical learning. 'He has fallen in love, *Klebe*. Every time Ana comes aboard, he forgets everything but her.'

'But he is only a boy,' Tom had exclaimed. 'Ana is a grown woman.' Though in truth, as he thought about it, he realized there were only a few years between the two. 'Does Ana reciprocate his feelings?'

'She does not yet see him as he sees her,' Aboli had said. 'But it will be a long voyage. Perhaps he has reasons to hope.'

Tom sighed. Neither Francis nor Ana were in his charge: both were of age, and free to marry whom they chose. But he felt a responsibility for Francis, not far off what he would have felt for any son of his own. And he knew from experience that love affairs in the claustrophobic confines of a ship could have unwelcome consequences.

Sarah had arrived at his side. 'Francis,' she said sweetly, 'could you carry Miss Duarte's baggage to her berth?'

'You should not put him in the way of temptation,' Tom grumbled when they had gone below.

'Whether I do or not makes no odds,' she replied. 'What will happen will happen. You, of all people, should know that.'

Dorian strode up to them. 'She is a fine ship,' he applauded. 'God speed, brother, until we meet again.'

'Until then.'

Their plan, deliberated over many weeks, was that Tom and Sarah, with Francis and Ana, would sail the *Kestrel* to Madras. Dorian and Yasmini, with Aboli, would take the *Centaurus* up the coast of Africa to the Arab ports at Gombroon and Mocha. They would rendezvous at the Laquedivas islands, a small archipelago a hundred miles off the southern coast of India, and sail home in company together.

Tom embraced his brother. 'Farewell.'

'Come back safely.'

'I have to,' said Tom. 'It has cost us too much to do otherwise.'

He felt a pang as he watched his younger brother go. For almost ten years, he had believed him dead. To be parted again, even briefly, sent a tremor through his heart. *What if this is the last time I see him?*

'Has Uncle Dorian gone?'

Francis had appeared through the companionway. Tom wondered how long he and Ana had been below.

'You are just in time to say goodbye.'

The boat cast off, with Dorian, Aboli and Yasmini waving from her stern. Tom gave the order to weigh anchor, and the crew leaped to the capstan. He felt the familiar thrum of the deck beneath his feet as the anchor came free and the ship got under way.

He loved the freedom of the sea. Even so, the knowledge of his debts weighed on him. He had never in his life been in debt to any man, and it sat uncomfortably with him. He longed to finish the voyage, take his profit and pay back what he had borrowed. Then he could breathe easily once again.

The ocean smiled on them. Though it was late in the season, Tom could not remember an easier voyage. The rough seas that had given the Cape of Good Hope her other name, the Cape of Storms, were nowhere in evidence. The *Kestrel* lived up to her name, flying before the wind as if the sea beneath her keel were thin as air. Every day, Tom discovered something new to delight him about his ship.

He spent much time with Francis, teaching the boy everything he could, just as his father had taught him on their first voyage. He schooled him in navigation: how to shoot the sun and plot their latitude; how to use the log line to measure speed and the compass to measure heading, and how to peg out their progress on the traverse board by the helm.

'For no man has yet devised a way to measure longitude, though many of the finest minds have tried,' he explained to Francis. 'The sun can tell us how far east or west we have gone, but not how much north or south. For that, we can only estimate that by our speed and our heading.'

In the afternoons, during the dog watch, they sparred with swords. Francis had been well taught by his stepfather, and he had his father's natural agility. Under Tom's tutelage, he blossomed into a truly fearsome fighter.

They also exercised with heavier weapons. The *Kestrel* carried ten nine-pounder cannons, and every day Tom trained his men to use them. He hardly dared hope that they would reach India without incident, and he was determined to take no risks. He worked the crews until they could fire as quick as an English man-of-war, a broadside every two minutes. Francis laboured with the crew, until he could sponge out, load, aim and fire a cannon as well as any man aboard.

'For if it comes to it, we shall need every pair of hands to work the guns,' Tom said one evening. 'I have wagered my fortune on this voyage. I will not have some pirate snatch it from me.'

'You think we will meet with pirates?' Tom saw the look on Francis' face and had to hide a smile. The boy could not hide his eagerness, to test himself in battle.

It's good, Tom told himself. *You were like that, at his age.* He remembered begging Big Daniel Fisher, his father's chief warrant officer, to be allowed to sign on – and his joy when his father finally allowed it.

'It is not only the pirates,' he cautioned. 'If Guy hears of our little interloping expedition, he will call the East India Company's entire fleet down on us.'

Francis squinted into the glare of the sun. 'Why does Uncle Guy hate you so much? You never told me in Cape Town.'

'It is a long story.' Tom hesitated, wondering what he should say. There were few things in life he shied away from, but talking about his brother was one. 'When we were your age . . .'

A sail billowed. One of the clew lines had come loose, the rope end darting around the deck. Instantly, Tom felt the change in momentum ring through the hull.

'I must attend to that.' He clapped Francis on the shoulder. 'Some other day, I promise I will tell you.'

Francis didn't ask again. Partly, that was because he sensed Tom's reluctance to touch on the subject. Mostly, though, his head was full of thoughts of Ana. He had long since learned to be suspicious of the fair sex. By the time he reached an age where he might be considered eligible, his poverty had become too obvious. A few girls had shown an interest in him, impressed by the grandeur of High Weald, but that rarely endured beyond their first visit, when they saw the bare walls and empty rooms inside.

Yet with Ana, he felt none of that. She had seen him without pretensions or privilege, and it had not repelled her. She spoke to him kindly, plainly and naturally. Though that brought its own torment, for he could not tell what feelings underpinned her words. He nursed the memories of her kindnesses, while if she was ever short, or did not seem to notice him, he teetered on the edge of despair. Each time she came on deck, he could concentrate on very little else. He fumbled with the traverse board, and lost his position in the back-staff tables he had to consult to read the angle of the sun.

'You have put us somewhere in the latitude of Greenland,' Tom reproved him one afternoon, when Francis' calculation was unusually wide of the mark.

'I'm sorry, Uncle.'

'Have you heard of Admiral Sir Cloudesley Shovell? Two years ago, he miscalculated his position and ran his fleet aground on the Scilly Isles. He lost four ships and near to two thousand lives, including his own, which at least saved the Admiralty the trouble of having to shoot him.'

Francis hung his head. 'I see.'

Tom softened his tone. 'You must understand, Francis, that there are only three men aboard who can shoot the sun accurately. If something were to happen to me and Alf Wilson – a storm, a pirate attack, a falling block – you would be the only man who could navigate the ship to safety.'

'I had not taken that into account, sir.'

'I did not insure this ship. The underwriter in Cape Town works for the VOC, and would have charged me more than I paid for her. All my fortune and more is bound up in this vessel. If she sinks, so do we all.'

'I worry about his stepfather's influence,' Tom told Sarah that night, lying in their bed in the stern cabin. The ship had come fitted with a single, high-sided cot, but Tom had ordered the carpenter to extend it to accommodate the two of them. They lay side by side, both naked in the clammy tropical heat. 'A gambler like that must have been a slave to his appetites. What if Francis learned the same habits?'

'Then he will unlearn them.' Sarah rolled on her side, laying her head on his chest and listening to his heartbeat.

'And he has Billy's blood running through his veins,' Tom went on.

'And my father cared only for the profit he could turn, and my mother could never enter the same room as a cream cake without devouring it. Yet am I such an incontinent monster?'

Tom stared at the low ceiling. Above, he heard the measured tread of the men on watch pacing the deck.

'What makes a man?' he wondered aloud. 'Is it what is in his blood, or what he learns from those around him?'

Sarah propped herself up on her arm. She was a little past thirty now, but if anything more sensual than ever. Her golden skin remained flawless, her breasts smooth and firm and her eyes as clear and blue as the Devon sky.

'Whatever Francis was made and whatever he learned, he will be his own man. And all you can do, Tom Courtney, is help him to find the right path to follow.'

Her long hair spilled across his chest, tickling him. She traced the outline of the muscles with her finger, working her way steadily lower. Tom found his thoughts drifting to other things.

Sarah kissed him on the lips. Her eyes sparkled. 'I must confess, though, that I am not wholly free of my mother's influence. In some ways, I am quite insatiable.'

Their luck held almost to Cape Comorin, the southernmost tip of the Indian subcontinent. Once there, they would be safe from the monsoon winds that would soon make any navigation on the west coast impossible.

'And once we clear the Cape, it is a fair run around Ceylon and up to Madras,' said Tom, pointing to the chart spread out on his cabin table. He touched the wood to ward off bad luck. They had arrived right at the turn of the monsoon, and the wind had been stiffening all afternoon. They were not safe yet.

'There are sapphire mines in Ceylon,' said Ana. 'The most beautiful, most precious stones in the world. It is said King Solomon gave them to the Queen of Sheba to woo her.'

Across the table, Tom saw Francis start, and guessed what he was thinking. He glanced at Ana, wondering if her comment had been deliberately aimed to plant thoughts in Francis' head.

'Could we call in at Ceylon?' Francis asked.

'Maybe on the return voyage,' Tom said. He meant to make a joke of it, but it came out sounding brusque. 'At present, we could not afford a lump of cheese.'

'There is a fortune to be made in gemstones,' said Ana. Looking in her eyes, Tom saw no guile or games: only a merchant's desire to take profit where it could be found. 'A few years back, the Governor of Madras, Sir Thomas Pitt, bought a diamond that weighed nearly a full quarter-pound, four hundred and ten carats.'

Even Tom was interested now. He let out a low whistle.

'It had been smuggled out of the Golconda mines by an Indian labourer. He had to hide it in a suppurating wound inside his leg, so that the mine guards would not find it. Pitt paid twenty-thousand pounds, and when the stone is cut and polished it will fetch upwards of a hundred thousand.'

'Is Golconda near Madras?' Francis asked.

'Two hundred miles inland. But all the best stones come to Madras.'

'Then let us hope we make enough profit on our cargo to bring some back to Cape Town,' said Tom. 'I'll wager—'

He broke off. Something had changed: he felt it through the timbers of the ship. He started to rise, even before the knock came at the door.

'Beggin' yer pardon, sir,' said the mate. 'Wind's backed, and weather's boiling up ugly. The master says there's a storm coming.'

Tom ran out on deck. Even in the short time they had been below, a fearsome change had come over the sea. The waves swelled large around them; the wind hummed in the rigging with a high-pitched wail. An eerie, bruise-red light flooded the ocean as the sun tried to penetrate the angry clouds massing on the horizon.

'Take in all sails except the main and mizzen staysails,' Tom ordered. 'Clew up the forecourse, but keep the yard half raised for steerage way. Prepare sea anchors and have them ready.'

The men sprang to their work, racing up the ratlines to furl the sails. Tom called Francis.

'Sound the level in the well.' The well was a depression in the centre of the ship, where all the water from the bilges collected. Even in calm seas, water would find itself into the soundest of ships. With the storm, Tom knew, the pressure on the ship's timbers would be immense. Waves would batter her hull and shift the planks; inevitably, leaks would spring. If the water was not pumped out promptly, the water would weigh down the ship, making her harder to steer and more vulnerable to waves crashing over her decks. Eventually, it might even sink her.

Francis returned, holding the dipping stick they used to measure the well. 'Six inches, sir.'

'Not too bad.' But Tom wouldn't take any chances. 'Once the sails are furled, double the men on the pumps, and relieve them every half hour.'

'Yes, sir.' Francis ran to obey. Tom turned, to find Ana and Sarah wrapped in their shawls.

'Are we in danger?' Sarah asked calmly. The wind blew her hair in wisps around her face.

'Given our position, we should have a hundred miles of open sea ahead of us,' said Tom. '*Kestrel* is a fine ship. With a little luck, we can scud before the storm until it blows itself out.'

'And for now?' asked Sarah. 'What can Miss Duarte and I do?'

'Get below and batten the hatches. And pray this storm relents.'

The wind rose. The sea heaved. Now the waves were so high, he could no longer see over them. The *Kestrel* bucked and wallowed, her deck pitched so steeply Tom could barely stay upright. Night came, though the day was so dark it made little difference. No one slept. Tom prowled the deck, helping the helmsman manhandle the wheel against the heavy seas, watching for falling spars and tackle. The storm had come up so quickly, he had not had time to strike her topmasts: he could not dare to hope he would escape without some part of his ship being carried away.

Nor did he. Somewhere in the middle watch, well after midnight, an almighty shudder hit the ship with a noise that cut through the howling wind. Alf Wilson came running out of the darkness.

'We've lost the bowsprit.'

'Cut it away *now*.' Already, Tom could feel the ship coming around as the fallen bowsprit dragged on her bow. If she turned broadside to the wind, the waves would roll her over like a barrel. The helmsman fought the movement, trying to correct course, but he could not stop her momentum. The sea was so strong it would snap the rudder.

Tom led the men himself, battling the waves that poured over the prow. It was impossible to resist them: if not for the rope tied around his waist, he would have gone overboard. The heavy sea slapped him in the face and stung his eyes. He could hardly see to wield his axe on the tangle of ropes that still bound the bowsprit to the ship. Another wave pounded over him.

He swung his axe at the forestay, the long line that ran from the foremast to the bowsprit. It was stretched taut to breaking: if it didn't give, it would pull the whole mast down.

His axe cut through it. Relieved of its tremendous pressure, the loose end whipped through the air. Tom darted out of its path as it lashed past, inches from his eyes, and struck the man behind him in the face. The man cried out and fell, just as another wave surged around him. The foaming water carried him towards the side.

He was wearing a safety rope, but if he went overboard it would be no protection. The waves would dash him against the hull. Tom ran, slipping on the planks. He threw his arms around the sailor's waist and dragged him back, just as the next wave broke.

A thud shook the deck. For a terrible moment, Tom thought they'd lost a mast: he looked up, expecting to see it crashing down over him. But the mast was still there, a ragged sail flapping from its yard.

'Did we hit something?' There should not be any reefs or

rocks in these latitudes – but the storm had driven them so hard he no longer knew where they were.

'Bowsprit, sir,' shouted Alf. 'Must have struck the hull as we cut it loose.'

Tom moved aft. Francis emerged from the companionway and staggered towards him. His hands were covered in blisters.

'Water's rising.' He had to bellow every word to be heard over the storm. 'It's coming in faster than we can pump it out.'

'Keep trying. I am relying on you.'

The night seemed endless, and the storm never relented. Dawn slipped almost unnoticed over the horizon. The first Tom knew of it was when he realized he could see the rain. He rubbed his salt-crusted eyes as he took in the damage to his ship. As well as the bowsprit, she had lost her fore and main topgallant masts, and her main topsail yard. The sails he had set had been torn to ribbons: the *Kestrel* now ran under bare poles, though it hardly slowed her speed. The wind blew as violently as ever.

'It could have been so much worse,' he consoled himself. The ship was afloat, and all her crew had survived. They had enough canvas and spars to patch the damage and reach Madras. The water in the well was still rising, but with daylight they could start trying to patch the cracks in the hull. Francis had been down in the hold all night, taking his turn on the pumps and encouraging the men tirelessly. Tom was proud of him.

The day grew lighter. Sometimes, as the ship tottered on the crest of a wave, he could see some hazy semblance of a horizon. Perhaps the storm was passing.

'What's that?' said the helmsman.

Tom looked up. 'Where?'

They both waited as the ship plunged into another trough. When she crested the next wave, he saw a smear of white on the horizon.

'Breakers,' shouted the mate. 'Breakers dead ahead.'

Tom grabbed a spyglass from the rack. 'That's impossible. We should be fifty miles from any land.'

The horizon disappeared as the *Kestrel* plunged into the next trough between waves. A moment later, she was thrown back up onto the next crest. This time there was no doubt about it.

'Land.' In fact, the land remained invisible, shadows against the dark sky. But there was no mistaking the line of breakers, chewing the horizon like a row of gnashing teeth.

Whether it was an uncharted reef, or the edge of a coast that should not have been there, Tom could not tell. At that moment, it was the least of his concerns.

The cabin door opened and Sarah appeared, carrying a ship's biscuit and a piece of salt pork. She moved nimbly across the deck, absorbing the ship's movements.

'You have not eaten all night. You must have food.' She saw the look on his face. 'What is the matter?'

'There is land ahead,' he told her. 'I cannot tell how. The currents must have pushed us further north than I realized.' He shook his head, aware he was wasting precious seconds. 'It makes no odds. That land is there, and if we do not act soon we will be driven onto it.'

Sarah read the look on his face. In all the years she had known him, through all the terrors they had faced, she had rarely seen him so distressed.

'Is it so bad?'

'We are trapped on a lee shore, in heavy seas, and we have no sails. It is about the worst position any ship can find herself in.'

He ran up on deck. 'We must bring the ship about.'

Alf Wilson stared at him. 'In this weather? You'll dismast her – or worse.'

'If we don't, we will be driven onto that shore and smashed to pieces.'

No one could argue with that. Sailors raced up what was left of the rigging, trying to bend on sail. The wind made their work almost impossible. The canvas bucked and snapped, resisting all efforts to tame it. The main topsail was carried away and vanished into the storm.

'It'll be a man overboard next,' said Alf.

'If we do not get canvas on her, we will all drown.'

Without sails, they could not hope to get on a tack against the wind to carry them away from shore. Even under canvas, it would be a close run thing. They would have to put the ship about, through mountainous seas and in the face of a gale. And they had precious little time left to them.

'Coast's getting nearer,' said Alf. With the low visibility brought on by the storm, Tom hadn't realized how close they had already come. Now he could make out a strip of white sand, individual palm trees bending like swan's necks in the gale.

Pray God there are no rocks or reefs between us, he thought to himself. He looked at the pattern of the waves, reading them for more danger.

A sailor thudded to the deck. For a moment, Tom feared he had fallen. He got up, rubbing his hands where he had burned them sliding down the backstay.

'Sail's set, sir.'

Above, Tom saw the forecourse finally unfurled. It hung askew, spilling wind where it had not been sheeted home. It would have to do.

'Put her about.'

'We don't have the steerage way,' Alf warned.

'We'll club haul her,' Tom decided. Club hauling was the last resort, a brute way of forcing the ship's bow against the wind. Now they had no choice. At the bow, men tied a second hawser to the anchor and fastened it to the lee quarter.

'Are you sure?' said the mate. 'If we lose the anchor, we'll be at the mercy of the wind.'

'We have to get away from that shore.' Tom raised his voice. 'Anchor away.'

The anchor dropped overboard. At the same time, the helm went hard over. Slowly, slowly, the bow came around. The ship heeled over as it came broadside-on to the waves, rolling heavily.

'Cut the cable.' Men with axes chopped through the forward anchor cable. The ship jerked free. The stern cable took the tension, keeping the ship swinging around.

But not enough. Against the onslaught of wind and wave, she did not have the momentum she needed. Her bows started to slip back downwind.

Two more men joined the helmsman. Together, they hauled on the wheel, fighting to keep the ship's head up. Suddenly, they fell to the deck. The wheel spun round and round, no longer bound to anything.

'Rudder's gone,' shouted the helmsman.

'And the sail,' said Alf. The forecourse had split down the middle, billowing open like a shirtfront.

With no steerage way, the *Kestrel* slipped back. Waves battered her hull, turning her broadside to the surging seas. Tom looked to larboard, and saw a huge wall of water bearing down on them.

'*Grab on.*'

The wave hit the *Kestrel* square on her side, putting her on her beam ends. The world changed. Her deck rose almost perpendicular to the sea, while her masts heeled over so far they touched the waves. Men who had not had time to take hold found their footing swept from under them. They fell into the sea surging around the gunwale. Some managed to grab on to rigging; others were carried away. Tom saw the heavy timber of the anchor stock strike a man on the head. He went under and did not reappear.

A cannon on the starboard side broke from its lashings. It rolled down the deck and crashed through the opposite gunwale. The other guns strained on their tackles.

'Cut the masts,' Tom cried. In a moment, the ship would roll back, and then the top weight of her masts would act as a murderous pendulum, increasing the roll and turning her right over, turtle-fashion.

Some of the men still had their axes. They made their way to the mainmast, sliding and slithering across the foaming deck. It didn't take much. As soon as two of the stays had gone, gravity and the sea did the rest, carrying the mast away in a welter of cordage and canvas. The men had to leap clear or risk being snared.

The *Kestrel* began to roll again. Her deck turned back through ninety degrees and kept going. Further, further . . . Waves boiled over the side.

The wrecked mast saved them. Hanging in the water, it acted as a giant outrigger, steadying the ship and stopping her from rolling over. It was small respite.

I've lost her, Tom thought. The starboard side had collapsed; the sea was flooding in. Soon she would be sunk. Even so, he could hardly bear to give the order.

Francis seized his arm. Tom had not seen him come on deck. 'The bilge is flooded; the pumps are overwhelmed.'

The words crushed Tom's last hopes. 'Abandon ship,' he ordered. 'Into the jolly boat.'

There was no thought of lowering the boat. The davits had been swept away. As soon as Tom cut away the ropes that held it, it slid down the tilting deck into the water. The men scrambled headlong to climb into it before the sea carried it away.

Sarah had come up from the cabin. Something flashed in her hands, bright even in the dark of the storm. The Neptune sword, in its gilded scabbard. Tom felt a surge of gratitude. She knew if there was one thing he would want to save from the wreck it was the sword.

'Get in the boat.' He held her hand, guiding her across the slanting deck so she would not fall. A surging tide moved the boat away; she leaped, almost capsizing it as she landed, still clutching the sword.

'You next,' Tom told Francis. Again, he helped him across the deck to the splintered wreckage that had once been the side.

'Jump.'

Francis paused. 'Where is Ana?'

Tom looked around. The deck was empty.

'She must be in the boat already.' There was no time to delay. Tom lifted Francis and hurled him into the boat, then leaped himself. He landed on top of Francis in a heap of limbs, while the boat bucked and tossed beneath.

Francis shook him off and sat up. 'Where is Ana?' he said again.

Tom scanned the faces around him. Ana was not in the boat.

'She came down to the cabin with me,' said Sarah.

Francis looked stricken. 'Did she come up?'

'She said she was going to look for you.'

The ship shuddered. With a groan like a wounded beast, the foremast snapped and toppled over into the sea, so close to the boat it nearly smashed it to splinters. Tom put his hand on Francis' shoulder and shouted in his ear, 'You cannot save her now.'

'I must.'

A wave lifted the boat high into the air, so close to the ship's hull they almost touched. Before Tom could stop him, Francis leaped. Tom cried out and watched in horror as Francis hurtled over the boiling sea. His outstretched arms flailed in the spray; a wave surged over the ship and buried him. Tom lunged, but the same wave caught the jolly boat and swept it far away from the ship.

But Francis had survived. As the foam subsided, Tom saw him with his arms wrapped around the shrouds, clinging on and pulling himself up against the water pouring off the ship.

'We must go back and help him,' Tom yelled to Alf Wilson.

Even as he spoke, another wave carried the boat still further away. Half the oars were missing, and the other half broken. If they tried to fight the sea, the boat would flip and they would all drown.

Francis was on his own.

Francis hauled himself over the *Kestrel*'s shattered side and crawled across the sloping deck, praying no more of the cannons would break loose. He crouched by the hatch and peered down. The ladder had torn away. Down below, he saw deep water sluicing around the hold. It chilled his heart. Could anyone have survived down there? He doubted it.

All he saw was black water.

'Ana?' he shouted.

No answer.

The ship lurched further over as more of her hull gave way. He had no time. He braced himself against the opening and lowered himself through, into the water. In the heeling ship, water filled the lower side to the ceiling, but there was still air on the upward side. He crawled along, clinging on to the ship's ribs and keeping his head just above water.

If she rolls over, I'll be trapped, Francis thought. He forced himself not to panic. He put out his hand to steady himself and felt—

Flesh. Cold and wet, but unmistakeably human flesh. In the darkness, he could not even tell if it was Ana. He pulled the body towards him, feeling all around until he found the head. He put his finger to the neck and sensed a feeble pulse beat.

The ship lurched again, settling deeper in the water. The last pockets of air disappeared. Francis just had time to take a last breath before he was submerged.

Get to the hatch, he told himself. The water pushed him against the low ceiling. Holding the other body under his arm, he dived, forcing his eyes open against the stinging salt water to find his way to the ladder. He saw the brightness of the open hatch and kicked desperately for it. Flotsam banged into him; he almost caught his eye on an iron hook suspended from a beam. But he was there and now, finally, the ocean helped him. The rising water lifted him through the hatch, over the broken ladder and out onto the deck.

Now at last he could see who he had rescued. It was Ana – though that would matter little if they did not make good their escape. He knew they had but seconds. The ship was going under.

'We must get off this ship,' Francis shouted. But the water around the hull was thick with wreckage. If they tried to swim through it, they would most likely be dashed to pieces. But the mainmast made a bridge across the debris, its rigging like roots tethering it in place.

Ana stirred in his arms. She opened her eyes.

'What—?'

'No time.' Francis thumped her back. Great gouts of seawater spurted out of her mouth. 'Can you move?'

Ana nodded. 'I think so.'

'Then let's get off this ship.' Francis heaved Ana onto the mast. Without having to be told, she started crawling out along it, across the churning water. Francis followed her.

It was like riding a wild horse, unbroken and unsaddled. The mast was in constant motion, twisting and writhing with every wave that struck. Francis wrapped his arms and legs around the trunk, inching forward. Sometimes he crawled on top, other times he clung on upside down like a monkey dangling from a branch. Waves snapped below him.

Ahead, he saw the bulk of the main top spreading out from the mast. He crawled through the lubber's hole and there, at last, was shelter. He crouched against its side with Ana, cupped in its railings and protected, a little, from the storm.

But they could not stay there. The wrecked ship was still shifting in the headwinds of the storm; at any moment the mast might roll over and trap them underwater. They were free of the worst of the debris, but any one of the waves was enough to dash them to pieces. Francis looked out into the storm for the jolly boat, praying that Tom and the others had survived. He could not see them.

'Can you swim?' Francis shouted at Ana.

She shook her head. Francis did not hesitate. Wrapping his arms around her, he jumped into the water. He could see the shore, a few hundred yards away, but he did not make straight for it. Instead, he used all his strength merely to stay afloat in the surging sea. He cupped his arm under Ana's shoulders to keep her head above water. He let the undertow take them, pulling them away from the broken ship until the wreckage thinned out. Only then did he start to swim.

After all Francis had suffered, he barely noticed the waves. He didn't fight them; instead, he let them push him under, then kicked back to the surface to draw breath when they released him. Abruptly, he felt firm sand underfoot. The waves, which had done so much damage, finally took mercy: they lifted him up and threw him down on the beach.

With the last of his strength, he dragged Ana away from the water and to safety, before the sea could reclaim them. Further up the beach, a fringe of palm trees offered shelter from the rain, but he kept clear. The wind was bending their trunks like reeds, stripping away leaves and fruit. A falling coconut was as fatal as a cannon ball.

Francis' body ached, and his legs were so weak from fighting the sea he could barely stand upright. The storm winds battered him. All he wanted was to bury himself in the sand and wait for the storm to pass. But he couldn't. Tom was out there; and so was Sarah, and the rest of the crew.

Francis left Ana where she lay, barely conscious. Half crawling, half running, he worked his way along the beach. Warm rain stung his face. The wind whipped up sand that flayed his skin. He never thought of stopping. He searched the beach, shouting Tom's name with every aching breath. He looked at the crashing waves, and doubted that the little jolly boat could have survived in such turmoil.

Ahead, further down the beach, he saw a cluster of wreckage spread across the sand. As he hurried closer, he saw it was the jolly boat – battered and overturned, but still in one piece. The dark shapes around it were people, lying where they had fallen from the boat. He ran between them, turning each over until he found Sarah and then, at last, Tom.

'Thank God you are here.'

'And Ana?' said Tom, scanning the sea fearfully.

Francis pointed back to where he had left her. 'She is safe.'

'Where are we?' Sarah croaked, her throat ravaged by the salt water she had swallowed. Beside her, pressed into the sand, Tom saw the gleam of the Neptune sword. Through all that, she had somehow clung onto it.

Tom shrugged. 'Alive – and that is all that truly matters.' He forced himself not to think of the unfortunates who had gone down with the ship. There would be time for that later.

Sarah tried to stand but the effort was too much. Her face went white, she dropped forward onto her hands and knees and vomited into the sand.

'Wait here,' said Tom.

Tom and Francis went to fetch Ana – though when they reached him, she had come to, and insisted she was strong enough to walk by herself. She stood, swayed, and fell into Francis' arms.

'I thought I was dead.'

'I would not let that happen.'

The storm had changed him, Tom realized. Francis carried himself with a new sense of inner strength. As he helped Ana regain her balance, Tom saw the way she gazed at Francis, a look that carried far more than gratitude. She no longer saw him as a boy, but as a man. Suddenly, Tom felt as if he was intruding.

'We should return to the others.'

The day drew on. The winds dropped, the rain eased to a drizzle, but the waves never relented, pounding the beach, each one breaking with a sound like thunder. The jolly boat had vanished, dragged out by the tide and smashed to matchwood. Tom was exhausted, but he continued scouring the beach until he had found all the men from *Kestrel*'s crew who had made it ashore. To his relief, Alf Wilson was among them. He gathered them together as far up the beach as he dared, huddling together to protect each other from the rain.

Out to sea, he could see *Kestrel*'s hulk with the waves breaking over her, so low she often disappeared into the surging sea. One look at her, and Tom knew she would never sail again. Her back had broken, cracking open her hull. Her foremast was a stump; her main and her mizzen had been carried away. Half her planking seemed to have washed up on the beach. Seabirds settled on the flotsam around her, like vultures picking over a corpse.

He could hardly bear to look. Then he thought of the men he had lost, and felt ashamed. He would have traded the ship and all her cargo twice over to bring them back.

'What shall we do now?' said Francis.

'We will find a way,' said Sarah. Her colour had returned. Now, she was able to move about, binding the sailors' wounds as best she could with cloth strips torn from their clothing, and splints cut from driftwood.

'I never found that sitting feeling sorry for myself improved matters.' Tom stood and strode a few paces up the beach. He pointed to scars on the palm trees, where knives had cut the coconuts.

148

'Someone has harvested those. There must be a village nearby.'

A little way down the beach they found a creek that opened up the interior. A path ran along its banks, trodden to mud by many feet.

'Francis and I will go and explore.' Tom hooked the Neptune sword to his belt. 'Sarah and Ana will wait here with Alf and the men.'

'No,' said Sarah firmly. 'We have come too close already to losing each other today. Ana and I will come with you.'

Tom knew better than to argue. Leaving Alf in command of the remaining crew, the four of them followed the path along the creek. It led through a forest of palm and jack trees, bright green against the red soil. The rain had released the odours of the forest, and the air was heavy with smells of vegetation and damp earth.

They had not gone far when Francis let out a yell. Ahead, they saw a thorn fence surrounding a low, mud-walled house and a yard. Beyond it, more houses straggled along the creek-side, each standing at a distance from the others in its own compound, so that the whole village stretched more than half a mile. Out in the creek, a woman stood waist deep washing clothes. Gaunt, and naked except for a small cloth tied around her hips, she seemed impervious to the pelting rain.

'Have they no modesty in this country?' Francis wondered.

'We are a long way from London society here,' Tom pointed out.

'There is no shame in nakedness in their religion,' Ana explained. 'And, in this climate, little need for clothes.'

The woman heard them speaking and looked up. With a cry, she gathered her laundry to her and waded ashore.

'Wait,' called Tom. She ran into one of the huts, shouting unintelligibly. Before Tom could follow, a man came striding out, dressed little differently from the woman. Others, hearing the commotion, emerged from their huts. Soon the whole village had gathered around them, chattering and pointing.

A wizened old man with white hair and a long beard stepped forward, evidently the chief or headman. Ana spoke to him in Portuguese, and then in an Indian language. The headman remained impassive. He replied slowly.

'Can you understand it?' he asked Ana.

'They speak a dialect of Malayalam,' she answered. 'It is similar enough to Tamil that I can make out what he is saying.'

'Tell him we need food. Ask him where the nearest port is.'

Ana spoke. When she had finished, the headman gave orders. A skinny boy ran off through the trees. Several of the women went to fetch food. Another woman went into the nearest hut with a lump of what looked like dried mud. She rubbed it over the beaten-earth floor, and then over all the walls.

'What is she doing?' asked Francis.

'Cleaning the house.'

'With mud?'

Ana gave a sly smile. 'It is not mud. It is cow dung.'

'Dung?' cried Francis, astonished. 'Do they clean their houses with filth?'

'The cow is holy to these people,' Ana explained. 'Even its excrement purifies the house.'

The woman came out. The headman pointed them inside.

'He invites us to enter.'

Tom peered in. The door was low, and there were no windows. The only light came through cracks where dung plaster had flaked off the wicker frame. But it was dry, and out of the rain, and a small fire smouldered in a stone circle.

Even so, it was more like an animal pen than a house. In an unknown country, among strangers, Tom's instincts warned against letting himself be confined.

'I'd rather sit outside.'

Ana put this to the villagers, but either they didn't understand or it was some grave breach of etiquette. They crowded around the Courtneys, herding them in through the doorway. More than one of them touched the Neptune sword on Tom's belt, marvelling at the intricacy of the workmanship, and the enormous sapphire in the pommel.

They sat on the floor, while the villagers waited at the door, ignoring the rain that soaked their skins. Naked children pushed through their parents' legs to stare at the strangers. Women brought them balls of rice and lentils served on broad vine leaves. Tom devoured the food. His stomach craved more, but looking at the tight ribs and spindly limbs of the children he guessed they had already given more than they could afford.

When they had eaten, Tom moved to the door. The crowd gave no ground.

'They say we have to stay here,' said Ana.

'Why?'

'From what I heard, I think they have sent to their local chieftain,' Ana explained. 'Perhaps he will be able to help us.'

Tom went back to his place. He drummed his fingers on the earth floor in frustration. 'Have they even told you where we are?'

'No. Can you not tell from our last course and heading?'

Tom shrugged. 'That storm drove us so hard, I could not place us within fifty miles. It might be Ceylon . . .'

'It is not Ceylon,' said Ana. 'Their language is different.'

'India, then. The Malabar coast.'

Ana nodded. 'I think so – and that is to our benefit. The British and Portuguese have trading factories all along this coast. We will find one.'

'Will they help us?' Francis wondered.

'Our ship does not lie in deep water,' said Sarah. 'Perhaps, when the storm calms, we could salvage her cargo and buy their aid, if they will not give it freely.'

'Most of our goods will be spoiled, I fear,' said Tom. 'But we may retrieve the ivory. Also, Dorian and Aboli have *Centaurus*, and a good cargo of their own to trade. When we do not arrive at the rendezvous, they will return to Cape Town. If we can find passage back there ourselves, we may yet survive with only a few bruises.'

They waited. Rain drummed on the roof. The villagers never moved.

'They look as if they're waiting for something,' Francis remarked.

'Their overlord,' Ana suggested. She sat beside Francis, nestling against him for warmth. 'These people live in terror of their masters. They will do nothing without permission.'

'I hope this overlord has a set of dry clothes that will fit me,' said Sarah. Her skin itched from hours in her wet, salt-ridden dress, but she had nothing to change into.

'And a ship to carry us home,' Francis added.

'And a haunch of mutton,' Tom suggested drowsily. He leaned against the mud wall. The fire had started to warm him. He had not slept in two days. His eyelids started to droop.

Stay awake, he told himself. *You are not safe yet.*

He pinched his own cheek to keep himself awake. But felt no pain. He could resist no longer. He dropped into a deep dark hole in his own mind.

He woke to feel hands shaking him. He had been dreaming of Sarah, and for a moment he thought it was her.

His eyes snapped open. They were no longer alone in the hut. A group of villagers had entered and were tugging at him, pulling him to his feet. He looked around for Sarah and the others, but they were gone. Suddenly he was fully awake. He jumped to his feet, shrugging off their hands. Then he ducked under the door jamb and stepped outside.

Sarah, Ana and Francis were standing in the centre of a wide circle of villagers. In front of them were seven strange men mounted on horseback. Their faces were grim and scarred; they wore body armour, and their turbans were wrapped around steel helmets. All of them were armed heavily. They wore pistols and short swords on their belts. Four of them carried lances, the other three swords.

Tom stepped in front of Sarah and Ana to shield them. 'Who are these people?' he demanded.

The lead rider kicked his horse forward. He circled the four of them, peering haughtily down at them. He wore a yellow feather tucked into the band of his turban, and the inlay on his breastplate was gold. A thin white scar snaked down between his eyes and along his nose. It gave his face a crooked look, as if his head had once been split in two, and then clumsily reassembled.

He shouted something at the headman, who replied in a nervous high-pitched voice, bowing and clasping his hands in front of his eyes.

'The arrogant one is named Tungar,' Ana translated. 'He is a *Subeldar* in the army of the local ruler, the Rani of Chittattinkara.'

Tungar stared enviously at the sapphire in the Neptune sword. Tom put his hand on the hilt and stared back at him.

'Tell him we were shipwrecked. Tell him we ask only for a little food, and safe conduct to the nearest European settlement.'

Ana spoke, but Tungar showed little interest in what she had to say. Before she had finished he interrupted her brusquely.

'What is he saying?' Tom asked.

'He says that all travellers in this country must pay a tribute to the Rani.'

'Tell him we have lost everything we own in the wreck.'

Ana translated but Tungar sneered at Tom in response, then leaned forward in the saddle and pointed at the Neptune sword with his riding whip.

'No,' Tom shook his head firmly, 'not the sword. It is a family

153

heirloom. However we have a cargo of ivory on the wreck. When the sea is calmer, we will dive for it and present some of it to his queen.'

Tungar unfurled the long lash of the whip. Then shot it out like a live serpent. The tip of it wrapped around Tom's wrist and jerked his hand from the hilt of the sword. Then with his spurs Tungar backed his mount, keeping the whip lash taut. Two of his men jumped from the backs of their mounts and ran forward to grab the sword. Tom kicked at them, twisting away. Two more men dismounted and circled around Tom, levelling their lances at his chest. Defiantly Tom drew the sword left-handed from its sheath and menaced his assailants with the blade.

But Sarah screamed at him, 'Let them have it, Tom! The Good Lord knows it is not worth dying for. There are six of them to your one. They will cut you down like a rabid dog.'

Tom lowered the sword. Then he tossed it towards Tungar. The point of the bright blade pegged into the ground and it stood there quivering upright. With a single shake of his wrist hilt Tungar unwrapped the lash from Tom's wrist, and spurred his horse forward.

He leaned from the saddle and seizing the hilt of the sword he jerked it free. Then he spurred his mount onwards, riding straight at Tom with the point of the blade aimed at his face. Tom stood unflinching. Sarah screamed again and ran forward to try and interpose her own body. But both Ana and Francis grabbed her arms and held her.

At the last possible instant Tungar lifted the blade to the vertical and slammed the glittering blue sapphire on the pommel into the centre of Tom's forehead as he swept past him. Tom dropped to his knees, clutching at the wound, while blood dribbled down his face and balled into the dust of the yard.

Tungar wheeled his horse back to stand over Tom. Tungar

was grinning, not bothering to hide his triumph as he mocked Tom.

'What is the arrogant swine saying now?' Sarah was weeping bitterly.

'He says that his mistress, the Rani, may her name be exalted for all time, will be amused by his gift. She may even reward him with the crust of bread for which he is begging, before she sends him on his way again.'

Tungar lost interest. He spoke sharply to his men and they fell in behind him. Before he rode away, he shouted something at Ana, and then he urged his horse into a gallop. In a thunder of hooves he led his men out of the village and away along the bank of the river.

Sarah crouched beside Tom. 'Are you hurt?'

Tom wiped the blood from his forehead. He would have a mighty bruise, but the cut was not deep. 'I have had worse.'

Even so, he winced as he came to his feet. 'What was that parting quip of his?'

'He says there is a settlement of hat-wearers a few miles down the coast. Perhaps the village head man can have one of his men take us to him.'

'Hat-wearers?' Tom shook his head to clear it.

'That is their name for a European. They wear turbans and we wear hats.'

'I suppose that makes sense,' Tom conceded.

Ana negotiated with the village elder for the services of a guide to lead them to the European settlement. Tom offered the guide as a reward the cross belt which had supported the blue sword. It was no longer of use to him, but the guide was delighted with it.

They left the village and went to find Alf Wilson and his surviving crew members on the beach on which the *Kestrel* had floundered.

Then their guide led northwards through the coastal forest,

along almost-obscured footpaths and stretches of open beach against which the surf thundered. At times they were forced to wade through the creeks and backwaters that dissected the coastline.

All of them were famished and weakened with fatigue, although they found a few rotten mangoes under the trees where the reapers had discarded them.

At last they came to the bank of a broad river running into the sea. On the opposite side stood a stout stone fort. On her flagstaff fluttered the English East India Company's standard, red and white stripes with a Union Jack in the corner.

Heavy breakers burst and foamed on the beach in front of the fort. On the coral sands, above the tideline, were drawn up a number of sharp-prowed surf boats. Beyond the fortress stood half a dozen godowns, warehouses for the Company's goods, surrounded by a cluster of palm-thatched cottages.

'I never expected I would be so happy to see that flag,' Tom remarked.

Their guide whistled, and several of the native boatmen ran to the surfboats and shoved them into the river to ferry them across. By the time they reached the far bank of the river, a small group of spectators from the fort had gathered to welcome them. Tom saw the red coats of a dozen or more East India Company soldiers, the blue coats of English merchants and three or four ladies peeking out from under their parasols. It seemed that they had at last reached civilization again, and that their ordeal was almost over.

A stout fellow in a tight-fitting scarlet waistcoat strode out from among the spectators. Even in the monsoon heat, he wore a wig. The light rain washed trickles of powder down over his face and clothing, leaving white snail trails.

'Who the Devil are you? What are you doing here?' he demanded in English.

'Do not use my real name,' Tom whispered to the others.

156

'These may be Guy's men. You know what will happen if Guy hears that we have arrived on his front lawn.'

'Tom Weald,' he announced to the fat man. 'My nephew, Francis; my wife, Sarah; our travelling companion, Ana Duarte.'

Tom was aware of how ragged and dishevelled they all appeared. The man stared at them with ill-disguised distaste.

'Lawrence Foy,' he said. 'I am the Governor of the British factory here at Brinjoan.'

'Our ship was wrecked in the storm,' Tom explained.

'Ship?' Foy peered at Tom suspiciously. 'What ship is that?'

'The *Kestrel*. Outward bound from Cape Town at Good Hope for Madras.'

'I know of no Company ship by that name, what?' Foy complained. 'I hope that you are not interlopers?'

Tom sidestepped the question. 'At the moment, sir, we are little better than castaways.'

Foy sniffed. 'Good God, sir. You smell frightful.'

'We would be grateful for a change of clothes,' Tom conceded

Foy pursed his lips. He had a pained expression on his face – as if he wanted to pass wind but was unable to do so. Tom smiled inwardly. No doubt he was wondering whether there was any way, in all decency, that he could rid himself of these unwanted guests.

'You had better come and explain yourselves,' he gruffed at last.

He led them into the fort. Discipline was lax, Tom noted as he looked about him. There were no sentries posted at the gates, and the only lookout he could see was on the ramparts, huddled under an awning to escape the rain. The Governor's house in the inner courtyard was made of wood, with palm-frond thatching that would burn like a bonfire in the dry season.

'I trust you have amicable relations with the locals,' Tom asked.

Foy swatted away a fly. 'They give us a little trouble now and then, but a sharp slap on the wrists shows them the error of their ways.'

Tom thought of the horsemen in the village who had deprived him of his sword, but he kept his own counsel as they entered the house. The floor underfoot was gritty with sand, and the air was stifling. A young Indian boy, naked but for a loin cloth, sat in a corner and waved a fan of matted palm leaves. It stirred soft currents of the air, without having any noticeable cooling benefit.

Foy slumped in a chair. A tray of dates sat on his desk. He stuffed three in his mouth, but did not offer them to his guests, who stayed standing. Tom's stomach turned with hunger.

'Now,' Foy said through a mouthful of fruit. 'You were ship-wrecked, you say. What was your cargo?'

The question took Tom by surprise. 'I hardly think that is relevant, sir.'

'On the contrary, it is of the utmost relevance.' Foy fixed him with a keen stare. Beneath his country-parson manner, Tom realized, lurked a mean and vicious intelligence.

'Ivory. Lace. Some worked goods.'

'*European* goods.'

'We bought them in Cape Town.'

'So you say. You have logbooks? Manifests? Receipts that can support your story?'

Tom tried to control his temper. 'All our papers were lost with the ship.'

'How convenient.' Foy spat the date stones onto the floor. 'You know what the Company does to interlopers. I could have you locked up and shipped back to England in shackles. I could send you to Bombay, and give you over to Governor Courtney. Bombay is a long way from the English courts. There, the Governor's word is absolute law.'

Foy went silent and thoughtful for a few moments, and then

he leaned forward over the table. 'Unless, perhaps, we could reach an accommodation.'

He wants a bribe, Tom realized. He relaxed. This was a situation he had been in many times and understood fully.

'Alas, since the shipwreck we have nothing.' Tom adopted a forlorn expression.

Foy steepled his fingers. 'That is a great pity.'

'However,' Tom continued, 'we carried a substantial cargo of ivory. If the storm did not rip the bottom out of our ship, it may still be there. She lies in shallow water. In consideration of the loan of a boat, we could give you a quarter of anything we retrieve from the wreck.'

'What manner of offer is that?' Foy composed his face so that Tom could see the insult he had taken. 'I could salvage it myself and claim the entirety of your cargo.'

'But you would have to travel to the Admiralty Court in London to claim it,' said Tom, calling up memories of his conversation with Captain Inchbird on the *Dowager*. 'I have powerful friends in London. While the case was heard, we might seek a lien on all your exports. An entire season of your trade could be lost.'

Foy made a growling noise, uncannily like a dog. 'Do you presume to threaten me, sir?'

'Not at all, sir! I wish only to show you how we can come to a mutually beneficial arrangement.'

Foy frowned, staring at the papers on his desk. He popped another date in his mouth and chewed it noisily.

'Half,' said Foy.

'Half,' Tom agreed. 'And you will give us board and lodging until we find a passage home.'

'You may lodge with the garrison, and eat at the Company table. I will deduct the costs from our final settlement.' He flapped his hand irritably. 'Now if you will excuse me, I have correspondence I must attend to.'

Tom wondered if he was about to write to Guy to inform him of this turn of events. He paused at the door. 'You mentioned Governor Courtney in Bombay. Are you acquainted?'

Foy puffed up. 'I pride myself we are most intimate. Guy Courtney is my patron – nay, my friend. It was he who secured me this position, after I rendered him some small service in a dispute with the Surat merchants.'

Tom gave inward thanks he had not told Foy his true name. 'Is he well?'

'In rude good health. He seems quite at home in this damnable climate.'

'And his family? He has a son, does he not?'

Beside Tom, Sarah stiffened. She kicked his ankle, but Foy was too keen to show off his connection with Guy to notice.

'Alas, his son is a great disappointment. A great disappointment,' he repeated. 'He defied his father and ran away to sea. He has not been heard of since. I believe Guy blames his mother's influence.'

Tom wanted to ask more. But Foy, belatedly, had gauged the interest in Tom's voice. He shot him a jealous look.

'Are you and Guy familiar?'

'A long time ago,' said Tom. 'Does he ever call at this factory?'

'Alas, so far he has not graced us with his presence.' This was clearly a matter of some concern to Foy. 'But his brother-in-law is with us. Here, in this very fort.'

A chill went through Tom. Had he been recognized? How could Foy have known? And why say 'his brother-in-law'? Tom and Guy had married sisters, but they were brothers above all else.

'I beg your pardon,' said Tom with a glassy stare. He scanned the room for a weapon, anything he could use. Could he take a musket from the sentry on the door? If shots were fired, how long would it take before the garrison arrived?

Foy mopped his brow, entirely oblivious to the effect his

words had had on Tom. 'Captain Hicks and his wife have been here in Brinjoan since January. Though I do not think Guy sent them here for their personal benefit.'

Tom paused. *What do you mean?* he wanted to shout. But before he could betray himself, Sarah spoke up.

'Of course,' she said brightly. 'Captain Hicks married Agnes Beatty, the sister of Guy's wife Caroline. Dear Agnes. She and I were the greatest of friends growing up in York together.'

Tom leaned on the desk. 'You mean to say Agnes Beatty is here?'

'Agnes Hicks, as she is now. I saw her this very morning. Her husband is captain of our garrison.' Foy looked at the Courtneys with new appreciation. Clearly, they were of more importance than he had assumed, though he could not tell precisely how much importance. That fact made him anxious. His entire career had been built on Guy Courtney's coat-tails, and he knew his master's temper if he did anything to disappoint him. Equally, though he was not as intimate with Guy as he pretended, he knew well enough that he bore little love for his family. This would require all his tact.

First, he had to get rid of his guests. He put on a broad smile. 'You asked for lodgings. I am certain Captain Hicks and his wife would be delighted to entertain you in their home. I will take you there at once.'

Tom's natural curiosity couldn't resist examining the fortifications as Foy led them out. The walls were strong, stone-built with triangular bastions giving interlocking fields of fire – but they were built on sand.

'Do you have fresh water in the fort?' he enquired.

'We get our water from the river.' Foy, sweating heavily once again, pointed along a well-worn path to a place on the riverbank, about four hundred yards away.

'You would go thirsty in a siege,' Francis pointed out.

'Oh! It would never come to that. The darkies have no stomach for a fight. At the first musket shot, they'd run screaming into the jungle.'

Sarah sneezed. They were passing the godowns, and the smell of black pepper tickled their noses. The warehouse doors were locked, for there were no ships in the bay.

'Now the rains have started, the coast is impassable. We will see no commerce until the autumn,' Foy lamented.

'Is pepper the chief object of your trade?' Francis asked.

Foy nodded. 'It does not pay so well as formerly, but the East India Company requires its ships to carry a certain weight as ballast. Our treaty with the natives gives us a monopoly on all the pepper this country produces, so we have captive markets on both sides of the ledger. Enough that with sound management we may hope to realize a small profit.'

Tom could imagine what Foy meant by 'sound management'. From all he had heard, the Governors of these small outposts of the Company's empire ran their stations as personal fiefdoms, cheating their own employers as much as they cheated the natives. Whatever profit Foy turned, little would find its way back to Leadenhall Street.

'Are the local merchants happy with the arrangement?' Ana wondered.

'Happy?' Foy looked appalled at the notion. 'If they were happy with the price I gave them, I would regard it as a personal failure.'

'A trade must benefit both parties if it is to endure.'

'I repeat, these people are ignorant savages. A month ago, some of the local merchants refused to sell to me. I broke a sword over their heads and sent them packing. And they have no choice. The Rani, their queen, commands it.'

Tom stiffened. 'The Rani of Chittattinkara?'

Again, Foy shot him a cautious look. 'Do not tell me you are acquainted with her, too?'

'We encountered some of her servants when we were shipwrecked. They stole something valuable from me.'

'Valuable, you say?' Foy's face lit up with interest. But at that moment, they stopped at the door of a broad, one-storey house in the Indian style called a *bungalo*. 'Here we are.'

Foy knocked. Behind him, Sarah and Tom exchanged an anxious glance. Sarah had not seen her sister since she was sixteen. Who knew how she might have changed?

A dark-skinned Indian servant girl opened the door. She curtsied to Foy, lowering her eyes.

'Tell your mistress she has some unexpected guests.'

Almost before he had spoken, a woman came to the door. She stared at the group on her doorstep, blinking.

'Sarah?' she breathed. 'Can it really be you?'

A shudder of recognition convulsed her. She went white; Tom stepped forward for fear she would faint.

'Dear Agnes,' said Sarah, trying to control the emotion in her voice. 'I did not know if you would recognize your old friend Sarah Weald.'

Foy looked suspiciously between them.

'Did you not have a sister named Sarah, Mrs Hicks?'

'Poor thing, she died years ago.' Agnes collected her wits. She grabbed Sarah's hand and led her inside. 'You must come in my dear. And your friends.' She beckoned in Tom, Francis and Ana. 'No doubt we will have so much to talk about. Will you join us, Mr Foy?'

'Alas, I have urgent correspondence that demands my attention.' He touched his hat. 'Good day to you all.'

As soon as he was gone and the door was shut, Agnes threw herself at Sarah, clutching her so tight Sarah gasped for breath.

'Sarah,' she cried in a low whisper. 'Can it be possible? I thought you were dead in Africa.'

'I nearly was – more than once.' Sarah stroked Agnes' hair back from her face. It came away damp with tears. 'But here I am.'

'Why did you never let me know that you were still alive?'

'I knew not where to reach you. And I could not be certain that any letter I posted you would not fall into Guy's hands.'

She pulled away a little and inclined her head towards Tom. 'Do you remember Tom Courtney?'

Agnes had lost the capacity for wonder. She simply stared at Tom, then said softly, 'So the story Caroline told me was true – that you and Sarah eloped together from Zanzibar.'

Tom bowed. 'It is a long time since we all left Plymouth on the *Seraph*.' Sarah and Agnes had been little girls then, so irrelevant in Tom's scheme of things that he could hardly tell them apart. He was enraptured only by their elder sister, Caroline, who had eventually married Guy. Since then, the intervening years had emphasised their differences. Agnes had darker hair and lighter skin than her sister Sarah, with tense lines on her face that spoke of many cares. She was a long way from the carefree child she had been back then. But perhaps they all were.

They sat in Agnes' parlour. Tom and Sarah told her everything from the moment they had fled from Guy in Zanzibar harbour fifteen years earlier. They related their adventures in Africa, their marriage in Cape Town, everything, right up to their meeting with Francis in Cape Town and their shipwreck on the coast of Brinjoan.

Agnes listened, completely entranced, clutching Sarah's hand as if she feared her sister would vanish again if she ever let her go.

'I cannot believe you are here,' she said hoarsely in the end. 'And William Courtney's son Francis also, all grown up. It is nothing short of a miracle!'

'It was a strange twist of fate that brought us here,' Tom agreed. 'But now we must consider how we can make our escape. Do you trust your husband?'

Agnes nodded. 'Captain Hicks is no friend of Guy Courtney. In Bombay, Guy took every opportunity he found to slight us:

164

I think we are an embarrassment to him. It was Guy who stationed my husband here in this miserable outpost.'

'And Mr Foy?' asked Francis.

'Mr Foy cares only for himself. As Governor, he is legally in command of the garrison here, and he does not let my husband forget it. Nor does his wife. But my husband and I will see that they learn nothing of the truth of our relationship.'

'Then we are safe,' said Sarah. 'Thank the Lord.'

And with that, she toppled over in a dead faint onto Agnes' lap.

'Poor thing,' cried Agnes. 'What have I done? You sit here, starving and soaked in your wet clothes, and all I do is prattle on. You need good food and complete rest.'

Tom and Francis lifted Sarah between them. Her skin was warm and feverish to the touch; Tom cursed himself for all the hardships he had put her through. They laid her on an upstairs bed, and covered her with a blanket despite the heat. Agnes brought a broth of lentils and lemon, and sat beside her, spooning it tenderly into Sarah's mouth.

The front door crashed open. In the hall, a man's voice called for Agnes. A few moments later, he appeared in the doorway. A tall, lean man, with close-cropped sandy hair and a skin weathered red by the sun. He wore the red coat with green facings of the Bombay regiment.

'Foy told me we had unexpected guests.' He ran his eye over the visitors and put out his hand. 'Elijah Hicks, at your service.'

'Tom . . .' Tom hesitated. 'Tom Courtney.'

'Courtney?' Hicks' voice thickened with surprise and suspicion. He turned to Agnes. 'Did you know . . . ?'

'They are family,' she said. She stroked Sarah's cheek, pale and hot. 'This is my sister, Sarah. I have not seen her in almost twenty years. And our nephew Francis Courtney, William's son.'

Hicks was at a loss for words. He shook hands with Tom

and Francis, and bowed to Ana. Then Agnes shooed them all out. 'Sarah needs peace, not a company of men all crowding around her. Go!'

They left the women, and returned to the parlour. Hicks fetched shirts and breeches for the men to change into. They fitted Francis well, though Tom struggled to fasten the buttons on his shirt. Hicks poured them a sweet white wine. The maid-servant brought a dish of fish and rice.

'This cursed heat,' Hicks complained. 'God knows how I have survived it this long.'

They sat, awkwardly, drinking the wine and watching the soft rain fall on the settlement. Hicks was a man of few words, and he seemed at a loss to know what to say to these most unexpected arrivals.

Tom tilted his glass towards the fort. 'The factory seems lightly defended.'

Hicks scowled. 'That is Foy's doing. He is so jealous of his dignity, he assumes any order I give must necessarily be some stratagem to undermine him, and so he countermands it. I cannot suggest I should drill my men, or reconnoitre the countryside, or even see to the fort's upkeep without him devising some ploy to prevent me.'

Tom was glad that Agnes' husband was not to blame for the garrison's meagre defences. On first impressions, he warmed to the man, with his no-nonsense demeanour and honest way of speaking. A good man to have on their side.

And he is my brother-in-law, he thought, wondering again at the chance that should bring Agnes and Sarah together in this distant land after so many years.

'Are the local people friendly?'

'Not so much as I would like. Foy provokes them constantly. He has eyes only for his profit, and is too blind to see what harm he does. He will not concede one peppercorn from his due, though the men who bring it are starving. He forces the

166

merchants to sell at whatever price he stipulates and God help them if they refuse.'

'I am surprised they are not more vocal in their grievances.'

'Foy believes the Rani will keep them in check.'

Tom grimaced. 'That is the third time I have heard of this Rani. Who is she?'

'The local queen. She is very young, but from what I have seen she has the mind of a serpent. Her court is divided between those who would trade with us, and those who would drive us into the sea. She holds them in check – but it is an uneasy balance.'

'If my experience of the Rani's men is any guide, they do not treat gently with Englishmen.'

Tom told of his ordeal at the village. Hicks nodded.

'I know that man, Tungar. He is one of the Rani's captains. He hates the English: his uncles used to control the pepper trade, before we arrived.'

'He took something precious to me. A sword that has been in my family for generations. I must retrieve it.' Now that they were safe, dry and fed, his thoughts turned instinctively to the blue sword. More than a weapon, in his mind it represented the whole honour and legacy of the Courtneys – all that survived of them, now High Weald was gone. Tom made an oath there and then: that he would not leave this place without the blue sword in his hand.

'Foy intends to make an embassy to the Rani in three days,' said Hicks. 'Tungar has been making trouble for us again, and Foy hopes to bring him to heel. You may try your suit with the Rani then – though you may find she is more minded to receive gifts than to dispense them. She is as jealous of her dignity as Mr Foy.'

'Then it should be an interesting encounter,' Tom conceded thoughtfully.

* * *

That night Tom slept like a dead man and woke to find the rain had eased. Sarah's condition had improved, too, though when Agnes brought her breakfast she could eat no more than a few spoonfuls of her porridge.

A servant arrived with a note for Tom from Foy. Tom wondered that he could not be bothered to walk the few hundred yards from the fort to the cottage to deliver it himself.

'I trust you have not forgotten our arrangement,' said the note.

'He wants me to go and look at the wreck,' Tom deduced. 'No doubt he is concerned we shall become a burden on him if we do not pay our bill.'

'I will come with you,' Hicks offered.

'I should be glad of it,' said Tom gratefully. 'If you can be spared from your duties here.'

Hicks snorted. 'For all the good I do, I may as well be picking coconuts. Mr Foy will be pleased to see the back of me for the day.'

Tom found eight of *Kestrel*'s crew who were strong enough to make the journey. Hicks complemented them with four sepoys from his company, led by a *hubladar* named Mohite who had a magnificent moustache that dangled below his chin. A *hubladar* was the equivalent of a sergeant in the Bombay army, and Tom could see by the easy respect between the two men that Hicks relied on him utterly.

They sailed out in a borrowed *gallivat*, a native craft as big as a longboat, but sporting a triangular sail like a dhow. Tom watched the weather anxiously, but the storm seemed to have relented. The *gallivat* glided along under the onshore breeze, her lateen sail bending eagerly to the tack.

'I wish Dorian were here,' grinned Tom. 'He would know how to get the most from her.'

'With luck, he will soon be drinking coffee with Aboli on the waterfront at Gombroon and toasting the fortune he has made,' said Francis.

Having arrived in Brinjoan by land, Tom recognized nothing of the coast. They sailed for some hours, always watching the horizon. The sky hung low and grey, and it would not be long before the next tantrum thrown by the monsoon made landfall.

They doubled a small headland, and came around into a long, shallow bay. Tom gave a cry. There was the *Kestrel*: a dark, broken hulk. The wind and the waves had pushed her close to shore, into water so shallow her shattered deck stood clear of the sea.

But she was not abandoned. Three men stood on her deck, pointing and shouting to a larger group of men on the beach. They had gathered around a team of oxen who were harnessed to traces that ran into the sea towards the wreck. As Tom watched, the drivers urged them forward, beating them with switches. The beasts shuffled forward. The chains slithered out of the sea, dripping wet. The oxen carried on, so far up the beach that they disappeared into a gap in the trees that looked newly cut for the purpose.

'Are they trying to drag the whole ship ashore?' Francis wondered.

Hicks had been studying the shore party through his telescope. He passed it to Tom. Through the lens, Tom saw a dark shark-like shape beneath the waves.

The oxen dragged it from the surf and he saw that it was the long barrel of one of the nine-pounder cannon. As soon as it came out of the water, men ran to it and levered it onto a set of wooden logs so it could roll freely.

'What are they doing with that?'

'European cannon are like hen's teeth to the natives,' said Hicks. 'Their princes would pay their weight in gold to have one, but even your brother Guy draws the line at selling them arms. Whatever the profits, he fears the guns might be turned on his ships and factories one day.'

Tom scanned the beach again. The cannon had reached the

trees. The oxen had been unhitched and were being coaxed back to the shoreline, while two men waded out to the wreck with the ends of the chains. Evidently, they intended to salvage her whole armament.

With the telescope, Tom found the group's leader. Tall and broad shouldered, he towered above the other men. He was naked to the waist, with pistols hanging from the bandoliers crossed over his chest, and a pair of swords on his belt. He directed his men with short, confident commands, and Tom noted how they leaped to obey. They were more than well drilled – they feared him.

'He looks a perfect villain,' Tom muttered. Something about the man unnerved him. 'Who is he?'

Hicks took the telescope back. 'I have not seen this one before. Perhaps he is new to the Rani's service.'

'Or a bandit.'

'It would be a brave bandit who looted a shipwreck on the Rani's coast. And taking cannon is not like dipping for travellers' purses. To bring that many men, a whole team of oxen . . . to say nothing of the difficulty of transporting the guns away. They could not do it without her knowledge.'

'Then it looks as if we shall have more than just my sword to ask her for when we visit.'

Hicks frowned. 'I do not like it. This portends some mischief, I'll warrant.'

On the beach, the men had seen the *gallivat*. They waved and shouted, though whether they were beckoning her in or warning them off, Tom couldn't tell. He took the telescope again.

'Keep to your course,' he told Alf Wilson on the tiller. 'They are too many for us to engage, and they must not know we have seen anything amiss.' He did not think the men on the beach had a spyglass; with luck, they might not have discerned that the men in the boat were Europeans.

170

Hicks read his thoughts. 'If we are to convince them we are innocent passers-by, you had best put away that telescope. Native fishermen do not usually carry such instruments.'

'Of course,' said Tom, feeling slightly foolish. He hoped the men on the beach had not seen it; there was little sun to flare on the lens.

Even so, he could not resist one last look at the man in charge. Perhaps, even at that distance, he caught the movement; perhaps it was pure chance. Either way, as Tom put the telescope to his eye the man looked up, and for a moment they came eye to eye in the lens. Tom was certain he had never seen him before, yet when the stranger's face leaped into focus a chill ran down Tom's spine. Some intuition, an inexplicable flash of recognition. Almost as if he had looked in a mirror.

He lowered the telescope away, and slipped it into its leather case. It was a foolish fancy, he decided, or perhaps something he had dreamed.

Once again, he remembered the flash of brilliant green on the horizon at Cape Town. *A spirit returning from the dead.*

Without the telescope, the man on the beach was little bigger than an ant. But still Tom could not take his eyes off him, until they had rounded the point and he disappeared from Tom's sight.

And all the way back to Brinjoan, he could not forget Hicks's warning. *This portends some mischief.*

Lying on his belly, Christopher crawled forward to the edge of the escarpment. He peered over a rotting tree stump and saw the caravan below. A curtained palanquin led the way, carried on the shoulders of eight slaves. Twenty armed men followed behind.

Tamaana came up beside him. 'I told you we were wise to wait.'

They had watched the same caravan pass by three days earlier travelling in the opposite direction. Christopher had wanted to attack then, but Tamaana had counselled patience. 'They are taking cloth to the English factory at Brinjoan,' she had said. 'When they come back, they will have traded all those heavy bales of cloth for gold.'

Now Christopher could see the truth of it. Three days ago, almost a hundred native bearers had followed the palanquin, balancing bulky parcels of fine-spun cotton cloth on their heads. Now they had been dismissed, replaced by a single mule straining under the weight of its saddle bags. Christopher was surprised the beast could move at all with so many guards clustered around it. He edged back a little.

He felt a flicker of misgiving, and wondered why. It certainly wasn't conscience. In the six months since he had joined Tamaana's bandit company, they had done this more times than he could count. They had robbed and murdered single travellers, and routed well-guarded caravans. Success had brought attention, both useful – their band had now swelled to a dozen men – and unwanted. Only three weeks ago they had moved north into the kingdom of Chittattinkara to escape a ruler who was determined to capture the bandits who infested his roads.

'Are you sure we should attack now?'

Tamaana gave a devilish smile. 'That poor mule's back will break if we do not relieve him of his burden. Are you frightened?'

'Of course not.'

'Then we should spring the trap, before they escape.'

It was the obvious place for an ambush. The road twisted through a narrow gully worn deep by the rains. Broken rocks littered the slope above, giving ample cover. The guards knew it. Watching, Christopher saw them loosening the swords in their scabbards. The captain – a huge man in a red turban – barked an order. The men who had guns – four of them – lit

the matches for their firelocks and clamped them to the serpen-
tines of their weapons. They scanned the steep slopes that
hemmed them in, alert to any sign of movement. Christopher,
well-practised in the art of remaining unseen, held his breath.

The caravan came around a bend and stopped with cries of
dismay. A tree had fallen across the road, blocking it completely.
The guards formed a defensive circle, facing outwards around
the litter and the mule. Christopher saw the captain check the
base of the tree. He knew his business. If the trunk bore the
marks of an axe, he would know it had been deliberately felled.

There were no axe-marks. That was intentional. Christopher's
men had spent hours digging out the roots until the tree fell
of its own weight, spreading the earth so it would look like
natural erosion.

It deceived the captain. While the men with matchlocks kept
guard, the others put aside their weapons so they could drag
the tree out of the way. They worked quickly, spurred by fear
for their lives as much as their captain's barked orders. In
minutes, they had rolled the heavy tree away, and with it the
weight of their anxiety. The road stood clear. Christopher saw
smiles and heard the laughter, the relief of men embarrassed
by their own fears. A hand extended from the curtained palanquin, waving them forward.

The first arrow hit the captain through the throat. The second
hit the mule. Tamaana's men had guns, but they always used
bows for the first assault. It left the victims disoriented, with
no tell-tale puff of smoke to mark from which direction the
attack had come.

Without their captain, the guards' discipline dissolved. They
fired blindly, wasting precious shots and blinding themselves
with their own gun smoke. Before they could reload, Tamaana
and her men charged down the slope. Christopher uncoiled
his *urumi* and joined them. Through the smoke that filled the
ravine, he saw one guard frantically trying to reload his match-

lock. The *urumi* sang through the air and opened his chest. With practised motions, Christopher drew it back, twitched the handle and caught another guard on the back of his knees, severing the tendons. He went down screaming.

Not long ago, Christopher might have been one of those guards. Now, he was the hunter. He strode through the smoke, barely needing to raise his sword as his men finished off the surviving guards. Soon, the only men from the caravan left standing were the litter bearers: eight broad-shouldered men, naked to their waists. In the speed and brutality of the attack, they had not even moved.

Armed, they would have made formidable opponents. But if Christopher had learned one thing about India, it was that the caste system was absolute. A litter-carrier would not fight, any more than a warrior would milk a cow. A man's birth was his destiny.

So Christopher felt no surprise when the bearers dropped the litter and fled. It was expected of them. Christopher let them go and approached the fallen palanquin.

The curtains parted. A short, fat man in a green silk robe stuck his head out. The anger on his face melted to abject terror as he took in the scene – and Christopher, standing over him with drawn sword.

The man started pulling off his rings and throwing them at Christopher's feet. Christopher enjoyed seeing him struggle to squeeze the tight bands over his plump fingers.

'It would be faster if I cut them off,' he suggested helpfully.

The man squealed and redoubled his efforts. A golden ring set with carnelian and rubies was so tight, it tore off a strip of skin when he removed it. Blood welled from the wound.

Christopher touched the blade of his sword to the man's throat. He went very still.

'Save your energy. I will take them when you're dead.'

The man cowered back into his litter. Christopher ripped

the curtains away, exposing a sanctum of sumptuously embroidered pillows that smelled of perfume. He wondered how much they would fetch. He should avoid getting blood on them.

'Please,' begged his prisoner. 'Do you know who I am?'

'No,' said Christopher. '

With his eyes calculating the man's wealth, he did not see the shrewd look that crossed the merchant's eyes.

'My name is Mahendra Poola. My brothers are all prosperous merchants: they will pay a handsome price if you free me.'

'We do not take prisoners,' Christopher explained gently.

'My brothers live not far from here. It would be a matter of a few days to arrange the payment.' The man dropped onto his knees and grovelled. 'The rains will start soon, and there will be no more caravans for you to plunder. Would you not benefit from a last coup to cushion you through the monsoon?'

'I will live quite comfortably on the gold you are carrying on that mule.'

The merchant's eyes widened. 'That is why you killed my men? For that?'

'Why else?' Christopher raised his sword for the kill, savouring the terror on his victim's face. Never mind the pillows. He would sell them to some scavenging peasant, who would not care about the bloodstains. He brought the sword down—

'Wait.'

Tamaana's voice halted the blade an inch from the merchant's neck. The only voice that could have checked Christopher. He turned, and saw Tamaana hurrying towards him holding a bulging saddle bag. The merchant burst into tears.

'What?'

Without answering, she hauled the merchant to his feet and put her pistol against his skull. 'Where is your gold?'

'Was it not on the mule?' said Christopher.

Left-handed, Tamaana upended the saddle bag. A small bottle

of cherry brandy fell out and smashed on the ground, followed by a bundle wrapped in paper that landed with a heavy thud. Christopher slit the paper with his sword revealing flat, black ingots stacked crosswise. He picked one up. When he tested it between his hands, it bent.

'Lead?'

The merchant put up his hands to ward off the expected blow. Christopher tossed the ingot away. 'Where is the gold?'

'There is none.'

'Then what happened to the cotton you took to Brinjoan three days ago?' Tamaana demanded.

'The English agent at Brinjoan is a thief. He takes my wares but does not pay me for them. He traded me this lead as part payment. Alas, I must wait until the dry season for what he owes me in gold.'

'You lie,' said Tamaana coldly. 'Strip him. And if we do not find the gold under his clothes, we will open him up and see what he has inside him.'

'No,' squealed the merchant. 'I am worth nothing to you dead. Alive, I could be valuable.'

'He wants us to ransom him,' said Christopher.

'We do not take prisoners,' Tamaana said flatly. 'And how would we collect a ransom without exposing ourselves? Your family would seek to negotiate a better price, and each time we exchanged messages we would risk being discovered.'

'No negotiation,' promised the merchant. 'Name your figure. I will send a message to my brothers and tell them to pay without question. They can leave it in a safe place, wherever you choose.'

'And why would they do that if they were not certain of getting you back alive?'

'Because otherwise, they would be certain of *not* getting me back alive.' The merchant seemed to have recovered some of his composure. He twisted the last of the rings off his finger

176

and held them out to Tamaana. 'I am a simple merchant. Why can we not strike a bargain to benefit us both?'

'I don't trust him,' said Tamaana.

They crouched behind a rock, talking in whispers. The night was dark, with a sliver of moon that gave the mere suggestion of light. That was no coincidence. Every detail of this meeting had been planned and argued over: the place, the time, the instructions to be given. They had considered and rejected a dozen options. More than once, Christopher had thought Tamaana would simply end the debate by killing their prisoner, Poola. She still might do so.

A low hoot sounded in the night air. It might have been an owl, but it was not quite like any owl that ever existed. Christopher stiffened.

'That is the signal.'

They had chosen a rocky hollow in the mountains, far from any village and the main roads. They had posted sentries along the path, watching for any sign of trickery or bad faith. Now they would find out if Poola was a man of his word.

'We should kill him anyway,' Tamaana fretted. 'He knows our faces and our names. As soon as he returns home, he will petition the queen and she will send out squadrons of her guards. Then we will have to move again.'

'He's a harmless fool,' Christopher countered. 'He will thank his gods he escaped with his life, and be content enough. Besides, if we kill him after taking the ransom, it will become known. Next time we take a hostage, the family will not pay the ransom.'

Tamaana shrugged. 'We have enough gold already.'

'There is no such thing as "enough gold".'

They fell silent as footsteps crunched the stone ground. Two porters came out into the hollow, almost damaging their backs under the weight of the chest they carried between them. They put it down, rubbing their aching arms and scanning the darkness.

'We have come for Lord Poola,' one said.

Beside him, Christopher felt Tamaana reaching for her pistol. He put his hand on her arm. 'There may be an explanation.'

'We said to only send one man,' Tamaana called. Her voice echoed off the stones, disguising her location. The porters looked around wildly. Even in the dark, Christopher could see they were terrified.

'The chest is too heavy for a single man to carry,' one of the porters pleaded in a high-pitched voice.

'Then we will relieve you of your burden.'

'What of our master?'

'We will release him when we have counted the money. Now *go.*' Tamaana raised her pistol and fired into the air. The echo made it sound like the volley from an entire company of fusiliers. The porters fled back the way they had come.

Christopher and Tamaana waited. The chest sat alone in the hollow like a pagan altar. Christopher scratched his palms with his nails, itching to open it, but he did not move until their watchman emerged from the path and signalled all was clear.

'They came alone,' he confirmed, 'and ran away as if a tiger was on their heels.'

Christopher went to the chest. It was extravagantly carved from heavy mahogany; it must have been used to store spices or medicines, for it smelled strongly of aniseed. He lifted the lid, and even in the feeble moonlight he saw the glint of gold.

He scooped a handful of the coins, enjoying the feel of the metal slipping through his fingers. Tamaana knocked them out of his hand and slammed the chest shut.

'Later. We must be away from here, before those messengers gather their wits and return in strength.'

'And Poola?'

From the glint in her eyes, he knew what she was thinking. She tested the edge of her curved dagger with her thumb.

Christopher kicked the chest. 'There is more money here than we would ever have taken from one caravan.'

'We could cut out his tongue to stop him describing us,' Tamaana murmured reflectively.

'He could still write.' Christopher pointed out.

'Then we could cut off his hands to prevent that.'

'His family might feel we had cheated on our bargain,' Christopher demurred. In this brittle mood, he could not tell if Tamaana was teasing him or giving it serious thought.

Without answering, Tamaana whistled to her men. They dragged Poola stumbling and tripping into the hollow. He was blindfolded, his hands tied behind his back. Even in the warm pre-monsoon night, he was shivering and shaking.

Christopher studied Tamaana's face, trying to guess what she intended to do with him.

'Why are we doing this, if not for money?' he asked quietly.

Tamaana nodded slowly. She pushed the dagger back into the sheath on her belt. Christopher breathed out carefully. He cared nothing for Poola; he would happily have inflicted any torture on him if he thought he could profit from it. But this was better business.

'You will stay here,' Tamaana told Poola. 'And pray someone finds you before the hyenas and snakes do.'

'Untie me and leave me a weapon to defend myself,' he begged.

'You will work those ropes loose eventually,' she told him. 'And I think your friends will soon come looking for you.'

She turned to go.

'Should we not count the ransom first?' Christopher asked. 'What if they cheated us?'

'Then we will find out where they live and kill them. We will kill their wives, their children, their brothers and sisters and

179

their servants. Last of all, we will kill *him*.' She kicked Poola. 'Do you understand?'

'Yes,' Poola whimpered. 'They would not cheat you, I swear it.'

'Every second we delay here we risk capture – and we cannot take the prisoner. He will only slow us down. Since you are so keen to leave him alive . . .' She nodded to the wooden chest. 'You can carry that.'

When Christopher tried to lift it, he discovered the porters had not exaggerated its weight. Strong as he was, he could barely lift it to his shoulder. He shouted at two of the men to help him. Each of them seized a handle but they staggered over the uneven terrain. Tamaana strode ahead of them, chiding them angrily to keep up.

They came down off the mountain and into the thick jungle on the lower slopes. Here there were few paths, used only by wild animals and bandits. The pain in Christopher's arms was excruciating. It made him hate Poola. He distracted himself from the pain by concocting fantasies of the ways he could kill him.

At last Tamaana called a halt in a jungle clearing. The pain in Christopher's arms faded miraculously as he opened the chest and started counting the gold coins. It took almost half an hour to count them, and by the time he had finished everyone was smiling or laughing. It was all there. Even Tamaana relented and came to sit beside him, resting her hand on his leg and stroking his thigh.

'But we cannot rest long,' she warned him. 'We must reach a town – a large town, where we will not be noticed or remembered. There we will buy supplies to last us through the monsoon. Then we find a secure place to wait it out, until the travellers and caravans take to the roads again.'

Christopher thought of the long, wet afternoons ahead of them, imaging how he and Tamaana might make good use of them. He felt a stirring under his tunic, and he took her hand

and guided it downwards. She smiled and nodded coyly. She stood up and opened one of the packs and from it distributed a bottle of arak to each of the men. Then she took Christopher by the hand and led him to a grassy hollow a little deeper in the jungle. She stamped her feet and beat the grass with her staff to frighten away the snakes.

Then suddenly and unexpectedly she dropped to her knees facing away from him. She bent over and with both hands pulled her skirts up under her armpits. Then she looked back over her shoulder at him and laughed to see the expression on his face turn from astonishment to rampant lust. She was naked from the waist downwards. Her buttocks were full and magnificently rounded. The skin was tinted the colour of ripe mangoes. Between them the dense curls of her pubic hair parted, and her vagina pouted out at him. Its opening was glossy with the love juice that oozed from the depths of her womb.

He dropped his trousers around his ankles and then fell to his knees behind her. She humped her back and reached behind with both hands to seize his rampant penis. It leaped and quivered in her grip like a creature with a life of its own. Her thumbs and fingers were only just able to encompass its girth, and it took all the strength of her wrists to direct the engorged head up between her brimming lips. She cried out with sweet agony as he forced the full length of it into her, and almost immediately she screamed again in ecstasy as she felt it pressing imperiously against the very mouth of her womb.

They awakened together and lay in each other's arms, uncertain as to what had disturbed them. The night around them was strangely silent, but the silence was menacing; fraught and terrifying.

'What is it—?' Tamaana started and then broke off as they both heard the dogs. They scrambled to their feet, reaching for their clothing to cover their nudity.

Christopher seized her hand, 'They are hunting, and we are the prey.'

'We must go back and get the gold.'

'We have to leave the bulk of it. It will weigh us down. We would not cover a mile before the dogs caught us. Come on!' They ran back to where they had left their comrades and the treasure chest.

The men lay sprawled around the clearing, all of them fast asleep. Most of them were still clutching an arak bottle. Christopher swore, and kicked the nearest of them.

'Get up, you drunken pigs.'

'Leave them, they deserve what is coming to them,' Tamaana ordered Christopher. 'Fill your pockets with as much of the gold as you can carry. Then we must run.'

The chest still stood in the middle of the clearing. They hurried to it. Christopher flung the lid back and they stuffed their pockets with gold pagodas.

'That's enough!' Tamaana slammed the lid of the chest, and they both paused to listen to the night. The baying of the dogs was louder and now Christopher thought he could detect the soft trembling of the earth beneath his feet.

'Horses!' he exclaimed. 'That makes it certain: they are after us.' In all the months that they had travelled these roads, they had not encountered more than five or six horsemen. Any man who could afford to own one was powerful enough to be feared. He cocked his head again to listen. It sounded like a squadron of cavalry was hunting them.

He grabbed Tamaana's arm and steered her into the jungle. The undergrowth was dense and many of the plants were armed with hooked thorns. Before they had covered half a mile they were both bleeding from lacerations to their arms and legs. Behind he heard the whinnying and neighing of horses being reined in, and the shouts of their pursuers as they discovered the drunken men and the treasure chest that they had abandoned.

182

Christopher looked to the sky and fancied he could see the first bloom of dawn through the tree tops. But he had lost all sense of direction in the dark of the night. He kept the sounds of the chase behind him and they ran on as the light strengthened.

Abruptly the forest opened directly ahead of them. They were both running as fast as the thorn bushes and treacherous footing would allow them. Christopher grabbed Tamaana, throwing an arm around her shoulders, and both of them teetered on the brink of a precipice that opened in front of them, dropping sheer for several hundred feet to a rocky dry river course.

In the monsoon rains it would be a wide and rushing river. But now it was a chasm lined with teeth of sharp black rock.

Tamaana stared down into it for a few seconds. Then she turned her head and listened back over her shoulder. The dogs sounded much closer, clamouring with excitement as the scent of the chase grew stronger.

'I am not going to let them take me.' Tamaana made up her mind suddenly and tried to tear herself from his embrace. 'I am going to jump.'

'No, my darling. I can't let you do it.' He tightened the grip of his arms about her. He could hear the horses and the dogs coming up behind them, the sound of running men blundering through the jungle.

'Better a quick death. If they catch us, they will make us suffer torments too terrible to contemplate.'

'I love you,' he shouted into her face. 'As long as we stay alive, we have hope.'

She twisted her head away from him. 'I listened to you once before. But never again. I will not let them take me.'

She almost succeeded in wriggling out of his grip, but he threw his full weight on top of her and forced her to the ground, just as the first team of dogs burst from the undergrowth behind them. After the dogs came uniformed men armed with clubs. They raced forward and fell upon the pair who were still struggling on the edge of the precipice, beating Tamaana and Christopher into a state of semi-conscious submission. Then they handcuffed their hands in front of them, and locked collars around their necks attached to steel chains. The ends of the chains were made fast to the saddles of two of the horses, and they were dragged back to the clearing where they had left Tamaana's drunken henchmen, and the treasure chest.

This was the first opportunity that Christopher had to examine their captors. They were obviously crack troops and first class horsemen. All of them wore similar uniforms of quilted armour, steel helmets and orange sashes about their waists. There was an air of self-confidence about them that was intimidating. Christopher determined at once not to make his own warlike training apparent, and adopted a meek and humble attitude, with downcast eyes and obsequious bearing.

Their erstwhile prisoner, Poola, stood in their midst, unrecognisable from the gibbering wretch they had left only a few hours earlier. He had changed into fresh clothes, combed his beard and stood erect and proud. He gave a satisfied smile as he saw Christopher and Tamaana brought in.

'Our situation has changed somewhat,' he observed drily.

'How did you find us so swiftly?' Christopher asked meekly.

'I can always follow the scent of gold.' Poola kicked the wooden treasure chest that still stood in the centre of the clearing. He lifted the lid and sniffed at the contents. 'I suppose you noticed that it smells rather strongly of anise? Did you think my family put the ransom in such a heavy chest merely to inconvenience you? Each time you put it down to rest, you left another trace of the scent on your path. Tungar and his dogs had little trouble following it.'

He gestured to the man beside him, his opposite in every way. Where Poola was short, urbane and plump, Tungar was tall and dangerous, with an ugly scar down the centre of his face. Christopher wondered how he could have survived the blow that made it. He wore a yellow feather tucked into his turban, and there was the unmistakable air of command about him.

'And who then are you?' Christopher asked.

'I am not any mere merchant,' Poola answered. 'I am an advisor to her highness the Rani of Chittattinkara – and she does not suffer her servants to be molested. You are about to learn how she treats those who displease her.'

Tungar's men loaded the treasure chest onto the cart they had brought with them. All Tamaana's men were chained behind horses, along with Tamaana and Christopher, and the column set off.

Christopher didn't know how long they walked. By the time Tungar, the captain, called a halt, Christopher's feet hurt so much he could barely shuffle forward. The prisoners collapsed in a heap at the roadside. Flies settled on Christopher; ants and beetles crawled over his scabbed and bleeding legs. He longed to swat them, but his manacled hands were useless.

Some of the guards went into the forest. Through his pain, Christopher heard the rhythmic thud of axes chopping wood. Perhaps they meant to make a cooking fire. He was ravenous.

'What will you do with us?' he asked Poola. A plan had begun to form in his head. 'Will you bring us to the Rani?'

Poola snorted. 'I would not demean her highness with untouchable scum like you.'

'You should take us to her,' Christopher pleaded. 'I have skills she might find useful.'

'Oh, she has a use for you,' Poola assured him unpleasantly. 'And it does not require any effort on your behalf – except a little patience.'

The guards emerged from the forest carrying a long sapling, about the thickness of a man's arm. They stripped the bark, and whittled one end to a needle-sharp spike. Others used their hatchets to scoop a small hole in the ground at the side of the road. The captured bandits stared, and even with the nooses around their necks they began to jabber with terror. They understood what their captors meant to do to them.

Poola stood over them. His hand hovered, half raised, pointing at each in turn like a man at a butcher's stall uncertain what joint to choose for his dinner. His eyes rested a moment on Christopher.

'You will be last,' he told him. 'When you have watched your friends die one by one.'

He pointed at the man beside Christopher, a swarthy individual named Vijay. Vijay had been charged with keeping watch over Poola, and he had not been gentle in his attentions. Now Tungar's men cut the halter that bound him to the others and dragged him to the middle of the road. He struggled, but they pushed him to the ground and held him face down. Tungar knelt beside him.

Tungar took a pouch of the mutton fat he used to oil his rifle cartridges, and smeared it on the end of the sharpened stake. His men laughed and made obscene gestures. Vijay squirmed, and screamed so loud the guards stuffed a cloth in his mouth.

The guards who held his legs spread them wide apart. Two others took the sharpened pole and pressed it between his buttocks. Christopher could not bear to watch. He closed his eyes, though with his hands bound he couldn't stop up his ears. Vijay had spat out his gag. Screams of agony split the jungle as the spike passed through his anus and into his body. The captors knew their business. Christopher could tell from the sounds Vijay made that they had avoided the vital organs. That would have meant too quick a death.

He opened his eyes. Vijay lay on the ground, still screaming, and the screams redoubled as the guards lifted the spike upright.

He slid down the pole, plunging the point deeper into his own entrails, but the guards had lashed a small cross-piece to the stake that kept him from penetrating too far. He sank down on himself, collapsing, until he was hunched like a chicken on a spit. Blood ran out of his anus and pooled at the bottom of the stick for flies to drink and savour.

They put the base of the stake into the hole they'd dug, and packed it with earth and rocks to keep the stake upright. Then they stepped back to admire their work, laughing and joking among themselves. Christopher heard them making bets as to how long Vijay would survive – most seemed to estimate two or three days. Vijay's screams had tailed away into choking sobs as the spike pressed the air out of his lungs.

Poola came across and looked down on Christopher with sadistic anticipation.

'It is twenty miles from here to Chittattinkara. I will do the same to one of your men, one every two miles, and when we reach the Rani's palace I will hoist you and your whore on each side of the gates of her palace. That will teach our people what happens to those who threaten the Rani's servants – and our commerce.'

Over the next two days, Poola made good his threat. One by one, the bandits were dragged from the group and impaled at the roadside. At last, as they approached the palace in the foothills, Christopher and Tamaana were the only survivors.

He had thought that repeatedly witnessing the ordeal might have brutalized him to what was coming. Instead, it only magnified his terror. He found himself watching with horrible fascination each time the spike went in, his anal muscles clenched, and he was unable to drag his eyes from the awful spectacle. With no food, and no rest, he began to hallucinate. He dreamed he was back in his father's study, breeches around his ankles, bent over a chair waiting for the strap while his mother sat sternly in the corner and told him to be brave. Once he dreamed he was making love with Tamaana. Her fingers stroked his back in ecstasy, but when she lifted her hands he saw she had torn away great bleeding chunks of his flesh.

They reached the palace gates in the late afternoon of the second day. Birds wheeled in the sky, as if they already scented the feast of carrion they would be offered, while the inhabitants of the palace came out to watch the spectacle.

Tungar's men already had the stakes, cut earlier in the day and sharpened to points. They stripped Christopher and Tamaana naked and pinned them down in the dirt, a few feet apart. Poola stood over them, speaking to the assembled crowd. In his high, pompous voice, he listed Christopher and Tamaana's crimes. The audience cringed and sighed, but through the sweat filling his eyes Christopher could see the looks on their faces. They were looking forward to the entertainment.

Poola finished his speech with a florid canticle of praise to the Rani. Christopher twisted his head, wondering if the queen had come to witness his execution, but he could not see her. Poola nodded to Tungar, who snapped an order to his men.

They brought the stakes, flourishing them so the crowd could admire their sharpness, and imagine the torments they would inflict. At the sight of the spikes, all Christopher's strength melted away. He began to babble, a hysterical stream of sobs and barely intelligible pleas. 'I will repent. I will crawl on my belly over hot coals to kiss the Rani's feet. I have skills. I can use them in her service. I can serve her well, only please God do not do this terrible thing to me.'

The spectators laughed and jeered and made monkey faces at him. In his panic, without realizing it, he had started speaking in English. Even Tamaana had never heard him speak the language before.

'Quiet,' she said in her own language. 'At least die with dignity.'

188

Poola frowned, and gestured to the men to hurry their work. They readied the stake. Gobs of mutton fat dripped from its tip.

But Tungar had other ideas. He accosted Poola and started speaking, gesturing angrily at Christopher. In his daze, Christopher could not understand what he was saying, though it seemed urgent. Perhaps they were devising some new refinement to his torture.

The stake pricked between his buttocks. After two days of mounting horror, he screamed the moment it touched him. He felt warmth between his legs as his bowels emptied. Pinned down, face in the dirt, he met Tamaana's eyes opposite. She kept perfectly still, making no sound.

'I love you,' she mouthed.

She made him feel ashamed. He bit his lip until it bled, trying to swallow the pain as the stake pushed into him. The guards were toying with him, inching it in, pulling back a little, enjoying every twitch and whimper. He wondered how long it would take to die.

He felt it slide out again, further than before. He tensed himself. Surely they were readying for the final push, ready to split him open and thrust it up through his entrails.

But the thrust did not come. Tungar was shouting at his men, and Poola was shouting at Tungar, and Christopher could not understand a word of it. The audience started to boo, but a glare from Tungar made them lapse into sullen silence. The crowd thinned.

The guards pulled him and Tamaana to their feet and dragged them away.

When they entered the palace dungeons, they were separated. Christopher was taken to one of the cells, but he had no idea of what they had done to Tamaana. They chained him to the stone wall and left him.

He lost count of the time that he lay in the dungeon. In his misery, bound in the utter darkness, he might as well have been in his grave. Only the pain assured him he still lived. His wrists and neck ached from his bonds, his buttocks were crusted with dried blood and faeces, and terrible hunger cramps wracked his stomach. Through a hole in the floor he could hear running water, a river that flowed beneath the dungeon in a culvert. With his mouth almost numb from thirst, it was the most perfect torture. He dreamed of diving into it, the cool taste of the water in his mouth.

At last, guards came, and they were not gentle. They cut his bonds and dragged him through the palace, still naked, along many galleries with gilded statues, and across courtyards screened by elaborate wooden shutters. At last, when he had lost all sense of direction, they came to a pair of bronze doors. The functionary who guarded them wrinkled his nose when he saw Christopher and tried to send him away, but his guards responded brusquely.

'The Rani has commanded it.'

The doors opened. The room beyond was larger even than the great reception rooms in Bombay castle, decorated with tapestries and beautiful paintings. His captors led him around a tiger skin rug in the middle of the floor, to the far end of the room. Poola and Tungar knelt there before an ornate mahogany throne, upon which was seated a beautiful young woman. Eyes downcast, Christopher barely caught a glimpse of her before the guards pushed him to his knees. However he knew from her surreal beauty and the magnificence of her crown and costume that she was the Rani of Chittattinkara.

Poola and Tungar were arguing. Poola was red in the face, while Tungar's scar seemed to throb, and both wore the expressions of men trying to contain their anger.

'We cannot afford to confront the English,' Poola was saying. 'We depend too much on them for our trade.'

'You mean *you* depend too much on them,' Tungar countered. 'How much did the English pay you to advise the Rani to grant them a monopoly?'

'I wanted to secure a market for our wares. Without the English, no one else will buy them.'

'There are other hat-wearers. They would probably give us a better price.'

They paid no attention to Christopher. He cowered on the floor, and wondered why they had brought him up from the dungeon.

The woman on the throne lifted her hand, clinking the golden bangles on her arms. Instantly, the two men fell silent and adopted subservient poses.

'The English traders at Brinjoan are jackals who feast on our people,' she declared. 'We have sought to mend their ways, and each time they heap insult upon insult upon us.'

Tungar smirked. Poola bowed stiffly to concede to her opinion. 'Your highness.'

'However, we are not a vengeful people. War should be undertaken only as a last resort,' the Rani continued.

Now it was Poola who nodded his approval.

'You are one of the hat-wearers?' said the Rani

Cowering on the floor, Christopher did not realize she had addressed him. Tungar reminded him with a sharp kick in the ribs. 'Answer her highness when she deigns to address you.'

Christopher pushed himself onto his knees and looked up. The Rani sat on her throne as still and beautiful as a Hindu goddess. Gold and ivory bangles covered her slim arms; her dress was stitched with gold thread and pearls. A diadem circled her head, with a pendant ruby hanging down between her eyes like a *bindi* mark. From his studies in the *kalari*, Christopher knew it represented the sixth *chakra*, the seat of concealed wisdom. Her almond-shaped eyes stared down at him, unreadable and ineffable.

'Yes.' He nodded. 'Yes, I am one of the hat-wearers.'

'Then how do you explain *this*?'

Her eyes flicked towards one of her servants, who held a leather bag. Attentive to her every movement, he stepped forward and turned out the bag. The *urumi* slithered out onto the floor with a soft whickering sound. Christopher stared at it, like a cat watching a bird, calculating the distance and the time it would take him to reach it.

Tungar put his foot on the *urumi*, and touched the hilt of his sword. The message was unmistakable.

'I ran away from home,' Christopher explained. 'An *aasaan* took me in to his *kalari* and trained me in the art of *Kalaripayattu.*'

'He is lying,' said Poola.

'Bring me any Englishman, and when he hears me speak he will know that we are of the same nation,' Christopher pleaded. He did not know why it mattered to them, but he understood that his life hinged on his nationality.

'Can you teach my guards to use the *urumi*?'

Tungar began to protest, but the Rani silenced him with a wave of her hand. She waited for Christopher's answer.

'I can teach it,' he declared. She wanted more. 'I can teach them to stand together in battle, as the hat-wearers do, and to fire faster than they ever have before. I will make them into such an army as has never been seen in this country.'

'This is unnecessary,' Poola protested. 'The path to greatness is commerce. War impoverishes all who indulge themselves in it.'

The Rani gave him a look that would have felled an elephant. 'The hat-wearers have offered my people many injuries,' she declared. 'They must learn that we are a proud people, unafraid of their ships and their guns. If they do not bow to me, we will teach them a lesson they will not soon forget.'

Tungar ran his fingers over his chin, stroking the scar that split his face. 'Your highness is wise and just.'

'But I must be sure of this creature's loyalty to me.' She spoke about Christopher as if he wasn't present. He only understood what she meant by the way all eyes in the room turned to him.

Christopher bowed. 'I will serve only your majesty.'

The Rani leaned forward from her throne. 'You have plundered the travellers on my roads, murdered my subjects and abused my counsellors. Can you imagine what punishment we reserve for men like you?'

Christopher thought of the men he had watched being impaled along the road. The first of them, Vijay, might almost be dead by now. He swallowed painfully, and nodded.

'Do you think you deserve better?' the Rani asked.

'I beg your highness's mercy. Let me prove my repentance in the zeal of the service I render you.'

The Rani considered it. 'One of your bandit companions still lives,' she observed.

She held his eyes, and in the power of her gaze he understood what she wanted. This was the ultimate test – perhaps his only chance to prove his loyalty and secure his life and his freedom. With the ruthless intuition of the truly powerful, she had fixed on the one thing that still meant anything to him. She wanted him to kill Tamaana.

Had he saved her from jumping into the ravine for *this*? He could not do it. He gave the *urumi* another sidelong glance. If he could get his hands on that, he could kill them all; fight his way to the dungeon, free Tamaana and escape the palace. There must be stables. They could take two horses, and ride – all the way to China, if needs be. *Another name, another new beginning.*

But then reason and reality washed over him in a cold dark wave. There were twenty guards in the room. He would die before he could even touch the *urumi* – or, worse, be returned to the dungeon. He remembered the pain and terror of the stake entering his body. He remembered the stygian darkness of the dungeon. He knew what his reply must be.

'I will kill the bandit,' he agreed. 'Give me my *urumi* and I will kill her and present you with her head.'

The Rani's expression remained impassive, but something like the ghost of a smile passed behind her eyes.

'I want you to kill one woman only, not every single person in my palace.'

She snapped her fingers, and a servant came forward, knelt before her and offered her an ivory inlaid teak box. The Rani lifted the lid and revealed a tiny dagger glittering on a silk cushion. The handle was a hollow golden ring, the folded blade was burnished steel barely two inches long. The Rani lifted it from the case and fondled it as a child would her favourite toy.

'This is the *bagh-nakh*. The tiger claw,' she told Christopher. 'I doubt you saw one like it in the *kalari*?'

Christopher shook his head. 'It is beautiful,' he whispered, in awe as the engravings that decorated the blade caught the light from the windows high above and shot out beams of reflected sunlight.

The Rani slipped the ring over the index finger of her right hand. The blade folded back against the palm of her hand, and she wrapped her fingers around it.

'An intimate weapon, for an intimate death,' she whispered.

She slipped the tiger claw off her own finger and passed it to Tungar.

'Give it to the hat-wearer,' she commanded, 'and let us see how it fits his hand.'

Christopher slipped the ring over his finger and folded his right hand over the golden claw. When he opened his hand it sprang out as of its own accord. He cut left and right with it and it hissed as it turned in air.

'Bring the woman to me,' he said, and his tone was impassive. The Rani nodded, and Tungar gave the order.

They waited in silence in the great hall. Nobody moved, not even the Rani.

Then finally there was the tap and scuffle of feet climbing the staircase from the rooms below and four of the Rani's bodyguard re-entered the throne room.

In their midst hobbled Tamaana, although Christopher could hardly recognize her. The soles of her feet had been whipped until they were raw and bleeding. They had stripped her of every shred of her clothing. Her wrists where tied in front of her. Her back was criss-crossed with angry red welts. Her hair hung to her waist; matted with sweat and dried blood. Her eyes had receded into the sockets of her skull, and were bloodshot. Her eyelids were swollen and almost closed. They had knocked out most of her teeth and her jaw was broken so she was unable to close her swollen and bruised lips.

She looked about her blearily, staggering to balance on her swollen feet. Her eyes ran over Christopher's face without her showing any sign of recognition. Her breathing whistled through her broken nose.

'Tamaana!' He called her name, and she looked about her with wild and sightless eyes, trying to trace the source of that familiar voice.

'They are going to set us free!' he told her, and her face crumpled as she began to weep silently, her chest heaving and her shoulders shaking.

'Fr—ee…' Her lips formed the word but could not utter it. He walked towards her, gesturing for her guards to release her. They backed away.

'Yes, free to go to a much fairer and finer place than this. Free to fly like the swallows.'

'Swallows . . .' she repeated, and now she was sobbing as she recognized him and staggered towards him with both hands outstretched. He went to meet her. The tiger claw in his right hand snapped open.

'No more bonds,' he told her gently. He cut the ropes that bound her hands. She fell into his arms and he kissed her broken lips. She clung to him desperately as he pressed the point of the tiger claw into her throat below her right ear, and drew it across the carotid artery and all the major veins. The blood erupted from the wound and cascaded over both of them. She struggled weakly but he held her tightly to his chest, and murmured soothing words in her ear while the life oozed out of her.

The Rani leaned forward on her throne, her expression avid, hugging herself as she watched Tamaana's death throes. No one else in the throne room moved or uttered a sound.

Suddenly Tamaana emitted a loud gasp that gushed from her severed windpipe and then she breathed no more, but relaxed in Christopher's embrace. Her head fell forward onto his shoulder, and her legs gave way. He lowered her corpse gently to the floor, and stood over her.

'That was beautiful!' cried the Rani and she clapped her hands. Christopher was astonished to see that she was weeping. 'That was one of the loveliest and most moving things I have ever watched.'

'Worm and sponge!'

Christopher stood in the palace courtyard and took his men through their artillery drill. He was unrecognizable from the wretched prisoner who had stumbled out of the dungeons a month previously. His beard was combed, and his hair bound in a white turban. He wore a clean robe, with a quilted waistcoat laced over it.

Tamaana's loss was still an ache deep in his heart, but Christopher had learned in the *kalari* to control his feelings. He would not forget; he would take his revenge when the time was right. A curved dagger and a keen-edged sword hung from the orange sash around his waist – a measure of how far he had come in the Rani's estimation. He did not imagine for one second that he was safe. The court, he had quickly discovered, was divided between two factions: those allied with Poola, who wanted to profit from the English, and those led by Tungar, who wanted war and blood. The one thing that kept him alive was the stalemate that the Rani imposed, playing one faction against the other to keep both in check. Christopher, unwittingly, had become a pawn in her game, but he knew that when the time was ripe he would be readily sacrificed. Christopher was not the only man in the palace biding his time for vengeance.

Christopher's life now depended on carrying out to the letter the tasks that the Rani imposed upon him. As the Governor of Bombay, his father also officially served as the Captain General of the Bombay army. He had paraded the troops at noon every Sunday, affecting to drill them, while the real officers sweated and cursed him under their breath. Christopher had been dragged along every week, stifling in a Sunday suit made for English winters rather than Indian summers, longing to be indoors. But now he was grateful for the training.

'Reload.'

The gun crew moved into position, but so sluggishly that he longed to whip the skin off their backs. The Rani would not permit that – not yet, at least. He had to content himself with shouting and abusing them as they fumbled the ramrod, mislaid the powder sack and dropped the ball.

'Sweet Jesus! If the English handled a cannon the way you do, then the Great Mughal would be living in London by now, and you'd be kicking my arse for not bringing your dinner on time.'

The roar of an explosion cut him short. The cannon had fired without warning. The men around the gun collapsed in a heap of torn flesh, kicking and screaming in their death throes. The *Subeldar* who had wielded the ramrod had been thrown a good ten feet away. He lay clutching his stomach, which oozed a mess of mangled intestines from where his own rammer had torn him open.

'You miserable vermin,' Christopher raged at the dying man. 'You did not sponge her out properly.' The wet sponge was essential to douse any sparks that remained in the gun barrel after it was fired, so they would not ignite the new powder charge when it was rammed home.

Predictably, it was at that moment that Tungar rode in with a squadron of his men. He swung down from his saddle, saw the split cannon and strode over.

'You were meant to train the Rani's army – not destroy it.'

But Christopher did not rise to the provocation. The gun, the screaming men, the Rani's displeasure: all were forgotten. He was staring at the new sword Tungar wore on his belt: a beautiful weapon with an immense sapphire in the pommel.

He knew that sword. He had seen it in the portrait of Sir Francis Courtney that hung in Guy's office in Bombay. He had spent hours staring at it in his youth, hours when he should have been concentrating on his work, imagining the magnificent weapon hanging on his hip, or sitting clutched in his right hand. More than once, Guy had beaten him for his daydreaming, but it had not deterred Christopher. He had pestered his father, until one day Guy told him the story of the Neptune sword. Hearing those famous names – Sir Francis Drake, Charles Courtney, his grandfather and his great-grandfather – was a roll of honour ringing in his ears.

'Where is the sword now?' he had asked Guy, full of wonder and desire.

'Your uncle Tom stole it from High Weald, shortly before he murdered William,' Guy had told him. That explained his reticence: Guy almost never spoke of Tom, and became furious whenever the name was mentioned. 'He must have had it with him when he died in Africa. Probably it has fallen into hands of some pirate captain or brigand leader.'

Christopher could not imagine how it could now have arrived on the Malabar coast; or how it had come into Tungar's heathen hands.

Tungar saw at once the effect it had had on Christopher. He drew the fabulous blade from its scabbard and cut with it left and right, making the glittering steel hum through the air, flaunting the weapon in Christopher's face.

'A ship of hat-wearers was wrecked in the storm some days ago. I took this sword from one of the survivors.' Christopher had to ball his fists and keep his hands behind his back to prevent himself from seizing it and stabbing Tungar through the throat with it. The sword was his – the eldest son of the eldest surviving son, the heir to the honour of the Courtneys. He was meant to have it: why else would fate have placed it in his path. Already, his calculating mind was turning over the possibilities of how he could take possession of it. It would be hard to get Tungar alone, for he lived with his men like a pack of dogs, roaming everywhere with them. But Christopher knew he had to find a way to possess it.

'What of the hat-wearers? Did you kill the survivors?' he asked, trying to keep his tone uninterested.

'I taught them to respect the Rani's servants – but I left them alive. Her highness is not yet ready to move against the English.' Tungar gestured dismissively to the wounded gun crew. 'Nor will she ever be, if this is the best you can do. Clean up your mess, before I make you lick up that blood with your own tongue.'

As soon as Tungar had gone, Christopher commandeered a horse from the stables and rode to the coast. The village headman cowered before him. Yes, he admitted, the hat-wearers had been here, but they had since left for the fort at Brinjoan. He did not want such people polluting his village. Everything they touched had to be cleaned and purified with cow dung.

Christopher left him. He knew he should return to the palace, but first he followed the path down to the beach. The storm had subsided, and the wreck was plain to see. The stumps of her masts jutted from the waves, and the sea was so clear he could clearly make out the dark mass of her hull looming beneath the surface. Not an Indiaman – he had seen so many of those in Bombay he would have recognized it the very instant he laid eyes upon her– nor an Arab corsair. She was a European ship, or had been. She was a private merchantman: an interloper more than likely.

His mind thrummed with possibilities. If she had come from England, she would have called at the Cape. Perhaps the sword had made its way there, traded from tribe to tribe along the African coast, arriving in Cape Town just in time to go aboard this ill-fated ship. How much had the captain paid for it? Had he won it on a wager – or perhaps killed a man for it?

It did not matter. The Neptune sword was his by right, and the sea had brought it to him. Now all he had to do was see off Tungar, and for a man who had trained in the *kalari* that would be little obstacle.

Still, he stared at the sunken ship. The storm had driven it hard onto the shore, so close he fancied he could almost wade out to it. The tide lapped at it, rocking the exposed timbers like a cradle.

He shaded his eyes with his hand. As the waves moved, he saw a long narrow shape poking from her side.

'That is a gun!' He was amazed at his own good fortune. The ship had been armed. It was probable that there were more guns aboard her. They must still be there, on or around the wreck. With a long rope, and a team of draught animals anything was possible.

He studied it for some time, working out the practicalities and possibilities of a salvage. Then he hurried back to where he had tethered his horse to a jack tree. He swung up onto its back and turned its head towards the palace.

Tungar would want to punish him for leaving his post without permission, but he would soon change his tune when he heard what Christopher had found. No-one could doubt his loyalty then.

Three days later, he stood on the same beach. Deep gouges showed where the cannon barrels had been dragged up the beach. It had been a good day's work: the Rani would be pleased. Yet he was not satisfied.

He looked again at the small boat loitering offshore. She had been there much of the day, apparently drifting aimlessly, making no attempt to come closer inshore. Probably fishermen, he knew, but something bothered him. A feeling of being watched, a charge in the air like static electricity ahead of an oncoming storm.

It means nothing, he told himself. He would bring the guns to the Rani, and she would reward him. She might even promote him above Tungar.

After the escape from the wreck, the monsoon storms returned for a full week. Tom and the others stayed cooped up in Agnes' cottage, with nothing to occupy them but their thoughts. Sarah's fever relented a little; although she was still frail and struggled to keep her food down. The Brinjoan factory had no doctor, so Ana and Agnes tended her as best they could.

Tom spent long hours sitting under the eaves watching the rain. When he was not thinking of Sarah, his thoughts always returned to the Neptune sword.

At least he was spared Lawrence Foy's attentions. All the Governor's time was spent preparing for his embassy to the Rani, prettifying his speeches and going over his accounts and manifests. Day after day, he was forced to delay the journey on account of the weather.

'For my husband cannot appear before the Rani like some drowned rat,' declared his wife. She had come to pay a call, ostensibly to check on Sarah's condition, but in reality – Tom suspected – to size up the new arrivals. 'She is very sensible of her husband's position,' Agnes had warned him, 'and she fears you mean to supplant him.'

Tom tried to placate her, talking earnestly about his desire to go home. He did not want this woman asking too many questions about him. But he could see his answers did not satisfy her. Several times, he caught her bright, bird-like eyes watching him closely. Her pert nose twitched as if she could sniff the evasions behind his assurances. She was an extraordinary creature: twenty years her husband's junior, just seventeen, but possessed of a poise that would have shamed a woman three times her age.

'She is already once a widow,' Agnes had confided. 'She came to India with her father, and had barely stepped off the ship but she was engaged to the factor at Tellicherry. He was a fat, loathsome old man named Crupper – when he came to Bombay, his hands would wander under the table at dinner. She was not yet fifteen. But he died inside a year, and left her his fortune – which became her dowry when she married Mr Foy.'

Now Tom sat in Agnes' parlour and tried to remain unobtrusive. He did not have to say much. Mrs Foy had a great many opinions and did not hesitate to share them; she dominated the room less by charm or personality than by sheer determination. She was not beautiful. Her nose was sharp, her eyes too round and her mouth too wide; she was slim, but with full breasts that did not quite fit comfortably into the tight bodice of her dress. Yet she had an undeniable energy that seemed to suck all attention in the room to herself. Tom saw Francis staring, until Ana gave him a discreet kick on the ankle.

'Once my husband has arranged matters with this upstart black queen, I am certain that Governor Courtney will reward him with an improved situation,' Mrs Foy said while she fanned herself with a paper fan. 'Perhaps at Madras, or Fort William.'

'If we ever reach the palace,' said Tom.

Mrs Foy narrowed her eyes. 'I fancy tomorrow the weather may improve.'

It did. The next morning dawned dry and hot. However the clouds pressed low, kettling in the heat: the whole earth seemed to steam with vapour. Tom had hardly risen from his bed before he was covered in a clammy sheen of sweat. He put on his coat with the greatest reluctance, an old one of Captain Hicks' that Agnes had let him have. Foy had decreed that every man must look his best.

They assembled on the sandy square outside the fort. Foy had gathered every able-bodied man in the settlement, the better to impress the Rani. A whole company of soldiers, their boots blacked and polished; all the Company's writers and traders in their blue coats; and a host of bearers and servants. Some of these last carried gifts for the Rani, though the rest seemed to be there purely to add numbers to aggrandize Foy's procession.

Those who were to stay behind watched from the side lines: a few old men and boys, the survivors from the *Kestrel*, and the women.

Foy stood at the head of his column, resplendent in a maroon coat and gold-buckled shoes, a long curling wig and a hat tufted with ostrich feathers. The effect would have been magnificent, if not for the obvious effort it took him. His face glowed almost crimson with the heat, and broad patches of sweat already darkened the shoulders of his coat. It was six miles to the Rani's palace. Tom wondered if Foy would survive it.

'He looks very fine, does he not?' he said to Ana, who was standing with them.

'He is a peacock,' she said vehemently. 'With a brain to match. I doubt he will even understand what the Rani tells him.'

'Perhaps you should translate for him.' Tom went over to Foy and suggested it. He looked appalled.

'The Devil, you say? These are weighty affairs – the business of the whole Company hangs on this. I cannot conduct it through a *woman*.' He placed special scorn on the last word. 'It would humiliate me.'

'I wonder if the Rani would agree with that,' Francis murmured in Tom's ear.

Tom saw Ana was about to offer a sharp retort. He steered her away.

'You must stay here and look after Sarah. If anything should happen to us, she will need all your care.'

The anger in Ana's eyes softened to concern. 'You think you are going into danger?'

'You saw how the Rani's servants handled me last time.'

'Then stay,' she pleaded. 'And Francis, too. Mr Foy's business is not yours.'

'I must go. I must have my sword back from that rogue Tungar, and this is my best chance. As for Francis, I would not make him go. But he is of an age where the prospect of danger only makes him more determined. I would not stop him even if I could. But Alf Wilson and the men will be here to protect you.'

They fell in behind Foy, walking with Captain Hicks at the head of the infantry. Glancing back, Tom saw Foy had not left so much as a single sentry to guard the fort. A shadow of misgiving crossed his conscience. Should he really leave Sarah, Ana and Agnes so undefended?

The sword, he reminded himself.

The column moved slowly. It comprised over a hundred

men, and the rains had softened the road to a quagmire. Soon Foy's gold-buckled shoes were invisible under their coating of mud, while the sepoys' breeches were spattered almost waist high. Even after an hour, they had travelled little more than a mile.

Tom noticed all the sacks and bags the native porters were carrying. 'Does Foy intend such generosity to the Rani? I did not think it was in his nature.'

Hicks laughed. 'Foy would not spend a drop of his own piss if he did not have to. Those bundles are powder and shot for the men.'

'They do not carry their own?'

'Mr Foy does not trust the men. He worries they are liable to turn on us.' He kicked at a pebble in the road. 'All he sees is the colour of their skins. He has no conception of their loyalty.'

Tom's misgivings deepened. He checked the priming on his pistols. He had borrowed a fine matched pair from Hicks, who had also lent him a blade, a serviceable army hanger that nonetheless made Tom itch to have the Neptune sword back at his side.

They struggled on. The whole country seemed to have turned to water. Tom imagined this was how the world might have looked to Noah when he stepped off the ark. Trees dripped down their necks, puddles yawned at the roadside, and the maze-like channels of the backwaters glistened through the trees. Yet, in so much water, their greatest enemy was thirst. Their woollen coats and hats weighed on them as they trudged through the mud. The heat was like a gun deck in the thick of battle. Tom felt as if all the fluid in his body had been wrung out of him into his clothes.

'There is a well at the next crossroads,' said Hicks. 'We can refresh ourselves there.'

Tom tried to distract himself by studying the country they

passed through. He was used to the wildernesses of Africa, but this was entirely different. Trees and flowers he had never seen before grew in lush abundance. Screw pines, tottering on their roots like stilts; custard apple, guava and papaya; a bush with leaves like holly and bright blue flowers.

'It is a veritable garden of Eden,' Francis exclaimed.

'A fortnight ago, this was a parched country,' said Hicks. 'The rivers were mere trickles, and the plants had withered. When the rains come, it is made new almost overnight.'

They passed a few villages, similar to the one they had found when they were shipwrecked. Palm-thatched huts straggled along the banks, while fishing nets dried on bamboo poles. Small channels diverted from the rivers fed into networks of pits, filled with brown pulpy masses. Hicks explained that these were coir pits, where coconut husks were steeped for months to prepare them for being spun into the yarn that would one day make the ropes and cables of ships. In other places, Tom saw women beating the fibres with short sticks.

Children and adults alike ran from their tasks and gaped at the procession snaking through the forest. But Tom could not help feeling there was more than curiosity behind their staring faces. Even away from the villages, he could hear movement in the undergrowth; sometimes he glimpsed dark bodies running ahead of them through the forest. He had faced danger often enough in his life to trust his instincts. Now, he felt like a hunted animal.

They reached a crossroads, where a makeshift wooden bridge spanned a creek. A small shrine to the monkey god Hanuman stood among a grove of yellow hibiscus flowers, and beside it was a well.

Foy called a halt and hurried eagerly to the well. But when he looked in, he gave a cry.

'It's dry.'

Tom joined him and peered down. Blocks of stone and rubble

had been thrown down the shaft, filling it so deep that not even the high monsoon water rose above it.

'It does not matter,' said Foy irritably. His face had gone past scarlet and was now almost white with the effects of the heat. 'The Rani will entertain us when we reach the palace.'

Tom sidled closer to him so the men would not hear. 'I do not like this,' he cautioned. 'Someone has blocked the well deliberately. They know how the heat saps our strength: they want us weak and parched by the time we arrive at the palace. We should turn back.'

'Go back?' said Foy loudly. 'Are you mad? We have over a hundred men – what harm can the Rani and her rabble possibly do us? Perhaps an *interloper* flees at the first sniff of trouble, but gentlemen in the Company's service are made of sterner stuff.'

For a moment, Tom let himself contemplate what he might gain by tipping Foy into the well. He restrained himself. All his instincts told him to return to safety, but the sword was a siren-song calling him forward.

The road climbed into low red hills, the first risings of the Western Ghats. Paddy flats and coconut gardens mingled on their slopes. Ahead, in a valley nestled between wooded hills, loomed the palace.

It was the first stone building Tom had seen since they left the fort. At least, parts of it were stone. The whole edifice was a rambling complex that had spread over decades like weeds colonizing a garden, throwing out wings and courtyards and turrets according to the mood of its rulers. Tom could see them rising behind the long, wooden wall that separated the Rani from her subjects.

Foy drew up the column outside the gate. A dozen guards marched forth, wearing quilted jerkins over long white surcoats tied with orange sashes. Silvered helmets with long cheek flaps and nose guards hid their faces. They made two files, holding their firelocks erect. A man strode out between them.

Tom stiffened. His fingers automatically went to the pistol in his belt. It was Tungar. He had changed from his warrior habit into a silk gown with intricate embroidery, his helmet replaced with a turban, but there was no changing that evil face with the dislocating scar down the centre.

Hicks laid a hand over Tom's. 'Not now,' he whispered.

Tungar addressed them in Malayalam, speaking with exaggerated smiles that only served to show his blackened teeth. A young Indian boy came up from the back of the column to translate.

'He says Rani not well. Too much toddy. You wait.'

'Now look here,' said Foy sternly. He mopped his forehead. 'We have travelled many miles with gifts for your poxy queen, and we do not expect to be kept waiting, d'ye hear?'

Tungar's smile widened ingratiatingly. He spoke again.

'You wait,' repeated the interpreter.

'Damn you, I will not. I—'

Tungar turned his back and sauntered away. Foy made to follow, but the Rani's guards closed ranks, staring him down. The gate closed from the inside.

'Now what are we supposed to do?' demanded Foy.

'You wait,' said the interpreter.

The hours dragged on, but Foy kept the column standing to attention in the full heat of the day. When Hicks suggested letting the men fall out, Foy rounded on him in fury. 'Do you wish to embarrass me in front of the Rani? I am certain she will receive us at any moment.'

But the gates stayed closed.

Tom's tongue felt like a dry brick in his mouth. Looking at Francis, he could see the boy was dazed with thirst. Anticipating a short march, they had brought no food: by mid-afternoon all the men were faint with hunger. One of the porters, a scrawny boy no more than eleven or twelve, collapsed. His friends tried to revive him, but Foy ordered them to leave him where he lay.

Were it not for the Neptune sword, Tom would have taken Francis back to the factory that instant. Already, he wondered if there remained enough daylight to make the return journey.

'When we see the Rani, I hope you will remember to enquire about my sword,' he said to Foy.

Foy gave a scornful laugh, though his mouth was so dry it sounded more like choking. 'This is a diplomatic embassy. I will not risk the entire trade of this province for the sake of some gewgaw you have lost.'

Before Tom could reply, the gate swung open. Tungar reappeared behind the line of guards. He bared his teeth in a grin.

'The Rani is pleased to see you.'

'You see,' said Foy. 'I told you all would be well.'

Tungar's guards led them through the gate, across a square and through another low archway. Tom hesitated. Everything felt wrong. But Francis and Hicks had already passed inside, and the sepoy column was pressing up behind him. Tom had to hurry to catch up.

As he crossed the square, he became aware of some kind of commotion at the gate behind him. It seemed not all the bearers had been allowed inside, and now the gates were closing. He tried to see what was happening, but the flow of men pushed him under the inner arch.

He came out into a courtyard. In a strange way, it reminded Tom of a coaching inn back in England, though on a much grander scale. At ground level, the square was ringed by an arcade, though most of the arches had been covered with coir mats and hangings so you could not see what was inside them. Guards with long pikes were stationed all around. Above, the high walls were ornately carved with foliage and animal figures. Figures moved behind the lattice screens that covered the windows, though Tom could not make them out clearly.

Directly opposite him, on the first floor, a balcony looked

down into the courtyard. Another six guards, with gold-plated helmets and bronze firelocks, flanked the door that led inside the palace.

The courtyard could barely contain all the men. The porters who had got through the gate struggled through to deposit their gifts next to Foy, who stood at the front facing the balcony. The men pressed and jostled behind him. Tom searched the crowd for Tungar, but he had vanished.

They waited. The interpreter reappeared at Foy's side.

'Tungar says when the Rani comes, your men fire salute.'

'Of course.' Foy shooed him away. 'Does the fellow think I'm entirely ignorant of protocol? Bit of sound and thunder makes a great impression on the blacks.'

Tom edged away, squeezing through the packed men to the perimeter of the courtyard. Something about the coir mats that masked the arcades made him uneasy. Leaning against the pillar of the arcade, he tugged the corner of the mat slightly aside and peeked in through the crack. In the gloom beyond he saw many men, lit by the steady glow of a slow match. They were standing around something large that was covered by a tarpaulin.

A firm hand on his shoulder pulled Tom away. One of the guards scowled at him and shook his head. He pointed to the balcony, where the doors had opened, and put a finger to his lips.

Tom shook his hand off his shoulder. He had to warn Foy that the Rani's men were up to something fishy.

But at that moment the Rani herself stepped out onto her balcony in a flutter of gauze and a sparkle of gems. Forty sepoys presented arms, then aimed their muskets at the sky.

'Wait,' Tom shouted desperately. But even if Foy would have listened, the words were drowned by a crisp volley of gunfire as the sepoys made their salute.

The Rani smiled down from the balcony. She raised her arm

in a lazy wave, then she let it drop to her side. Tom realized that this was a signal. Around the courtyard, the coir mats fell away, revealing the mouths of black cannon staring out from the shadows.

Tom threw himself against the wall, just as the cannons fired in a blast of thunderous smoke. A volley of musket balls, scrap iron, and rusty nails swept through the ranks of the men who were packed shoulder to shoulder in the courtyard. The palace walls shook to the discharge.

In an instant the courtyard was turned into a shambles. Only the back ranks of men were screened by the bodies of their companions in the front rank. Those under direct fire, were cut down almost to a man. The screams of the wounded mingled with the shouts of the sergeants desperately trying to rally the survivors whose muskets had been discharged in the salute to the Rani. But then the marksmen on the balconies above the courtyard fired down into the milling confusion of sepoys, and the guards around the perimeter charged in with their pikes, joined immediately by the gun crews who abandoned the cannon and waded in to the fight with swords and axes.

And somewhere in the midst of all this was Francis. Tom could not see him, but he guessed the boy must be among a knot of men who had made a stand under the Rani's balcony, where the marksmen's fire could not reach them. He could see Hicks, his moustachioed *hubladar* beside him. The surviving sepoys formed a ring around them, desperately fending off the enemy. But they had discharged their weapons in the salute to the Rani, and their spare powder and shot was with the bearers locked outside the gate. Some had managed to affix their bayonets; others simply used their guns as bludgeons.

Tom drew his sword. In the first rush of battle, no one had seen him pressed against the column. He came at the attackers from behind. Their quilted armour and long helmets defended their backs and necks, but their legs were unprotected. He sliced one man's hamstrings, and, as he fell back, Tom ripped the helmet off his head and hacked through his skull. He snatched up the fallen pike and speared the next man like a wounded wild boar.

The man screamed and the enemy turned on Tom. One man rushed at him, with bared sword. Tom took his guard, but before he could engage, the man dropped to his knees with blood spurting from a bullet wound in his back. On the balcony above the yard, Tom saw a marksman almost hidden by a cloud of smoke. He realized that the ball had been meant for him.

At the same time he glimpsed Francis, in the front rank of the defenders under the balcony. Tom waded towards him, swinging and stabbing with the pike in his hands. Francis saw him and sallied forward to join him. He ducked under the swing of an axe, stabbed the guard who wielded it with a bayonet thrust in his guts, and dragged Tom into the knot of defenders. One of the Rani's guards tried to force his way into the gap, but Hicks stepped in front and fired his pistol into the man's face.

'We cannot stay here,' Tom shouted. Pinned against the wall, outnumbered and outgunned, they would be massacred. Their only real hope was to cut their way out of the palace and escape back to the Company factory.

'Do you still have the pistols I gave you?' Hicks demanded.

Tom nodded. He drew one and cocked it. Hicks reloaded the one he had just discharged.

'On my word… *Now*.'

They all fired at once, punching a hole in the ring of guards that surrounded them. The attackers fell back. Tom extended his sword and charged in, Hicks on his right and Francis on his left.

'Stay together!' he shouted. Once they left the shelter of the balcony, they came under fire from the marksmen again. A volley of musket fire crashed out and a ball knocked plaster from the wall beside Tom's head, a sharp fragment scored his cheek. Tom wiped the blood away with the back of the hand that held the pistol and in the same movement he aimed and fired. The ball struck the man who had fired down at him in the forehead. He toppled over the balcony rail and crashed down into the courtyard. Tom grabbed the gun from the corpse and cut the ammunition pouch from his belt. He threw them both to Francis.

'Keep those marksmen pinned down.'

Francis knelt, loaded and fired. A guard on the balcony stumbled back, clutching his stomach. The others retreated, wary of this new threat.

'Come on,' bellowed Tom. The ebb of battle had opened a gap for them. Forsaking caution, he charged forward, hurdling the corpses of the men who'd fallen in the first onslaught. He nearly lost his footing as he slipped in the blood that covered the stones. Shots cracked from the upper levels; two of the men beside him went down. A guard stepped into his path, wielding a long pike. The *hubladar* hurled his bayonetted musket like a javelin and it caught him in the throat. He dropped under their feet.

Tom scrambled over a low wall and into the arcade. The cannons still stood there, abandoned after firing the initial volley. Squeezing past one of them, Tom saw the hallmark stamped on the long barrel, the crossed swords of the foundry where it was cast. He recognized it. Just as he had feared, it was one of the cannon that had been on board the *Kestrel*. Salvaged from the wreck, cleaned and remounted, they had now been turned on Tom and his allies. The confirmation made him tremble with fury.

This was no time to dwell on it, however. The Rani's guards were already regrouping. A door opened in front of him: and without pausing to think where it might lead, Tom ran through.

Down a corridor, past open rooms, and into a courtyard filled with trees and tinkling fountains. Shuttered windows overlooked the garden. In one corner, a flight of stairs led to the upper floors of the palace.

Tom counted the men who had followed him. Francis was there, along with a young merchant, one of Foy's assistants whose name he did not know. The youth was snivelling like a child, his shirt stained with other men's blood. Tom had lost Hicks somewhere along the way, but he had the *hubladar* and six sepoys, though only four had kept hold of their muskets.

Rapid footsteps pounded down the corridor that had brought them here. Tom lifted the point of his blade. Hicks ran out of the corridor, pursued by a guard armed with a scimitar. Hicks spun around, aimed his pistol and shot the man in the chest. He fell to his knees. Francis stepped forward smartly and ran him through before he could regain his feet.

'Thank God you are safe,' said Tom. 'My sister-in-law would never forgive me if I did not bring you home safe and sound.'

'No more would mine,' said Hicks as he reloaded his pistols. 'Curse that idiot, Foy.'

'Where is he?'

'The last I saw of him was when he was kowtowing to that bloodthirsty bitch, the Rani.'

'Then he is probably dead by now.' Neither man suggested going back to try and rescue him.

Francis had made a quick circuit of the courtyard. He ran back to Hicks, his face grim.

'There are no doors. We are trapped here.'

As if to prove his words, shouts echoed down the corridor.

'Let's get the hell out of here,' Hicks suggested. 'Follow me.'

He led them up the stairs to the upper level. Even now, in so desperate a situation, he showed no signs of panic. Tom marvelled at his cool bearing. Agnes had chosen herself a good husband.

They rounded a corner at the top of the stairs and came into a long gallery. Through open doors, Tom glimpsed lavishly furnished state rooms. They ran on, choosing their course almost at random. Speed was all that mattered, never pausing to think, always driven on by the chasing pack behind them.

The noise of battle grew louder as they entered another room. Tom swore. All their turns had brought them almost back where they began, into the galleries above the courtyard. Smoke drifted through the wooden screens. Looking down, Tom saw grim evidence of the massacre: bodies strewn across the square, some piled upon each other; severed limbs and blood splashed over the cobblestones and halfway up the walls.

And in the midst of the carnage stood the man he had last seen on the beach, above the wreck of the *Kestrel*. From this angle, his face was hidden, but Tom knew him at once, purely by his bearing. He stood calm amid the dead, directing the guards who moved among the carcasses finishing off survivors. This was the man who had stolen his cannon and turned them on Tom himself.

Tom drew his pistol. But the lattice was too finely wrought to allow him a shot through it. Then, with the instinct of a fox, the man turned quickly and stared straight at Tom – although Tom must have appeared to him only as a shadow through the screen. Once again, Tom experienced the eerie sensation of looking at his own ghost. The man barked an order to one of the guards, who handed him a firelock. He cocked the hammer, and aimed the musket at Tom.

Tom ducked as he fired. The screen in front of Tom exploded in a cloud of splinters. Tom pushed the muzzle of his pistol through the jagged hole it had left, scanning the courtyard for his enemy.

But he had vanished.

'Come on,' called Hicks. Tom turned back to follow him – and almost collided with Hicks as he reversed course.

'*Guards,*' Hicks warned. Half a dozen of the gold-helmeted guards – and in their midst, bareheaded so that the scar down his nose was plain to see, was Tungar. The Neptune sword flashed in his hand, the sapphire glinting in its pommel. Tom drew the sabre Hicks had loaned him.

The gold-helmeted guards knelt and aimed a volley of musket fire. Their long-barrelled firelocks were cumbersome weapons, so heavy that each had a tripod fixed to the end of the barrel. Not the weapons for fighting in a confined space. Tom and the others threw themselves against the walls of the passageway. The volley flew harmlessly past them. Before the guards could reload, Tom and his men charged.

The guards dropped their muskets and reached for their swords, but the sepoys were on them before they could clear their blades. The sepoys showed no mercy. They bayoneted them or clubbed them with the butts of their muskets. Tungar would not stand and face Tom. He turned and fled and the surviving sepoys ran with him.

'Now's our chance to get out of this death trap!' shouted Hicks. He pointed to an open window that led out onto the tiled roof. 'There is a way out.'

But Tom knew he could not leave without the Neptune sword. The lure of it was a siren song that resounded in his head.

'You go ahead. I will follow you.'

Without waiting for an argument from Hicks, he chased after Tungar down the hall. He rounded the first corner, and almost stabbed a terrified servant girl who was fleeing towards him. He shoved her aside and raced on down a short corridor and through a pair of bronze doors which were standing open.

He paused and looked around him. He had come out into a room much larger and grander than any they had seen before. Rich tapestries draped the walls. At one end, a mahogany throne picked out in gold stood on a dais; opposite, double doors opened onto the balcony from which the enemy marksmen commenced the massacre. A tiger skin was laid out before the throne, its head tipped back and its jaws open in a silent roar.

Tom checked the balcony, but it was empty. He was about to run on through the next door, when he heard a creaking floorboard behind him. He spun around, to see Tungar advancing from behind the throne with the Neptune sword clasped in his right hand. Tom brought up his sabre, just in time to parry Tungar's lunge. He went on the counter attack, but the unaccustomed balance of his weapon hampered his movement, giving Tungar time to step back and recover his guard.

Tom had won many duels with that blue sword in his hand. Now he was on the other end of it, and he understood fully the advantage it had conferred on him. But now that wicked point was turned towards him, and he felt his courage quail before its glittering menace.

Tungar launched a series of swift, cutting attacks that Tom could barely keep pace with. But although he was driven back to the balcony he had survived. His courage returned to him, but cautiously.

He prefers to use the edge rather than the point. Tom knew that he could use this knowledge to his advantage.

He edged sideways, trying to turn Tungar towards his left hand. Tungar read the move and forced him back. He was trying to work Tom towards the balcony door where he would be easy prey for any marksmen in the yard below. Tom pirouetted away and regained the centre of the room. It was small advantage. It was like fighting with a leaden blade. Every movement dragged, every impact came a split second later than he anticipated. These were tiny amounts, but the fractions added up.

He feinted left, leaving an infinitesimal opening. But Tungar saw it instantly. The lunge would have been the correct stroke, but instinct induced him into the cut. He lifted his arm, just as Tom had anticipated. Before the blade came down, Tom drove forward, putting his whole weight into the thrust so that he came inside Tungar's guard.

Tungar pivoted. Tom's blade struck his armour a glancing blow and was deflected away, the sword spinning out of Tom's grip. In desperation, Tom wrapped his arms around Tungar's waist and drove him to the floor. They both went down. Tom put both his booted heels to Tungar's chest and shoved him over backwards. On hands and knees Tom went for his sabre, which was several feet away. He got his hand on the hilt and heaved. But the blade was stuck fast. It had been trapped in the open jaws of the snarling tiger's head. Tom tugged again, it would not budge.

Seeing Tom's predicament, Tungar rolled to his feet and lifted the blade of the Neptune sword over Tom's head. Once again he favoured the edge rather than the point. In the Malayalam language he shouted ugly and evil words that needed no translation.

He swung the Neptune sword down with all his strength behind the blow. Tom shot out one booted foot and it caught Tungar in the knee-cap. Tungar's litany of hatred was cut off abruptly and became a cry of pain. The sword blade hissed past Tom's head and hit the floor, but despite the pain of his damaged knee Tungar retained his grip on the hilt. He staggered back, limping on the damaged leg, while Tom bounded to his feet and rushed at him again.

Once more he locked both arms around Tungar, but this time from behind him and under his armpits so he could not reach back with the blue blade. Tom shoved him forward through the open doors that led onto the balcony, above the courtyard. With his damaged kneecap Tungar could not resist. Tom slammed him into the wooden guardrail, trying to force him to drop the Neptune sword.

However the guardrail was unable to withstand the impetus of both their muscular bodies. Whether gunfire in the battle had weakened it, or whether it was simply the force of Tom's charge, the rail splintered and gave way. Tungar crashed through. For a moment, he seemed to hang on the edge of the balcony, arms flailing for balance. Then he fell.

Tom's momentum almost carried him over too, but a firm hand on the scruff of his neck pulled him back from the brink.

Tom shook himself free, and glanced back. Hicks stood behind him, a musket slung on his shoulder, but Tom hardly registered his salvation. He peered over the shattered edge of the balcony.

Tungar lay on a pile of bodies. His right arm was flung out like a broken wing. And still clutched in his fist, was the Neptune sword. The resilience of the blade had survived the fall. It was unmarred and unmarked.

Tom measured the drop with a calculating eye, then he changed his stance, positioning himself to make the jump. But Hicks grabbed him again. 'Don't be a bloody fool. Tom! You will break both your legs, and probably your neck into the bargain. It's just a sword, not the Holy Grail.' They grappled for a few moments longer.

Then the people who had been looting the bodies of the dead and injured scattered around the square came running to cluster around Tungar. Some of them looked up, saw the two of them on the balcony and started shouting and pointing up at them. A few of them drew pistols and pointed them up at them.

Tom capitulated and allowed Hicks to drag him back into the throne room.

'I told you not to come back for me,' he snarled at him.

'It is as well I did,' Hicks remarked drily. 'And now we best make a run for home. Before the Rani and all her army come after us.' Tom realized that he was endangering the lives of all their men, and he acceded to Hicks' entreaties.

The two of them ran back down the galleries. While behind them they heard the clamour of the guards who were searching for them.

Finally, Hicks led Tom into one of the store rooms with barred windows. One of the grills had been ripped off. And beyond the opening was the tiled roof of an outbuilding. Hicks pushed Tom through the window and vaulted after him. They ran along the roof ridge to the far end. Open ground stretched beyond them to the outer palisade where Francis and the others were waiting for them.

The drop was not too daunting. Tom lowered himself to the full stretch of his arms, and then let himself go. He landed in a patch of soft muddy ground and then beckoned Hicks to follow him. Hicks dropped the musket down to Tom, and then crouched to lower himself over the edge.

Seemingly out of nowhere, a glistening steel snake shot out and wrapped itself around Hicks' neck. Hicks grabbed for it with both hands and struggled to pull it loose, but it clenched around his throat; dragging him to his knees. His face swelled and turned crimson. He opened his mouth to scream but uttered no sound. The steel band snapped back, pulling him off his feet, and as he fell Tom saw a ring of blood outline the halter of steel that encircled his neck.

As Tom watched helplessly, a figure stepped up behind Hicks. It was the man he had seen on the beach where the *Kestrel* had foundered, the man who had fired a shot at him minutes ago – and again Tom felt that strange intuition, the sense of destiny being fulfilled.

Still watching Tom, the man made another movement with his right hand. The ring of bright steel that encircled Captain Hicks' neck jumped tight. It cut down through skin and flesh, through veins and arteries, and then finally through sinew and vertebrae.

Hicks was decapitated completely. His head tumbled from his shoulders, and a bright fountain of blood shot from the stump of his neck. He slumped forward and fell from Tom's view behind the angle of the roof. His killer snapped his wrist again and the metal snake whipped back upon itself into a tight reel in his right hand.

Tom raised the firelock and aimed at him. He pulled the trigger, but the weapon misfired. The killer laughed down at him, and in that instant Tom recognized his features and the sardonic tone of his laughter. This man was the spitting image of his brother Guy Courtney, or rather as Guy had been when he last laid eyes on him over twenty years previously.

With another snap of his wrist, the killer unleashed the silver steel snake at Tom. It hummed in the air as it uncoiled down towards him. But then it stopped abruptly at its full extension, only a foot in front of Tom's face. Tom jumped back with a startled cry.

When he looked up again at the roof the killer and his infernal steel garrotte had disappeared. But Tom knew that he would never forget him.

A chorus of shouts sounded from the palace gate. A band of the orange-sashed guards came charging around the corner. With a pang of remorse, and the murderer's laughter ringing in his ears, Tom ran.

From the top of the outer wall of the palace Francis and the sepoys urged him on. They reached down and helped him over the wall, as a volley of musket balls smacked into the brickwork below them.

Then they were all over, but a long, long way from safety.

Forcing himself to put Hicks' fate out of his mind, Tom made a quick head count. Francis, the *hubladar*, five sepoys and the young Company factor who stared at the ground and fiddled with the buttons on his coat. They had four muskets between them.

'How much powder and shot?'

'Precious few balls. One flask of powder.' Unlike the British armies, Indian troops had not yet adopted the ball cartridge, which combined the musket ball and the correct amount of powder in a paper wrapper.

On the far side of the wall, Tom could hear the sounds of the Rani's army mustering. The gates began to open. He grabbed the young factor by the shoulders.

'Look at me.' He shook him. '*Look at me.* What is your name?'

'K . . . Kyffen, sir,' he stammered.

'Can you run?'

Kyffen nodded.

'Then get back to the factory as fast as you like. Tell them . . .' Tom hesitated as he remembered the force they had left behind them when they left the factory; a handful of old men, women and boys. How could he hope to defend the fort with them?

But what was the alternative? They had only the one small boat, and in the monsoon season it would be folly to trust it to the seas. On the other hand, the fortress's walls were tall and thick. Even with the *Centaurus'* guns, the Rani's men could not have salvaged much ammunition. The defenders might hope to hold out for some time, with luck and good tactics. Perhaps long enough for reinforcement to reach them from Madras.

Kyffen was still waiting for orders. Tom felt the weighty responsibility of his decision, of the lives that depended on the choices he made now in the heat of this moment.

'Tell them to prepare for a siege. We will delay the Rani's men as long as we can.'

Kyffen ran as if his feet were on fire. The others followed as far as the trees. Tom divided them into three pairs, each pair with a firelock, keeping one for himself.

'Fire in turns,' he ordered them. 'One pair fires, the second reloads while the third retreats. And aim for the officers, as best you can. Their lack of training and discipline is our best hope now.'

Afterwards, all Tom remembered of the retreat was the terror. Not for himself, but for Sarah and Agnes, the knowledge of what would happen to them if he failed. The journey was a constant blur of running, turning, firing, reloading and running again; always too slow, always conscious of their dwindling supply of ammunition, while the Rani's vanguard pursued them remorselessly.

Tom fired and ran back. He reached in his pocket for the next musket ball, but it was empty. He found Francis, crouched behind a tree waiting for his partner to reload.

'Do you have any more musket balls?'

'Two,' Francis replied with a grin. 'I can let you have one. If you promise not to miss.'

'Your generosity is overwhelming.' Tom tried to grin back at him, but the smile would not stay on his face.

They had not covered much more than two or three miles. With daylight fading, and the road a mire, they could not hope to outrun the pursuit. The Rani had cavalry. If she released them it would all be over before nightfall.

'We must give Mr Kyffen more time.'

An explosion rent the air, so loud it shook a shower of water droplets from the trees above them. Tom looked back, dreading that the Rani's guards had brought up their big guns. But he could not make out any pursuit. There was another deafening crash.

'Thunder!' Tom and Francis rejoiced together.

A fat raindrop stung the back of his hand. Then another, and another. Soon it was a deluge, the rain falling so hard it burst through the forest canopy and soaked the men beneath it. It fell so furiously that they could hardly breathe, and their vision was restricted to a dozen yards.

'They cannot fight in this, and neither can we,' Tom exulted. 'The gun powder is turned to paste and the wet flint will not spark.' He threw the useless firelock aside, gathered his men and ran with them, slipping and slithering through the mud, back towards the fort.

But the Rani's men had not given up the chase entirely. Whenever Tom paused to check his rear, he could make out their dim shapes through the rain.

They reached the bridge they'd crossed that morning, by the well and the shrine to the monkey god. Since they had last seen the river, it had risen five feet or more. The chocolate-coloured water was almost touching the underside of the rickety bamboo span.

Their pursuers were pressing them so hard that Tom almost led his band across the bridge without thinking. A few strides beyond, he realized the opportunity he was missing. He turned back and drew his sabre.

The leading guards had almost reached the bridge when they saw Tom confronting them from the far end. They checked for a moment, suspecting some trap, then grinned when they saw how few men opposed them. They drew their side arms and charged forward.

Tom didn't move until they were more than half way across, then he raised his sabre and brought the blade down across one of the coir hawsers which anchored the bridge to the bank. It took him three blows, and then the hawser parted with a crack like a musket shot and the bridge skewed around. Five or six of the attackers were catapulted into the racing waters and were whipped away immediately. The survivors clung desperately to the side rope, with their feet dangling into the racing waters. Tom turned his attention to the remaining support rope. With another four hacking strokes the rope gave way. The remainder of the pursuers who were on the bridge were dumped into the river, and almost instantly they were drawn under by the weight of their armour.

The guards on the far bank who had not yet reached the bridge saw their comrades drowned, and they drew back from the water's edge in dismay and confusion.

At that moment a rider on a black horse cantered out of the dense forest. Its rider reined in and stood up in his stirrups, gazing across the turbulent waters at Tom and his men on the opposite bank. Tom scowled as their eyes met. It was the man who had stolen his cannon and turned them upon him. The man who had decapitated Hicks with the steel snake.

They stared at each other, and the river was not wide enough to contain or mitigate their mutual hatred. The rider swept his gaze across the turbulent waters, judging whether or not he should attempt the crossing. Then he walked his mount to the very brink of the racing waters.

'You can never run far nor fast enough,' he called. 'I will come for you.'

With surprise, Tom realized he had spoken in English. Not faltering, nor with any trace of an accent: the confident voice of a man born and bred in England.

'Who are you?' he shouted across the rushing water.

The rider gave him no reply. Circling his horse, he galloped back into the darkness of the forest.

Night hurried on before the storm. In the dark and the rain, they could hardly follow the road. More than once, they almost plunged into the rising backwaters. Tom didn't dare stop. He knew, with cold certainty, that the man on the horse would not sleep nor rest in his pursuit.

But they were travelling blind. Soon, he realized they had lost the path. Even then, he would not let them stop to rest, but urged them on through the forest. Francis eventually accosted Tom when he had paused to catch his breath.

'We must stop. At this rate, we will find we have travelled in a great circle and come back right into the Rani's jail.'

Tom knew the boy was right, but he could not bring himself to accept defeat.

'Just a few more minutes. I am sure—' He paused. The rain and the wind had eased. Further off, he picked up a new sound. 'Listen.'

They both heard it: the low, rhythmic roar of the surf pounding a beach. 'The ocean,' they cried in unison.

Hacking a path with his sabre, Tom followed the sound through the trees. The jungle fell away abruptly in front of him, and he was out in the open, running along a beach with soft sand under his feet.

'Which way?' he shouted at Francis, but before Francis could answer Tom saw the lights of the fort burning brightly ahead of them, and he realized that Kyffen had delivered his message and the garrison were expecting their arrival.

Tom and Francis reached the gates together and hammered upon them. The gates creaked open and two old men stood before them, holding lanterns high and levelling muskets at them.

'Where are all the women?' Tom shouted at them, pushing the barrels of their muskets aside. 'Where is my wife?'

William Kyffen blundered through the forest, slipping and skidding in the mud. He had never been so afraid in all his life.

This was not how he had envisaged his career developing. When he had donned the blue coat of an apprentice writer for the first time, he had imagined a glorious future as Consul General to the Orient, riding elephants into the great palace in Delhi, receiving gifts of jewels any one of which would have been worth more than a year of his father's salary as a curate in Lincolnshire. Instead, he had found himself in this godforsaken outpost, answering the whims of a governor who treated him no better than the native servants.

The storm increased in strength. Every snapping branch and falling nut sounded like a musket shot in his ears. By the time he reached Brinjoan, and saw the reassuring bulk of the fortress on the shore, he could hardly credit that he survived the ordeal.

He stumbled to the gates. The whole settlement – all who remained – ran out to meet him. 'Where are Tom and Francis? Where is Mr Foy and Captain Hicks?'

'Mr Foy and Captain Hicks are dead. The men are massacred. I was the only one who escaped.'

Agnes went deathly pale and swayed on her feet. Ana caught her before she fell.

Mrs Foy took the news of her husband's death with more stoicism. She did not faint or cry out; she did not even shed a tear.

'Then we must make good our escape,' she declared at once.

Kyffen had bent over, trying to squeeze out the pain that wracked his side. 'Mr Weald said we should prepare the fort for a siege.'

'Tom is alive then?' Ana asked. 'But what of Francis?'

'They were both alive when I left them.'

'They will surely be dead by now,' said Mrs Foy brusquely. 'We cannot delay. Every minute we wait is a minute those terrible savages draw closer. Can you conceive what they will do with four gentlewomen such as ourselves?'

Kyffen's imagination baulked at the thought. Still, he hesitated. 'Mr Weald said—'

Mrs Foy's face changed, as if the full import of his news had only just sunk in, and she suddenly dropped to her knees. She threw her arms around Mr Kyffen's waist and stared up at him, wide-eyed.

'My husband is lost,' she wailed. 'Dear Mr Kyffen, only you can save us now.'

Kyffen looked down at the woman clinging to him, and blushed as he realized he was looking straight down the neck of her dress. Her breasts swelled against the fabric as she gasped in her shock.

For the first time in his life, Kyffen felt the responsibility of having a lovely woman beseech him for *anything*, let alone her life. Mrs Foy needed his protection and, like the gallant knights of old, he would risk all to save her. She was a widow, now – an extremely wealthy widow – and she would need a man's firm hand to guide her in her grief. In time, perhaps, her gratitude . . . but he would not allow himself to imagine such things.

He put his hand on her shoulder, amazed by his own daring. 'Do not worry,' he said stoutly. 'I will be your protector from now onwards.'

'We must flee,' Mrs Foy said. 'Prepare the boat.'

'Mr Weald said—'

'Mr Weald is not in charge here. *You* are.' She stared up at him, eyes imploring, and despite everything he felt the thrill of command. 'We rely on you to save us.'

Kyffen turned to the assembled men and cleared his throat. 'Prepare the boat for sea. Lay in stores, provisions, powder and shot. We must leave within the hour.'

The old men and boys moved to his command. But at the far corner of the courtyard, Alf Wilson and the rest of Tom's men stood aloof, with arms folded. Kyffen eyed them nervously. He did not like the look of the mate from the *Kestrel*. If there was one man in the settlement who might challenge his authority, it was him.

'Jump to it,' he barked. 'The Rani's men will have your guts for garters if they catch us here.'

Ignoring him, Alf went to Agnes and Ana. 'What would you have me do? Could Tom and Francis have survived?'

Agnes could not look at him for weeping. Ana spoke with

228

a confidence she did not feel. 'Go with half your men to look for survivors. Take no risks: if you meet the Rani's guards, fly at once. The rest of your men can help prepare the boat. Whether Tom and Francis are alive or no, I fear we will need it soon enough.'

Ana led Agnes back to her house. She wondered how she would break the news to Sarah, still confined to her bed by her sickness. Could Francis and Tom really be dead? They had seemed so strong, so full of life, it was hard to believe.

In the fort, Lydia Foy still knelt beside Kyffen, clinging to him and weeping. She opened one eye a little and saw that the men had gone about their tasks.

'I hope you will not neglect to bring some of the goods from the godown.'

Kyffen looked startled. 'Is this the time to think of commerce?'

'My dear, late husband gave his life for that commerce. It was all that mattered to him. It would blacken his memory to let his goods fall into the hands of his murderers.'

She rose and wiped the tears from her face. She stood a good three inches taller than Kyffen. She looked down at him with wide blue eyes that made his head swim.

'If we are to make good our escape, we must have the means to support ourselves when we reach safety. I do not intend to live out my dowager days in penury.'

'It will not come to that, ma'am. I, personally, guarantee it.'

She stroked his arm. 'Dear Mr Kyffen, you are too kind. But we have no time to lose.'

Kyffen ordered four of the stronger men to accompany her to the warehouse, and was gratified when they went without demur. He was unused to giving orders, less still to having them obeyed. Until that day, he had been the most junior factor in the settlement, clinging to the bottom rung of the Company ladder while other men trampled on him. Now, suddenly thrust into command, he found he rather enjoyed the sensation.

Soon enough, the boat was filled with the pick of the cotton cloth, some of the worked goods that had been sent from England, and the best of the wine and brandy casks. Mrs Foy oversaw the loading with a keen eye, making sure the goods were well stowed. When she was satisfied, she found Kyffen again.

'Come with me,' she said. 'There is something I must show you.'

Kyffen followed her willingly into the Governor's house. Despite their predicament, his imagination conjured all manner of intriguing possibilities – but she took him without ado into her late husband's office.

Kyffen hesitated at the doorway. Mr Foy might be dead, but the habits of deference died hard. Mrs Foy had no such scruples. She strode to the desk, gathered up a pile of leatherbound account books and deposited them in his arms.

'Are you certain we need these?' he asked in surprise.

'You can be sure that the East India Company will seek to blame us for what has transpired. We must ensure we have the evidence to refute their allegations.'

Kyffen could only admire her mental fortitude, to think so clearly in this intolerable situation.

'Also, there is this.'

She unlocked a small cupboard in the corner, built of solid teak. As the heavy doors swung out, Kyffen saw it was a deceit: the cupboard opened into a small brick vault built into the wall. Four ironbound chests, each fastened with stout locks, stood stacked within.

Mr Kyffen's admiration for Mrs Foy swelled still further.

'We will need men to carry those,' he ventured.

'Watch them carefully. Each of these chests contains a thousand pounds in gold.'

Kyffen began to wonder if the catastrophe that had befallen them might not offer some benefits after all.

'We must take to the boat,' said Mrs Foy. 'If we are not away soon, we will be trapped here.'

By now, Kyffen had all but forgotten Tom's instructions. Indeed, in his mind Tom was already dead, or at best a prisoner of the Rani. Still, he paused.

'The boat is so heavily laden; if we all go aboard, we will sink her.'

'Indeed,' said Mrs Foy. 'You must decide who should crew in the boat. The rest will stay here and defend the fort as best they can, until we can bring relief.'

By the time they had loaded the chests of gold into the gallivat, the boat rode so low in the water Kyffen wondered if anyone at all could go in her. All the men and women assembled on the sea front, already soaked by the rain. Alf Wilson and his party still had not returned.

Ana stared at the vessel. 'Is this your plan? To take what you can and abandon the rest, while Tom and Francis may still be out there?'

'I have made my decision,' said Kyffen, importantly. He felt the reassuring weight of the pistol in his belt, though the rain had probably rendered it useless. 'We will send away the women and the youngest children. The others will stay here to defend the Company's honour, and await any survivors.'

'A wise plan,' said Mrs Foy.

'At least wait for Alf Wilson and his men, to see if they have any word of Tom and Francis,' pleaded Ana.

Kyffen glanced at Mrs Foy.

'If they have not come back by now, they are surely dead,' she pointed out. 'And so will we be, if we do not escape now. Mr Kyffen is treating you more than generously, Miss Duarte. You arrived at our factory unwanted and uninvited; probably, you meant to injure our commerce. Yet now Mr Kyffen offers you an escape, and all the thanks he receives is carping and ingratitude.'

Agnes stepped forward. 'I will go. But Sarah is weak. I will need men to carry her aboard.'

Ana grabbed her sleeve. 'Wait,' she said. 'Surely you cannot go without the others.'

'Mr Hicks is dead,' said Agnes bitterly. 'I have no reason to stay here.'

'What about Tom and Francis?'

Agnes stared at her dully. 'Tom is not my husband. Most likely he is dead, too. I must care for my sister, Sarah.'

Ana was about to argue, when she realized Mrs Foy was lingering behind Agnes, paying more attention than she pretended. Even now, Ana feared to give away Tom's secret. With so much upheaval, she did not dare imagine where their fortunes might lead them next.

So it was that Agnes boarded the lifeboat. Three men carried Sarah aboard and laid her in the bow, resting on bales of cloth with a spare sail tented above her. Of the others, Kyffen chose two boys and eight of the strongest and most likely looking to man the oars, including all the men who remained from the *Kestrel*'s crew. The most senior of them, a boatswain named Hale, looked questioningly at Ana.

'We should be staying here waiting for the Captain and Mr Wilson,' he protested.

'Leave your two stoutest men here,' Ana replied. 'If Francis and Tom return, God willing, they will need all the help they can get. But if Tom were here, he would not want Sarah abandoned to the mercy of strangers.' She lowered her voice. 'I do not trust Mrs Foy and Mr Kyffen. At least if you and a few of the *Kestrel*'s crew are in the lifeboat, you can protect her.'

'Would we not be better keeping Mrs Courtney here?'

'Agnes is her sister,' said Ana. 'By rights, she must decide what is best for Sarah. And perhaps she is right. If there is to be a siege, it will be no place for a woman in her condition.'

'I thought she was getting better.'

'Her sickness is passing. But I think that may only be a symptom of—'

She broke off. The men in the lifeboat were already raising the sail, urged on by Lydia Foy.

'Go. God speed, and take good care of Sarah.'

Hale knuckled his forehead. 'We'll treat her like one of our own, miss.' All the crew had served the Courtneys many years – some going back to Tom's first voyage on the *Seraph*. They knew Sarah better than their own mothers. When they had wounds or injuries that needed tending; when they had trouble with their womenfolk ashore, or difficulties with money, it was always her they went to. They loved her, and would die to protect her. Even the few weeks that Ana had spent with the Courtneys had left her in no doubt of that.

'Will you not join us?' called Agnes.

Ana shook her head. 'I will wait for Francis.'

'Leave her,' said Mrs Foy. 'If the silly thing cannot look to her own best interests, I most certainly will not.'

The boat slipped away into the gathering gloom. Watching from the shore, Ana could hardly breathe for all the doubts and foreboding roiling inside her. She prayed she would see them safe again.

She saw movement at the edge of the forest. Could the Rani's men have arrived already?

Alf Wilson and his men emerged from the forest. Covered in mud, hunched over with exhaustion, she barely recognized them.

'No sign of Tom and Francis,' he reported. 'We went as far as we dared.'

'Thank you.'

'That doesn't mean they aren't alive.'

'I know. Thank you.'

Alf Wilson peered out to sea and pursed his lips. He took in the situation.

'Suppose we're planning on staying here, then?'

His calm acceptance was the most comforting thing Ana had heard all that terrible day. Again, she marvelled at the Courtneys, that they could surround themselves with such loyal men.

'I think we may be here some time.'

'Then we'd best make ready for visitors.'

By the time Tom had heard the story of the boat's departure, Ana and Alf had come to see what the commotion was about. Ana had been sleeping in the Governor's house; Alf had lain down for a brief nap, and was furious with the defenders who had abandoned their posts.

'If we were aboard the old *Seraph*, I'd have the skin off their backs,' he growled.

'Leave them be,' said Tom. Inside, he shared Alf's anger, but when he looked at the men in the fort he could see that there was no use undermining them further. Their superiors had abandoned them: no wonder they lacked the discipline to keep watch. If they were to defend the fort against the army that was surely coming, he would need to give them every shred of self-belief they could summon.

He had been awake a day and a night; had fought through the hell of the palace and the jungle, only to find Sarah gone. If there had been a boat, even the ship's jolly boat, he would have taken it in a trice, he was so worried. His body craved rest, warmth and food, while with all his soul he longed to be with Sarah.

Tom forced himself to ignore it and mustered the men in the fortress yard. He could hardly hide his dismay at the tally. Twenty-one Company men, of whom roughly two thirds were above fifty and the rest under fourteen. Add to them the *hubladar* and the four sepoys who had escaped the Rani's palace, Alf Wilson and four more men from the *Kestrel*, and Francis – that made thirty-two men, including himself.

'How are we equipped for weapons?'

'We won't want for powder and shot, sir,' said Alf, who had made an inventory as soon as he realized their predicament. 'The Company gave them plenty, for they knew they might go months without supply.'

'How about muskets?'

'Not so many, but more than we need. Also a fair number of pikes and swords – Captain Hicks kept his armoury well stocked, rest his soul. And of course, we're not short of cannon.'

If only we had the men to serve them, Tom thought. He tried not to let his misgivings show as he surveyed the rag-bag army he had inherited. The irony that he had become the unlikely defender of the East India Company was not lost on him.

They looked back at him, and he realized they were waiting. They expected him to speak; they *needed* him to speak.

What do you say to men who are almost certainly doomed to die, and want reassurance?

He stepped up on a mounting block.

'I know you did not come here to fight,' he told them. 'But our enemies are coming, and so a fight we will give them. We have stout walls, provisions and no shortage of weapons. Most of all, we have ourselves. Rely on each other, defend each other to the death, and we will make the Rani wish she had never dared defy us. Her attack was cowardly and unprovoked. Now, you have the chance to make her pay for her treachery.'

The men gave a ragged cheer – the best he could have hoped for under the circumstances. At least they did not look defeated yet.

Tom divided the men into teams, mixing the young, the old, the sepoys and the able-bodied men from the *Kestrel*. Alf Wilson commanded one team, Francis another and the *hubladar* the third.

His greatest concern was water. 'Fetch every cask, butt and

bucket you can find and fill them from the river,' he ordered Francis. 'Hunger and thirst have ended more sieges than gunpowder ever did.' A second group fetched in sacks of rice and salt fish from the stores.

Tom sent the rest of the men to man the defences. They cut loopholes in the gates low and wide enough to accept the mouths of cannon. One of the men had been a carpenter, and he fitted them with lids like gun ports to disguise them from the outside. They rigged tarpaulin awnings over the guns to keep off the rain.

When that was done, he had them strip the palm thatch from the roofs of the Governor's house and the other storehouses inside the fort. The moment they dried out, they would be tinder waiting to burn.

He went up on the walls and inspected the fort, studying the angles of fire and lines of attack. With the roofs off, the buildings were nothing more than shells; sand had started to blow into them, as if the beach had already begun to reclaim this spit of land that the East India Company had presumed to call its own.

Not for the last time, he cursed the Company for their carelessness – a symptom of their casual arrogance, the sense of entitlement that allowed them to monopolize the trade of an entire subcontinent. The godowns were too close to the fort: they would make perfect gun emplacements for the enemy besiegers. Worse, there was a cottage standing almost in the shadow of the north wall, from where marksmen could cover an assault. He would have to get the men to demolish it.

Movement at the edge of the forest caught his eye. A dozen of the Rani's cavalrymen rode out from among the trees. They cantered along the beach, kicking spray from the surf, and reined in a little over two hundred yards away from the front of the fort. One pulled out a brass telescope and studied the fort through the lens.

'Bring me a musket,' Tom called, and was pleased to see how quickly the boy brought it to him, already loaded. He sighted it on the nearest rider and fired.

He knew they were out of range. He saw the ball kick up a plume of sand as it struck the beach a few paces in front of the men. The horses skittered back; one reared up, nearly throwing its rider. The others retreated.

Tom lowered the musket. He hadn't expected to hit them, but at least now they knew they wouldn't take the fort without a fight. He tossed the musket back to the boy who'd brought it.

'Get that reloaded. We will need it again before long.'

Two of the horsemen galloped off, no doubt to warn the army that must be following them. The others began riding a lazy circle around the fort towards the settlement, careful to keep safely out of musket range.

'Are all the men inside?' Tom called.

'Water party's still out.'

'*Francis.*' He ran around to the landward side of the walls. Francis and his men were straggling back from the river, bent double under the weight of the casks they carried. Blocked by the godown, they had not seen the Rani's riders approaching.

Down by the river, Francis tried to maintain a bold face. In the last twenty-four hours he had witnessed more brutality than he could possibly have imagined; he had gone without food or water. But he could feel the men's eyes on him, craving his leadership. He knew he had done little to deserve it, yet he was determined to prove worthy of their trust. He waded knee deep into the stream with them, fending off the floating logs and branches that the storm had washed down, helping steady the casks against the current, encouraging and cajoling the men. He had made a point of learning all their names, and he noticed how their faces glowed with pride when he used them.

237

They had taken one load of water back to the fort and were filling a new set of casks when one of the men pointed upstream. A log was floating towards them.

'What is that?'

Francis stared in horror. It was not a log but a raft, three long planks fixed together in parallel. But they were not bound with ropes. They were joined by a naked human body, nailed across them in a crude representation of a crucifix.

'It's Mr Foy,' cried one of the men, a book-keeper named Ilkley.

Or it had been, before the Rani's people captured him, thought Francis. Foy's body bore the marks of the horrific tortures they had inflicted upon him. His mouth gaped open: an empty hole in his face. His executioners had cut out his tongue and nailed it to his chest.

'I reckon they didn't like how he talked to them,' said Ilkley.

The crude raft floated by, almost within arm's reach. No one tried to take hold of it. The current carried the body on. It rounded a bend, and washed up on a small sandbar near the mouth of the river.

'We should bury him,' one of the sepoys said.

Francis forced the horror from his mind. He had to take control of himself. 'Leave him,' he said brusquely. 'If we have time, we may bury him later. For now, we must secure the living.'

No one challenged his decision. They knew Foy had authored this disaster, and that their hopes for salvation hung by a thread.

'Are all our casks filled?' Francis asked, and when his men confirmed this he called them back to the fort.

The men carried the casks slung between poles. Even with two men apiece, the weight was immense. Legs buckled; shoulders ached. They paused often. The two boys followed with smaller casks, rolling them across the sand. They reminded Francis of children he had seen in the village playing hoop and stick.

A musket shot broke the sultry silence that hung over the settlement. One of the men dropped his pole, spilling water from the open bung. Francis looked at the fort, then back at the treeline, but saw nothing.

'Hurry,' he told the men. He tried to force the pace, but the weight of the casks made it impossible. The sand dragged on their footsteps, while the poles were slippery with their sweat in the humid air.

He felt a tremor in the ground beneath his feet. He looked up, and saw the gates of the fort opening. Someone was standing atop the gatehouse, waving and shouting. Was it Tom?

Just then six riders swept around the corner of the godown. When they saw Francis and his men they wheeled about, drew their sabres and charged.

The men threw down their barrels, careless of the way the precious cargo spilled across the sand. They turned to flee.

'Stand fast,' Francis shouted. He knew that if the men scattered, they would be ridden down like animals. 'On me.'

Two of the biggest casks had fallen side by side. Francis gathered the men behind them. They had five muskets, but only two were loaded.

'Give those to me.' He almost snatched the muskets out of their hands, took one himself and passed the other to the sepoy. There was no time to load the others. 'Fix bayonets,' he ordered.

The cavalry bore down on them at terrifying speed. Francis levelled the musket, aimed into the chest of the leading horse and fired. The beast was so close he could see its nostrils flaring; he felt a twinge of sympathy for the dumb animal, but it did not spoil his aim. The ball struck the point of the animal's shoulder, dead in line with the heart. Its forelegs buckled and it went down, throwing up a cloud of sand. The rider screamed as one of his legs was trapped beneath his mount, and his fibula and tibia bones shattered at the impact. The other riders swerved to avoid him. But one of them was too close behind

239

the leader, could not change course in time. He went down as well.

The remaining four riders reined in their mounts and sawed their heads around until they were facing Francis and his sepoys. At that moment the sepoy standing beside Francis threw up the second loaded musket and fired without dwelling on his aim. His ball struck the Rani's cavalry subaltern squarely on the bridge of his nose. He threw his arms wide, and slid backwards over his horse's rump. One foot caught in his stirrup when his horse bolted and dragged him down the beach with his head bumping over the stones that littered his path.

Francis slotted the bayonet over the musket muzzle and twisted it into position. Three of the riders were down, but the remaining three still presented formidable odds. One of them was loading a pistol.

And then, without firing, he tucked it back in his waistband. He said something to his companions and twitched the reins. Then all three of them wheeled their horses away, forded the river and galloped into the jungle.

Only when they had vanished did Francis think to turn around. The fort gates stood open, and a dozen men with muskets were running towards him. Tom was at their head. When he saw Francis and the others safe, he gave a great whoop of joy. He had not dared order his troops to fire, for fear they would hit Francis and his men. He did not trust their aim.

He ran to Francis and hugged him as he would his own son. 'Thank God you are alive.'

Francis' face had gone white, as the surge of battle fever left him. Tom felt him shaking in his arms. He held him a moment longer to steady him.

'You did well,' he murmured, so the other men wouldn't hear. 'Many men with more experience would have broken, fled and died.'

Francis pointed to the casks strewn about them. 'We lost more than half the water.'

'It matters little. We can refill them. It is *you* who are irreplaceable.'

'Lets hear three cheers for England,' he called. 'Three cheers for the red, white and blue. Hip hip—'

The huzzahs died on their lips. Across the river, the cavalry had reappeared – except where there had been three riders before, now there were a hundred, spread out in a long screen trotting out of the forest.

'Back to the fort,' Tom cried. 'Not point in lingering here.'

Abandoning the casks, they ran for the gates. The Rani's cavalry rode back across the river. However, they pulled up their horses long before coming in range of the fort's guns. Perhaps if they had known how few men remained, they would have risked it: but for now, they were ignorant.

Tom reached the gate and waited there until the last of the stragglers was inside. Francis stayed with him, urging the men to hurry. When all were in, the Courtneys slipped through. Alf Wilson slammed the gate and barred it.

The enemy's army spread itself in a loose cordon, sealing off the sandy spit upon which the fortress stood. Some of the soldiers went into the settlement, and emerged with furniture and valuables. The defenders in the fort had to watch, impotently, while their homes were ransacked and looted.

Later in the day, the artillery trains arrived: teams of a dozen bullocks, each hauling one of the guns salvaged from the *Kestrel*. There were other guns, too, but they were feeble weapons: merely bamboo tubes bound with iron hoops.

'Those will be more danger to their own gunners than to us,' Tom said, watching the Rani's men manoeuvre them into position. He cursed the fate that had allowed his cannon to fall into the enemy's hands, along with the Neptune sword. 'If they did not have our guns, we could withstand a siege until the next monsoon.'

'But they do not have your powder,' said Ana, standing beside him.

'They have their own.'

'Indian gunpowder is not nearly as potent as English. Your guns will have a greater range.'

'Good heavens, madam, you are a useful woman to have in a tight spot.' He called for the *hubladar*.

'Miss Duarte believes that our guns enjoy a greater range than those of the enemy. Perhaps you could have your crews demonstrate that fact.'

The *hubladar* saluted and called his men. Tom looked approvingly at the way they sprang to their task, though with more enthusiasm than skill. It took them a full ten minutes to load and train the gun; while his gun crews on the *Centaurus* or the *Kestrel*, would have done it in two.

The men stood back, the *hubladar* put his taper to the touch-hole, and the gun roared and the carriage sprang back against its restraining tackle. Through the smoke, Tom saw the ball fly well past the enemy guns, then skipping over the sand dunes and into a platoon of infantry who were coming up to support the guns, throwing them about like rag dolls and tearing at least one man's leg from his body. It finally came to rest half-buried in the side of one of the dunes, where it lay steaming and crackling in the heat generated by its own trajectory.

Soon afterwards, Tom was gratified to see the Rani's troops returning with their bullock teams to haul their ordnance away to a safer distance.

Tom had never endured a siege before – not from the inside. In the cut and thrust of a sea battle, or an ambush, he could act; here, the hours and days of waiting sapped his strength. He became irritable. If Sarah had been there, she would have known how to soothe him. But she was far away, and that only added to his cares.

What sort of man am I? he mused to himself. An army a thousand strong surrounded him, and he lived every minute of every day knowing they intended to murder him. Yet the primary emotion he felt was not fear or anger: it was boredom. After that first skirmish on the beach, the besiegers did not mount an assault. Each day, they would fire a few desultory shots with their cannon, and the defenders would answer with their own, but none did much damage. The Rani's men were content to delay their assault. Soon, Tom positively yearned for it. Anything to break the stalemate.

But he did not sit idle. He could see the same lassitude he felt creeping in among his men, and he knew he had to fight it. He put them to work digging cistern pits to catch rainwater, which he lined with timbers from Foy's dismantled house, and oakum from the stores. With no prospect of an assault by sea, he brought down one of the seaward-facing guns into the courtyard, and drilled the men in servicing it until they could clean, load, bring it to bear and fire in two minutes. He was pleased to see how the teams he had established in those desperate first few hours had taken root. The men ate together, stood watch together, gossiped and laughed together. He raced them against each other on the guns, and delighted in the pride they took in each other's achievements.

If I had a hundred more like them, I could overrun the Rani's camp and chase them all the way back to the palace, he thought.

In the first weeks, their greatest trouble was the weather. Storms rolled in from the ocean, day after day, and the open fort offered no protection. The men huddled in the lee of the walls, shivering and soaking; if the Rani's army had attacked then, they would have carried the fort without a shot being fired. Later, the storms gave way to a gentler, more constant rain that lasted longer than Tom thought possible. When the clouds finally parted, and the sun emerged, he stared at the blue sky like a prisoner getting his first glimpse of freedom.

But it was scant respite. No sooner had they dried their clothes and their powder than they found that the sun was a worse enemy than the rain. Through long hours in the middle of the day, the fort became an oven. Men pressed themselves against the searing stones to find the merest fragment of shade. The cisterns, which previously had overflowed, now dried up.

The dry spell reinvigorated the besiegers. They burned the nearest godown, and used the rubble to make a platform for their guns. Tom tried to blast them out, but they brought up their cannon in the night, and by morning were able to commence a sustained bombardment that kept his men pinned down.

'They mean to come for us,' he told Francis, some six weeks after the siege had started. 'Load every musket, and ready your weapons.'

Under cover of their artillery, the Rani's troops had begun to advance, digging an entrenchment in the soft sand. Tom watched them through the loophole in the gate, paying special attention to their commander. It was Tungar, no doubt about it. The telescope brought him so close he could almost touch the scar down the middle of his face. He limped along the battle lines, shouting orders at his men: the fall from the palace balcony had hurt him, but not killed him, and he still wore the Neptune sword. He often consulted with the tall man beside him, who Tom recognized as the man who had killed Hicks with his strange, steel whip. The man who had spoken perfect English. Tom wondered how an Englishman had found his way into the Rani's service. Perhaps another castaway.

Tom longed to take a shot. But the East India Company's muskets were inferior weapons, without rifling to spin the ball and make it fly accurately. It would be a waste of powder.

Behind Tungar, the army was forming up into lines.

'They mean to throw their full strength at us,' Tom announced. He surveyed his men, paraded in the courtyard. Burned red by the sun, gaunt from short rations, they did not look like warriors. And they were so few.

'Keep low, and do not give them easy targets.' He was about to say, 'Sell your lives dearly,' but thought better of it. They did not want to sell their lives for this scrap of the East India Company's vanity. They wanted to save themselves.

'Fight for each other, and we will come through this together.'

He assigned the men their stations. He took the east wall, facing the enemy; the *hubladar* and Alf Wilson took the north and south respectively.

'You stay in the courtyard and man the gate guns,' he told Francis. He saw the disappointment on his face.

'If you are trying to protect me, Uncle . . .'

'I am trying to protect us all. Your platoon is our reserve.' He shook his head ruefully, filled with admiration and anxiety. Had he been any different at that age? 'You will get your fight, I promise you that.'

The enemy cannon had fallen silent. The men ran to the defences. Looking through the loopholes, Tom saw the Rani's men had come under the fort's guns, so near that the defenders could not depress the barrels far enough to aim at them. Thinking they were safe, they charged forward, bunching together on the neck of the spit of sand.

'Run out your guns and fire at will,' he called to Francis.

The attackers had not seen the gun ports built into the gate. The first they knew of it was the hatches lifting open, and the barrels of the two long nine pounders rolling out.

'Fire,' Francis shouted.

Tom had prepared for this. Ana had sewn old rice sacks into small bags, which they had filled with musket balls. Fired from the muzzle of a cannon, the bags disintegrated, fanning the balls out in a lethal arc. The front rank of the men on the

245

beach went down. The second rank, pushed on by the men behind, tripped on their corpses and fell, slowing the attack still more.

'Reload,' Francis ordered, but his men needed no encouragement. All the weeks of suffering and waiting were over. All their training, working the scorching hot guns until their hands blistered, came into its own. *Worm and sponge. Ram the cartridge. Home! Wadding. Shot. Prick the cartridge and prime the hole.* No need to aim, because the target was vast and everywhere in front of them.

'Fire.'

The second volley did more damage than the first. The targets had spread out, giving the balls more space to work their havoc. At the fringes, some of the attackers had waded out into the shallows to get away from the guns. It did not save them. The gentle waves turned red with their blood; some died drowned by the weight of dead men above them.

But still they came. From the walls, Tom could see Tungar on horseback, his face hidden by the cheek-pieces of his helmet. He urged his men forward, stabbing the Neptune sword towards the fort. A soldier, panicking, tried to flee. He leaned down from the saddle and opened the man's chest from his shoulder to his hip, then trampled him with his horse. No wonder the men were more frightened of him than the fort's guns.

Smoke blew over and hid the commander from view, before Tom could attempt a shot. And now he had trouble nearer at hand. Even with all their training, Francis's men could not reload fast enough. The Rani's men had almost reached the walls – and the closer they came, the narrower the cannon's field of fire. They did not approach the gate, but spread around the walls like waves breaking on a rock. Among them, Tom saw men carrying long bamboo scaling ladders.

'Stay with the guns,' he called to Francis. Though the big guns could not touch the men around the walls, they still commanded the little isthmus which any reinforcements would have to cross.

The attacking army surged around the walls on three sides of the fort. The top of a ladder appeared at one of the embrasures. Tom reached out, fired his pistol blind straight down, then pushed the ladder back. Screams sounded as the ladder toppled, and as it landed in the mass of besiegers Tom and his platoon rose from behind the battlements and fired down into their midst.

He threw the spent musket to one of the boys and took a fresh one. But when he stood to fire, a hail of shot came back at him, chipping the parapet and flying about his ears. He ducked quickly back.

'They will not give up easily,' he muttered. As if to prove his words, another ladder rose up and slammed against the top of the wall. This time, Tom let the attackers come. A bare head appeared; two dark hands reached for the parapet. Before the man could get a purchase, Tom grabbed him by the throat and lifted him off the ladder, holding him up as a human shield. The body twitched as musket fire from below struck him. Tom's platoon rose and fired a volley down among the attackers.

Tom threw the riddled corpse to the ground. The next man on the ladder tried to gain the walls, but one of the boys reached through with a pike and stabbed him through the heart. Tom pushed the ladder back again but could not move it: this time, the men at the bottom threw themselves against it to weight it in place.

Along the inside of the parapet, together with the piles of weapons and powder and shot, stood a dozen of Foy's wine bottles. They had been emptied, then refilled with powder, nails, and all the scrap metal that could be scavenged in the fort. A rag, soaked in spirits, protruded from the neck.

Tom cocked his empty pistol, held it next to the bottle and pulled the trigger. The flint struck sparks from the frizzen, which showered onto the rag and set it alight. Tom lobbed the bottle over the wall. It landed at the foot of the ladder and exploded among the men holding it. A cloud of steel splinters tore through them, ripping off eyes and ears and fingers. The ladder fell.

The attackers retreated from the walls. That made them easier targets for the men at the top, who poured volley after volley into them, driving them still further back to where they came in range of the cannon at the gate.

Tom looked about. Through the clouds of smoke that gusted about the fort, he saw the *hubladar*'s men on the south wall. They seemed to be holding their own. But on the north wall, Alf Wilson was waving frantically, shouting for help.

Crouched low, Tom ran around the rampart. Without having to ask, he saw the danger at once. A small stone cottage stood opposite, about twenty yards from the fort, and from its windows there came an unremitting fusillade of musket fire peppering the wall.

'We must dislodge them,' Tom shouted. 'If they hold that house, they will have perfect cover for an assault.' With their greater accuracy and range, the Indian muskets would be able to sweep the walls clear, allowing the besiegers to raise their scaling ladders unopposed.

This was what he had feared. His men were stretched so thin, there was nowhere he could take reinforcements without risking disaster.

He yelled down to the courtyard to get Francis' attention. He raised four fingers, indicating four men, and beckoned Francis to him. That left enough men to serve one of the guns – enough, he hoped, to make the attackers think twice before trying the gate.

Francis and his men came up to the rampart and crouched beside him. Musket balls rattled on the stonework and whistled overhead. Tom explained what was needed.

248

'But how can we get down?' Francis asked.

'Ropes.'

'And up again?'

'I will solve that problem when I face it.'

'You mean "we"?'

'Not you,' said Tom. 'You will stay on the wall to provide covering fire.'

He saw the hurt on Francis' face, the refusal coming to his lips. 'There is no time. If anything happens to me, the men will look to you for leadership.' For an instant, he remembered another siege at another fort, on the far side of this same ocean. Tom had taken command when his father's legs were blown off by the force of an exploding mine.

Dear God, let that not be my fate, he prayed.

They fetched ropes and fastened them to the iron rings which studded the parapet. Tom carried two pistols in holsters in his cross belts, two more on his belt, and a musket slung over his shoulder. He gathered up half a dozen of the wine-bottle grenadoes and put them in a sack.

'Ready your men,' he called to Francis. '*Now*.'

The men fired in unison, a sharp volley that deafened his ears and almost blinded him. The smoke was more protection than the musket balls. Clouding the parapet, it hid them for those vital seconds when they stood exposed atop the rampart. Then they leaped.

The men he had picked were all sailors from the *Kestrel*: they could burn a backstay in their sleep. They slid down the ropes before the attackers even saw them. Tom landed in the sand, rolled away and scrambled to his feet. A furious fusillade erupted over his head as Francis' men fired another volley, pinning the attackers down.

Tom drew his sword and started cutting his way towards the house. Alf Wilson fought beside him, wielding an axe he had fashioned by cutting down one of the sepoys' halberds. The

Rani's troops, surprised by this sudden counter attack, fell back.

But the marksmen lodged in the building held their nerve. Through the melee, Tom saw smoke blossoming from the windows as they fired without care for their own men. Tom saw a tall Indian swordsman felled when a musket ball took off the back of his head. But not all the shots went awry. One of Tom's men was hit in the arm; another was dropped by a clean shot between the eyes.

In front of them, the beach sank into a low gully where the wind had been funnelled between the fort and the house, and scoured away the sand. Tom threw himself down into it and gestured his men to do likewise. If they pressed themselves into the ground, the rise offered just enough cover to protect them against the musket balls whistling over their heads. Behind, Francis' men maintained a steady fire from the walls, keeping the enemy at bay.

Tom pulled three of the wine bottles from the sack. He pointed to one of the sailors, a Cornishman named Penrose. 'As soon as these grenadoes go off, you follow me. Alf, maintain a steady fire.' He handed him two of his pistols. 'Ready?'

He struck a spark. The cloth fuses in the bottle necks flared into life. Keeping as low as he could, Tom lobbed them towards the house. One landed short and went out on the sand; the second struck the cottage wall and shattered. He cursed. No alternative: he would have to risk it.

Alf saw what he intended and nodded. He raised his musket and fired. At the same instant, Tom popped his head up from the shelter of the gully, sighted himself on the nearest window and hurled the bottle. He threw himself back to the ground, as half a dozen musket balls tore the air where his head had been.

The bottle sailed through the open window. Lying in the gully, he did not see it enter, but he knew he had aimed true by the muffled sound of the explosion. In fact, he had timed it perfectly. It exploded just before it struck the floor, spraying its lethal contents around the small room.

A heavy weight struck Tom's shoulder. For a moment, he feared he'd been hit. But it was Alf Wilson. He had been a fraction of a second slower than Tom getting down, and had paid the price. He lolled against Tom, blood flowing from a wound on his collarbone.

Tom had no time to tend him. The Rani's men would already be regrouping. He cut a sleeve off Alf's shirt and stuffed it into the bullet hole to staunch the bleeding. That was all he could afford. They could not defend the gully for long. If they got trapped there, they would all die.

Tom rose and ran forward. Penrose followed, while the last of the *Kestrel*'s men stayed with Alf and kept up a rapid fire. Again, the smoke hid them from their enemies. Tom weaved across the beach, cutting down any man who resisted, judging his course through the fog by the steady report of musket fire ahead and to his right. His grenadoe had not emptied all the defenders from the house.

The smoke cloud around the house was so thick Tom almost ran straight into it. He had come around its end, where an oak door opened inside. Half a dozen of the Rani's guards were gathered there. Tom shot two of them with his pistols. A third ran at him with his musket. Tom sidestepped, wrestled the weapon from his hands and clubbed him over the head with it. As the man dropped, he reversed his grip and swung the musket like a bat into the next man's throat, breaking his neck.

Penrose had dispatched the other two. Tom kicked in the door and leaped through, sword in hand. This was where the grenado had done its work. Three men lay dead on the floor, their gore splashed high up the walls. A second doorway led through to another, longer room, which echoed with gunfire, the rattle of ramrods and the thud of the butts as they reloaded.

If he had brought one more grenado, he might have cleared

251

them out in a single blast. But he only had his sword, and the empty musket he had taken. The fire coming from the fort had slackened. Francis' men must have been picked off, or else run out of ammunition. If the attackers could make themselves secure here, and regroup, they would overrun the fort in minutes.

More men than he could count were squeezed into the room. Some firing, others reloading, others bringing fresh powder and shot. Impossible odds, but he had no choice. He nodded to Penrose.

The two of them burst into the room, closing so fast none of the marksmen had space to bring a musket to bear. Tom slashed and thrust with his sabre, while Penrose swung Alf Wilson's boarding axe to bloody effect in the confined space. Soon, even those proved too unwieldy. The press of bodies became a scrum, nothing more than men grappling and pushing each other.

This was a fight they could not hope to win. Tom was wrestled back. Penrose took a knife to his belly, fell and was trampled beneath the Rani's soldiers' feet. Before Tom could help him, the surge of battle pushed him away.

He took another step backwards – and felt hard stone against his back. He was trapped. The Rani's troops made a semi-circle around him. Their captain, a huge man with a black turban stepped forward. He took a long-barrelled pistol from his orange sash and aimed it at Tom's face.

Tom flinched as he heard the shot, but he kept his eyes open. The cock on the pistol had not moved, but the captain's face dissolved in a mask of blood and bone.

Francis stood in the doorway, a pistol in each hand and with two men from the fort flanking him with bayonet-tipped muskets. Before the Rani's stunned soldiers could respond, Francis' men charged in, stabbing with the well-practised movements Tom had drilled into them over the past weeks. Stunned by the reversal, the soldiers hardly resisted. They fled the building, diving out through the windows and abandoning their arms in their haste.

'I told you not to come,' Tom said to Francis. 'But thank God you did. Now let us finish our business. We are not safe yet.'

The Rani's troops had prepared the house for a long siege. Around the back, Tom and Francis found a hoard of powder kegs.

'This is more than any musketeer would need,' said Tom. 'They meant to bring their big guns up. Now we shall use their arms against them.'

They piled the kegs inside the house and laid a fuse. From the east side of the fort, Tom could hear blasts of gunfire, but here on the north side the Rani's men had given up the fight. Tom lit the powder trail, and they all ran for the walls. Crossing the little gully, Tom saw the impressions in the sand where he had taken cover, and the blood where Alf Wilson had fallen.

Now the gully was empty. 'Did you rescue Alf?' Tom asked Francis. 'I left him here.'

Francis shook his head. 'There were none here when I came.'

Before Tom could think any more of it, the house exploded. Stone debris rained down on the beach. Some travelled as far as the fort, rattling off the walls. When the smoke cleared, Tom saw the house had been flattened to its foundations.

'They will not lodge any guns there again,' said Tom with grim satisfaction.

The explosion had broken the attackers' last will to fight. Beyond the corner of the fort, Tom saw them streaming back across the narrow isthmus towards their camp on the mainland. A couple of parting shots from the guns at the gate hastened them on their way: the men in the fort had not lost their taste for battle.

Tom leaned on the musket he was carrying. He ached: he

was not as young as he had once been. He looked at Francis: hair tousled, face black as a powder monkey, shirt torn and drenched with sweat. He felt as proud as if he had been the boy's father.

'You should not have come to rescue me,' he muttered.

'I didn't,' retorted Francis. 'I thought you were dead. I was going to finish the job you had started.'

Tom put his arm around the boy, and together they picked their way among the corpses to the gate.

'You did well,' he said. 'But we have only won a single battle. No doubt, they will try again soon. We had best be ready for them. Now, where is Alf Wilson?'

But no-one in the fort had seen him.

'He was wounded,' Tom said urgently. 'Someone must have brought him back.'

'I have not had him in my care,' said Ana. She wore a dirty apron over her dress, her arms wet with blood from the wounds she had already bound that day. 'They would have brought him to me.'

'Then where—?'

A sick dread churned Tom's stomach. He ran to the walls and shielded his eyes, scanning the bodies around the fort for any sign of his friend. Clouds of flies buzzed about the fallen.

'Look,' cried Francis. 'They've raised the white flag.'

Four horsemen rode across the blood-soaked sand towards the fort. One carried an upright lance, with a white cloth hanging limp from the tip. Tungar rode beside him. Behind them, two riders trotted forward with a prisoner stumbling between them. Taut ropes around his wrists fastened him to his captors' saddles, so that if he tripped he was dragged through the sand.

They reined in before the gate. The prisoner collapsed to his knees.

'That's Alf Wilson,' cried Francis.

'Quiet,' Tom hissed, but down on the beach Tungar had heard. He gave an evil smile.

'This man is your friend?' he called up.

'A member of my crew.' Tom tried to sound unconcerned, and hoped Alf would understand why he had to be so callous. Tungar was not fooled.

'I offer you a bargain. Surrender the fort, and I will let the prisoners go.'

'And where will *we* go, if we surrender the fort?'

'I will give you safe conduct to a nearby village. From there, you may make your way down the coast to the English settlements at Travancore or Cochin.'

'The same safe conduct you gave to Mr Foy when he brought his diplomatic mission to the Rani's palace?'

Tungar did his best to sound regretful. 'The Rani laments that there is war between our peoples, and wishes only for peace.'

Tom could guess what sort of peace he meant: the peace that came at the point of a sword. He tried not to look at Alf but couldn't help himself. Alf raised his head, and shook it imperceptibly. Wounded, beaten and captive, his face still burned with pride. He could see the lie for what it was. He would not want to be the cause of their downfall.

Tom gripped the hilt of his sword so hard the wire grip left welts in his skin. Only the deep-rooted habits of honour, learned over so many years from his father, kept him from breaking the truce and loosing a shot at Tungar.

'We will not surrender the fort,' Tom declared. 'And if you harm so much as one hair on his head, I will come to your camp and visit such tortures on you as you cannot imagine.'

Tungar gave an unpleasant laugh. 'You do not know what I can imagine. But you will soon find out, if you refuse my offer.'

'Go,' shouted Tom. 'Before my patience expires. But heed my warning: not one hair on his head.'

255

Tungar grinned. 'I swear I will not touch him.'

He turned and left. Alf Wilson gave one, last plaintive look at the fort before the guards dragged him away.

Tom went down into the courtyard, profoundly troubled by what he had had to do. He had not gone far when Francis, who had stayed on the walls, called out, 'What are they doing to Alf?'

Tom raced back up the steps. At the edge of the beach, beyond the enemy camp, the guards had stripped Alf Wilson naked and were tying him to a palm tree. When he was made fast, one of the guards took a clay bowl and seemed to daub him all over with a liquid that glistened in the sun.

'What devilry is this?' Tom wondered.

'He's coming back,' said Francis. Tungar had mounted his horse, and was cantering across the beach, the white flag fluttering from his lance. This time, he came alone.

'What have you done?' shouted Tom angrily. 'You swore you would not touch him.'

'Nor have I. I am merely letting nature take her course.' He swung the horse around and pointed the spear at the tree where Alf was bound. 'The coconut palms produce a sweet liquor called toddy. The natives cannot resist it, but nor can wasps, or the red ants. When the liquor is running, early in the morning, those insects swarm over the trees in their thousands. As the sun rises high and the day grows hot, they retreat to shelter. The ants descend the trees, and bore their burrows into the soft roots.' He smiled. 'Unless, of course, on their way down they find something sweeter. The soft, yielding flesh of a man. They will burrow inside him, and I assure you their bite is every bit as painful as the stinging of the wasps, who will be drawn to the honey I have painted on his skin.'

'Fetch me a musket,' Tom whispered to Francis. '*Go.*'

'It can take a man three days to die that way,' Tungar

continued. Most of the fort's defenders had come up on the walls to listen, but he pretended not to see them. He raised his voice.

'Give your men this message. The first man who opens the gate to me, I will reward with lands and gold. The others will die – but not before they have wished a hundred times over they were dead already.'

'I will make you wish that, and then I will make you wish it a thousand times more.' Tom grabbed the musket Francis had brought and aimed it through the embrasure. But Tungar had read his intention. He kicked the horse, and galloped away across the sand. Tom's shot fell harmlessly behind him.

Tom reloaded, and trained the gun on Alf Wilson. Alf kept still, either bound too tight or not yet aware of the terrible fate that awaited him. But Tungar's torture was complete: even the Indian matchlocks, with their superior range, could not cover that distance.

In sheer anger, Tom pulled the trigger. The musket recoiled, and the ball flew into the sea, the little splash invisible among the little whitecaps.

'What now?' asked Francis, his face as white as the sand.

'He dies,' said Tom.

It took Alf Wilson three days to die: three terrible days that dragged like a nightmare. No one spoke; none of the defenders would meet Tom's eye. In the evenings, when the breeze came off the land and blew the screams to them, Tom thought about slipping out in the dark and cutting Alf free. But Tungar had posted a double line of pickets, and at night they lit huge bonfires so that no one could approach unseen. Even after Alf was dead, they left the corpse bound to the tree until it was unrecognisable as the man he had been.

Tom longed for the next assault. He craved the release of battle, the chance to seek out Tungar and avenge Alf. But it did not come. Days passed with only the most desultory exchanges of cannon fire to remind each other they were still there.

'They are trying to starve us out,' Tom guessed. He had cut the rice ration again that morning, and now that the rains had stopped they were down to their last half cask of water. He had already heard men complaining. Soon they would be desperate.

'The enemy are losing heart,' said the *hubladar*. 'In this country, armies do not fight sieges to the death. No one is so loyal to his lord that he would die for him. If a castle falls, it is because it is betrayed.'

Francis looked appalled. 'Are men so fickle here? No Englishman would ever disgrace himself that way.'

'Peace,' said Tom, surprised by his nephew's idealism. 'No race is immune from cowardice and self-interest. If you look back through the annals of old England, how many of our own castles were taken by treachery or deceit?'

'My guess is that the Rani is troubled,' said Ana. 'She needed a complete victory before the monsoon ended. Soon, the new trading season will open. If she is at war with us, her merchants will have nowhere to sell their pepper and cloth. They will blame the queen for losing their livelihoods, and she will lose her revenues from the customs. The whole kingdom will be impoverished. She knows this.'

Tom gave her an admiring look. Even in the extremes of hardship, she had a cool head for business. He glanced at Francis. He had seen how the boy followed her about, sitting long hours talking with her when he was not on duty, saving little portions of his rice ration to give her. He marvelled that he could carry on his courtship in such circumstances.

'The monsoon will turn soon.' Tom had already felt the change in the air, a new coolness as the prevailing winds shifted. 'Perhaps then the Rani will reconsider her policy.'

* * *

258

A quarter of a mile away, Christopher sat in Tungar's tent. Through the open flap, he could see his battery of nine-pounders sitting impotent in their emplacements. The sight enraged him. They ought to have reduced the fortress to rubble by now, and buried all the defenders beneath it. But the Rani's powder was feeble, and instead of iron balls she only had stones, which shattered against the well-engineered walls.

'The Rani is most displeased with your lack of progress,' said Poola. He had arrived unannounced that evening, with a retinue of fifty of the Rani's bodyguards. According to Christopher's spies, he had been spending more and more time in the Rani's council chambers. Perhaps that explained the glittering profusion of gold rings that had sprouted from his fingers like fresh shoots in spring.

I should have cut off your fingers when I had the chance, Christopher thought sourly. *And your tongue.* He gave a blank smile, and poured his guest another cup of toddy.

'We would have carried the fort weeks ago, were it not for the accursed hat-wearers who were shipwrecked,' Tungar protested. 'Their leader is a *djinn*, a devil.'

Poola nodded to the Neptune sword that hung from a peg on the tent pole. Light from the lamps smouldered in the depths of the great sapphire. 'Perhaps if you had not taken his sword, he might have joined our cause. Instead of thwarting us.'

'Why have you come here?' said Tungar brusquely. A beetle flew down and landed on the plate of dates he had laid out for his guest. It crawled over the fruit, antennae twitching.

'The monsoon is nearly over. Soon the seas will open, and the hat-wearers' ships will return. If our weavers and pepper-farmers have no one to buy their goods, they will starve.'

'You mean they will not pay the Rani's taxes,' retorted Tungar.

'And who do you think pays for your army?' said Poola. He coughed; Christopher smelled the sickly sweetness of the toddy on his breath. 'I counselled against this war, but you prevailed with the Rani. Now that you have had your way, you had better see it to a favourable conclusion. If you fail, do not think you will be welcome in the palace at Chittattinkara. This ill-advised war has cost the Rani a year's revenues.'

'No doubt it cost you a pretty penny too,' said Christopher.

'The Rani is a river, and all wealth flows from her,' said Poola unctuously. 'I would not expect you to understand.' He looked at Tungar. 'This is what comes of waging war with pirates and bandits.'

The beetle was still clambering over the fruit plate. Suddenly, Tungar slammed down his fist to kill it. The plate shattered, spilling dates over the floor. The beetle flew away, buzzing around the lamp in the corner.

Tungar picked up a fragment of the broken plate and crushed it to dust in his fist. 'We will win this war,' he promised. 'I will mount the hat-wearers' heads on spikes every mile from here to Chittattinkara, and when we reach the palace I will mount yours right above the gate, to warn all those who would speak treason to the Rani.'

Christopher stayed silent. He knew it was only the stalemate between Tungar and Poola that kept him alive. If the war was lost, Tungar would surely lose his head – and Christopher with him.

Poola stood to go. 'I do not think we have anything more to discuss. I bid you good night.'

He lifted the flap of the tent. The beetle, drawn by the sudden brightness of the watch fire outside, fluttered out. It flew into the flames and vanished in a puff of smoke.

Poola smiled. 'You see? There is more than one way to destroy your enemies.'

After he had gone, Christopher sat by the fire in thought. The safest course, he knew, would be to vanish into the forest, for this could not end well for him. Tungar would send men to hunt him, but Christopher could evade them.

But there was the sword. Always the sword, with its fathomless blue sapphire promising him his inheritance. How many times in those past months had he contemplated murdering Tungar, seizing the sword and fleeing? But Tungar had many enemies, and guarded himself well. In all those months, Christopher had never once caught him alone – and he never let the sword out of his sight.

A challenge rang out in the darkness beyond the fire. He heard an urgent exchange of words, then three guards appeared with a prisoner between them. The prisoner's sandy hair betrayed him as a white man, though months of exposure had tanned his skin as dark as a native. His cheeks had sunk in, his legs were thin as matchsticks and bony ribs pressed against his tattered shirt.

How have we let these men defy us so long? Christopher thought angrily. He wondered again about the English captain, the man who had staggered out of the sea with the Neptune sword and thwarted all their plans. If the fort fell, there were many questions he would ask him before he died.

'We found this man trying to infiltrate our lines,' said the guard captain. 'He says he wants to speak to you.'

'To me?' said Christopher, surprised.

'He has heard that you speak the language of the hat-wearers.'

Christopher considered the prisoner. Was he a spy? He considered whether he should torture him, to find out what he knew.

There would be time for that later, if necessary.

'Speak,' he said in English. 'Before you suffer the same fate as the last man I captured.'

The prisoner fell to his knees, pleading in a wheedling voice, 'Bless you, sir, there's no need to talk that way. I saw what you did there, and I don't want that happening to me. I come here of my own free will to make you a proposition.'

'What is it?'

'My name's Ilkley, sir. I kept Mr Foy's accounts. I did hear, sir, that the man who gave you the fort might expect some gratitude. A reward, so to speak.'

'Yes.'

'I can be that man, sir. I can open the gates for you.'

He stared hungrily at Christopher, and Christopher stared back. He wondered if this might be a trap: again, he considered torturing Ilkley to be sure of his sincerity. But the fort commander had so few men. He would not have risked one on this errand – not when he knew what fate awaited them.

'When will you do it?'

'Tomorrow night, sir. Dark of the moon – they won't see you approach.' He clasped his hands. 'There will be a reward, won't there?'

'You will get your due,' Christopher assured him, hiding his smile.

Ilkley nodded gratefully. 'I'd best be getting back, sir. It's my shift on guard, and if I'm not there when the relief comes, the captain will give me a buttock-stirring about it. He's a hard bastard. Has us drilling our guns till our arms drop off. Me, sir.' He looked affronted. 'An accountant.'

Christopher had stopped paying attention to the man's complaints – but the mention of the captain got his attention.

'Tell me,' he said. 'What is your commander's name?'

'Tom Weald. He was shipwrecked just at the start of the monsoon season. Why, sir? You know him?'

'No. But he seemed . . . familiar.'

Christopher had revealed more than he intended. He straightened.

'If that gate is open tomorrow night, you will have your weight in gold.' He stared into the man's dull eyes and liked what he saw: avarice, hunger and fear. 'If not, so help me, I will melt the gold and pour it down your throat.'

* * *

Francis woke without knowing why. He'd been dozing in a corner of the fort, body pressed against the warm sand. Automatically, he reached out and felt the musket lying beside him. With the new moon, the night was black as pitch: they had long since run out of candles and oil for their lamps.

Soft footsteps approached. He sat up.

'Francis?' Ana's voice came out of the dark, soft and cool as night. She sat down beside him, smoothing her skirts under her. Francis could hardly see her, but he felt the heat coming off her bare arm, an inch from his own.

'I couldn't sleep,' she said. 'I had a dream. I was running through a great fortress, looking for you, but I could not find you anywhere. Men were chasing me, always on my heels, and I knew that if I did not find you they would kill you.'

Without even thinking, Francis reached out and cradled her to him. He stroked her hair.

'It was only a dream.'

She gathered herself. 'I am sick of this terrible place.'

'Soon we will go. Just before sunset, I saw a sail out on the ocean. The seas are open again. If Sarah and Agnes got word of our situation to Madras, the governor there will send help as soon as he possibly can.'

'I wish a ship would come here and carry us far away.'

She stared into the night, then straightened. Francis, embarrassed, lifted his arm, but she had only moved to bring her face level with his. She leaned in, her mouth searching his in the dark.

Her lips were paper-dry. She brushed his mouth, parting his lips with her tongue. Francis wrapped his arms around her, feeling her breasts firm through the thin fabric of her dress. He ran his fingers through her hair, and—

He broke away. Ana sat up, wounded. 'I thought—'

He hushed her. 'Do you smell that?'

She wrinkled her nose. 'It smells like . . . sulphur?'

263

'It is match-cord.' Francis rose, all thoughts of romance driven from his mind. 'But we do not use it for our guns: we have flintlocks. Only the Indians use matchlocks.'

Ana understood the gravity of the situation at once. 'Who is on watch?'

'Ilkley.'

Francis felt his way along the wall until he found the steps. 'Wake my uncle,' he told Ana. 'It may be nothing, but . . .'

By now he knew the fort so well he could run up the steps in perfect darkness. He stepped out onto the rampart – and stopped dead.

The night was not so dark as he'd thought. In the west, beyond the clouds, he could see stars shining through; on the eastern horizon, a dim smudge gave the first hint of dawn. But that was not what made him stare. Below him, clustered in front of the fort like sparks around a forge, a hundred orange pricks of light glowed on the beach. He knew what they were. The smouldering cords of the enemy matchlocks.

He ran back down and almost collided with Tom at the foot of the stairs. 'They are here,' he gasped. 'Scores of them, maybe hundreds, just outside the gate.'

'How did they get there unseen? Where is Ilkley?'

'I don't know. I did not see him on the walls.'

A creak sounded by the gate. Tom and Francis turned. Dawn was coming quickly, as it does in the tropics; the gatehouse was now visible as a shadow against the lightening sky. Something moved at its base.

Ilkley did not hear them approach. At the beginning of the siege, Tom had buttressed the gates with beams taken from Foy's dismantled house. Now, Ilkley strained to pull the heavy timbers away, sweating even in the cool pre-dawn air. He had not allowed enough time for this, and the Rani's men had lit their matches too soon. He worked with feverish haste, his mind clouded with thoughts of what the enemy captain would do to him if he reached the gates and found them barred. After three months in the fort, wasting from hunger and thirst, Ilkley had lost all hope. The fort would fall: it was only a question of time. He intended to survive it.

The last of the beams came free. Ilkley's slippery hands lost control; it fell away and landed with a thud. Ilkley did not have time to wonder who might have heard. The enemy captain was waiting on the other side of the gate. The moment he saw it open, he would launch his attack.

He lifted the bar that locked it and let it fall on the sand. He put his shoulder against the gate and heaved. Rusted by rain, jammed with grit and disuse, the hinges resisted. He pushed harder, drawing on a desperate strength he did not know he had.

A hand on his shoulder spun him around. Tom and Francis stood behind him, both with drawn swords. Beyond, he saw the rest of the garrison stirring to life, repeating Tom's orders in whispers, to keep silent and grab their weapons.

'What have you done?' said Tom in anguish.

Ilkley wanted to answer, but the words wouldn't come. He stuttered and stammered. 'I just—'

It was too late. His last, frantic shove had finally shifted the gate. Only a foot or so, but it was the signal the enemy had been watching for. Through the opening, Tom saw a host of glowing sparks rise from the ground like fireflies taking wing. They ran for the gate.

'They are coming,' shouted the *hubladar* who had gone up to the walls.

Tom threw Ilkley aside and hauled on the iron bracket to close the gates. The day was light enough now that the attackers saw him. A musket fired; a ball whistled through the opening just over Tom's head.

Francis dragged him back, as a second ball hit the gate. A

six-inch splinter tore through the space where Tom's eyes had been a second earlier.

Tom looked at the two cannon. They were kept loaded, but there was no powder in their touchholes. He grabbed a powder flask hanging from a nail in the wall and poured it in, spilling it in his haste. Francis brought a match.

The attackers were already scrabbling at the gates, heaving them open. Tom touched the match to the first cannon, and leaped out of the way as it thundered back. The blast blew the gate off its hinges, scattering the attackers backwards. The second wave poured in to the breach, but only in time for Tom to reach the second cannon. They died on the bodies of the fallen.

But there were more behind – and no time to reload the cannon. Tom's men grabbed the timbers that had buttressed the gate and piled them in the gateway. With the corpses that choked the entryway, the cannons, and the broken remains of the gate, it made a rough barricade they could crouch behind.

Even woken from sleep, the discipline Tom had instilled over the past months repaid itself now. The men knew what to do, and the cannon blasts had bought them just enough time. Half the men knelt behind the barricade, keeping up a steady fire, while the others reloaded the muskets. Behind them, two of the boys crouched in the sand, digging out a shallow trench where Tom had ordered.

But as fast as the men could shoot, the enemy kept coming. Clambering over the corpses of their comrades that choked the gateway, they were now so close that the men on the barricade had no time to reload. They fixed bayonets. The battle became a close-up, savage slaughter: hand to hand combat that left every man covered in blood.

The boys had finished their trench and filled it as Tom directed. They brushed sand over to conceal what they had buried, then took up cudgels to join the fray. Tom waved them away. He could see how the tide of the battle was running. Now that the two sides were face to face, the enemy commander could bring his weight of numbers to bear. He was forcing his men forward, driving them through the gate like a nail into a hole. However hard the defenders fought, they could not resist the sheer pressure of so many men. Soon they would be overwhelmed.

'Back to the redoubt,' he ordered.

From the beginning of the siege, he had feared it might end this way. He had prepared a redoubt, a last refuge they could retreat to. He had fortified the north-west bastion, furthest from the gate, and provided it with a supply of powder and shot. He was under no illusions: he knew he could not last long. On the tower, they would be vulnerable to enemy musket fire. As soon as the enemy gained the walls, they would be finished. All he could hope for was to make their attackers pay so dearly they gave up the fight.

'Back,' he shouted. 'Back.'

His bellowing voice penetrated even the chaos of battle. The men on the barricade disengaged, leaped back and ran so fast that their assailants lost their footing and fell. Those in the front rank of the attackers, who had fought most bravely, were crushed under the weight of men pushing in behind.

Tom was last to go. He stooped, and fired the fuse that led into the shallow trench the boys had dug. Then he ran.

Men poured into the courtyard behind him. They might have caught Tom, but their numbers worked against them. Pressed together, they hindered each other from running, or from levelling their muskets. And they did not see the fuse.

The flame reached the powder kegs the boys had buried in the trench just as Tom reached the stairs. The powder exploded in a cloud of flame, sand and blood, as if a giant fist had reached out of the ground. Such was its force, even the bones of dead men became lethal projectiles. The attackers were eviscerated.

267

The explosion echoed around the courtyard. Through the screams, Tom heard a new sound: a gathering roar that shook the earth with even more force than the original explosion. It rose to a crescendo like a thunder clap, then slowly rolled away in the rumble of settling stones.

Tom gained the top of the tower and looked down into the courtyard. Smoke and dust choked the air, but from that height he could see enough to make out what had happened. The gatehouse had disappeared. Battered by the enemy's artillery over the last three months, the explosion almost directly beneath it had been the final straw. It had collapsed, burying the bodies of living and dead alike.

Instinctively, he looked around for Francis and Ana. Both were there. Ana knelt beside one of the men, dressing his wounds, while Francis had come up right beside him. He was shouting something, but Tom's ears were still ringing from the explosion and he could not understand.

The dust had started to settle in the courtyard. With a sinking heart, Tom saw that his last gambit had failed. The explosion had not deterred the attackers: they were still coming on, scrambling over the debris where the gate had been and charging towards his last redoubt. It would not be long now before they overran the walls and all was lost.

He reached for the pistol he carried – but it was gone. It must have been knocked out of his belt in the melee. He raised his sword, and steeled himself for the end. Still, he refused to give up. He would not surrender, for while he breathed he could hope he would see Sarah again. But it would not be long now.

Francis was still trying to tell him something. Making no impression, he grabbed Tom's arm and turned him, pointing him out to sea. For some unaccountable reason, he seemed to be grinning like a madman.

Then Tom saw, and no pain or battle-weariness could keep

the joy off his face. A ship had appeared in the bay, her furled sails bunched like clouds from her yards. A row of cannon gleamed from her gun ports. From her stern hung the red-and-white striped ensign of the East India Company. She had lowered her longboat, which pulled through the surf towards the beach filled with red-coated marines.

One of her guns bellowed. Tom saw the ball skim over the water and carve a bloody gap in the Rani's army. The beach erupted in a fountain of sand. Another gun fired, and another, staggered shots that gave the Rani's men no respite. In an instant, victory turned to a rout. They ran headlong through their camp and into the jungle, abandoning their weapons, their stores and their big guns. Even their officers joined in, making no attempt to rally the men.

The only man who resisted was Tungar, standing up in his stirrups, shouting at his army to stay and fight. When words did no good he used the Neptune sword, laying about his men with the flat of the blade. But the fleeing soldiers simply ignored him, abandoning all discipline as they melted away into the jungle. One of the men grabbed his stirrups and tried to unhorse him, but Tungar fended him off with a cut that left him clutching his eyes.

The ship fired again. One of the balls passed so close to Tungar's mount it almost took its head off. The beast reared up, teeth bared, and only Tungar's superb horsemanship kept him from being pitched onto the sand.

With a final roar of rage, he circled the horse and spurred it away. Tom saw the Neptune sword waving above the fray as he used it to cut a path through the fleeing throng.

This was his last chance, Tom realized. If Tungar reached the jungle, let alone the palace, Tom might never have another chance to retrieve the sword – or to avenge Alf Wilson, and all the men who had died because of Tungar. He ran down the stairs, across the courtyard, and clambered to the top of the

269

rubble pile that blocked the gate. The stones were still warm from the heat of the blast.

He scanned the battlefield. Where was Tungar?

Christopher staggered away from the fort. Dust and sand choked his mouth; his ears were still ringing from the sound of the blast. When he touched his hand to his scalp, he felt only blood and bare skin. The explosion had burned his hair off.

He had been at the gate. Tungar had insisted he lead the assault – no doubt because he did not trust Ilkley's story, and hoped to rid himself of his inconvenient ally. If so, the plan had almost worked to perfection. Christopher had seen Tom Weald on the far side of the gate, had been ready to charge in and capture him before the Rani's soldiers butchered every man alive. Just in time, some instinct had stayed him. The Devil takes care of his own, his mother would have said. Christopher knew it was fate, saving him to reclaim the sword. He had held back, long enough to see his men blown to pieces by the mine, the survivors crushed under the falling arch, and Tom Weald out of reach again on the tower. Thrown down by the force of the blast, he had not even risen when suddenly he became aware that the tide of the battle had turned decisively. His men were in full retreat, and as a cannon ball tore one man's head off he saw the ship in the bay and understood why.

He felt no disappointment. He owed no allegiance to this army – and this was a moment he had long planned for. Instantly, he sought out Tungar. Tungar stood on his horse, a little distance away, screaming at the men to stand their ground. He might as well have shouted at the waves.

Even in the chaos of battle, Christopher felt a chill blast of triumph. Tungar was finished. If the English did not kill him, the Rani certainly would. Now all that mattered was getting the sword.

He ran for Tungar, pushing past the wounded who limped and struggled too slowly. He saw one of the soldiers trying to commandeer Tungar's horse, but a blow from the Neptune sword put paid to that insolence. Watching, Christopher did not see the fallen firelock on the sand. His boot caught it, tripping him on his face. Two men rushed past him, and as he got to his feet he saw a cannon ball shatter their bodies, right in front of him. If he had not tripped . . . Again, he thanked the dark fate that protected him.

But now even Tungar had seen it was hopeless. He turned to flee, swinging the golden sword like a scythe to cut through the mass of men who choked the neck of land that led back to the river and to safety. Even he could not force a path. The horse, terrified by the crowd and the roar of the ship's broadsides, refused to move.

Christopher slipped through the crowd, moving closer to his target. He uncoiled the *urumi* that he had prudently worn around his waist. In the press of men, he had little space to wield it. He waited for an opening, then let fly, unspooling it over the heads of the men in front.

The steel blade closed around Tungar's wrist. Christopher snapped it tight and yanked it back. The force cut Tungar's hand clean from his arm. It dropped to the ground, still clutching the Neptune sword, while a jet of blood fountained from the stump. Tungar screamed. He let go the reins to staunch the flow, but the horse was already too close to panic. It felt the bridle loosen and reared up on its hind legs. Tungar fell and landed hard on the sand. The horse bolted, trampling men beneath its hooves in its haste to be away.

The crowds around them were thinning. Most of the men had already reached the trees, or died in the attempt. Christopher could see the Indiaman's boat approaching the beach, filled with red-coated marines. If they caught him here . . .

The Neptune sword lay in the sand, glittering like buried

treasure. Christopher reached for it. Even among all the wreckage of defeat, he felt the sweet thrill of victory. All the horrors he had suffered, the terrible things he had seen and done, were justified in that moment. The sword was his, inches from his grasp.

A hand closed around his ankle and hauled him back. Christopher overbalanced and fell onto his knees. He lunged for the sword, but the hand gripped him with a ferocious strength and dragged him away.

It was Tungar. Christopher twisted around and saw him, his severed stump pressed against the sand to staunch the bleeding, while his left hand held Christopher fast. He clenched the skull-handled dagger in his teeth, so tight the blade cut the corners of his mouth.

'Traitor,' he hissed through the blade. 'You may have defeated me, but I will send you to Shiva the Destroyer before I go myself.'

With a howl of pain and hate, he pushed himself up on the stump of his right arm. At the same time, he let go Christopher's foot, grabbed the knife from his mouth and plunged it into Christopher's leg in a single motion.

Once again, the skills he had learned in the *kalari* saved his life. The moment Tungar let go, Christopher used all his strength to leap onto his feet. When the knife came down, he was already standing. The blade struck a glancing blow, drawing blood but missing the muscles beneath.

Now Tungar was helpless. He tried to stand, but Christopher knocked him back down. He pried the knife from his grip and tossed it aside. Straddling Tungar, he put his hands around his throat and squeezed. Tungar flailed and kicked; he reached for Christopher's face to gouge out his eyes, but his arm was not long enough. Christopher caught his hand in his mouth and bit down on his fingers until he felt the bone crack. Tungar opened his mouth to scream, but no sound came. Christopher's chokehold was unrelenting. He pressed his thumbs against Tungar's windpipe.

Tungar's eyes bulged. His face went red, so bright Christopher thought it might split down the seam of its scar and spill out his brains on the sand. His tongue pressed through his black, betel-stained teeth, gasping for air that would not come.

His windpipe snapped. His eyes rolled back, his head lolled and his mouth hung slack. Christopher gave the body one last squeeze to be sure he was dead, then stood. Ignoring the wound on his leg, he gathered up the sword and ran for the safety of the trees.

The marines had come ashore. They shouted at Christopher but he did not listen; he only knew they were firing at him by the blooms of sand that erupted on the beach around him. He glanced back. Uncertain of the situation, the marines were not giving chase. Beyond them, he saw a figure standing on the rubble at the fort's gate, and he knew instinctively it was Tom Weald.

He had defeated Christopher. But Christopher had the sword, and that gave him new strength. He reached the trees and vanished from sight.

A little way inside the forest, he found Tungar's mare. The fleeing army had given no thought to taking her. She stood in a glade, spattered with blood and grime, chewing on grass.

Christopher caught the bridle and murmured soothing words in her ear, until she allowed him to mount. He knew pursuit would not be far behind. He rode hard, fording the backwaters and following twisting paths until he was sure he was alone.

The horse was breathing hard, her wet flanks steaming in the heat. He slipped out of the saddle to give her some respite, and walked a while, leading her by the bridle. He thought furiously.

He could not go back to the Rani. With her army routed and the fortress relieved by the East India Company, her stratagem had failed. She would have to sue for peace, and the Company would be in no mood for leniency. They might even demand she hand over Christopher, for exemplary punishment. The thought of being taken back to Bombay in chains, of being thrown down before his father and having to beg for his life, made him shake with rage and fear.

Walking had brought him to a crossroads. A few shabby huts stood among the trees, though the villagers had heard his horse and made themselves invisible. They knew nothing good happened when powerful men came to their village. Christopher ducked into the huts and took the food he found: a few balls of rice, and some dried fish. He didn't bother looking for money. The villagers lived little better than animals. He could feel their eyes on him, watching from the undergrowth, but he was unconcerned. The Neptune sword would deter them from mischief.

He pulled it from its scabbard, thrilling to the balance of the weapon. He turned it in his hand, so that the gold inlay on the blade caught the sunlight coming through the trees. The sapphire in the pommel glowed like a single, blue eye looking into his soul. He had lost nearly everything – but so long as he had this, he felt invincible.

He stood there for a time, pondering what he should do. A fragment of that last conversation with Tamaana came into his head.

Where could we go, if we were free? If we wanted to be together, somewhere nobody knew our past?

Tiracola, she had answered. *A land without laws or constraint. A place you and I could be truly free.*

Perhaps one day we will find ourselves there, he had said.

He remounted the horse, and turned her head north.

* * *

Tom found Tungar's body lying on the blood-soaked sand. His right hand had been cut off, but he saw no mortal wound. Tom approached carefully, wondering if he might yet be alive.

A fly crawled out of Tungar's mouth, along his lolling tongue, and Tom saw he had nothing to fear. He found the severed hand a few paces away, where the ground was thick with hoof marks. But of the sword it had carried, he saw no sign.

The last of the Rani's troops had reached the edge of the beach and were disappearing into the jungle. One caught his eye – a tall, bald-headed man who seemed familiar. At that distance, shaded by the palm trees, Tom could not see the sword in his hand.

Disappointment seized him – only for a moment. One of the soldiers must have looted a sword from the battlefield, but Tom did not give up hope. Such a prize could not be kept hidden. Men would talk, and when they did he would make sure he heard of it. If the Rani tried to withhold it, he would burn her palace to the ground.

'Put down your weapon!'

Tom turned, and saw two dozen muskets all trained on him. The marines had come ashore. They stood formed up in a line, the sun behind them, their stockings still wet from the surf.

Tom raised his weary arms. 'Peace,' he called. 'I am a friend.'

His voice was little more than a croak – but the marines recognized the words. Their sergeant ordered them to lower their weapons.

'My apologies,' said a new voice. A blue-coated man wearing the uniform of a captain in the East India Company strode out from among the marines. 'When word of your plight reached Madras, we feared we would find no Englishmen left alive.' He halted. 'Good God. Can it be . . . ?'

Tom shaded his eyes against the sun. After everything he had endured, he needed a moment to place the captain's face:

the weatherbeaten cheeks and stern blue eyes, the russet hair streaked with grey.

'Captain Inchbird?'

'We meet again, and this time I am able to repay the debt I owe you.' Inchbird eyed him keenly. 'How the deuce did you come to be here?'

'A long story.'

'I cannot conceive of what you have suffered.' Inchbird gestured to the fort. 'To have held out so long, against such odds. Your name will be the toast of Leadenhall Street.'

'I do not need their gratitude. I did it to save myself and family. If it were not for the Company's high-handed avarice, the Rani would never have been provoked to war.'

'Nonetheless,' said Inchbird wryly, 'there is nothing the merchants in London love quite so much as a hero. Especially one who saves their dignity and their profits.'

'All that matters is my wife and Agnes – Mrs Hicks. Were they well, when you left them?'

Inchbird's face clouded. 'I do not take your meaning.'

'You sailed from Madras, yes?'

Inchbird nodded.

'Then surely you saw them. How else did you have intelligence of our plight here?'

'No survivors reached Madras. We had our news from Tamil traders coming overland.'

'But Sarah and Agnes sailed months ago,' cried Tom. 'They must have arrived by now.'

'It is possible they arrived after we sailed.' Inchbird saw Tom's stricken face and softened his tone. 'The seas have not been easy, this monsoon season. Very likely, they put in to some safe harbour to wait for kinder weather.'

But Tom heard his reassurances for what they were: empty words, without real hope. Despair gripped him; he almost wept. What use was surviving the siege if he could not find Sarah?

Terrible fears for what might have befallen her crowded his mind, each more dreadful than the last.

Yet against the darkness, one glimmer of hope held out. If Sarah had died, he would surely have felt it in his heart. She had to be alive.

'I must find them.' Tom looked into Inchbird's eyes and saw his sympathy. 'You spoke of the Company's gratitude to me. If that means anything at all, take us to Madras.'

Tom, Francis and Ana anchored in the Madras roadstead three weeks after leaving Brinjoan. It reminded Tom of pictures he'd seen in books of medieval cities. Hard stone walls the colour of rusty iron ringed the town, engineered with many batteries and half-moon bastions for protection. A great variety of fine buildings rose within the walls, while to north and south stretched the low, ramshackle towns where the native merchants who had flocked to the Company's trade lived.

The anchor had barely touched bottom when a great flotilla of small boats and catamarans rushed out from the shore, offering coconuts, rum, fruit and fish. Some of the women who thrust them up to the waiting sailors were almost naked; Tom guessed *they* were for sale too.

'They have marked you as *orombarros*,' said Inchbird. 'Men who are strangers to the town. They will expect to make a good penny from you.'

'Then they will be disappointed, for I do not have a penny to my name,' said Tom. 'When will you send the cargo ashore?'

'We will wait until the morrow to unload,' said Inchbird. 'I must secure the ship and procure refreshment for the men. But the Governor will expect me to send my packet ashore forthwith. I should be obliged if you would deliver it for me.'

Tom understood what he was doing, and was grateful. He clambered into one of the small boats with Francis and Ana.

277

The planks, tied together with ropes rather than nails, shifted and squirmed under their weight; water oozed through.

'Will we even make it ashore?' Francis wondered. 'This boat seems designed to tip us into the sea.'

'They know what they are doing,' Tom countered. 'Unlike our longboats, these craft are made to flex in the surf. You may get wet, but they will not overturn.'

And so it was. The boat brought them damp but safe to the jetty by the Sea Gate. They had no difficulty gaining admittance with the ship's papers to deliver. Directly inside the gate, they stepped straight into a market. The sandy street was thronged with traders, standing around and shouting bids at each other, while bills posted on the wall advertised when the next ships were due. Some of the merchants broke away when they saw Ana and embraced her warmly. Tom was pleased to see the affection they had for her. Francis stood back, frowning.

Ana spoke to them rapidly in their own language. Her face was grave. 'They have had no news of Sarah or Agnes. But they say a ship brought a man from Brinjoan last week – an Englishman. He is at the citadel.'

'Then I will go there,' said Tom 'You and Francis see what else you may discover on the docks.'

In the centre of the walled town, the citadel was like a larger model of the fort at Brinjoan – though twice the size, and with an imposing three-storey house in its centre. Tom felt a pang of memory as he passed under the archway, an echo of those last desperate moments in the fort when he had feared all was lost.

Inchbird's correspondence got him as far as a waiting room. He handed the packet to a servant, and waited as he disappeared into the large first-floor office.

The minutes passed. The grandfather clock in the hall struck the hour. Tom stared at the door with furious concentration, willing it to open. He gripped the arms of his chair to keep from launching himself at the door.

When he thought he could not wait one more second, the door opened. The footman beckoned him through, into an airy room with high windows. The walls were decorated with antique weapons, fixed in patterns: a rosette of muskets, a fan of swords, and crossed pikes. It reminded Tom of the weapons in the library at High Weald, which he had not seen in so many years.

A man strode to meet him, arm outstretched. 'William Fraser,' he introduced himself. 'I am the Governor of Fort St George. You are Thomas Weald?'

Tom nodded. Fraser clasped his hand firmly. 'Then I and the whole Company owe you a great debt of gratitude. Captain Inchbird's report leaves no doubt that but for your gallant intervention, the fort would have been lost and all her garrison enslaved or slaughtered. The damage to the Company's prestige, to say nothing of her commerce, would have been incalculable, if the blacks got it in their heads they could bloody our noses with impunity.'

Tom went uncharacteristically quiet. He had not expected to become the East India Company's champion: the irony was not lost on him. Nor the danger. In these comfortable surroundings, after months of suffering, feted as a hero, it would be too easy to drop his guard. If anyone recognized him, or if Guy got to hear of it . . .

'I am sorry more of your men did not survive,' he muttered. 'Mr Foy did not leave many to save.'

'He has paid the price for his recklessness.'

'So did a great many others. And they had no choice in the matter.' Tom felt all the frustrations of the past months boiling up inside him. He wanted to tear down the heavy curtains, smash the pictures on the wall and sweep all the paperwork off Fraser's desk.

He forced himself to keep his temper.

'Before we were besieged, one of the factors escaped in a

boat with the women from the settlement. Foy's wife, Captain Hicks' wife and my own. They were making for Madras.'

Fraser's face grew solemn. 'Until last week, I would have counselled you to fear the worst, for I had heard no intelligence of them. Now I can tell you more, though whether you think it better news I cannot say.'

Tom's ribs seemed to crush against his heart. He gripped the rim on Fraser's desk, knuckles white. 'What is it?'

'Sit.' Fraser gestured him to a chair. 'You may hear it from the horse's mouth, as it were.'

He rang a bell. Tom slumped into a high-backed chair. He heard the door open, tentative footsteps approaching.

'Mr Kyffen,' the footman announced. He closed the door.

Kyffen was halfway into the room before he glimpsed Tom in the chair. He recoiled; his head jerked around as he darted a furtive look at the exit.

'Mr Weald,' he exclaimed, with no warmth at all, when he saw he could not escape. 'Thank God, sir, that you have survived. I dared not hope I would live to see you again.'

The last time Tom had seen him, they had been running for their lives from the Rani's palace. The intervening months had been kind to neither of them, but Kyffen had come off worse. His nose was heavily scabbed where the sun had burned it raw. His eyes seemed to bulge from their shrunken sockets, and his fingers trembled.

There were many things Tom could ask him, but only one he cared about. 'Where is my wife?'

Kyffen shuddered. He sank into a chair, angling it so he would not have to look Tom in the eye.

'I fear, sir, you will not like what I have to tell you.'

The boat barely moved on the flat sea. Eight men and three women sprawled in her heavy-laden hull. The men were stripped to the waist; the women's dresses were torn to the very limits of modesty. Four oars dipped and pulled with little conviction on the glassy water. Soon they would stop, for they had long since learned there was little point trying to row through the heat of the day.

The sun shone from a cloudless sky. The monsoon had been feeble that year. The storms that heralded it had come on schedule, but not the rain that usually followed. Inland, peasants would be scratching the dry earth, and praying they would survive to the next season. In the boat, they did not know if they would see the next week.

Since the age of ten, Agnes had lived her whole life in India. The soft hills and gentle rain of her native Yorkshire were memories so distant they might have been dreams. She had survived more than twenty years – twenty feverish monsoons, twenty parched summers where the heat seemed to set her bones on fire. She had borne five children, and buried each one before the age of three. She had known hardship.

But nothing in her life compared to this. She had spent three weeks crammed with ten other people in a thirty-foot boat, so heavy laden the gunwales barely broke the water. There was no shelter, and no privacy. After the first monsoon storms had passed, Leigh – the *Kestrel*'s boatswain – had rigged a piece of canvas as a modesty screen at the stern, and another as an awning. But another storm had blown up out of nowhere and torn them away, together with the mast and the sail. After that, they had had no choice but to put in long days on the oars. Agnes took her turn, when she was not nursing Sarah, until her hands were as calloused as any tar's.

'I should help row,' Sarah protested that morning. Her fever had passed and she could sit up, though she was still very frail.

'Nonsense,' said Agnes. 'In your condition, you would not be able to lift the oar.'

'But it would show the men I value what they do. Everyone else takes his turn.'

'Not everyone,' said Agnes. She shot a dark look at Lydia Foy, who sat in the bow of the boat with the Company's strongboxes. Kyffen sat beside her, affecting an air of command. Even by the cramped standards of the boat, they were inseparable, squeezed together under the parasol which Lydia refused to share.

'The men know how much you care for them,' Agnes told Sarah. 'All they want is to bring you to safe harbour.'

Sarah smiled weakly. 'Then I suppose—'

She broke off with a cough that became a retching. She just got her head over the side before the small portion of rice and salt pork she had eaten for breakfast came up and was vomited over the side.

Agnes sighed, and held her sister until she had finished. This happened every morning.

'We should not waste food on her if she cannot hold it down,' said Lydia Foy tartly. 'Not when the rest of us are starving.'

'Sarah gets her share like all the rest,' Agnes insisted. Of all the people in the boat, Lydia seemed to have suffered least from the meagre rations they shared. Her complexion was healthy, and her breasts filled her bodice as amply as ever. Agnes suspected Kyffen had been slipping her extra morsels – and perhaps more. Some nights, she had heard strange noises coming from the bow of the boat.

'I do not wish to be a burden,' said Sarah. She lay back, her stomach still heaving with its exertions. Agnes sat beside her, positioning herself so that she shaded Sarah's face. She tipped a cup of water to her sister's lips. It was a fine, porcelain cup painted with willow leaves, the most incongruous vessel to have in their circumstances. Agnes had been shocked when she discovered that Mrs Foy had managed to stow her entire dinner service in the boat.

'Careful,' said Lydia. 'Unless it rains again, we will run short before long.'

It was one of the many cruel ironies of their predicament. When the rain came, it fell so hard it almost filled the boat. All hands had to abandon their oars and bail furiously to keep from being swamped, literally throwing water away. But they had no casks to store it in, so when the rain ceased and the sun came out, they were soon parched with thirst.

Agnes stared at the nearby coast, the dense forests broken by golden beaches. After the storms, they had kept close to land for fear of drowning.

'We should go ashore,' she said. 'We might find water – or a village. Perhaps we could get food from the natives.'

'Food?' said Lydia, with a withering look. 'Why should they help us? More like they would cut our throats and steal all our possessions.'

'We have gold enough. We could buy it from them.'

'You are touched by the sun. I would not give these natives one *fanam* of my gold.'

'It is the Company's gold,' Agnes pointed out.

'It was my husband's,' Lydia insisted.

'And it will do you no good if you are dead.' In all her years in India, Agnes had learned to play the dutiful wife. To ignore Guy's snubs, and the slurs from her sister Caroline that only became more barbed as Caroline grew older, fatter and unhappier. To bite her tongue, for the sake of her husband's career.

Now she could feel those old restraints falling away. If it was the loss of her husband, or the heat of the sun, or merely the extremity of her situation: she did not care. The anger rose inside her and she did not try to check it.

'My sister needs sleep and a place to lie,' she said hotly. 'All the men want food, shelter and rest. I will not let you sit smug on that chest of gold and deny them what they need to survive.'

The men on the oars paused their rowing and looked up. Lydia glared down the length of the boat. 'You forget yourself, Mrs Hicks.'

Agnes turned to Leigh, sitting in the stern at the tiller. 'Alter course to larboard, if you please. We are going ashore.'

'To be robbed and enslaved by natives?' Lydia tugged at Kyffen, who had fixed his gaze elsewhere to keep out of the argument. 'Mr Kyffen! You are in command here.'

Kyffen looked uncertainly between the two women. 'Mrs Foy is correct,' he mumbled. 'Hold your course. We cannot risk going ashore.'

'Beggin' yer pardon, ma'am, but wearing the Company's blue coat don't make you a captain,' said Leigh. He put the tiller over. The men on the oars started to row.

Lydia blazed with fury. 'This is mutiny. When we reach Madras, I will inform the Governor of this and he will have you strung from the nearest gibbet.'

Leigh stared her down. 'I'll take me chances. If we make Madras.'

'Mr Kyffen,' screeched Lydia. 'Will you permit this insolence?'

'I am sure he will not,' said Agnes coldly. 'Seeing as you have been so free with your favours, you have him by his privies.'

Agnes heard the words come out of her mouth and hardly believed she'd dared say them. Lydia's face went white with anger. She looked at Kyffen, but he simply gaped at Agnes in astonishment.

With a squeal, Lydia reached under her skirt. Her hands emerged clutching a small, ivory-handled pistol. She trained it on Agnes.

'Mr Leigh, return to your previous course, if you please,' she ordered. The pistol did not waver.

No one moved. Leigh looked beseechingly at Agnes. The men on the oars stared between the two women. The only sound was the soft slap of waves against the hull, and water dripping from the raised oars.

'*Sail.*'

Sarah's voice shattered the false calm. Unnoticed by all, she

284

had sat up, and now pointed out to sea, her mouth open in wonder. Her voice was so hoarse it barely registered, but it cut through the tense silence that gripped the boat.

In an instant, the quarrel was forgotten. They all turned where she pointed, shading their eyes as they took in the white sails that broke the horizon.

'Thank the Lord, we are saved,' cried Kyffen, mopping his brow. Beside him, Lydia Foy cast a keen eye at the approaching ship.

'Is she English?'

'A *grab*, by the looks of her,' said Leigh.

A *grab* was an Indian style of ship, named from the Arabic word for raven. Like the birds, they could fly in the lightest of winds, with two square-rigged masts that made them formidable sailors. The most distinctive feature was the prow, which was cut away to leave a low, flat foredeck, affording her bow chasers an unimpeded field of fire.

'Could she be a country trader?' said Agnes. The 'country trade' was how the English termed the internal commerce of the Indian ocean.

'Not many merchants would risk their cargos at this time of year,' said Leigh doubtfully.

Their euphoria subsided. They stared anxiously as the ship closed with them – suspended between hope of salvation, and the excruciating fear of a yet worse fate.

'She's raising a flag.'

A red pennant ran up to her main topmast. A gust of wind caught it, stretching it out so they could see the serpent design rippling on the crimson cloth.

Agnes had never seen the flag before, but she knew its fearsome reputation. Many nights in Brinjoan at the Company table, talk had turned to the pirate Angria, the scourge of the Malabar coast. Every trader and sailor had a story of a shipmate killed in battle, or captured and made to suffer unspeakable torments in his dungeons.

'Make for shore,' cried Kyffen. 'Flight is our only hope.'

The men bent to the oars. But they were few, and weak. The *grab* bore down on them, gliding effortlessly across the flat sea.

'They've got the Devil himself blowing them along,' gasped one of the men.

'Quiet,' ordered Leigh. 'Don't waste your breath.'

'If we get closer to shore, perhaps she will not be able to follow us without ripping out her keel,' said Kyffen hopefully.

Agnes shook her head. 'I have seen ships like this moored at Brinjoan. They are built with a shallow draft.'

A flame flashed from the *grab*'s bow. A second later, they heard the flat boom of a cannon. The ball skimmed across the water and splashed down about thirty yards off their beam.

'Those savages cannot even aim aright,' said Lydia Foy. She still held the ivory-handled pistol.

'That was a warning shot,' said Leigh. 'The next will be closer.'

As if the pirates had heard him, the *grab* fired again. This time, the ball landed so close that they felt the touch of its spray.

'We are overloaded,' said Leigh urgently. 'One hit and we will all go under. Can you swim, Mrs Hicks?'

'A little. But we would never get Sarah ashore.'

They stared at the onrushing ship. She was so close, Agnes could see the sun gleaming on the muzzles of her guns, and the crew massed in her bow. They jabbed their weapons in the air, uttering shrill battle-cries that spoke of terror and torment.

'What shall we do?'

Slumped in the chair in the Governor's house, Kyffen stared at his lap. The tropical sunset pouring through the high windows cast him in an almost crimson light.

'Naturally, I resisted the pirates as best I could. But we were famished, and wasted by so many days at sea. The pirates soon overpowered us. They took the women hostage, and set me

286

adrift in a small boat. They averred, in their savage way, that they wished me to deliver a message to Madras. A ransom demand for the prisoners. And that is how, after much drifting and facing death more than once, I came here.'

While he told his tale, Tom had risen from his chair, pacing the room. He paused now, leaning on the windowsill and staring out at the sun setting over the lagoon that lay to the west of the town.

'How much?' he asked.

Kyffen shifted uneasily in his seat. 'I beg your pardon?'

'How much is the ransom they demanded?'

'It . . .' Kyffen's jaw flapped like a fish. 'Five thousand rupees.'

'And how is it to be paid? Where are they holding the women?'

Kyffen twisted his fingers together until Tom thought they might snap. 'I do not recall. The situation . . . Everything was so terrible, you understand. I barely escaped with my life.'

'Angria's lair is the fortress at Tiracola, south of Bombay,' put in the Governor. 'He will almost certainly have taken them there.'

Tom ignored him. He turned from the window and advanced on Kyffen, until he completely overshadowed him. The little man cringed into the chair.

'You're lying.'

Without warning, Tom grabbed him by his coat lapels and jerked him to his feet. He spun him around, carried him kicking across the floor like a recalcitrant child, and slammed him into the wall. Fraser started to protest, but the strength of Tom's fury held him back.

'Tell me the truth,' Tom demanded.

Kyffen had sunk so far down inside his shirt he was almost buried in it. He babbled, flailing his arms and legs. 'Let me go,' he squealed.

Tom let him go. He dropped to the floor with a thump and a cry.

'You are a coward and a wretch,' Tom told him. 'If you had obeyed my orders, and not simply thought of saving your own skin, we might all have escaped in the boat. A good many men who are now dead would be alive, and I would have my *wife*.'

Rage overtook him; the final word came accompanied by a kick in the ribs that had Kyffen squealing anew.

'Mr Weald,' said Fraser, appalled. 'I will call my guards.'

Tom stepped back, breathing hard. He stared at the wall, for he knew if he looked at Kyffen again he would do him more violence.

'The pirates did not let you go, and they did not give you a message. *Did they?*' He raised his fist; Kyffen whimpered and cowered into the skirting board.

'Mr Weald,' Fraser cautioned.

'I was fighting pirates in these oceans when you were fighting toy soldiers. To them, every prisoner is merchandise. They would no more let one go than they would a sack of gold. So I ask you again: *what happened?*'

Kyffen sat up. Blood dribbled from his nose. He gave Fraser an imploring look.

'Will you allow him to treat me this way? Call your guards – lock him in prison. He is a villain and a lunatic.'

'Answer his question,' said Fraser.

Kyffen stared between the Governor and Tom. Defeat dawned on his face as he realized he had no friend in that room.

'I did not fight the pirates,' he whispered.

'And they never captured you?' pressed Tom.

'I jumped overboard,' Kyffen said miserably. 'We were close enough to land, I was able to swim. The pirates were too busy securing their prize to concern themselves with me.'

'You abandoned the women?' said the Governor.

'Yes.' Kyffen hung his head. 'What could I have done against a hundred pirates? I thought I might find help, raise the alarm.'

'You thought no such thing,' said Tom, struggling to control his anger. 'You thought only to save yourself.'

Kyffen did not deny it. 'I found a village and threw myself upon their kindness. When the pirates had gone, fishermen brought me down the coast – village to village, week by week, until I came here. And you must believe me,' he added piously, 'that not a single day has passed since then that I did not pray God to spare those poor women. If I could have exchanged my situation for theirs, I would gladly have done so.'

Tom cut him short with a fierce glare. He stared at the man snivelling on the floor, remembering how his own father Hal had dealt with one of the Company's servants who had betrayed the family to pirates. He had forced a confession from him at the point of his sword, then hung him naked from his own window.

But even if Fraser would have permitted it, Tom did not have the heart to make Kyffen suffer more. Kyffen was a coward, no worse. He had not asked for the responsibility that had been thrust upon him. Blood and snot had crusted on his upper lip, like a bawling child who had been pushed over by bigger boys.

'Get out of my sight,' he hissed.

Kyffen crawled away, trembling in fear of another blow, and fled through the door. Tom turned to Fraser.

'How can I get Sarah and Agnes back?'

Fraser looked uneasy. 'If Angria has them, he will have sent his ransom demands to Bombay.'

'And what will happen then?'

'Governor Courtney does not believe in treating with pirates. He says it merely serves to encourage them.'

'Then what? Will he attack the fortress?'

Fraser hesitated. 'Angria is the most powerful pirate on the Malabar coast, and Guy Courtney's forces are limited.'

'Do you mean to say he will let them rot? One of the women is Agnes Hicks, Guy Courtney's sister-in-law.'

'I cannot speak for him.' Fraser saw the anguish in Tom's face. 'But I will give you passage on a ship to Bombay. You may plead the case with Governor Courtney yourself. If he will not put up the ransom, there may be merchants there or at Surat who will advance you the money.'

'Against what?' said Tom bleakly. 'I have no collateral and no prospects. I risked my life saving your Company's precious property, and what is my reward? To have my wife left to rot in some pirate's dungeon?'

Fraser spread his hands. 'I wish I could do more. As you know yourself, these pirates are men of business, and hostages are their stock in trade. Find the ransom Angria asks for, and he will treat fairly with you.'

'And if I can not?'

'Then he will cut his losses, and make an example of his prisoners to those who would not pay.'

They had to wait a week in Madras. Every day Ana took Tom and Francis down to the markets to talk with merchants she knew. All offered sympathy, but none had money to lend.

'It is the wrong time,' said Ana. 'Until this year's ships arrive from England, all their capital is tied up in their merchandise.'

They sailed at last, slow weeks beating around Cape Cormorin and up the Malabar coast to the rhythm of the winds. In the mornings, the air came off the land, pushing them out to sea; in the afternoons a sea breeze would get up and drive them back inshore.

They passed Brinjoan, a speck on the horizon. From the seaward side, it showed no sign of the devastation it had suffered. Tom was glad to see the back of it. Further north, Ana pointed out Kidd's island, where the notorious pirate captain had once paused to refit his ships.

'I wonder if he buried any treasure there,' Francis wondered. 'We could certainly use it.'

The palm-fringed beaches gave way to a more jagged, rockier coastline. Thickly wooded promontories shot out one after another all the way to the horizon, split by hidden coves and river estuaries. Stone castles guarded many of them, and often Tom glimpsed boats in the secluded anchorages at their feet.

'This is a contested country,' Ana explained. 'Some thirty years ago, the Maratha people rebelled against the Mughal emperor and carved out their own kingdom. But now they are locked in a civil war among themselves: the dowager queen has rebelled against her step-son. Angria flourishes in the chaos, playing one side against the other.'

As the ship slipped past a headland, a new promontory came into sight at the end of the next bay. White waves foamed around its base, while high above gulls circled around a black-stone fortress that covered the entire summit.

'There,' said Ana. 'That is Tiracola, Angria's stronghold.'

Tom seized a telescope. He stared at the slit windows, in the vain hope Sarah might be looking out. His soul ached; he could hardly bear the anguish of being so close, and so impossibly far. On the other side of those unforgiving walls, Sarah and Agnes would be lying in God knew what condition, waiting for him to rescue them. In a wild moment, he thought of diving overboard, hauling himself up the rocks and climbing the sheer cliff into the castle.

'It looks impregnable,' said Francis in a small voice.

The vessel's master had joined them. 'Those walls are eighteen-foot thick. The last governor but one, Sir Nicholas Waite, had a mind to bring Angria to heel. He gathered a fleet of bomb vessels and brought them down here. The walls are too high to bring regular cannon to bear from the ships, so he fitted them out with coehorn mortars to lob exploding shells inside. It did him no good. The shells just cracked like eggs on the rocks, spilled their powder and lost their fuses.'

Tom scanned the fortress and its surroundings. High towers guarded every corner. The walls' lower reaches had been carved from solid rock, while the masonry above fitted as neat and tight as anything he'd seen in Europe. He saw few guns, but that hardly mattered. The position was unassailable.

Past the promontory, the coast receded into a deep cove at the mouth of a river. Tom counted a dozen ships, including several of the larger *grab*s that were nearly the size of frigates. They sat behind a long boom made of tree trunks chained together.

'Make more sail,' the master ordered, anxious at being so close to the pirate's lair. But the boom stayed down, and none of the ships ventured forth. Today, evidently, Angria had other business to distract him.

Tom watched the fort recede behind them. 'I will come back for you,' he promised. The wind whipped his words away.

Deep in the bowels of the castle, Sarah Courtney stirred. She sat up, feeling the iron fetters bite her wrists, and stared out into the gloom. Water dripped like a ticking clock; some of the other prisoners moaned or wept. She ignored them all, listening through the rock. Hoping, against all reason, it had not been a dream.

A tremor went through her body, like the flicker of a candle in the gust of a passing servant.

'What is it?' said Agnes, alert to any change in her sister's condition. The vomiting had passed; Sarah had no trouble keeping down the meagre rations their captors allowed them. In fact, she had put on weight. But now Agnes had other concerns. 'Is it the fever again?'

Sarah shook her head. 'I thought I heard Tom's voice. I dreamed he had come to rescue us, that he stood in that doorway with the Neptune sword in his hand, and cut through our chains.' She sighed, resting her hand on her stomach. 'It must have been a dream. Even the sword is lost, after all.'

She had no concept of the time they had spent in the dungeon, though by now it must be weeks. No daylight penetrated this far down, not even a crack by which they might count the days. They were in a cave, a network of caverns so deep in the promontory Sarah sometimes fancied she could hear the waves beating outside. The dank walls were hewn from raw stone that ran with water whenever it rained. The only light came from a single lamp in the adjoining cave. When the oil ran out, it sometimes took days for the guards to replenish it.

'He will come,' said Agnes. 'If he were snatched up by the winds and driven to the far side of the world, and though all the hosts of the Great Mughal himself stood between you, still he would come for you.'

'What if he is dead? We do not even know if he escaped the massacre at Chittattinkara.'

Agnes placed her hand over Sarah's heart. 'If he had died, you would know it here.' Even in the few days she had lived with Tom and Sarah at Brinjoan, she had seen how profoundly they loved each other. She knew Tom would not abandon them.

From the opposite corner of the cave, she heard a derisive hiss of breath.

'Do not rely on your husband. If he is alive, most like he has already forgotten he was married.'

'I have faith in him.'

'I had faith in Mr Kyffen,' Lydia retorted, 'until the coward hurled himself overboard. Who would have thought a gentleman would abandon three ladies, and all their worldly possessions, to those pirates?'

'Tom is different,' said Sarah softly. Though she thought of

Tom constantly, she tried not to speak of him too often. It would be cruel to dwell overmuch on her husband, when Agnes had not even had a chance to grieve the loss of Captain Hicks.

'If we are to be saved, it can only come from Guy Courtney,' said Lydia. 'Though I cannot comprehend the delay.' She pointed to Agnes. 'You are Guy's sister-in-law. Why has he not ransomed us already?'

'If you rely on Guy's love for me to save us, you will be disappointed,' said Agnes. 'I committed the worst crime in his book: I passed up an opportunity to advance his career. He wanted me betrothed to some high eminence in the East India Company. Instead, I married Captain Hicks, a humble soldier. He has never forgiven me. That is why he exiled us to Brinjoan.'

She sank back against the cold wall. This was not a new conversation: they had debated it every day since the pirates seized them. But this time, Lydia did not let it pass. She sat up straight, wriggling her wrists in the manacles, and fixed Agnes and Sarah with a sly look.

'Why do you pretend that you are not sisters?'

Lydia laughed at the shock on their faces. 'Did you think you had hidden it from me? I have discerning eyes. I watch and I listen. Even before we left Brinjoan, I had my suspicions. In our current confinement, you could hardly hope to conceal it. Your care for each other; the words you whisper when you think I am asleep. I know your secret – and the other matter you do not discuss.'

She raised her head, so her sharp chin jutted towards them. 'Can you deny it?'

Though it hardly mattered, Agnes felt a stab of betrayal. In their prison, all they owned were their secrets. Now she had lost even that. And she did not trust Lydia.

'It is true,' said Sarah flatly. 'Agnes and I are sisters. I had not seen her for near twenty years before we landed, unlooked for, in Brinjoan.'

294

'So you must also be a sister of Caroline Courtney, the Governor's wife.'

Sarah nodded.

Lydia raised her manacled arms. 'Then tell our captors who you really are. If Guy Courtney knew they held both his wife's sisters – to say nothing of the widow of his loyal friend Mr Foy – he would pay whatever ransom they demand.'

'You are mistaken,' said Sarah. 'If Guy knew my real identity, he would pay Angria to keep us here the rest of our lives. Or if he did ransom me, it would only be to inflict worse punishment than ever Angria would visit on me.'

Lydia leaned in, like a bloodhound catching the scent. 'Why?'

Too late, Sarah realized she had said too much. Fatigue and despair had lowered her defences. 'It does not signify.'

'If it is the reason I am left rotting in this dungeon, it signifies everything.' Lydia crawled forward. 'What does Guy hold against you?'

'Nothing.'

'Did he love you?'

Sarah shuddered. 'Never.'

Lydia considered this. 'He did not forgive Agnes for marrying beneath her station. Perhaps you committed the same offence?'

Sarah did not trust herself to speak.

'But that would not explain the hatred,' Lydia mused. 'There must be more. Your husband, perhaps. Some enmity between your husband and Governor Courtney?'

Her nose twitched. 'But what would provoke him so? An interloper? A rival?'

'He was an interloper,' said Agnes. 'You know how Guy despises the men who steal the India trade from him. That is the reason.'

But she had spoken too hastily. Lydia heard the lie. 'No. I do not think that can be it.' A triumphant smile parted her lips. 'When we were loading the boat at Brinjoan, I heard one of the men call you "Mrs Courtney". Now why should they do that? And the boy who travelled with you – Guy's nephew, Francis Courtney. A remarkable coincidence, is it not?'

'You misheard,' said Sarah.

'I fear I did not. And if you are Mrs Courtney, then your husband must be . . .' She thought a moment. 'Tom Courtney.'

She saw the stricken looks on their faces, and laughed. 'You are Mrs Tom Courtney – not only Guy's wife's sister, but also his brother's wife. Now I begin to understand. I have heard of Tom Courtney, during my days in Bombay. It was said he and Guy had become such enemies that they tried to kill each other. I heard Guy once threw a man from the roof of the Governor's house merely for mentioning his name.'

'I do not pay attention to gossip,' said Agnes.

But Lydia had not finished. 'There was another story I recollect now. A veritable scandal. I had it from a friend, who had it from Caroline Courtney's maid that came with her from England. According to the serving girl, Caroline was no maiden when she married Guy – in fact, she was already ripe with child.'

Lydia's face loomed out of the gloom. The privations of the past weeks had only sharpened the lines of her angular face, giving her a terrifying appearance.

'They said the child – young Christopher Courtney – was not Guy's at all. They said Caroline had been rather free with her charms on the voyage from England, and that though it was Guy who drank the nuptial wine, he was not the first to pop the cork. His brother Tom, they said, had that pleasure.'

Even in the darkness, her eyes shone with triumph. 'That is why Guy hates you. Though I wonder,' she added spitefully to Sarah, 'that you are so loyal to your husband, after he made so free with your sister. I am sure I would not content myself with being any man's *desserts*.'

'Please,' begged Agnes. 'Now you understand why Guy cannot know who Sarah is. You must not reveal this to anyone.'

Lydia sank back into her corner, her cheeks flushed dark with the thrill of the hunt.

'You may rely on me,' she said. 'Your secret is safe. And the other matter, of which you do not speak.'

'What do you mean?' said Sarah dully.

'You are with child. You never say it, but it is as plain as the bulge in your belly. The way you could not keep your meals down in the boat, and now how you grow fat even on the thin fare the pirates allow us. And there are other signs, which any woman would notice.'

Sarah clenched her fists.

'Why do you not tell the pirates?' Lydia asked.

'Tom and I have wanted a baby these last fifteen years,' said Sarah sadly. 'In all that time, only once did I conceive, and that child I lost. That it should happen now, in these surroundings . . .' She trailed off.

'If the pirates knew, they would surely find some way to exploit her vulnerability,' said Agnes. 'That is why we do not talk of it, and why I implore you, Mrs Foy, to say nothing to the pirates.'

'As you wish,' said Lydia. She curled into a ball and smiled to herself, though in the dim light the others could not see it. 'Besides, whom could I ever have to tell?'

Far above them, through many levels of rocks and into the parts of the castle built of stone, the pirate Angria sat in his hall. He had a slight, lithe build, but no man who saw him could mistake the intensity that glowed in his eyes. A knotted turban covered his head, and a long moustache turned across his cheeks and almost joined his sideburns.

He had not been born a seafarer. His father had been a *deshmuk*, a minor lord charged with the care of a hundred villages. His business had been passing judgement on farmers' disputes, and protecting villagers from the depredations of brigands. But Angria was not made for the stiff rituals and proscriptions of rural life. The peasants grovelled to his father, his father grovelled to his overlord, and all that ever mattered was the next rice harvest. There was no glory. The first time Angria had seen a ship, a Portuguese merchant scudding across the bay in full sail, he had known that was his destiny. To fly free, unencumbered by laws and custom, unanswerable to anything but the wind and the sea – that was his dream. Twenty-five years later, he had achieved it with infamy.

The hall was testament to his success. Trophies from the ships he had taken lined the walls – Dutch, English and Portuguese ensigns, ships' bells and lanterns, and even the carved figurehead of a bare-breasted mermaid. Thickly woven rugs covered the floor, sometimes piled three deep. His men lay sprawled out on them. Usually, they would be playing at dice, drinking arak or smoking the hookah pipes they imported from Arabia. Now, though, all were quiet, their attention fixed on the man who stood before Angria.

He had arrived that afternoon, riding up to the castle on a horse that had once been a fine mount, but was now lamed by weeks of hard riding. He had a long, dark beard, though the hair on his head had been burned off, leaving him bald. Even when he dismounted his horse, tossing the reins to a stable boy, he towered over the other men in the castle. He had demanded to speak to Angria. The guards admitted him, for who could deny a man with such a fabulous sword about his waist?

Now Angria studied him from the dais where he sat. Beneath the beard, and the fresh scars that shone pink on his skin, the visitor was still almost a boy, not yet twenty but already battle-hardened. A warrior, no question. Perhaps the way Angria had looked at that age, before he learned to appreciate the merits of subtlety, as well as strength.

'What is your name?' the pirate asked.

'Raudra,' said the visitor. Raudra was an avatar of the god Shiva. Looking at the youth, the wildness in his eyes, Angria could imagine him as an incarnation of that god, the destroyer of worlds.

'Why have you come here?'

'To serve you.'

'What do you offer?'

'I have studied the ways of the hat-wearers,' said Christopher. 'I have sailed their ships, and I can train your men to fight as they do – with discipline and precision.'

Angria shook his head. 'I have fought the hat-wearers more seasons than you have lived. I do not want my men to fight as they do. I need men who fight in our own fashion, with spirit and bravery. You cannot teach a tiger to spit like a cobra.'

'I have trained in the *kalari*. I can fight like a tiger, or like a cobra.' Christopher drew his sword. 'I will take on any man in this hall to prove it.'

At that, half Angria's men were on their feet, clamouring for the chance to put the rascal in his place. A few, though, stayed seated: older, wiser heads that had taken the measure of the new arrival, and saw plenty in him to give them pause.

Angria stood and quieted his men. He stepped down from the dais and approached Christopher, circling him like a buyer at a country fair.

'That is a fine sword,' he said. The lamps in the hall shone on the sapphire. 'You must be a brave man, to bring such a weapon into a house full of strangers.'

'I trust to your honour,' said Christopher.

Angria nodded, accepting the compliment.

'And if any man touched it, he would lose his hand that instant.'

A growl went through the room – though no-one moved to take the challenge. Angria hushed them again.

'How do I know you are who you say? I have many enemies. You might be a spy sent by the rajah Shahuji, or an agent of the hat-wearers whose ships I plunder.'

Christopher stared him down. 'How can you be sure of any of your men?'

That brought several of them to their feet again, knives in their hands.

Angria laughed. 'Truly, a spy might be expected to try to ingratiate himself more with his hosts. Unless, of course, that is what you wish me to think.'

He made a gesture with his hand. A side door opened, and four guards bustled in a gaunt man with unkempt hair and a wild beard. He was naked, except for a breech clout around his middle, and judging by the scars and scabs on his body he had suffered many torments. The guards threw him down between Christopher and Angria.

'This man was caught stealing from my treasure store,' said Angria. 'What should his punishment be?'

The prisoner whimpered. Christopher looked bored. 'If he stole from you, he should die.' He drew the sword. A soft gasp went around the room as the men saw the perfection of the blade, and the gold inlay rippling down it. 'Do you wish me to do it for you?'

'Put your blade away,' said Angria. 'That would be too easy. I keep a special place for men like this, down at the foot of the castle by the water gate. I have had an iron collar fixed to the rocks so I can bind the traitor there, near the high tide mark. You said you were a sailor?'

The question caught Christopher off guard. 'Once.'

'You know of the spring tides?'

'Twice a month, at the time of the new and the full moons, the tide sinks lower and rises higher than usual,' said Christopher.

Angria nodded. 'The collar keeps the man's head fixed where it will not be covered until the flood of the spring tide. Each day, he comes a little closer to drowning. The rocks down there are covered with limpets and barnacles. The waves dash him against them, flaying his skin on their razor-sharp shells. When the tide goes out, the sun shrivels his skin and dries the salt into his wounds. Salt water gets in his mouth – he is so thirsty, he cannot help but drink it – but it only makes him sick. If I put him out at the time of the lowest tides, halfway to the full moon, it might take a fortnight for the water to come high enough to drown him. And, by the time it does, he will thank me for my mercy.'

The prisoner had started to speak, mumbling pleas and imprecations under his breath. One of the guards silenced him with a slap across the face. Above him, Angria and Christopher gazed at each other. Looking into the pirate's eyes, Christopher saw nothing but a limitless appetite for power. He did not know that Angria, returning his gaze, saw almost the same reflection.

'I offer you a bargain,' said Angria. 'You came here freely, and freely I will let you go. You may walk out of my castle without hindrance. If you stay, and serve me well, you will be a rich man. But if you betray me, then you will pay such a price that even the sharks will have little left to feast on.'

Christopher hesitated. Angria thought he was frightened.

'If you have any doubts, there is no place for you here,' he warned.

But Christopher had none. Looking on the treasures and trophies in the room, he knew this was where he belonged. He knelt before Angria. A servant put two dishes of rice and milk before him. He dipped the rice the milk, ate it, and repeated the oath that Angria administered.

'I will eat rice and milk, and remain always at your feet.'

* * *

They reached Bombay without misadventure. Tom paid close attention as they sailed in to the harbour, observing the master as he lined up the seven trees on Malabar point to steer a safe course through the reefs and islets that guarded the approach. Features Tom had only seen on charts slid past: Sunken Rock, the Oyster, the Middle Ground. And so they came into Bombay roads, under the castle on Dungarey hill.

Tom stripped down to his shirt and breeches, and removed his stockings so he looked like a sailor in short trousers. Going ashore, he pulled on an oar with the other men, while Francis and Ana sat in the stern with the master. Tom felt exposed, more vulnerable even than in the fort at Brinjoan. This was Guy's domain, and he did not know what eyes might be watching unseen from the Governor's house behind the walls.

The stench of swamp mud and rotting fish rankled his nostrils. As they beached the boat, he averted his face. The waterfront was quiet, that afternoon. The lascars and stevedores lounged in the hot shade, with no great enthusiasm for unloading the ship.

Francis, Ana and the master fell into conversation with a group of Company officials. They were exceedingly surprised to find Guy Courtney's nephew so suddenly come ashore; they mopped their faces and shot each other anxious looks, each calculating how this new arrival would change the balance of power in the settlement. Guy ruled the island as absolutely as the Great Mughal in Delhi ever ruled his empire, and his courtiers survived by reading the shifting tides of his mood.

The Company men bustled Francis off to the Governor's house. When he was sure no one was watching, Tom slipped away towards the little cluster of taverns and punch houses in the lee of the castle. He found the busiest, and took a seat in a corner. A few minutes later, Merridew – one of the few sailors who had survived the wreck of the *Kestrel* and the siege at Brinjoan – ducked in.

'No one followed you, sir. I'll keep a watch outside the castle for Master Francis.'

Tom nodded, and settled down to wait.

Francis stepped through the castle gates, and felt a shiver of apprehension as they rang shut behind him. His misgivings mounted as he crossed the courtyard, past various store rooms and guard huts, and climbed the steps towards the imposing Governor's house, which stood against the southern wall of the castle overlooking the harbour.

News of his arrival had raced ahead of him. He was admitted straight away to the Governor's office on the top floor.

He had never met his uncle Guy before. The one picture he had seen of him, a painting that had hung in High Weald, had showed a cherubic boy dressed in a white smock, standing beside a puppy. It was a far cry from the man who sat in front of the great windows now: tall and slim, dressed in a dark green coat with tailoring that was so impeccable it seemed almost unnatural. Even seated, he carried himself with grace and menace, like a cat pretending to sleep. He was handsome, with fine features and a full head of hair, yet the cast of his eyes warned against intimacy. Francis searched the face for any echo of his twin brother Tom, and found nothing.

'Step into the light where I can see you,' Guy growled. He studied Francis, with an appraising gaze that made him feel like a piece of livestock at an auction. 'Yes. You are Billy's son, no doubt of it. I will try not to hold that against you.'

Francis hardly dared speak, lest his voice betray him. Looking around the room, his eye was caught by a portrait on the wall. Sir Hal Courtney, dressed in the fashion of the late King Charles with a flowing wig and a feather in his hat. One hand rested lightly on the hilt of the magnificent sword he wore. The artist had painted it with rare skill, capturing every facet of the sapphire in the pommel.

Guy followed his gaze. 'You like my painting?'

'I liked it better when it hung in High Weald,' said Francis, despite himself.

Guy chuckled. 'Recognize it, do you? I had it from your stepfather. He was only too happy to part with it, given his need for ready money.'

He put down the quill he had been writing with. 'I confess, I have been expecting you these several months. I received a letter commending you to the Company's service before the last monsoon.'

'I was detained in Cape Town.'

Guy studied Francis. Even before the boy had left London, Childs had written to Guy in secret, informing him that Tom was alive in Cape Town, and that he had dispatched Francis to kill him. The news had left Guy in a black mood, caught in a vice of uncertainty and hope. He had awaited further news for months.

'I understand Lord Childs gave you an errand to run in Cape Town,' he said.

Francis marvelled that Guy could discuss the murder of his own twin so casually. Again, he wondered what could have come between the brothers.

'I did.'

'And did you conclude it successfully?'

Francis nodded.

'I have had no report of it.'

'We hid the body on the mountain. The jackals and hyenas will have ensured no-one can identify him. Afterwards, I took passage on a country trader, but she was shipwrecked in a storm, near Brinjoan. I reached the fort, only to be swept up in the events I am sure you are well aware of.'

'Indeed.'

'Perhaps you know that my aunt Agnes and her husband Captain Hicks were at Brinjoan.'

'Captain Hicks' death was a terrible blow,' said Guy, without emotion.

'And – I do not know if this intelligence has reached you – Agnes has been captured by the pirate Angria.'

Guy stroked his chin with the plume of his pen. 'In fact, I have known it for some time. We received a ransom demand from Angria weeks ago. As well as Agnes, he holds Foy's wife, and another woman he claims is Captain Hicks' sister.' He frowned. 'I was not aware Captain Hicks had a sister.'

'She sailed on the same vessel as I from Cape Town,' Francis improvised hastily, trying to allay Guy's suspicions. 'She lived in Dorset, but had been widowed, so came to seek succour from her brother.'

The lie served its purpose. Guy lost interest.

'May I ask,' said Francis, 'how much ransom Angria expects for the three ladies?'

'Thirty thousand rupees.'

Francis gaped. 'That must be more than five thousand pounds.'

'Nearer six thousand,' Guy answered.

Francis marvelled that Guy could keep so cool. 'How are you to pay it? Have you made arrangements?'

'Arrangements?' Guy laughed as though it was the most astonishing notion he had heard in months. 'I sent back to Angria and told him the only payment he could expect from me would be in lead, from the mouth of a cannon.'

'Then you intend to attack the fortress?'

'Certainly not. Tiracola is impregnable. If we attempted the assault, and failed, it would humiliate us before the world. Every pirate from Bantam to Zanzibar would have license to prey on us. The damage to our commerce would be inestimable.'

'Then what will you do?'

Guy twiddled his pen, until Francis understood. 'But surely

you cannot mean to abandon the prisoners? Agnes Hicks is my aunt – your sister-in-law.'

Guy gave him an icy look. 'Do not think you can play on my heartstrings. I have had my damned wife pleading with me every night this last month, begging me to relent, until I had to beat the notion out of her. I would not expect a woman to understand the dictates of business, but you . . .' He fixed Francis with a stern glare. 'You come here seeking my patronage, asking for employment with the Company. I should have hoped you would appreciate the delicacy of the situation. It would be a shame if I had to write to Lord Childs to say I could find no position for you here.'

Francis bit back his anger. It would not help advance his cause. 'I apologize, Uncle. I will not question you again. I am new to this country, and ignorant of its ways.'

'Yet you have already seen much action.' Guy leaned back in his chair, eyes half closed. 'Tell me about the man who saved the fort at Brinjoan. I have had various reports, but none seem to know who he really is.'

Francis froze. His mind raced, thinking what he could say without betraying Tom to Guy.

'His name is Tom Weald. He was master of the vessel I boarded at Cape Town. In truth, I know little about him. He kept his own counsel.'

'Even in those long months pent up in the fort? I should have thought men who survived such a siege together would know each other's most intimate secrets.' He folded his fingers together and rested his chin in his hands. 'The men I spoke to said you were most familiar. That he relied on you like no other.'

'Every man did his duty.'

'They said you called him "uncle".'

'They are mistaken. I called Captain Hicks "uncle". The men must have confused their memories.'

306

Francis forced himself to look Guy in the eye, hoping his face would not reveal the deception.

'And this Mr Weald. He accompanied you to Bombay?'

There was no gain in lying. Guy would already have seen the ship's manifest. 'He did.'

'And do you know where he intends to stay?'

'He did not say.'

'No matter.' Guy looked pleased. 'Bombay is a small settlement, and he will not be hard to find. I should very much like to meet this man, who emerges from the sea to save the Company's trade and honour. No doubt we shall have much to discuss.'

'If I see him, I shall inform him of your interest.' Francis made to take his leave. 'But now, if you will excuse me, Uncle, it has been a long voyage. I will find lodgings in the town.'

Guy pretended shock. 'I will not hear of it. You are my nephew – and a hero besides. You will stay in this house as my honoured guest, until I can find a home that befits a member of my family.'

Francis tried to conceal his horror. 'You are too kind,' he demurred. 'But I have already sent my effects to a boarding house. I shall retrieve them, and rejoin you forthwith.'

'I will have a servant fetch your baggage,' Guy answered. Then he seemed to reconsider. 'But you are a young man, and you have been a long time at sea. I know you will be eager to explore the delights Bombay has to offer.' He winked at Francis, with a knowing leer that made Francis shudder. 'Go with my blessing. We dine at six.'

'I shall see you then, Uncle.'

As soon as he had gone, Guy rang the bell and summoned one of his clerks. A young blue-coat boy entered, a lanky lad with greasy hair and a face scarred by small pox. His name was Peter Peters, and Guy had already established there was little he would not do to advance his career.

'Follow young Francis and see where he goes,' Guy ordered him. 'Report back on any men he associates with.'

Peters wiped his face on the back of his sleeve and bowed. 'Of course, sir.'

'Most especially, see if he contacts a man called Tom Weald. If you see this Weald, do not approach him, but bring me word at once of his whereabouts.'

Guy stood and stared out at the ships in the harbour. A fly crawled across the windows. A terrible thought had been growing in his heart, ever since he had word of the mysterious saviour of Brinjoan. That he had arrived in Bombay with Francis only added more fuel to his burning suspicion.

Would he dare come here, after all this time? Would he risk his life in Bombay, the seat of Guy's authority?

Yes, he thought grimly. Tom had proved more than once that he had no shame, no depths he would not plumb to take what was rightfully Guy's.

With a sudden movement, Guy lashed out with the flat of his hand. He crushed the fly, smearing it against the glass. When he looked at his palm, he saw a streak of blood.

You will not escape this time.

Francis found Merridew loitering outside the castle. Together, they went to the punch house where Tom was waiting. Tom's face darkened as Francis recounted his meeting with Guy.

'I would not expect him to lift a finger for Sarah,' he said. 'But to abandon Agnes, after her husband lost his life defending the Company.' Not for the first time in his life, he wondered how he and Guy could have shared the same mother's womb, yet emerged so different.

'But we cannot delay here,' Francis went on. 'Guy asked many questions about you – I think he suspects that "Tom Weald" is not all he makes himself out to be.'

Tom groaned. 'I should have chosen a better pseudonym. A child could see through that.'

'You could not know you were destined to become a hero of the East India Company.'

'But I knew I had entered Guy's domain. It was folly to think he would not get to hear of me.'

'I think he is as yet uncertain. I told him I killed you in Cape Town, though I am not sure he believed me. But he will speak to the men from Brinjoan, and the ship we sailed on, and it will not take him long to piece together the story.' Francis stared at his drink. 'What are we to do?'

Before Tom could answer, Ana entered the room, leading a gangly man with a stooped back and a bright red nose. She pulled two stools up to their table.

'I went to the bazaar and spoke with some trading acquaintances,' she said, without preamble. 'They introduced to me to Mr Berry.'

The gangly man gave a formal bow. At a nod from Tom, Francis went to the bar and fetched two more glasses of punch.

'Thank you kindly,' said Berry, slurping down the liquor. 'Much obliged.'

'Mr Berry worked for Governor Courtney,' explained Ana.

The others stiffened. 'Can we trust him?' said Tom.

Berry took no offence. 'I have no love for Governor Courtney. But I know a thing or two about his money.'

'That is no use,' said Francis bitterly. 'I saw my uncle. He would not pay a shilling to save Agnes, or the others, from Angria. He said he would not treat with pirates.'

Berry looked up from his drink. 'Ha,' he spat. 'Governor Courtney says he'll have no truck with pirates, but that's not the real reason he refuses to pay the ransom.'

'What do you mean?' Francis demanded.

Berry studied the inside of his glass, which was already empty.

Tom took the hint and slid his own drink across to him. Berry winked.

'I was a bookkeeper at the *bunder*, the Company's warehouses over by the pier. I did well for myself, steady promotions. One day, going through the books, I noticed some discrepancies. Goods paid for that never came in, goods marked "lost in transit", that I'd seen with my own eyes. Of course, being an honest man, I brought it to Governor Courtney's attention.'

'I presume he did not thank you for it,' said Francis.

'Threw me out on the street, he did.' Berry looked around the table, inviting their sympathy. 'Told me he'd see me dead of the flux in three months.'

'That sounds like Guy,' said Tom. 'But what has this to do with Angria?'

Berry held up his glass to show it was empty again. Tom waved to the serving girl, who brought another. Berry reached for it, but Tom was faster. He held it just out of the man's reach.

'Tell me about Guy and Angria. Then I will buy you enough liquor to drown yourself in, if you so wish.'

Berry tottered on his stool. Tom put out a hand, thinking he might fall, but Berry regained his balance. He straightened himself, and a crafty look came over his face.

'How much is Angria asking?'

'Thirty thousand rupees,' said Francis.

'Pah.' An alcoholic mist of punch and spittle sprayed across the table. 'Thirty thousand rupees is nothing to Guy Courtney. In the vault in the castle, beneath the Governor's house, he has built a strongroom filled with wooden chests. Each chest contains one *lakh*. You know what a *lakh* is?' He leaned forward, jabbing his finger on every syllable. 'A *hundred thousand* rupees.'

'Then why will Guy not pay the ransom?' said Francis in frustration. 'He would hardly notice such a sum.'

'If even one penny dropped through a hole in his purse, Guy Courtney would feel the loss. But that is not his game. The reason he does not move against the pirates is because it suits his plans to have Angria at large, threatening the seas.'

'But that is nonsense. They threaten his own commerce,' Francis protested.

'The Indiamen are the biggest, best-armed ships in these seas. Angria leaves them well alone. Instead, he preys on interlopers and country traders.'

'Thus removing Guy's competitors, and driving up prices.' Tom whistled, though he knew he should not be surprised. For as long as men had taken to the sea in ships, the Indian Ocean had been a hunting ground for the world's most fearsome pirates. Only a few years earlier, an Englishman named Henry Every had captured the Great Mughal's treasure ship on its pilgrimage to Mecca. The pirates had taken three days to loot it, and the treasure had never been recovered. But even in that villainous company, Guy was as ruthless a man as had ever sailed those waters.

Berry drummed his fingers on the table. 'That's not the half of it. You have heard of Shahuji?'

Tom and Francis shook their heads.

'Shahuji is the Rajah of Satara, the king of the Maratha people,' Ana explained. 'For the past thirty years, they have waged war against the Great Mughal, to free themselves from his empire and create their own kingdom.'

'But what has that to do with Guy?' asked Francis.

'Shahuji controls most of the ports on the Malabar coast,' said Berry. 'And all the routes overland. Guy Courtney wants to negotiate a *firman* with him, a treaty to guarantee safe passage for his goods and reduce the customs he pays. Now, Shahuji's sworn enemy is Angria. Guy dangles the possibility that he could take action against Angria as part of his negotiation with Shahuji. But until he has the *firman*, Angria's piracy weakens Shahuji and strengthens Guy.'

Tom began to get an inkling of the labyrinthine web of

politics that bound the region. No doubt Guy was a master puppeteer, pulling strings across the continent and setting one man against another to further his own interests. But to Tom, it was a distraction.

'All this talk of *firmans*, rajahs and Mughals serves no purpose,' he declared. 'All that matters is to rescue Sarah and Agnes.'

'How?' said Berry. 'You sailed here from Madras: you'll have seen his fortress. It's impregnable.'

'I do not intend to take it. Angria is a man of business. I will buy their freedom, for thirty thousand rupees.'

Francis slammed the table in frustration, rattling the cups. 'But we do not have the money! All this talk has simply brought us back to where we began.'

Tom grinned, feeling a familiar devilry warming his blood. 'On the contrary – we have moved on considerably. We now know where Guy keeps all the money we could possibly need.'

The others stared at him. 'You mean to rob his strongroom?' said Ana slowly.

'It is no easier to penetrate Guy's strongroom than Angria's fort,' Berry warned. 'There is only one key, and Guy keeps it hidden in his office.'

'But unlike Angria's fort, we have a man who knows the way in.' Tom turned to Francis. 'Round up the rest of the men, and have them assemble at the docks. It is time Guy learned to support his family.'

His confidence affected them all. They left the punch house happy, fired with a new sense of purpose. Francis and Merridew went to find the others – the four men from the *Kestrel* who had survived the storm and the siege – while Berry took Ana and Tom to a man who could supply arms, and the other things they would need. Even if they did manage to get into the strongroom, Tom did not think they would escape without a fight.

In their good mood, no one noticed the pox-scarred man

sitting in the corner of the punch house. He watched them go, then hurried away.

A little before six, just as night was falling, Francis sauntered into the castle. The sepoy guards saluted punctiliously, fear in their eyes. Word had already spread that this was Guy's nephew.

They closed the gates behind him. Halfway across the courtyard, Francis swerved off into a small store room under the walls. He emerged a few moments later and hurried back to the entrance.

'I left my purse in the punch house I visited,' he stammered, feigning embarrassment. 'If my uncle Guy finds out, he will be furious with me.'

The sepoys unbolted the gate. As it swung open, Francis half turned and glanced over his shoulder.

'Look,' he cried.

Caught off-guard, the sepoys spun about. Smoke was billowing from the store room. Flames licked out through the open door.

'Fire!' shouted Francis. The others took up the cry. At once, the courtyard became a frenzy of panicked shouts, men running everywhere to fetch buckets and pumps.

In the confusion, no one noticed the open gate – or the three men who slipped through. Tom, Berry and Merridew followed Francis to the Governor's house and through the door. No one challenged them. From the hallway, Tom saw the servants busy in the dining room, hastily packing the silver and other valuables in case the fire spread.

Francis led them up the grand staircase to the third floor, and along the dimly lit gallery to Guy's office. He had hoped the fire would have attracted every man in the building – but he was disappointed. A sepoy guarded the door, musket held erect before him.

'What is happening?' he demanded. He had heard the shouts from outside, but did not dare leave his post to see what they portended.

'Fire,' said Francis briefly. 'Governor Courtney sent me to see his papers were secure.' He stepped forward, showing his face to the light. 'I am his nephew, Francis Courtney.'

As ever, the family name worked like an incantation. The guard stepped aside – then paused.

'Who are they?' he asked, gesturing to Tom and Merridew. 'I do not recognize their faces.'

'Tom Weald. The hero of Brinjoan.'

The guard stood his ground. 'Governor Courtney did not tell me about him.' He glimpsed Berry, trying to hide behind the others, and angled his musket towards Francis. 'I cannot permit you to enter.'

Francis did not flinch. 'I have a note from my uncle that will explain the matter.' He opened his coat and reached in. The guard leaned closer to see.

Francis' coat shielded his arm, so the guard never saw the punch coming. It connected with his jaw and knocked him off balance. Before he could recover, Tom stepped forward and gave him a sharp blow that laid him flat on his back.

'That was a smart trick.' Tom stepped past the unconscious guard and put his hand on the door. Downstairs, the servants were rushing to and fro, seeing to Guy's valuables. Soon, someone would surely think to look in the office.

Yet still Tom hesitated. What if Guy was on the other side of the door, frantically gathering his precious papers? What would he do if they came face to face?

An old thought echoed through his mind. *The last two times you met, he tried to kill you, and if you meet a third time you know one of you will die.*

He gripped the handle and pushed open the door.

314

The room was empty. Tom felt almost sick with relief – but he had no time to waste.

'Guy keeps the key for the strongroom somewhere in here. We must find it.'

They spread out across the long room. Tom made for Guy's desk, then stopped, transfixed by the portrait of Sir Hal Courtney on the wall.

'My father,' he murmured. Hal had died almost twenty years ago, but the sight of him here, so sudden and unexpected, brought a pang of loss. 'That belonged . . .'

'. . . in High Weald,' said Francis.

Tom gazed at the Neptune sword in the painting, the soft glow of the sapphire in the canvas. Frustration boiled inside him, to be confronted with the legacy that had been torn from him. As soon as he had rescued Sarah, he would return to Brinjoan and find the man who had the sword.

But that was for another time. He put the thought aside. Francis had already begun to search Guy's desk. He pried open drawers with his dagger, scattering papers to the floor. 'The key must be somewhere.'

Berry stared out of the window. 'We do not have much time. They are bringing the fire under control.'

Tom heard him. He knew he had to act. But the picture hypnotized him. To find his father and the sword here, in Guy's office, brought such a collision of memories it left him dizzy.

But he could not linger. Reluctantly, he tore his eyes away from the painting – and, as he did so, noticed something. He stepped up to it and ran his hand along the side of the heavy gilt frame. Two hard lumps bulged out of the line of the wood.

'Hinges,' he exclaimed. He felt the other side, running his knife up the crack between the frame and the wall. Halfway up, the blade caught.

'There must be some kind of lock or mechanism.' Tom jiggled the knife, prying and twisting to force the latch.

Something gave with a crack. The knife blade fell and struck the floor, an inch from his foot.

Francis had come up behind him. 'Will it open?' he asked.

Tom showed him the broken hilt of his knife. 'The lock is stronger than my blade.'

He tried to work his fingers into the gap, but it was too narrow. Francis stood back and studied the frame.

'Does Guy have a pen-knife or a letter-opener?' Tom called to Merridew.

Francis reached forward and took a firm grip on a piece of the frame's gilded moulding. He twisted it in a half circle. With barely a whisper, the frame swung out on its hinges.

Tom gave Francis an admiring look. 'That was smartly done.'

They all crowded round. Behind the painting a recess opened in the wall, piled with ledgers and papers. Tom took them out one by one, passing them back to Berry and Francis.

Berry turned the pages in one of the books. 'These are Guy's secret accounts,' he said in wonder. 'All the transactions he makes to his own profit, away from the eyes of his masters in Leadenhall Street.'

'Never mind that,' said Tom in excitement. 'This must be what we need.' He held up a brass key, with many teeth that bespoke an intricate lock. 'Now to find the vault.'

'I can take you there,' said Berry. 'If we can find a way past the guards.'

By the noises outside, Tom could tell the fire was coming under control. Soon the garrison would return to their duties. Tom took the pistol from his belt, and wished he had a better plan.

'We may have to—'

The door to the office slammed open. A dozen guards in the red coats and green facings of the Bombay army burst in. Before anyone could react, they made a line across the front of the room and levelled their muskets at Tom and his companions.

316

'Stay where you are,' bellowed their sergeant. 'Nobody moves until Governor Courtney arrives.'

All four men stopped where they stood. Looking at the sepoys, Tom saw they had not been called from fighting the fire. There was no soot on their faces or their gleaming white cross belts, no sense of haste or surprise. They had been waiting for him.

Despair crawled down Tom's spine. He glanced at Berry.

'Did you betray us?'

But one look at the fearful shock on Berry's face told him it could not be true. He was as surprised as the rest of them – and even more terrified.

It did not matter now. However Guy had learned it, he had them trapped. And he was coming.

Tom started to back away. He reached his hands behind him and felt the pistol, tucked in his belt in the small of his back.

'Stand your ground,' the sergeant roared. Sweat beaded on his brow. He would not want to open fire before Guy arrived to see his prisoners – not unless he had to. Tom edged back another foot.

The others took their cue from him and retreated in step. The sergeant looked angrily from one to the other. 'If you move another inch, I will order my men to open fire and Governor Courtney's orders be damned.'

Tom kept his eyes locked on the sergeant's, even as he moved again. Now he was behind Guy's desk, almost against the back windows. The sergeant relaxed a fraction with the knowledge there was nowhere else for Tom to go.

'Governor Courtney has a chamber in his dungeon for men like you,' he told Tom. 'By the time he has finished with you in there, you would eat your own shit if he ordered it.'

Outside the door, a heavy footfall sounded on the stair. The sepoys stiffened, aiming their muskets straighter.

'They are going to fire in a moment,' Tom told his companions. 'Be ready.'

'The Devil you say,' the sergeant snarled. 'I would not give you so easy a death.'

The footsteps reached the top of the stairs.

Tom glanced at the others. What he intended was a desperate plan, but it was his only hope. If Guy caught them, he would visit a lifetime of hatred upon them, and Tom most of all. Worse, it would kill all hope of ever rescuing Sarah and Agnes – unless, in the torments of the dungeon, Guy discovered who they really were. He might ransom them purely so he could use them to torture Tom.

And I will not kill Guy, Tom promised himself. *I will not repeat the mistake I made with Billy.*

The feet approached the door: the ponderous gait of a heavy man in no hurry at all. *He is savouring his victory*, Tom thought. He edged the pistol out of the belt, trying to hide the movement. He would only have one shot.

'Are they all there?' Guy's voice boomed down the hallway. 'This is an acquaintance I have long waited to renew.'

At the sound of the voice, Tom almost lost his nerve. The last time he heard it he had been sailing out of Zanzibar harbour in a small felucca, clutching Sarah, with a hundred of Guy's musketeers firing on them. Guy's parting words were still seared in his memory.

One of these days you will pay what you owe in full. I will see to that. I swear it.

'I'm sorry,' said Tom. In a single, fluid movement, he raised the pistol and fired straight into the sergeant's heart.

The response was almost instantaneous. The sepoys were already on edge. At the sound of the pistol shot, they all fired their muskets in a furious fusillade.

Tom had expected it. Even as he fired the pistol, he had already started to dive behind the desk. He landed on the floor

318

as the musket balls sailed harmlessly over his head. To the deafening report of the guns was added the sound of glass shattering, as the balls struck the long windows overlooking the bay.

Smoke choked the room. Tom shouted for Francis and Merridew, but with the shots ringing in his ears he could hardly hear himself speak. A figure came out of the smoke – Francis – bleeding from a cut on his face where a piece of glass had struck him, but otherwise unhurt. Merridew followed.

Tom pointed to the window. He charged towards it and jumped, spinning in mid air so that his back went through first. The jagged glass tore at his shirt, but only for a split second before his momentum carried him through and out into mid air.

When they had sailed into the bay that morning, Tom had studied the fort carefully. Now, the attention repaid itself. He had noted the high windows facing the harbour, and assumed that Guy would place himself where he could observe all traffic. But between the windows and the harbour stood the castle wall, low enough that it did not impede Guy's view from the third storey, but high enough that the rampart ran only a few feet below the windowsill.

Tom landed there in a shower of broken glass. He started his feet, and was promptly knocked down again as Francis came down on top of him. Merridew landed beside them.

'Berry?' Tom mouthed. Francis drew a line across his throat. Berry had reacted a moment too late, and paid the price.

Tom glanced up at the window. Smoke billowed out; he heard shouts, then a shot. Without the sergeant to keep discipline, the sepoys must be shooting at shadows – or each other. But they would not be deterred for long. Tom looked along the wall for a stair or a ladder.

They were trapped. Jealous of his privacy, fearful of being overheard by a sentry under his windows, Guy had caused this stretch of wall to be bricked up at either end. There was no way through.

From above, Tom heard Guy bellowing orders. If the sepoys reached the window and looked down, they would find Tom and his friends trapped like rats in a barrel.

'Into the sea,' Tom shouted. 'It is our only chance.'

He clambered onto the embrasure between two battlements. Below, white surf frothed on the rocks where the sea lapped the foot of the wall. He did not know these waters. How quickly did they drop off?

'I command you to halt,' shouted a voice from the window. Tom did not even bother to look. He knew whose it was. He crouched, tensed his arms against the battlements on either side, then leaped, springing as far from the wall as he could.

He fell for what seemed an age. The moment he hit the water, he was kicking and flailing upwards, terrified of breaking his legs on the submerged rocks. He broke the surface, unharmed, just in time to see Francis splash down behind him.

Merridew followed. Fortunately, he was a strong swimmer, and together the three men kicked out into the bay. The tropical night had fallen sudden and complete, hiding them from the guards in the castle. Occasional musket shots sounded from the walls, but none came anywhere near them.

Ahead, Tom heard the squeak of rowlocks. He pushed his head well out of the water and whistled the first few bars of 'Spanish Ladies'.

Ana's voice came straight back out of the darkness. 'What happened? Are you hurt?'

Tom felt giddy with relief. According to their plan, Ana and the other survivors from the *Kestrel* were meant to stand off in the harbour until Tom and the others had stolen the gold from the strongroom. On a signal, the boat would have come in to the water gate in the castle walls and they would have made their escape. But Ana had heard the shots, and brought the boat in sooner.

She steered the boat towards them. Tom let Francis and Merridew go aboard, then heaved himself over the gunwale. 'Guy knew we were coming.'

'Did Berry betray you?' asked Ana.

'If he did, he paid for it with his life.' Tom shook his head to clear the water from his ears. 'But I think otherwise. It was folly to think we could come to Bombay, right into the heart of Guy's dominion, without him hearing of it somehow.'

Tom looked back. The castle hid the pier from sight, but he did not doubt it would be busy. 'Guy knows we went into the water. He will have boats looking for us, even if only to gloat over our corpses. We must make our escape while we can.'

'What about the gold?' said Francis.

'Perhaps another time . . .' said Tom. But even as he spoke, he knew it was futile. Guy would be waiting, and every man in Bombay would be watching for Tom and Francis. Even if they did penetrate the fort again, there would doubtless be a whole battalion of sepoys guarding the strongroom now.

The boat had a small sail. Merridew and the men raised it, catching the evening breeze that blew off the sea.

'We could try to rendezvous with Dorian and Aboli,' suggested Ana. 'If they have had a profitable voyage, they might have the gold to pay Angria's ransom.'

'That could take months,' said Tom. 'We do not have a ship to reach the Laquedivas Islands, and even if we did, we are later than we arranged. Dorian might have given us up and sailed for Cape Town already.'

'Then what can we do?' blurted Francis.

Tom looked out across the water. Even now, the fire in the castle was not wholly tamed. It smouldered in the courtyard, filling the sky with a red glow that silhouetted the Governor's house. Ahead, across the channel, the sea lapped the mangrove

321

swamps and open beaches of the coast of mainland India. Somewhere along that coast, Sarah and Agnes were waiting for him to save them. He could not fail them.

'We cannot buy their freedom,' he mused. 'Therefore, there is only one alternative.'

'Free them by force?' said Francis incredulously. 'But Angria's fort is impregnable.'

Tom sat forward on the thwart. 'Is it? Everybody says so, but how can they be sure? It is rumoured to be impregnable, so no one ever assaults it. No one captures it, so men continue to insist it is impregnable. The reputation sustains itself. But I have never yet seen a fortress that could not be taken.'

'Maybe if we had an army at our backs,' said Francis doubtfully.

Tom clapped him on the shoulder. 'Exactly.'

He took the tiller from Ana, and steered the ship towards the dark Indian shore. Francis stared at him.

'Where are we going?'

'To find ourselves an army.'

Though it was always night in the caverns beneath Tiracola castle, Lydia Foy had learned to infer the passage of time and the rhythm of the days by the faint sounds that reached her sharp ears. Even through the massive stone walls she could differentiate between the ebbs and flows of the castle coming to life, the activity of the days and the long stillness of the night hours.

Now the castle was asleep. By the light that seeped in from a distant lamp, Lydia saw the two sisters lying together, Sarah with her head resting on Agnes' chest. By now the bulge of Sarah's belly was obvious, even in the gloom: she could not pretend to hide it any longer. Both women slept, breathing softly.

It was time for Lydia to act now. She lifted her skirts and

wrapped them around her manacles so that the chains would not rattle when she moved. Neither Agnes nor Sarah stirred when Lydia padded through the cave to the gate that barred the entrance to the dungeons. A lamp hung from a bracket on the outer wall. Through the grille, she saw the guard slumped on the stairs, snoring.

She found a small pebble on the floor and threw it at him. It struck him on the forehead, and he started with a grunt; his hand jerked to the pistol musket propped on the wall beside him. He scowled at Lydia and waved her away with the gun, but with his other hand he rubbed his forehead. Lydia refused to move.

'I must speak to your captain,' she said in halting Portuguese.

The guard inspected his fingertips for traces of blood, ignoring her. She could not tell if he had understood or not; she tried the few Indian words she knew. 'Subadar? Jagirdar? Havaldar?'

The guard shook his head and snarled at her persistence.

Lydia reached a hand under her skirt. The guard's expression changed to one of interest. Lydia felt around between her legs. The guard licked his lips and rose to his feet. He came to lean against the gate from where he could get a better view.

Lydia brought her hand out from under her clothing with a bright golden pagoda held between her fingers. She had secreted the coin inside herself when capture by the pirates seemed inevitable. She wiped it on her skirt, and then proffered it to the guard. He grabbed for it, but Lydia snatched it back through the iron grille. The guard glared at her in frustration.

'Havaldar,' Lydia repeated. And then, in Portuguese, 'I have something he must hear.'

The guard hesitated, but the lure of her gold was irresistible. He took a ring of keys from the wall and unlocked the gate.

He held out his hand for the coin.

'*Havaldar*,' Lydia insisted, keeping the coin clutched behind her back.

The guard did not insist. He led Lydia up many flights of stairs. The construction of the walls changed from hewn rock to slabs of cut stone. The lamps were hung at more frequent intervals. Tapestries and cloths began to appear on the walls, so ornate and beautiful that they could only be plunder. Despite her predicament, Lydia found herself valuing them with a knowledgeable eye.

Finally they reached the guardroom, where half a dozen or so men were playing dice. Their captain had angry words for the guard when he saw Lydia, but she held herself erect and looked him firmly in the eye.

'Can you understand me?' she said in Portuguese. 'I have important news for your leader.'

The captain shrugged. Obviously he did not understand – and he did not care. He said something to his men, who laughed unpleasantly and the captain fondled his own crotch. Lydia subdued her own unease, and stamped her foot.

'Does anyone here speak English?' she said in a show of anger. 'I have intelligence your captain must hear.' She knew they would not understand her words, but hoped they could read the sense of them.

The captain squinted at her and nodded. Then he snapped an order at his underlings.

Two of his men sprang to their feet and grabbed Lydia's arms. She started to scream, but the third man stepped behind her and clamped his hand over her mouth. The captain drew the curved dagger from his belt and held it to her throat.

He ran the point of the knife down inside the neck of her dress. She went still, as she felt the steel cold against her skin. Then he drew the blade sharply downwards, her bodice fell open as far as her waist. Her breasts bulged out, heavy and pendulous. Her arms were pinned behind her, she could not cover herself. She stared at the captain, trying to shame him with her gaze.

He smiled and ran the knife back into its sheath on his belt. Then he reached out and took one of her breasts in each cupped hand. He weighed them as though they were ripe papayas. Then he pinched one of her nipples so sharply that she winced. The captain reached down to his own crotch; and despite herself Lydia's eyes followed his hand down as he began to massage himself. She could see the bulge of his cock swelling and stiffening under his *dhoti*.

Lydia rocked back in the arms of the men who held her from behind. Instinctively they pushed her forward again, and she used the impetus to drive her right knee up into the captain's crotch with all the savagery of her anger and outrage.

The captain screamed like a girl and reeled back against the wall, clutching his damaged genitalia with both hands. But he retaliated almost immediately and launched himself back at Lydia. His face was twisted into a mask of agony, and in his right hand he clutched the knife that he had drawn from the sheath on his belt and held poised to strike her down.

'Stop.' A loud and authoritative voice rang out. 'Release that woman at once.'

The guards responded instantly. They backed away from Lydia with their hands clutched behind their backs, and their expressions terrified and abject. Even the captain of the guard opened his hand and dropped his knife to the floor, then cringed back against the wall.

All of them were staring at the man who had entered the guardroom and was standing in the doorway.

One of the guards muttered a name as he touched his forehead submissively. 'Raudra.' In the weeks since Raudra had appeared in the castle, he had risen astonishingly fast in Angria's service. First, he had gone to a village that had resisted Angria's demands for tribute, and come back with two years' worth of tribute, and the headman's head mounted on a stick. Next, he had been sent out on a raiding expedition with one of Angria's captains; when he returned, it was with five captured vessels, and over a hundred thousand rupees in plunder. Angria's captain was dead. In the smoke of battle, no one could say exactly how he had been killed, but men cast suspicious looks at Raudra, and muttered when they thought he could not hear. When Angria heard the rumours, he only laughed, and said, 'A man must be bold to survive a nest of vipers.' He promoted Raudra in the dead captain's place, and nothing more was heard of the rumours – especially after one man, who had spoken less carefully than the others, was found floating in the sea at the foot of the walls.

Now Raudra stared at Lydia. 'Who are you?' he asked in perfect unaccented English that startled her. He was tall and broad-shouldered. There was a fresh burn scar on his head which had left a bald patch on his scalp. However, his beard and his eyebrows were dark, dense and bristling. He was naked to the waist, with only a leather cross belt slung across his muscular chest. Lydia realized that he was much younger than he looked, but even more dangerous than he seemed.

'My name is Lydia Foy,' she told him, hugging her arms across her chest to cover her nudity. Then before he could lose interest, she hurried on. 'I have news that your lord would want to hear.'

'What news?' he demanded.

'I wish to speak to you in confidence.' She nodded, significantly, at the other men. 'Somewhere we can be alone.'

Christopher acceded and led her to his chamber, high in the north-east tower. It had been uninhabited when he found it. Like wolves, the common pirates mostly hunted, ate and slept together in packs. They shunned such lonely places. But for him, the solitude was perfect.

And now it afforded him privacy. He told himself that he had brought her here only so he could hear Lydia's story without interruption, but that was not the whole truth. He could not forget what he had seen as he stepped into the guardroom: her naked breasts, her dress torn open down as low as her thighs. Now, she had managed to tie the laces of her bodice together to give herself some semblance of modesty, but he could still see bare skin through the gaps in the fabric.

He had not been with a woman since the morning Poola captured him with Tamaana. Not for lack of opportunity – the pirate castle attracted plenty of whores and other, willing women – but he had not felt any attraction towards them, as he did for this woman.

'What do you have to tell me?' Christopher asked.

Lydia was once again perfectly poised despite her disarray. 'How is it that an Indian pirate comes to speak such refined English?' she asked him.

'I served some time on a coastal trader,' he explained.

'Were you ever in Bombay?'

Christopher tensed. Could she know him? But that was impossible. He had glimpsed his reflection in a bucket of water that morning: his own mother would not recognize him.

'I have visited Bombay,' he answered carefully.

'Then you have heard of Governor Courtney?'

'Yes,' he said tightly. 'Of course I have.'

'Are you aware that two of his wife's sisters are held prisoner in this castle?'

Christopher stared at her speechlessly. Lydia, who missed nothing, saw the astonishment on his face, but could not guess the reason for it.

'Their names are Sarah and Agnes. Except that Sarah will not reveal her identity, because . . .' She had been about to tell him the truth, to explain Sarah's fear of Guy, but her good sense made her cautious. 'Because she fears Angria will take advantage of the connection to increase the ransom he demands,' she lied.

'You are betraying her confidence,' Christopher observed, but his tone was not judgemental.

Lydia edged towards him, so close her full breasts almost touched his bare chest and she could feel the heat coming off his body.

'Please,' she implored him. 'My husband was killed in the massacre at Chittattinkara, and I am all alone. I do not expect charity; all I ask is a chance to earn my freedom.'

She bit her lip, like a small girl, and opened her eyes wide. She touched his forearm, feeling the hardness of his muscles. 'I do not know how you came to be here, but it can only be providence that brought us together. I am sorely in need of a good man to give me protection.'

Christopher stared down at her. Her statement had left him in turmoil, yet at that moment, all he wanted was to have her; and it was clear that she was reciprocating his attraction to her.

He reached for her, and untied the laces of her torn bodice and drew them apart. She made no effort to pull away as he bowed forward and took the nipple of one of her breasts in his mouth, sucking on it as he undid his own belt and let his *dhoti* drop to the floor. Lydia's wrists were still manacled: she raised her arms and looped the chain of the manacles over his head so they were bound together. Then she moved backwards, drawing him after her, until she felt the back of her knees come up against the mattress of his bed.

'Be gentle with me,' she murmured, but Christopher barely heard her. With both hands he reached down and spread the lips of her sex. He ran his forefinger deeply into her; and she was wet and lubricious, slippery to his touch. She toppled over backwards onto the bed, and he was drawn down on top of her. She opened her legs and immediately felt his penis probing blindly at her. She wanted to take it in hand and guide it into herself, but of course her hands were manacled.

'Put it into me,' she whispered urgently into his ear, 'Quickly! I can wait no longer.' He reached down and she felt the glans of his penis pushing her lips apart. 'Yes, like that!' she whispered urgently.

Abruptly he speared his full majestic length deeply into her and Lydia screamed with terror and ecstasy. For the first time in her entire life all the cunning and duplicity that she had built into a formidable bulwark against the world were swept away like so much trash before the roaring flood of her lust.

She carried Christopher with her into the tempest, so that they climaxed at the same moment in time. Her cries almost matched his animal roarings. Afterwards, still manacled to him, she fell at once into a death-like sleep.

Christopher could not sleep. He lay beside her stroking the long braids of her hair, trying to make sense of what Lydia had told him.

Though he had only dim memories of his Aunt Agnes, from before she left Bombay, he could imagine how she might have been captured and brought to Tiracola. But Sarah Courtney?

Caroline, his mother, seldom ever spoke of her second sister; Christopher had been twelve years old before he heard her name mentioned. When he asked, his mother had told him that Sarah had died many years earlier in Africa, with her husband; his uncle Tom Courtney.

But now it seemed that she was not dead. And if she was alive, might Tom not be also?

The moon beamed through the turret window and shone on the Neptune sword that leaned against the far wall. The gold inlay showed silver in the moonlight. Could Tom have brought the sword to India? Was he here now? And if so, what did that signify for Christopher?

Guy hated Tom. Christopher hated Guy. Did that mean that

he and his uncle could join forces against his father? Could he use Sarah, somehow – bring her to Tom as part of a bargain? Or should he pass on Lydia's intelligence to Angria? It would bring a better ransom, and he would rise in the pirate's favour.

The moon dipped, the stars turned and the sky outside his window began to brighten. Christopher slipped out of the circle of Lydia's manacled arms and stood up stiffly. He gazed down at Lydia, her skin so pale and smooth. His loins stirred again. There was time, all the time in the world; he told himself.

He lay down behind her. He squeezed her breast, and she moaned softly. He kissed the nape of her neck, and she pushed her naked buttocks back into his belly. Even in her sleep she was seeking out his manhood.

A low sound drifted through the window like thunder. In an instant, Christopher was on his feet. It had sounded far away, but he knew that noise better than his own breathing. It was the distant roar of cannon.

He went to the window and peered out. Beyond, past the castle walls, across the narrow promontory that connected it to the mainland, the sun was rising over a low hill. And on that far hill war banners fluttered from the tips of thousands upon thousands of upraised lances. They fluttered in the morning breeze, while the horsemen who carried them reined in their mounts and gazed down on Tiracola castle.

A mighty army was on the march.

The travellers made their way along the passes through the mountains. The paths were narrow so they walked mostly in single file, dark shapes in the mist making for the great fortress that crowned the mountain ahead.

Tom Courtney led the way, with Ana and Francis following him. Merridew and the four other sailors who had survived the wreck of the *Kestrel* came after them. They had travelled many days since leaving Bombay, following the coast until they reached the foothills and this path which led them into the high peaks of the Western Ghats.

'It is like some fairy-tale kingdom, where a terrible curse has befallen the land,' Francis remarked. As a boy, he had devoured the romances of the Arthurian knights he had found in the library of High Weald. The landscape they had passed through reminded him of the wasteland where the Fisher King lived in the Grail Castle. So soon after the passage of the monsoon all should have been green and verdant; instead, the pastures were blackened and barren. Most of the villages had been abandoned: sometimes they passed three or four days without seeing a soul, and at night very few fires or lamps pricked the darkness. The people they did see were mostly naked and starving, crawling out from their mud hovels like animals from their holes to stare at them as they passed. The only signs of civilization were the forts that overlooked every valley, perched on the mountaintops like the nests of eagles.

'What has happened here?' Francis wondered on their second morning in the wilderness.

'War,' said Ana. 'This is the kingdom of the Marathas. They have been fighting for survival against the Great Mughal these past thirty years, and it has cost them dearly. And now they have their kingdom, they cannot agree who should rule over it. They are wracked by civil war.'

Now at last they had reached the fortress of Satara, climbing a road that wound steeply up the face of the mountain. Guards challenged them at the gate. Tom stepped forward. The time for hiding his identity had passed. He spoke slowly and clearly, pausing while Ana translated.

'I am Thomas Courtney, the brother of Guy Courtney, the Governor of Bombay. I have come to speak with the rajah, Shahuji.'

From the guards' impassive faces, Tom could not tell if the name meant anything to them. However, they were led into

331

the fortress and admitted to an antechamber, while servants scurried deeper into the castle precincts.

'What do you know of this rajah?' Tom asked Ana. 'His kingdom is in ruins. Will he have the stomach for more fighting?'

'Do not underestimate him,' Ana warned. 'There was a time when the Great Mughal's army captured this fortress. To prove they meant to stay, the Mughal general brought his wife and children. Shahuji besieged it. He captured the Mughal commander's wife and daughters, and tied them over the mouths of his cannon below the walls. In full view, he primed the touch-holes and had his gunners light their linstocks.'

'What happened then?' Francis asked.

'The Mughal commander surrendered. Shahuji regained his capital, and he has stayed here ever since.' She swatted a fly that had landed on her arm. 'Also, I have heard that he is a master of letting men see in him only what he wants them to see. Whatever impression he gives you, do not be deceived.'

She fell silent as the servants returned. Guy Courtney's name evidently carried much weight. Leaving Merridew and the men, Tom, Francis and Ana were led through more corridors and anterooms into the very heart of the castle.

'What does this mean?' Francis asked in a whisper.

'It speaks of Shahuji's self-confidence,' Tom answered. 'A lesser man would have sought to impress us with his authority by keeping us waiting.'

At the top of a grand staircase, and through a pair of ornately carved doors, they entered the throne room. It was austere, by Indian standards, though that was still lavish enough to make any European palace seem like a convent. In the centre of the room, surrounded by courtiers and guards, a throne stood on a raised platform. It seemed to be made of solid gold, draped with lion and tiger skins. The man who sat on it wore rich robes, ivory silk sewn with silver threads and strung with pearls, lapis lazuli and garnets.

He was younger than Tom had expected, not yet thirty, his youth accentuated by his clean-shaven cheeks. He held himself erect, tense, conscious of his image, proud of his estate. He studied his three visitors. His gaze was inscrutable. The only sound was the clicking of the magnificent pearls on a string around his neck, as Shahuji shuffled them between his fingers.

'You are Governor Courtney's brother,' he broke the silence at last. It was a statement, not a question. He spoke in Portuguese, the *lingua franca* between India and Europe. Tom had learned a little of it from the Portuguese settlers he had traded with at Mozambique and Sofala, on the east coast of Africa, but he let Ana translate. He did not want any misunderstandings.

'I am Guy Courtney's twin brother.'

'He has sent you to claim the *firman* he demands of me?' Shahuji suggested.

'I am not here on my brother's behalf,' Tom admitted. 'I am here to suggest to you how you may gain an advantage over him.'

The rajah blinked. 'If you are Guy Courtney's brother, how can you wish to betray him?' Tom remembered what Ana had told him of the civil war among the Marathas, how Shahuji's aunt had tried to wrest the kingdom from him.

'I believed you would understand, your highness, how different branches of a family do not always work in accord with each other.'

Tom waited patiently while Ana translated. He wondered if perhaps he had gone too far, if the rajah would take umbrage – or worse. The shuttered eyes gave him no hint. Shahuji stared at him for a while, and then he leaned forward a fraction on his throne. 'What is it that you have really come to me for?'

'I wish to speak to you in private,' Tom said boldly. He knew

333

that the throne room was a political theatre, not a place for real bargaining.

Shahuji pursed his lips. Then, without a word, he rose and stepped down from his throne. The courtiers parted; a door in the far wall opened before him. Tom and the others followed, out onto a high stone balcony overlooking the valley. Tom remembered Ana's story of the Mughal general's family. Was this where he had stood, looking down as his children were tied over the mouths of the guns? Had their cries risen high enough that he could hear them here?

The guards left them there and retreated into the throne room, and closed the doors behind them. The only sound was the wind across the mountains, and the clicking of the rajah's beads.

'Why do you wish to betray your brother?' Shahuji posed the question without judgement, as calmly as if he were enquiring about Tom's health.

'I believe you and I have an enemy in common.'

'Governor Courtney is not my enemy.'

'I was speaking of the pirate Angria. He molests your shipping and terrorizes your coasts. He is also an ally of your mother-in-law in her campaign against you.'

Shahuji gave the merest fraction of a nod.

'Angria has captured my wife and her sister,' Tom went on. 'He holds them in his castle at Tiracola.'

A flash of annoyance passed over Shahuji's face; the first emotion he had showed. 'Tiracola is my castle,' he said.

'That is why we have come to you,' said Tom quickly. 'You desire to have your castle back. I want my family back.'

Whether Shahuji was intrigued or insulted, Tom could not tell.

'My brother Guy wishes to make a treaty with you,' Tom said. 'He allows Angria to commit his crimes with impunity, so you will be forced to negotiate. But if we drove Angria out of Tiracola and broke his power, you would have the upper hand over Guy. And further more you would recover your castle.'

'Why do you tell me this?' Shahuji asked.

'Because Angria offered to ransom the hostages, and Guy refused to pay the ransom money,' Francis intervened hotly. 'Only you have the power to seize Tiracola from Angria and free our family.'

Tom shot Francis a cautioning look, although Shahuji gave no sign of having taken offence. He merely raised an eyebrow.

'Why do you not think that if I had the power to take Tiracola, I would not have done so already?' He stared down the mountain, into the mist that still swirled through the valley. 'Let me explain to you about my kingdom,' he continued. 'In the lands you passed through to come here – did you see any crops?'

Tom and Francis shook their heads.

Shahuji continued, 'Why grow crops when your lord cannot defend your village? Once, this was a rich kingdom. Now, the peasants farm only what they can take with them when they flee into the jungles. For thirty years, my grandfather Chhatrapati Shivaji fought the Mughals for this kingdom. When he died, my aunt proclaimed her son the new king, though in fact the throne was mine. Now the Great Mughal is dead and his empire is in disarray, but we cannot have peace because we fight amongst ourselves. We call this *bhalerai* – the rule of the spear. Every local chieftain thinks he is a warrior. They gather their own war-bands, and fight each other for the scraps. In places, my authority is less than the lowest *patil* – the headman.'

He picked a loose piece of stone off the parapet and let it fall into the void below where they stood.

'Ever since my grandfather started his war, the Mughals dismissed us as bandits. "Rats in the attic," they called us. I have seen how rats, when they have nothing else to eat, will devour each other. Perhaps the Mughals were right, that's what

335

we are.' He never once raised his voice or allowed any emotion to inflect it.

'You triumphed over the mightiest empire in the world,' Tom pointed out.

'Have you ever seen a Mughal cavalryman?' Shahuji did not wait for a response. 'Their horses are the biggest and strongest mounts that exist. They are bred that way, for the weight of a cavalryman and his armour is immense. Our horses are small, light-footed beasts made for mountain paths and quick escapes. We never fought the Mughals in open battle. When they sent armies against us, we let them pass, and then harried their supply lines. When they besieged our fortresses, we let them in, then burned our crops and slaughtered our own livestock so that the occupiers would starve. That is how we wage war. Against a fortress such as Tiracola, we would smash ourselves to pieces.'

'Have you no pity?' Francis protested angrily. 'My aunt has already suffered for weeks at the hands of those pirates. Would you leave her to die in that dungeon?'

Shahuji gave him an impassive look. 'As a boy I was sent as a hostage to the court of the Great Mughal. I lived my whole childhood there. Every morning for eighteen years, I woke wondering if my guards would cut me down; and every evening, I went to bed unsure if I would see another dawn.'

'I did not know that,' Francis dropped his gaze, chastened.

'When I was eleven, the Great Mughal captured my father. My father refused to do homage, so the Mughal had him torn limb from limb by a pack of hunting dogs. He made me watch. Then he made me sit at his right hand at the celebratory banquet. So, you see, I know what it is to be a prisoner.'

Francis mumbled an apology. Tom bowed his head in acknowledgement. Now he understood why Shahuji could discuss the ruin of his kingdom with such bloodless calm. Growing up a hostage, a sword always inches from his neck, he must have learned to bury his emotions so deep they might never come to the surface.

'I do not ask for sympathy,' Tom began.

Shahuji said nothing, but his eyes flickered with impatience.

'But I believe our interests have aligned.'

Ana joined in the discussion, 'The pirate Angria supports your aunt, and her son the pretender, in your civil war. If you are ever to unite your kingdom, you must destroy Angria first.'

'My father wore out the Mughals. I will defeat Angria the same way – by attrition. Tiracola is impregnable.'

Tom grunted with exasperation. 'Every man I meet says that. Has anyone ever attacked it?'

'No one who has lived to tell the tale,' said Shahuji with the ghost of a smile.

'Give me an army, and I will break open the fortress for you and for my family.' Tom spoke flatly.

'I have heard you are well-schooled in withstanding a siege. Are you so confident you can prosecute one as well?'

Tom saw the look Shahuji gave him, and finally began to get a measure of the man. The siege of Brinjoan had been fought hundreds of miles away, in a distant kingdom and under a false name, yet Shahuji knew of it, and knew Tom had been there, though he had only arrived that morning. Tom could not help but be impressed.

'Did you ever hear of another pirate named al-Auf?' Tom asked.

'The evil one,' Shahuji translated effortlessly from the Arabic. Growing up at the Mughal court, he must have learned the language fluently. 'I confess I have not.'

'That is because he died many years ago. Until his death, he was the most feared pirate in the Indian Ocean. Even the mighty ships of the East India Company were not safe from him. He ravaged their trade from a great fort on the island of Flor de la Mar, defended with mighty batteries and a garrison of a thousand pirates. Men said that it was impregnable, too. But my father and I burned his fleet and broke open the fort. I myself severed al-Auf's head from his shoulders.'

It was the last battle Hal Courtney had fought. He had lost his legs in the explosion that blew open the gate, and soon gangrene had set into his wounds. But Tom did not mention that.

Behind Shahuji, a ray of sun pierced the cloud and lit up the mist, like the glow of cannon fire in the smoke of battle. Tom looked at the rajah, but his smooth face gave nothing away.

He seemed to reach some decision. He straightened, and called over Tom's shoulder. Turning, Tom saw half a dozen retainers standing at the back of the balcony, though he was certain they had not been there earlier. The servants bowed, and gestured to Tom and his companions to follow them. Evidently, the interview had finished.

'What did he say?' Francis asked Ana, as they were escorted back inside the palace.

'He announced he wishes to go hunting.'

Francis stopped short in the corridor. 'We came to make war, not hunt,' he protested.

'You do not understand,' said Ana. 'The one is preparation for the other. The rajah is considering your proposal, but he is allowing himself options. When he summons his lords for the hunt, they will bring their retainers, their captains, and their arms. He is assembling his army, without committing himself. Also, success in the hunt will be a good omen for battle.'

'And if the hunt is unsuccessful?'

Ana shrugged, 'Let us pray that it is not.'

Over the next few days, from where Shahuji lodged them in the palace, they watched dozens of bands of armed men climb the treacherous road up the mountainside. Soon the castle rang with the sounds of a great host, while the elephants trumpeted from their stables at the foot of the cliff, and the horses kicked up their heels and frolicked in their paddocks.

Tom chaffed at the delay. Shahuji was a generous host: he sent them plentiful food and drink, served by beautiful attendants with inviting smiles. But the Courtneys were not allowed to leave the precincts of the palace. Tom sent the serving girls away and spent hours at the window, watching the legions assembling. When he tired of that, they played chess. Francis was a tolerable player, Tom had played since he was a child, so the main conflict was between him and Ana.

'If only taking a castle were as easy in real life,' she said, as she swept Tom's rook off the board. The pieces were all carved from ivory, beautifully detailed, unlike any set Tom had ever played with previously. All the pieces were shaped like elephants or gods or common soldiers, with ever more elaborate distinctions of rank.

Tom retaliated by attacking swiftly with his queen. In quick succession, he took two pawns, a bishop and her rook – then found his king isolated.

'You play like an Englishman,' said Ana, amused. 'Like all the hat-wearers. You charge in, and do not fear for the consequences. The Indian way is to wait and be patient.'

She picked up her knight, kissed it and took his queen with it.

'Patience is so pathetic,' Tom told her. His bishop slithered across the board into the square guarded by his knight, and brought her king under attack, leaving it with no avenue of escape.

'Checkmate.' He smiled at her.

* * *

On the morning of the hunt, Shahuji's attendants fetched them, and carried them on palanquins down the mountain, and some miles through the jungle to Shahuji's hunting lodge, which was a many-storeyed pagoda set in a walled garden by a limpid lake.

As boys, Tom and Francis had both been hunting and shooting on the High Weald estate. The routines were familiar: the gathering of the beaters, the blare of horns and the excitement that charged the air as the hunters assembled. However this was on a different scale to anything they had seen before. The beaters numbered in the hundreds. Musicians played trumpets and stringed instruments, and serving girls gave them cups of arak spiced with cinnamon, and trays of dates and almonds. Elephants stood placidly, munching the great bundles of leaves their keepers fed them. They carried ornately decorated boxes mounted on their backs, which Ana told them were called *howdahs*.

'That is how we will ride out,' she said.

Francis stared at the huge animals. 'Is it safe?'

'Considerably safer than coming eye to eye with a tiger,' she assured him.

The beaters, armed with sticks and small axes, trooped off into the forest. The others waited as the morning wore on. The musicians had stopped playing; the laughter and talk had lapsed to a few quiet conversations. The loudest sound was the elephants, masticating their leaves. All the hunters watched the forest, and listened expectantly.

'Should we not mount up and chase the tiger?' Francis wondered.

Ana put this question to the rajah.

'You cannot simply venture into the jungle and seek a tiger,' he explained. 'You must lure him out. My men have tethered water buffaloes at different places in the forest. When a tiger comes for the kill, they will inform us, and then we will go to that place.'

Shahuji was in a happier mood that morning, more relaxed than he had been in the palace. Though he still bore himself with the same dignity, he could not hide his pleasure and excitement in the hunt. Tom could imagine how the freedom of the forest, the simple pursuit of man against beast, would appeal to a man who had spent more than half his life as a noble prisoner.

Then a messenger ran in to the clearing in front of the lodge. He was drenched with sweat and panting for breath. He babbled out his message, and then he collapsed to his knees.

Shahuji turned to his guests, his face lighting up with excitement. Already, the attendants were readying the elephants and guns, and making the final preparations.

'The tiger has made his kill,' they shouted to each other.

Tom had shot more elephants than he could count, but this was the first time he had ridden on one. It was smaller than the great African elephants he was accustomed to, but still majestic: a big bull with a crimson caste-mark painted between his eyes that gave him a wise, almost human air. Out of habit, Tom found himself sizing up the tusks, and calculating how much they would fetch in Cape Town.

The mahout, the driver, patted the elephant's flank to make it kneel. Tom stepped onto the animal's outstretched hind leg, then onto his haunch and finally into the *howdah*. A young boy clambered in carrying a pair of fine firelocks with silver chasing. Tom squinted down the barrel, and saw it was rifled for greater speed and accuracy.

The mahout vaulted over the elephant's head like an acrobat, settled on the neck and tucked his knees behind the beast's ears. He barked a command in a high, lilting voice, and the elephant lumbered to his feet. Tom looked back and saw that Francis and Ana had climbed onto their own animals, while the Rajah led the way in a magnificent *howdah* with gilded woodwork and a cloth-of-gold awning.

341

Tom soon got used to the elephant's rolling gait as it stamped through the jungle. He marvelled at the animal's ability. If a branch threatened to catch the *howdah*, the elephant would reach up with his trunk and snap it off. Sometimes, where the way became narrow, he pushed over whole trees to make a wider path. When the way became boggy, he lowered his head and felt the ground with his trunk for the safest footing.

After a few miles, they crested a ridge and came down into a gully, formed by a dry river bed. They followed it another mile or so, winding through the jungle. In the mud and river sand, Tom read the tracks of many varieties of animals. Monkeys screeched from the trees; jungle fowl preened themselves at the river's edge. A muster of peacocks flew low overhead, their necks gleaming brilliant sapphire-blue in the sunshine. The sight gave Tom a pang, as it reminded him forcefully of the jewel in the pommel of the Neptune sword.

The rajah called a halt, at a place where a dry stream met the river bed. The elephants knelt, and the hunting party dismounted. Tom stretched his legs and looked around, scanning the undergrowth for any sign of their prey.

Shahuji missed nothing. 'Have you ever hunted the tiger before?' he asked, through Ana.

'I've hunted lions.'

Shahuji nodded. 'I have seen lions. The Great Mughal kept them for his pleasure at the court in Delhi. But the tiger is more dangerous. He is larger, stronger and fiercer. The lion hunts in packs, but the tiger hunts alone, so he must be stronger and more cunning. I have seen a tiger kill a buffalo and pick it up in her jaws like a cat carrying a mouse.'

He saw the sceptical look on Tom's face. 'Once, in Delhi, the Mughal arranged a fight between a lion and a tiger. It was the talk of the palace: all the nobles arrived in great excitement to see such a contest. When the beasts were unleashed in the arena, every man was on his feet.'

'What happened?' asked Francis.

'The tiger killed the lion with a single swipe of his paw. His claw severed the artery in the neck, and he bled to death.' Again, Tom saw Shahuji's ghostly smile, the most emotion he ever permitted himself. 'The emperor was furious. You have never seen so many disappointed *amirs* and *jagirdars*.'

While he spoke, his attendants had unstrapped the royal *howdah* and unloaded it from the elephant's back. They carried it between them to a tall tree, where they rigged ropes and hoisted it ten feet into the air, so that it came to rest on the outspread branches. They erected a ladder beside it.

'This will be our *machan*,' said Shahuji. 'Our hide.'

They climbed the ladder. The servants had rigged two *howdah*s side by side, one for Tom and Shahuji, and one for Francis and Ana. The gun-bearers and other servants perched in the branches behind them, all of them constantly scanning the jungle from their raised viewpoint.

'The tiger likes to follow the water courses,' Shahuji explained. He pointed to the place on the opposite bank where the stream joined the river. 'If the beaters drive him correctly, he will come out there.'

Tom began to understand why the hunt was such fine preparation for war. With over eight hundred men spread across miles of jungle, all hunting an unseen prey, communication was paramount. If one portion of the line moved too quickly or too slowly, it would create a gap for the tiger to slip through. If the tiger changed course, the whole line would have to wheel about. The understandings that developed, the practice in transmitting orders between the different commanders and manoeuvring the units, would be priceless in battle.

The mahouts led the elephants away. 'They will join the beaters,' Shahuji explained. 'They are trained to take branches in their trunks and clash them against the trees, to make a noise to frighten the tiger.'

They settled down to wait. A symphony of birdsong rang through the forest. Insects buzzed about them and crawled over their skin. Tom stayed as still as possible. A nilgai, a small-horned antelope, grazed along the river bed. Tom sighted his gun on it, but did not waste the shot.

'I have a previous history with Angria,' Shahuji said suddenly. 'Perhaps you know of it?'

Tom shook his head.

'Before Angria became a pirate, he was a captain in my navy. With the Mughals pressing us hard by land, the sea was our one refuge, vital for our supply and communication. Then, when we needed him most, Angria spied his opportunity. He mutinied, took his ships and crews, and overthrew our garrison on Tiracola. From there, he scoured the coast, seizing our fortresses and capturing our ships, while we were too hard-pressed by the Mughals to retaliate in strength. I can never forgive him, for in his greed, he nearly destroyed our kingdom, in order to make his own lawless empire of the sea.'

Shahuji's fingers drummed on the stock of his gun.

'Yet, I was willing to forgive him. For the sake of the kingdom, I would have put aside our quarrel. I sent emissaries, under a banner of truce, to offer peace. Do you know what he did?'

Even the memory made his face grow pale with anger.

'He sent my men back. He had put out their eyes, and branded their foreheads with his sign. So deep, you could see the mark burned into the bone of their skulls. So deeply had he burned them that their brains were damaged, and they were like little children again; unable to talk, and incontinent, so that they soiled their clothing.'

Tom tried not to think of Sarah and Agnes in the hands of such a man.

'It would gladden my heart to see Angria trampled by elephants,' Shahuji went on, 'as the Great Mughal sometimes executed his prisoners in Delhi. But I will be candid with you.

344

You see me on a golden throne, amid hundreds of courtiers, and you think I am a great man.'

He thumped his fist on his chest. 'I *am* a great man. I have taken the sacred thread, and I am the *Chhatrapati*, the emperor of the Marathas. And yet . . .' A mournful expression flitted across his face. 'Beyond my palace, my power is not what it ought to be. In a civil war, every man's loyalty is in play. If I attacked Tiracola, and failed, it would strike a mortal blow against my authority.'

'Guy Courtney makes the same argument,' said Francis. 'He would rather men believed him to be strong, than risk his dignity proving it.'

He spoke ardently, but Shahuji did not take offence. 'When you are older, you will understand that the appearance of power is often more real than its substance.'

'But if you have power, and do not use it, it is no power at all,' said Tom.

Shahuji did not answer. A new sound had penetrated the din of the jungle, a percussive clanking like a thousand blacksmiths hammering on their anvils. Tom wondered if it might be some unknown species of bird. Then, from Shahuji's reaction, he realized it must be the beaters, tapping their axe heads to drive the tiger towards the *machan*. To Tom, it was merely noise, but from the way Shahuji listened he could see the rajah was following the sound precisely, working out exactly how the hunt was progressing.

Clapping and shouts started up on their left. It was the stops, men placed in the treetops to stop the tiger veering off course. Shahuji took a gun from his bearer. Tom, Francis and Ana did likewise. Tom felt the thrill of the hunt rising in his blood.

A furious roar rang through the forest. The noise of the stops increased, beating the tiger back towards the river bed and the waiting guns. Like a flash of golden sunlight, the tiger burst from cover. For an instant, Tom forgot the gun in his

345

hands as he marvelled at his first view of the creature. It was an enormous animal, moving much too fast for him to even hazard a guess at its size. But it was much bigger than any of the lions he had seen in Africa.

It bounded across the clearing in the forest not twenty paces from where they stood and snarled when it saw the men in its path. It spun around. The white ruff around its head was erect and bristling. The fangs in its jaws sparkled as it roared.

Even at such close range it was a difficult shot, but the rajah fired. Tom saw the ball strike, but much too far back behind the shoulder blade. The heavy ball bowled the animal over. But in the same movement it somersaulted back onto all four feet, and kept on running without seeming to miss a stride. Both Tom and Francis fired simultaneously, but the tiger was moving too fast and their shots kicked up dirt and dead leaves several feet behind it. The tiger reached the forest edge and disappeared into the dense vegetation.

Shahuji jumped down from the tree, heedless of his own safety, and ran to the place where he had hit the tiger. He scanned the ground for a blood trail.

'He is hurt,' he declared, 'but not killed. This is when he is most dangerous.'

'What do we do now?' Tom demanded.

'The tiger will be thirsty after the chase and the wound I inflicted upon him. There is a water hole, not far from here. I think he will go there.'

Before Ana had finished translating, the mahouts had brought up the elephants. There was no time to rig the *howdah*s. They all clambered on to the elephants' backs, sitting on folded blankets and clinging to the rope that circled the girth as the animals strode forward.

In a short while, the gully opened into a wide meadow, with high grass that brushed the elephants' bellies. Up on its back, Tom felt as if he were on a ship, sailing through a rustling sea.

He gripped his firelock, and searched the ground ahead for a blood trail or pug marks. He knew that the tiger itself would be invisible. His stripes would blend almost perfectly with the long grass.

One of the huntsmen, running along ahead of the elephants, shouted and pointed at the ground without checking his speed.

'He has found the tiger's trail,' Ana called.

The mahouts kicked the elephants into a faster pace. Soon, the grass gave way to bare earth, trampled by many hoofs and paws. Even from high on the elephant's back, Tom could make out the tiger's tracks. Ground water was oozing into the freshly made depression that its paws had left, and the animal was beginning to bleed. Dribbles of bright blood sparkled in the sunlight like rubies.

'He is a male in his prime, about fourteen years old. But he has lost the toe on his left front,' Shahuji mused softly, and Ana translated.

Tom gave the rajah an approving nod of the head. To have gleaned so much from a casual glance high on the back of an elephant demonstrated his exceptional hunting skills.

The tracks ended at the edge of a muddy hole, half filled with water. A pair of kites watched from a lone, bare tree. The tiger was nowhere to be seen.

Every nerve in Tom's body tingled with anticipation. This was the overwhelming thrill of the hunt, and he had never lost his addiction to it since the first time his father put a gun in his hands.

The tiger must be near. The elephants had caught its scent. They twitched and shuffled anxiously, huffing through their trunks. The motion would make any accurate shooting well-nigh impossible. Shahuji slid down to the ground. Tom and Francis followed him.

Shahuji consulted with his huntsmen. 'There is another watercourse, a little to the north,' Ana translated. 'It leads through a ravine into the next valley. The tiger may attempt to go that way to escape our net.'

While they were talking the beaters started to catch up with them, and within minutes there were a hundred or more half-naked men in the clearing, armed only with sticks and machetes.

The rajah's elephant was thirsty. Without warning, it walked to the edge of the pool and began slurping up water through its trunk. The mahout shouted and hauled on its rope; more of the attendants clustered around it, but the beast was immovable. Distracted, everyone turned to watch.

This was when the tiger took the moment to attack its tormentors. It had been lying hidden behind a bank of low saplings, no higher than a man's knee, so thin that Tom could hardly believe it had hidden the huge creature so effectively. Even in the African lion, he had never seen such lethal speed. It charged in with snarling jaws and bristling white whiskers. Its tail was held like a scimitar curled over its back. Its great paws, each the size of a soup plate, with claws fully extended tore up the loose earth with each bound. It knocked down one of the mahouts and bit him in the back of his neck as he sprawled, severing his vertebrae and killing him instantly.

But the tiger did not fixate on the corpse beneath it. With its next bound it bore down upon a second running man and killed him with a bite that took the top off his head; and then he took down another man and another. Total pandemonium reigned over the field with men running and shouting and the elephants trumpeting and squealing, knocking down and trampling anyone who stood in their way.

Tom ran sideways, trying to get a clean shot at the tiger but the frenzied crowd blocked his line of fire and threatened to knock him off his feet. He saw Francis throw up his gun and chance a fleeting shot at the enraged beast, but one of the beaters ran in front of him as he fired and took the heavy ball squarely in the chest. He was thrown backwards with his machete spinning from his hand, dead before he hit the ground.

Shahuji stood his ground in the rout and turmoil, holding his firelock at high port, shouting at the tiger to attract its attention; 'Come to me, Shaitan! I will send you as a messenger to your foul gods! Come!'

The tiger seemed to hear him, and it swerved towards him. It opened its mouth as it roared at him, as if it accepted his challenge. Its fangs were encrimsoned with the blood of the men it had killed and it flattened into its charge. Shahuji leaned forward and raised the butt of his gun to his shoulder, his trigger finger poised, ready for the precise instant to fire his shot.

Only then Tom realized that Shahuji had not seen the elephant. It was one of those that had been drinking at the pool and it had been panicked by the scent and the roars of the tiger. It was rushing down blindly on the rajah.

Tom shouted a warning, but Shahuji was oblivious to all but the great cat in his gunsight. Likewise the elephant had the scent of the predator in its nostrils and the sounds of its roars ringing in it ears, and was oblivious to the man standing in its path. One of its great swinging feet struck Shahuji in the back, lifting him off his feet and throwing him in a heap fifteen feet away. The loaded and cocked gun was sent spinning from his hands and by chance it landed at Ana's feet. She stooped and swept it up.

The elephant rushed away into the long grass. The tiger had lost sight of the rajah and now it checked its charge, and swung its head left and right seeking an alternative quarry to savage.

It saw Francis. It swung towards him and roared. Francis was fumbling with his weapon, and Tom saw by the pallor of his face and his staring eyes that he was terrified witless. He had probably never fired a heavy gun before, and he had certainly never stood down the charge of a great ravening beast such as this.

349

From where Tom was standing it was a long and awkward shot; furthermore Ana was in the line of fire. But Francis was in mortal danger, and Tom had to take the chance. He swung up his own gun, and fired in the same movement. Yet he knew at once that something was dreadfully wrong. Smoke spurted from the muzzle of the gun but there was no recoil at all. Either his *shikari* had not loaded the ball on top of the charge, or the ball had been shaken loose from the barrel when he dismounted from the elephant.

In any event the tiger was untouched, and continued its charge at Francis. At the last possible moment Francis seemed to rally his wits and his courage. He flung up his gun and fired in the same movement, but his eyes had been fixed on the tiger and not on the gunsight. Tom saw the ball kick up a spurt of damp earth six feet behind the charging animal, and at least three feet to its left.

Untouched by the shot the tiger was still charging in on Francis, who threw down the gun and began to turn away. The great striped beast launched itself into the air, springing at him with its jaws wide open and Francis covered his face with both hands and stood helplessly, screaming, 'No! No!'

Another shot boomed out from nowhere, and the tiger seemed to crumple up in mid-air. However its momentum carried it onwards and it crashed headlong into Francis, slamming him to the ground and piling up on top of him.

Tom reached the man and beast only seconds later. He seized the tiger's head and, by some superhuman effort, dragged the massive carcass off of Francis.

'Are you all right?' he shouted at Francis.

'I think so,' Francis stammered as he crawled back onto his knees. 'You saved my life. Thank you, Tom.'

'Not me! My gun was not even loaded with ball . . .' He looked around him and for the first time became aware of Ana. She was standing ten feet behind where Francis was lying. She was still holding the butt of the rajah's long gun to her shoulder, and a cloud of blue gun smoke seeped from the muzzle.

'Ana Duarte!' Tom went to her and took the gun from her trembling hands. 'Did you fire the shot that killed this monster?' She nodded, too overcome to speak. 'That was a shot of which any man could be proud.'

Tom reached down and seized the tiger's head with both hands and twisted it around. Ana's musket ball had struck the great animal squarely in the forehead and gone on through the centre of its brain.

'And a shot of which any woman should be doubly proud!' Tom went on.

'I had to do it; Francis is the only man I have,' Ana explained reasonably, but her voice was shaky.

Tom's skin prickled as he entered the courtyard of the Rani's palace at Chittattinkara. He thought of the men who had died there, Captain Hicks, Lawrence Foy and so many others. Then he wondered if he might have dreamed it. The bullet holes in the brickwork had been patched up, blood scrubbed from the stones, and the shattered balconies replaced. The only sign that a battle had ever taken place was the fresh plaster on the walls. It made him angry to remember the carnage that they had lived through.

The throne room brought back many more bitter memories. The last time he had been there, he had fought Tungar for the Neptune sword, and nearly died for it. Now, the Rani received him cordially, as if history were a blank page. Like Shahuji, she had the ruler's art of forgetting everything that was no longer convenient. Tom was not sure if he detested her for it, or envied her.

He did not waste time with pleasantries.

'The Rajah of Satara, Chhatrapati Shahuji, demands the return of the cannons you seized from the wreck of my ship.

He has a vessel standing off the coast near Brinjoan ready to take them aboard.' This was the same ship that had brought Tom from the coast near Satara. Francis and Ana had stayed with Shahuji as he mustered his army and prepared for the siege of Tiracola.

The Rani smiled at Tom's outburst. She was so lovely when she smiled that Tom was thrown off his stride for a moment.

'The cannons were mine by right of salvage,' she explained reasonably. 'All wrecks on this coast, and their cargoes, belong to me.' She lifted a hand to stay Tom's retort. 'I assure you, Captain Courtney, that I have no quarrel with you. On the contrary I find myself exceptionally well disposed towards you. If it were within my power I would return your guns to you without quibble. But, alas, I no longer have them. When my men fled the siege of Brinjoan, they also abandoned the guns there. The hat-wearers have them. My scouts report they have mounted them on the ramparts of their fort.'

Tom cursed inwardly. He had feared that might be so, but had come to the Rani first in hope of being mistaken. If Guy had sent word to the fort of Brinjoan of his escapades in Bombay, he could expect a hot reception if he ventured there to reclaim them.

'I am sorry you have wasted your time by coming to me,' said the Rani. 'But from my own point of view I have enjoyed renewing our acquaintance. Is there any other way that I might be of service to you?' She leaned forward on her throne and the movement accentuated the size and shape of her bosom.

'There is another matter.' Tom was confused and mollified by her change of attitude towards him, so he decided to take full advantage of it. 'Your captain, Tungar, stole a weapon that belonged to me. It belonged to my grandfather and my father before me. I place a very high sentimental value upon it. It is a gilded sword, with a sapphire in the pommel.'

'I know it well.' She nodded. 'It is truly a magnificent weapon.

Tungar was inordinately proud of it. He carried it into battle.'

'Yes!' Tom agreed. 'But I found his body after he was killed in the assault on Brinjoan. Tungar did not have the weapon with him.'

'One of your men must have looted it.'

'None of them had reached his corpse before I did. If it was looted, it must have been a man from your army.'

The Rani made an elegant but dismissive gesture. Tom watched her hands; they were lovely, almost as beautiful as her face. 'No subject of mine would dare hide such a treasure from me. And what would a peasant do with such a weapon, and where could he sell it that I would not hear of it? If it has not been found, that is because either the sea took it, or it has been looted.'

Tom flinched at the thought, though he knew she spoke good sense. He had one more question.

'There was a man in your service – he spoke English, and wielded a strange sword with a blade like a whip. What became of him?'

'His name was Absalom. He disappeared in the final battle. We did not find his body. Perhaps he lies buried under the rubble of the gatehouse.'

Her words hit Tom with surprising force. Of course it did not matter – Absalom was just another pirate – yet his mind refused to let it go. He had some unfinished business with the man Absalom: avenging Hicks, certainly, but something else besides.

He turned to go.

'Wait.' The Rani's tone was imperative. Tom paused. 'There are many hat-wearers who have settled in India to sell their skill as warriors.'

'I serve the Rajah of Satara,' Tom answered.

'Whatever he pays you, I will triple it. I could make you a great man in my kingdom. You would want for nothing.'

Her cheeks had flushed lightly. Her jewelled hand reached to her throat, resting on the valley between her breasts.

'Stay with me, Thomas Courtney.' Her voice sank to a whisper. 'I have need of you.'

He was riven by guilt and temptation. He felt the very foundations of his honour shaken. She was so very beautiful, but also so very evil.

Tom doffed his hat and made her a courtly bow. 'Alas, your highness, I must leave you now to rescue my wife.'

Returning to the fort at Brinjoan was even stranger than revisiting the Rani's palace. The sentry on the gate stared at Tom as if he were a ghost.

'Mr Weald?' he stammered.

Tom recognized him – one of the sepoys who had survived the siege. He tried to remember the man's name. 'Akal?'

The sentry beamed with pleasure at being recognized. 'Welcome back, *sahib*.'

'Is the new Governor here?'

'He came three weeks ago.' He grinned, as if at a private joke. 'However, I do not think he will be happy to see you.'

'Then take me to him.'

The East India Company had been busy repairing the fort, though the work was not yet finished. Gangs of half-naked labourers toiled with stones and mortar, reconstructing the gatehouse, but the Governor's house which Tom had torn down was already rebuilt. He was glad to see that, this time, they had used bricks and tiles instead of wood and straw. One hard lesson learned, at least.

No one guarded the door to the Governor's office. 'Wait outside,' Tom told Akal. 'Better if he does not know you let me in.'

Without knocking, he stepped inside. The Governor's desk was stacked high with papers, but they could not have been

354

urgent. The Governor himself lounged on a day bed, half asleep, holding a goblet of wine against his chest. Some had spilled, leaving a red mark spreading across his shirt-front like a wound.

Tom slammed the door shut. The Governor woke and sat up with a start. More wine spilled from the cup. He gaped at Tom.

'Mr Weald?' he squeaked.

Tom nodded grimly, hiding his surprise. 'Mr Kyffen.'

'What – ah – why . . . ?' Kyffen scrambled to his feet.

'I have come for my guns,' said Tom baldly. 'The nine pounders the Rani salvaged from my ship, those that the Company recovered from the battlefield.'

Kyffen stared at him speechlessly.

'Are you going to tell me they are your property?' Tom asked. 'After everything I did for the Company, the least you could do is permit me to reclaim what is my own.'

Kyffen finally regained the power of speech. '*Hubladar*,' he shouted.

The door opened. Tom looked back, and saw another familiar face, the sergeant with the bristling moustache who had fought beside him in the siege. The man frowned. He drew a pistol from his belt, and trained it on Tom.

'This man is a murderer, a thief and an imposter, charged with high crimes in London and Bombay,' screeched Kyffen. 'Clap him in irons.'

The *hubladar* gazed at Tom while he twirled his moustache thoughtfully. Then he barked an order in his own dialect, and Tom heard the scurry of feet outside.

Tom's mind raced with possibilities. He had his own pistol, and a knife in his boot, but he had too much respect for the *hubladar* to think he could draw them quickly enough.

'I need those cannon to rescue Mrs Hicks and my wife from the pirate Angria,' he told Kyffen. 'The man who captured them because you abandoned them, while other men were dying to save your precious factory here.'

Two sepoys came in from the corridor, each with a pair of manacles. There was nothing Tom could do. He put out his hands. 'Is this how the East India Company shows its gratitude?'

Kyffen did not answer. As Tom was speaking, the *hubladar* suddenly switched the aim of his pistol from Tom to Kyffen. At the same time, the two sepoys stepped past Tom, seized Kyffen's wrists and snapped the manacles on him, passing the chain through the arms of his chair.

'This is mutiny!' cried Kyffen. 'When Governor Courtney hears of this—'

'It will not change Guy's opinion of me one jot,' said Tom cheerfully. He pulled a handkerchief from Kyffen's coat pocket, and stuffed it in his mouth to gag his complaints. Then he embraced the *hubladar*.

'Thank you, old friend,' he said, 'though you should not have done that. They will hang you for mutiny.'

The *hubladar* grinned, untroubled by the prospect. 'Is it true that Angria has captured Mrs Hicks?'

'I am afraid so; and also my wife, Sarah. They are being held at the fortress of Tiracola.'

'And you have a ship to carry the guns there?'

'She is waiting in the bay.'

'Then if you have space for another man aboard, I will join you.'

Tom clasped his hand. 'Bless you.' He looked down at Kyffen, squirming in his chair and struggling ineffectually against his bonds. 'I am going to take my cannons,' he told him. 'And while we are about it, perhaps we will relieve the Company of some of its powder and shot.'

Kyffen raged and writhed. He tried to spit out the gag, but Tom pushed it firmly back in and bound it in place with Kyffen's belt.

'When we have finished, I will free you. But if you are thinking that I cannot remove those guns alone – even with the *hubladar*'s help – be warned. If you so much as touch one sepoy because you suspect him of aiding me, I will get to hear of it and I will avenge it. You remember how the Rani treated Mr Foy? That will be as nothing compared to the torments I will visit on you. Do you understand?'

Kyffen stopped struggling and he nodded hopelessly.

'I will give your regards to Mrs Foy,' Tom assured him.

Flame spat from the cannon's mouth. Through a telescope, Tom watched the ball strike to the left of the castle gate. Another small shower of rubble trickled down from an area of wall that was already pitted and broken, speaking to the gunners' impressive accuracy. Behind him, Tom heard Merridew exhorting the Maratha artillerymen to work faster, to the chant of, '*Worm and sponge. Powder.*' He had already cut their reloading time from ten minutes to close to five, encouraging them with tales of the treasure to be had inside the pirates' castle, if only they could get inside.

It had been five weeks since Shahuji's army had arrived with the guns and powder that Tom had fetched from Brinjoan: five weeks trying to reduce those mighty walls. So many men had said the castle was impregnable, Tom had almost begun to believe it. But now, seeing it made real and with time to study its weaknesses, he had reason to hope.

True, any assault by sea would be sure to fail. There was no landing place at the foot of the sheer cliffs, save for a tiny jetty, and heavy floating booms had been strung across the little bay to the north where Angria kept his fleet anchored. Coral reefs ran far out to sea, showing above water at high tide, so that any ship which tried to bombard the castle would be in constant peril.

From the landward side, too, the defences were formidable. The promontory narrowed to a thin neck of land before the castle gate, making a tight approach which was well covered by falconets and other guns on the walls. Groves of prickly kalargi trees grew thick in front of the walls: not only would they impede attackers, but their springy branches would absorb much of the cannon shot. Iron spikes four feet long protruded from the gate, to counter the favourite Indian tactic of using elephants as battering rams.

But no attempt had been made to extend the defences further out. A low hill rose half a mile inland, offering a commanding field of fire over the fort. Angria had placed a small watchtower there, but that had mostly been to spy out ships at sea. Shahuji's cavalry had easily overrun it, driving out the defenders and claiming the hilltop, where his men had now dug gun emplacements and erected the battery of the *Kestrel*'s nine-pounders. Now, they kept up a barrage day and night, opening the breach inch by inch.

Tom prayed it would be enough.

Down on the jetty that protruded from the promontory, fishermen unloaded the catch from their boats. The siege had allowed them to increase their prices, with eager buyers on both sides of the walls. Every morning, the boats clustered at the jetty like birds on a freshly planted field, while the pounding of the guns sounded like distant thunder.

It had become such a constant background chorus that Christopher, supervising the unloading, barely noticed it any more. Spray splashed his face as a wave crashed onto the rocks by the jetty. Out at sea, he saw the sail of a merchantman slowly beating up the coast. He felt a surge of frustration at its brazen freedom. The Marathas did not have the resources to blockade the castle by sea, but still Angria could not let his ships out: he needed their crews and their guns to defend the castle. So the fleet stayed anchored behind the boom, and the local merchants could conduct their trade without fear.

The only reason Christopher had come to Tiracola was the promise of riches. Now, with the fleet confined to its anchorage and no hope of plunder or prizes, he chafed at the enforced inactivity and poverty.

He knew he was not the only man who felt that way. Many of the pirates had started to complain, quietly at first but now ever more audibly. They knew the Marathas would not take the castle – it was impregnable, after all, and they could not be starved out while they could be resupplied by sea – but they did not like losing their livelihoods while the siege dragged on.

Christopher had decided to do something about it.

Most of the fishermen had cast off, heading back to their fishing grounds for another catch, which they would take to the Marathas in the evening. For them, war was merely a commercial opportunity. The barrels of fish had been loaded onto a crane, which hoisted them up the walls to the keep. Christopher lingered, chatting to the boatmen, while the pirates drifted back to their stations within the castle walls.

When they had gone, Christopher took one of the fishermen aside. He knew he could trust the man: for the past week, they had been running a scheme whereby Christopher let him over-charge for the fish, and the two of them shared the extra profits. Now, Christopher led him to a place at the foot of the cliff, where the breaking waves blotted out their conversation.

'You will go to the Maratha camp later?'

The fisherman nodded.

'I want you to take them a message from me.'

Christopher said what he had to say, and made the fisherman repeat it twice. He did not dare commit it to paper.

'If you are caught, I will deny everything. If you betray me, I will find your family and I will gut them each in turn like one of your fish. Do you understand?'

The fisherman trembled. Christopher smiled, and clapped him on the shoulder.

'If all goes well, we will share the profits, and you will never need to cast another net in your life.'

* * *

359

That night, Shahuji summoned Tom to his tent. It was a magnificent structure, as befitted a king, with many spacious rooms draped with silk hangings and filled with gold and mahogany furniture. Incense burners smouldered in the corners to keep the stench of the camp from intruding. Inside, you could almost forget you were on campaign at all – except for the sound of the guns. Each time a cannon fired, the walls shivered, and gold plates and goblets rattled on their trays.

'How is the siege progressing?' asked the rajah.

'We are widening the breach,' Tom answered. 'It is slow work – the walls are fifteen feet thick in places – but the gunners are breaking it down.'

'Not fast enough,' said Shahuji. 'The powder and ammunition you fetched from Brinjoan is dwindling. My army are far from the mountains. Men who were eager to fight last week now grumble about missing their homes.'

'They will stop complaining when they see the pirates' treasure store,' said Tom.

'If it comes to that.'

Tom's eyes narrowed. This was the fear he lived with every hour that the siege endured, that Shahuji would lose faith or interest – or that he would no longer trust Tom.

'I hope you are not thinking of giving up the siege, your highness.'

Shahuji went over to a tray of dates. He popped one in his mouth, and dipped his fingers in a small silver bowl of water to wash them.

'I have heard that in your country, battles are fought to the death,' he said.

Tom thought of the battle of Blenheim, which had been fought a few years earlier between the armies of France, Britain and the Holy Roman Empire. According to the reports he had read and heard in Cape Town, the French had lost over thirty thousand men, more than half their army. He nodded.

'In India, we are more civilized,' said Shahuji. 'Sophisticated, perhaps. As our great sage Kautilya said, "Intrigue is a better way to win battles than force." Why beat down the door, if someone will open it to you from the inside?'

Tom started to understand where the conversation was going. 'Do you think there is such a man in Tiracola?'

Shahuji nodded. 'I have had a message.'

It had never been the Courtney way to profit from treachery. But Tom saw the sense of what he said. If the castle could be taken without a frontal assault, it would cost many fewer lives – and increase the chances of finding Agnes and Sarah unhurt.

'Who is this man?'

'A fisherman brought the message. He says the traitor is one of Angria's lieutenants. A man who entered his service seeking riches, and now understands he can be richer still if he betrays his master.'

'Can such a man be trusted?'

'We will buy his trust.' Shahuji took a small silk bag and tipped it out in his palm. A handful of cut diamonds glittered bright against his dark skin.

'How is it to be arranged?'

'He cannot escape the castle by land without being seen. But there is a water gate, down among the rocks, which Angria uses to bring in supplies. Tomorrow night, a fisherman will bring the traitor to a beach down the coast. You will go to meet him.'

'And if it is a trap?'

Shahuji funnelled his fist and let the diamonds trickle back into the bag. 'I am sure you will know what to do.'

The next night was calm and clear. A waning moon hung low in the sky, but the stars shone bright on the white sand and frothing waves. Tom hung back among the palms that fringed the beach, so as not to offer a target from the sea. He glanced up at the cliffs overlooking the little cove. He had stationed Francis and Merridew up there, armed with flintlocks so that the glow of matchlocks would not give expose them.

'Do you think he will come?' said Mohite, the *hubladar*, beside him. He had shed his East India Company uniform coat and replaced it with a traditional Indian *dhoti*. From somewhere in Shahuji's armoury, he had acquired a heavy mace.

Something squeaked out to sea. Faint, so that the rush of surf almost drowned it, but Tom's senses were sensitive to the least disturbance. He peered into the darkness, and saw a dim shape solid against the shifting sea. It was a small boat, one of the Indian *mussoolas*, so light and shallow that when it caught a wave the surf carried it almost clean onto the beach.

Two men leaped out and dragged it above the surf. One squatted down beside the boat and waited; the other strode confidently up towards the trees. He was tall for an Indian – almost as tall as Tom, in fact. By the starlight Tom could make out a full beard, a tightly wound turban, and a sword at his belt.

There was no reason Tom should ever have seen him before. Yet even in darkness, something familiar nagged at him. A shiver went down his spine – the same foreboding he had felt waiting for the tiger to emerge from the forest. He tried to see the man's face, but it was hidden in shadow.

'What is your name?' growled Mohite.

'Raudra.'

'Ask him how he will open the gates,' Tom said to Mohite.

Opposite him, Christopher was so surprised to hear Tom's voice he almost answered in English. He caught himself, and pretended to listen while the *hubladar* translated. His mind raced. Against the trees, it was hard to make out the man clearly, yet he knew instinctively he recognized him. *Was he someone from Bombay?*

The others were waiting for his answer. 'I cannot open the main gates. They are too well guarded, and you would be seen approaching.'

'What, then?' said Tom impatiently. 'Why did you bring us here?'

Again, Christopher forced himself to wait until the *hubladar* had translated. It gave him time to study the Englishman more closely. He was tall and broad-shouldered, with dark hair, a dark beard and a commanding, confident air. Not dissimilar to Christopher, in fact.

And with a sudden shock, he realized who the man was. Tom Weald, who had defeated him at Brinjoan; the man he had last seen across the smoking rubble of the fort. The man whose sword now hung from his belt, pressing against his thigh. *How could he be here?*

Weald was examining Christopher just as closely. Had he recognized him? Or was it simply the same nagging feeling of familiarity?

'Angria keeps his ships in the cove to the north of the castle, protected by a wooden boom,' Christopher said, forcing calm into his voice and looking down so that his face would be in shadow.

'We know that.'

'In three nights, when the moon is full dark, I will cut the boom. The ebbing tide will carry it away. You can enter the harbour in small boats, and cut out or burn his fleet. Without ships, he cannot protect his supply line. Better, if you can moor your own *grab*s or *gallivat*s in the cove, their guns can cover the approach on land. Angria does not wish to die a martyr. If he thinks he cannot win, he will sue for peace. It is the Indian way.'

It was a long speech. When it was translated, Tom took a small pouch from his belt.

'The Rajah Shahuji has given me these.' He tipped out the bag in his hand, so that the cut diamonds sparkled in the starlight. Christopher stared at them hungrily.

'If you do what you have said, Shahuji will see you are well rewarded,' said Tom. 'You—'

He broke off. As the pirate leaned in, drawn by the diamonds, the moon caught the hilt of his sword. White light gleamed off the polished stone set in the pommel, and the gold inlay traced down the scabbard – a pattern Tom had known all his life. It was the Neptune sword. The blue sapphire had turned jet black in the night, but he could see the cut of it. More, he knew the shape of that sword like the curve of Sarah's hips; as well as the bulge of the grip, the taper of the blade apparent even through its scabbard. It was his Blue Sword.

He almost snatched it off the pirate. 'Where did you get that sword?' he cried.

Christopher straightened up, and placed his right hand on the hilt. 'I won it in battle.'

But as he spoke, Tom suddenly knew why he seemed familiar. Everything was explained. This was the man he had seen at the Rani's palace, who had salvaged his cannon and killed Captain Hicks. And now, by some devilry, he had appeared here at Tiracola . . . and he had the Neptune sword.

He stared at the sword. After his return to Brinjoan, he had given it up. He knew the hurt of the loss would never heal, but he had resigned himself to the fact he could never hope to get it back. And now here it was, within arm's reach.

He knew he should keep silent, but he could not help himself.

'That is *my* sword,' he said fiercely. 'It belonged to my father, my grandfather, and his grandfather before that.'

Christopher stared at him. 'Your father?' He spoke in English, though in their mutual shock neither man remarked on it. The implications were so immense they left him numb, unable to comprehend the situation.

Christopher collected himself. 'The sword belongs to me,' he said curtly, 'and I would not give it up for all the diamonds in the Golconda mines.'

Tom's mind raced. With the *hubladar*, he had the advantage of numbers. Better, Francis and Merridew were watching from the cliffs with their rifles sighted on the pirate. All he had to do was call out, and the pirate would die. The sword would be his again.

He opened his mouth to give the command. Deep inside, part of his soul screamed warnings this was a mistake, that the cost would be something he would regret all his life. But the sword was in front of him, the sapphire reflecting the stars in its facets, winking at him. He had lost it, and now providence had delivered it into his power once again. What sort of man could pass up such an opportunity? It was his birthright – and, more than that, the whole honour and legacy of the Courtneys was at stake.

The pirate knew something was wrong. He stepped back; his hand went to the hilt of the sword. It would not save him from the sharpshooters. Tom filled his lungs with the warm night air to shout the command to Francis and Merridew.

But the words would not come. Tom's sense rebelled. If he killed the pirate, then the harbour boom would not be cut. The fort might not fall, and very probably Tom would never see Sarah and Agnes safe again.

And what was the honour of the Courtneys worth, if he would sacrifice the woman he loved most for it?

He closed his mouth, suddenly hardly able to swallow. Shame flooded through him, coupled with relief he had not given the signal to fire.

'Angria has two prisoners,' he said. 'They are two Englishwomen. You know them? Are they safe?'

Christopher relaxed his grip on the sword. He did not know what had come over Tom, but he had felt the danger in the air.

'Yes,' he muttered. 'Yes, the women are healthy and unhurt. One is . . .'

He had been about to say 'with child', but stopped himself. In the last five minutes, his situation had changed beyond recognition: he needed time to gather his thoughts. He should hoard his knowledge until he had decided how best to use it.

'One is a little thin, but she is not in any danger,' he said blandly.

'See that no harm comes to them,' said Tom. Inwardly, he was thinking: *who are you?* This man who spoke English, allied himself with pirates and brigands, and now possessed his sword? What strange fate kept pitting them against each other?

Opposite, Christopher did not need to wonder whom he spoke to. *The sword belonged to my father . . .* the man had said. If he spoke the truth – and the passion in his voice left Christopher in no doubt of that – he could only be one of Guy's brothers. William was dead, and Christopher knew from family lore that Dorian had had red hair. This could only be his uncle Tom Courtney to whom he was speaking

Christopher was immediately seized by a terrible fear that Tom would recognize him. It ought to be impossible – Tom had never seen him before in his life, possibly did not even know of his existence – but then Christopher had never thought it possible he would find himself standing on a beach talking to his dead uncle.

He had to escape. Without apology, he turned and hurried down the beach towards the boat. So abruptly, Tom almost gave the signal to his sharpshooters for fear of some trick.

'Wait,' Tom called. Christopher halted. Again, his hand went to the hilt of his sword as he turned, tensed like a panther about to spring.

Something flew through the air. Instinctively, Christopher reached out and caught it one-handed. It was the purse of diamonds – he could feel them bulging through the soft silk when he closed his fist around it.

'I had almost forgotten,' he mumbled in surprise.

'Be sure you do not forget to cut the boom,' Tom warned.

Waves rippled around Christopher's ankles as he slid the boat into the sea. The cool water clarified his thinking, waking him from the dream he had slipped into.

'I promise you, the boom will be open.'

* * *

Christopher scrambled out of the boat, gave the boatman a golden coin for his silence, and climbed the stairs cut in the rocks. They were slick with spray thrown up by the breaking waves; swamped by his thoughts, he almost lost his footing.

He swore, and forced himself to concentrate. He was not out of danger yet. He rapped on the little gate and called his name.

A face appeared at the small barred window in the door. 'Was she worth it?'

Christopher had almost forgotten the lie he'd told. He forced a satisfied smile. 'And more. You should try her.'

Heavy bolts slid back. The door opened. He gave the guard a gold coin, and thought of the little bag of diamonds tucked in his belt. 'Not a word to Angria,' he cautioned. 'If he knew I was out of the castle, he would kill me.'

'She must be something, to be worth risking your neck,' said the guard, hoping for details.

'Sweeter than honey and roses!' Christopher agreed.

He went up through the castle to the turret room. Lydia was waiting for him, lying on the bed.

He unlocked her manacles. It had become routine, now: during the day, she stayed in the dungeon, but each night the jailer brought her up to his chamber. Christopher did not understand why, but he craved her company more than he liked to admit. After so many months and years of living a deception, it was a freedom to speak English again, and be understood. But it was more than that. She had something that he responded to, a spark that touched the dry paper deep in his soul and set it alight.

She was also the most imaginative and uninhibited lover he had ever had – wilder even than Tamaana.

She stroked his back. She reached forward and slid her hand across his thigh, between his legs, taking his cock and rubbing it between finger and thumb.

He did not respond.

She came around and knelt in front of him. Lifting the skirt of his *dhoti*, she took him in her mouth. She was no ingénue – she had survived two husbands already, and ten times as many lovers – but she had never taken a man as well-endowed as Christopher. Though she had seduced him with clear-eyed determination to survive, she found he genuinely excited her. She spent all her days looking forward to the moment the jailer would come to take her to the tower.

She ran her tongue down the length of his manhood. It did not stir.

She rose, wrapped her arms around him and rubbed her breasts against his chest. She tipped her head back and stared up at him.

'Is something wrong?'

In his turmoil, Christopher hardly realized she'd spoken. He pulled away from her and took out the long Neptune sword, brooding on his reflection in the blade.

'Have I displeased you?' said Lydia anxiously. As much as she was attracted to Christopher, she knew she could not afford to leave him unsatisfied. Her life depended on it.

He looked up. 'I learned something this evening which I cannot quite comprehend.'

She stroked his arm with her long fingers. 'What is it, my love?'

'You would not understand.'

She felt the muscles in his shoulder, thick as anchor cables. Her fingers worked harder, probing into his flesh. He grunted with satisfaction.

'Try me, my love,' she said, in her most girlish voice. 'There is so much knotted up inside you. Why will you not let me share your burden?'

He had not meant to say it – but her touch released something, like uncorking a bottle. 'Tom Courtney is here,' he blurted out.

Lydia's fingers stopped moving. 'Tom Courtney?'

'Guy's brother. I saw him this very evening. He is here, with the besieging army.'

'How can you be sure?'

'He recognized the sword. He said it belonged to his father. It can only be him.' Now that he had started, the words spilled out of him like a river bursting its banks. 'You said one of your companions is Sarah Courtney. She is his wife – he must have come to rescue her.'

Lydia's mind raced, trying to absorb this information and discern its import.

'Do you think the Governor sent him?' she asked cautiously. 'Could it be that Guy has raised this army to free Agnes and Sarah?'

Christopher laughed. 'That is unthinkable. Guy hates Tom even more than he hates me. If Guy knew Tom was here, he would come himself and serve his head on a platter to Angria.'

'You know a great deal about the affairs of the Courtneys,' Lydia said tartly. 'Have you had intercourse with Sarah without me knowing?'

Christopher's face went dark again. He gazed at Lydia, raking her with his eyes so hard she suddenly feared for her life. In that mood, he might be capable of anything.

'Tell me, my love,' she begged. 'I am on your side.'

He could not keep it pent up inside him any longer. 'Sarah Courtney is my aunt,' he said. 'I am Christopher Courtney, Guy's son. Two years ago, I defied Guy and ran away from Bombay.'

Suddenly, everything became clear to Lydia. 'You must hate Guy very much.'

'With all my heart!'

The conversation was moving too fast. With so many possible paths, Lydia could no longer calculate her advantage. Perhaps she should keep the secret. But if she did not say it now, and Christopher found out later, he would never forgive her.

She leaned closer towards him. Even her self-control wavered at what she had to say.

'There is a reason that Guy hates you that you do not even know yourself. Guy is not your father.'

Christopher was so surprised he almost laughed. Then his face hardened, as if he meant to strike her. 'What mischief is this?' His voice rose. 'Do you think because I allow you in my bed you can insult me like this? I can have you chained back in your dungeon this instant – or give you over to Angria for his sport.'

'Sarah Courtney told me,' screeched Lydia. 'Her sister Caroline, your mother, lay with Tom when they sailed from England. She was pregnant before Guy ever touched her.' She saw the realization dawning on his face. 'With you.'

'That is impossible.' But even as he clung to the certainty, it disintegrated around him. The truth of it resonated deep in his soul, and he could not block it out. Everything came into place. Like a captain lining up the marks to guide him into harbour, he could chart the course of his life anew. Guy's moods, his resentment of his wife and his hatred of his son. The way the Company men whispered over his head, ever since he was a child, and the way they always fell silent when Guy entered the room. The fact that his father was red-haired and pale-skinned, while Christopher was dark and strong. *Did you think that came from your mother?* he chided himself. He was the mirror image of the man on the beach, Tom Courtney – if he had but seen it.

His whole life was rewritten. He leaned on the windowsill for balance, staring out into the night. Lydia wrapped her arms around him.

'Tom is your father,' she said again. 'And he is here, waiting.' She pointed out the window, to the watchfires burning in the besiegers' camp. 'Surely now you cannot deny him his wife, his aunt – and his own son. Let us go to him this very night. I am sure you could get us past the guards. He would be overjoyed to see you. He would embrace you as his son.'

She waited. Christopher rested the Neptune sword on the window, blade pointing to the horizon, and gazed out.

'This should have been mine by right,' he murmured. 'Tom Courtney had it from his father, and I would have had it from him. If he had not abandoned me.'

'Now he has found you,' said Lydia.

Christopher looked at her like a man waking from a dream.

'No,' he said softly. And then, with gathering certainty, 'No.'

Lydia had never seen such ferocity in his eyes. She shrank back. 'I do not understand.'

Christopher rammed the sword home in its scabbard. 'What sort of man is Tom Courtney?' he said viciously. 'He sated himself on my mother, and then discarded her like a dirty rag when she got with child. With *me*. No wonder my father – Guy – hated me so. However hard I tried to please him, whatever I did to win his affection, he could not love me because I was not his.'

'You could not have known.'

'How I loathed him.' The words came out ragged, each one wrenched out of him. 'I did not understand. He saved my mother's honour when he could have left her to her shame. It was too much to expect him to love me as well. I was a living rebuke, the proof of his brother's crime, yet still he accepted me as his own. He did his best, he treated me as his son, and all I repaid him with was hatred. And if you had not come to me, I would never have found it out.'

He held her face tight in his hands. Lydia did not breathe. She looked into his eyes, and could not tell if he meant to kiss her or snap her neck.

'I'm sorry,' she gasped.

Christopher kissed her on the forehead. 'You have done nothing wrong. Thanks to you, I have a great opportunity.'

371

Her hopes rose. 'For reconciliation?'

'For revenge.'

The boats made no sound as they glided in towards the harbour. Francis had had the men oil the rowlocks, and wrap rags around the oars to muffle them. The Maratha crew were mountain men, unused to boat work. Tom and Francis had drilled them all day, out of sight of the castle, and distributed the *Kestrel*'s men among them to guide. But at night, on the open water, they were still clumsy.

One of the rowers missed his stroke. Unbalanced, he let go his oar, fell off the thwart and landed on a pile of weapons stacked in the bilge. He cursed; the oar banged against the gunwale. The blades underneath him clashed and jangled.

'Quiet, there!' Francis hissed.

The man, chastened, scrambled back onto the thwart. The crew held their oars level for a moment, not daring to breathe, while they listened for any sign they had been discovered.

All they heard was the chatter of birds and insects from shore, the lap of waves and the dripping of water from their oars. Beside Francis, Merridew whispered a command, and the rowers took up the stroke again.

'I hope they can keep calm when the musket balls start to fly,' whispered Merridew. 'If the boom is not cut, we will need to row away in a hurry.'

'It must be cut,' Francis insisted, more to reassure himself than his crew mate. Off the starboard beam, the castle loomed high on its headland, black against the starlit sky. A solitary light glowed high in one of the towers. Francis imagined a watchman looking out from the window, and wondered if he would notice the small vessels stealing towards the boom. Four longboats, Indian *gallivats*, each packed with fifty armed men.

I wish Tom were here, he thought. For all they had suffered together, he felt safe with his uncle. He had assumed Tom would lead the attack – Tom had demanded it – but Shahuji had forbidden him. 'You are the man who brought us the great guns and showed us how to fire them like the hat-wearers,' he had said. 'If you went astray in the dark, or found a wandering patrol, or were sighted by the sentries – it would break the soul of my army.'

'My wife is out there,' Tom had protested, but before he could argue it further, Francis had stepped in. He knew what he had to do.

'I will lead the attack.'

Now, in the boat, he did not regret it – though he felt mortally afraid. Ahead, he heard the creak of ropes and timbers. They were approaching the anchorage. He scanned the darkness, looking for the boom and hoping it was not there.

'At least they do not seem to be expecting us,' Francis murmured. None of the ships carried lights, and no watch fires burned on the shore. Perhaps Angria had pulled all his men back into the castle.

He felt the sack at his feet. It contained clay pots filled with oil, each with a slow fuse protruding from its lid. They had not dared carry fire in the boats for fear of being seen, but in each boat they had a tinderbox. As soon as they were among Angria's ships, they would light the fuses and hurl the bombs aboard.

They had come past the promontory and into the cove. The land rose on both sides, solid black against the speckled sky. They must be nearly at the boom now. Or maybe they had passed it without realizing it. Perhaps the traitor had been as good as his word.

Francis rose from his bench, swaying with the motion of the boat. He stared forward. Was there something ahead, or was it just a patch of calm on the dark water?

With a bump, the bow struck something solid. Francis was pitched back and sat down hard on his seat. The men murmured in alarm; some let go of their oars and reached for their weapons.

'Is it the boom?' called Francis in alarm.

Merridew reached out and felt around in the darkness. 'It's a boat,' he answered. 'We are inside the harbour.'

Francis took a deep breath of relief. He did not doubt the traitor's greed, but still he had not trusted him. Until that moment, he had not been sure the boom would be open.

'Shall I make ready the grenadoes?' asked Merridew.

'Wait until we are further in,' said Francis. 'Once the first ship goes up, we will need all haste to make good our escape.'

He checked back to see that the other boats had followed. Rows of wet oars glistened faintly behind. 'Pass the order back for the last boat to wait here and guard our escape. For the rest – on we go.'

The boats worked their way through the anchorage. Merridew knelt in the bow with a boat hook, ready to fend off any unexpected obstacle. Now that they were among Angria's fleet, Francis could see the ships more clearly. Many were small craft, no bigger than his own *gallivat*, but several were the larger *grab*s, snub-nosed vessels whose masts towered over the men in the boat. Francis guessed they would carry substantial magazines of powder, unless Angria had taken it to supplement the castle's supply. He would want to be well away before those blew.

They rowed on. There were no more *grab*s ahead, now: they must have come to the shallower waters at the back of the anchorage, near where the river flowed in. Francis ordered the rowers to stop.

'This is far enough,' he declared. 'Ready the grenadoes.'

He hesitated. This was the moment of maximum danger – deep in the cove, with two score ships between them and safety. And now they had to spark a flame, announcing their presence to anybody with eyes to see.

But it was what they had come to do. Francis produced the tinder box and laid out a small pile of kindling. Merridew emptied the sack and lined up the grenadoes on the stern thwart. Francis scraped the flint against the steel.

374

The first spark had not yet touched the kindling when a shot shattered the still of the night. Francis' head snapped up, just in time to see the flash of a muzzle flare somewhere near the mouth of the bay.

'Was that our men?' But even as a second report reached his ears, he knew it could not be. The boat he had left to guard their escape should have been in the middle of the channel. The shot had come from nearer shore.

'Turn the boats around,' he yelled. 'We are discovered.'

The men dropped their weapons and grabbed for the oars. In the dark, many collided with each other. Some pulled in opposite directions and knocked their oars together; the boat spun in an aimless circle.

'Together, damn you,' Francis shouted. Everything before him was a dark chaos of bodies, blades and oars. He could not even see to straighten them out.

But suddenly, everything was illuminated. All down the bay, along both shores, huge bonfires burst into life. Their flames rose so high, so bright, Francis was temporarily blinded. More lights appeared on the moored ships, drummed on by the sounds of many feet rushing on deck from their hiding places below.

Night became day. As his vision adjusted, Francis saw the men in the boat frozen in their panic, as if glimpsed in a flash of lightning. Except the light only got brighter. More fires were lit, beacons on the hilltops. Lights came on inside the castle keep. From the ships, he heard the ominous rumble of cannons being run out through the gun ports.

'It's a trap!' Francis cried.

Tom could not sleep. Knowing Francis was out on the water, in the dark, risking his life to save Sarah and Agnes – he was not prone to anxiety, but now it devoured him. He had tried to lie down in his tent, hoping a nap would make the time pass quicker. In fact, it had slowed to a crawl, as every black thought and worry crowded his mind. What if the boom was not open? What if the pirate had played them for fools, or been found out by Angria and tortured to reveal their plan? What if—?

Eventually, he left his tent, and climbed to the top of the watchtower on the hill. From this height, he could see over the rim of the bay and down into the cove below, where Angria's fleet was moored and where Francis would be by now. Tom had no doubt he would be leading the way.

He was proud of his nephew. The last few months, they had rarely been out of each other's sight. Now, with Francis gone, he realized how keenly he felt the boy's absence. He had come to rely on him: his youthful passion, his determination, his calm good humour. A son any man could be proud of.

A pang of guilt twisted in his belly. Once more, he replayed that dreadful scene on the banks of the Thames, so many years ago. Seeing the pistol in the caped man's hand; hurling the Neptune sword like a javelin, and seeing it pierce the man's heart. Aboli lifting the dead man's hat, and finding Billy's face on the corpse.

I killed Francis' father. It was his original sin: the one, inescapable fact that confronted him every time he looked at Francis.

But *Billy would not have loved Francis as he is,* Tom thought. Billy would have hated the goodness in Francis' heart, and beaten it out of him until it deformed the boy's very soul. Francis would have become a twisted, cringing wreck. Or, worse, the mirror of Billy: a black devil who cared only for power, who drew his strength by inflicting pain on others.

I killed Billy. But I also saved Francis. The realization was like a key turning in Tom's heart, opening a lock that had been fastened almost twenty years. He had not understood how tight it had bound him until it fell away. His spirit seemed to grow inside him, filling out his body. The cool night air in his lungs felt fresh and clean. Smells in the night he had not been aware of were suddenly fragrant in his mouth.

The guilt for Billy's death would always be there. But now, at last, he had the promise of redemption also.

A light flared in the darkness below. Tom gripped the watch-tower's parapet, all thoughts of Billy driven from his head. Francis must have got past the boom, deep into the cove, and started hurling his incendiaries. Tom searched the night for Francis' small boats. This was the most dangerous part of the plan. If Francis could not make good his escape quickly, he would be trapped under Angria's guns.

But the flames had not come from the anchored ships. They came from shore: a huge bonfire shooting sparks into the night. A second one went up beside it, then another, and another, until the whole bay became a cauldron of light. Men appeared on the ships' decks: not drowsy nightwatchmen clumsy with surprise, but squads of well-drilled men who raced to the tackles on the cannons.

Tom stared, sickened. Then he acted. He slid down the ladder, burning his hands, and ran to Shahuji's tent.

'They were expecting us,' he blurted out. He did not have to explain. The boom of a cannon echoed through the tent walls, followed by many more: an unrelenting barrage. Tom could not bring himself to think of Francis in a small boat under those guns.

Shahuji rose from the couch where he slept and pulled on a robe. From the cove, the gunfire continued unabated.

'Give me five hundred men,' said Tom. 'I can lead them down into the bay and create a distraction – or at least try to draw their fire.'

Shahuji shook his head. 'I know your nephew is down there. But the cove's sides are sheer cliffs: you would never get down them in the dark. And the approaches are covered by the castle's guns. If they were expecting the boats, they will surely also expect us to try and rescue our men. Their gunners will be crouched behind those walls this very instant, waiting to cut you to pieces.'

Tom knew he spoke the truth. But fear for Francis drove all reason out of his mind. 'I will go myself.'

'You may do as you wish. But dying a martyr's death will not save your nephew – or your wife, in the castle.'

Tom paused, rebuked by the rajah's implacable calm. He should not need lessons in restraint from a man as young as Shahuji.

'You said if this attack fails, you may have to break off the siege,' said Tom.

'I told you once before, we are like rats in the attic. We nibble away at our enemies, and when the cats come, we run back to our holes. That is how we survive.'

The noise of battle sounded louder than ever. Tom felt the posts of the tent shivering with the vibrations. He had no time.

'Angria knew we were coming to attack the harbour,' he said suddenly.

'It seems so.'

'Then he will have sent men from the castle to reinforce the fleet.' A plan was hatching in Tom's mind: a desperate gamble, but he could think of no other. Francis, Sarah and Agnes – all their lives hung in the balance that night.

Shahuji saw the intent on his face. 'What are you proposing?'

'The last thing Angria will expect.'

The fires in the cove burned so high that their light touched the clouds. Smoke drifted across the water; the echo of the guns resounded around the bay.

At the back end of the bay, Francis' boats were caught like kittens in a sack. To escape, they would have to run the gauntlet past the line of Angria's anchored ships, the big *grab*s with their heavy broadsides. The men worked the oars to bring the

378

*gallivat*s around, but it was agonizingly slow work. Cannonballs sang through the air all around them. One took a man's head clean off and carried it into the sea like a coconut from a shy. Another scored a direct hit on the boat behind. It snapped in two, tipping its crew into the water. Screams added to the roar of battle. Few of the Marathas could swim.

Francis grabbed the tiller and put it over. The *gallivat*'s bow turned towards the line of anchored *grab*s.

'What are you doing?' bellowed Merridew. 'This is madness.'

'We must head closer in among the fleet,' Francis said. 'Their cannon will not be able to bear on us there.'

The men pulled on the oars. Facing the stern, they could not see where Francis was steering them, but they could tell by the deepening roar of the guns what he intended. Now they could feel the heat of the guns on their backs, blasts of hot air as the cannon belched fire behind them. Iron balls tore the air around them. Shot screamed overhead, terrifying, but it no longer threatened the men. The boat had come so close that the gunners on the *grab*s could not depress their weapons low enough.

The bass note of the cannons gave way to the crack of musketry. Some of the men aboard the *grab*s had climbed the rigging, taking position in the tops and the crosstrees where they could fire down at will. All around the boats, a heavy rain of lead struck the sea and made it boil.

Many of the shots went home. In an open boat, packed so tight, there was nowhere for Francis' men to shelter. Soon the bilge ran red with blood. The gunwales were ground to splinters; limp oars hung abandoned from their rowlocks, dragging on their progress.

'Aim all your fire on the nearest *grab*,' Francis shouted, though few men could have heard him above the screaming of the wounded. If they could not pin down the marksmen aboard the ship, the pirates would be able to empty their muskets into the small boat at will.

Francis looked ahead. The faces of the rowers stared back at him, hunched over their oars and spattered with blood. That they were still able to move at all, under that onslaught, was testament to their courage. But they were close to breaking. To take the fight to the pirates, they would need something more.

For the first time in his life, Francis understood the true burden of leadership. He would have to show them the way, even if he died in the attempt.

He rose to his feet, crouching to keep under the flight of the cannon balls. The wind they made ruffled his hair, scant inches overhead. As he stood, his foot knocked something hard in the bottom of the boat. It was one of the incendiaries, forgotten when the pirates sprang the trap.

He grabbed one in each hand. 'Get me a light.'

Merridew struck a flame and lit the wicks. Aiming carefully, Francis hurled the two pots at the ship. Under fire, from a boat that pitched and bobbed with the turmoil of wounded men, he could barely keep upright – but all their lives depended on it.

His aim was true. The pots struck the ship's bulwarks, just below the gunwale, and exploded in two great flashes of flame. The pirates at the side were thrown back, spattered with the flaming oil. Some caught alight, and rolled on the deck to try and smother the flames that leaped from their hair and their clothes.

The *gallivat* bumped alongside the *grab*.

'On me,' Francis yelled. A rope hung down over the side. He grabbed it, and swung himself up to the channels, the wooden platforms that fixed the standing rigging to the side of the ship. He had no time to be frightened. The oil had burned quickly but it had not set the ship alight. The pirates would already be regrouping.

He climbed the shrouds, leaped onto the deck and drew his sword. A pirate stumbled towards him, still blinded by the brilliance of the exploding oil. Francis aim a deft cut at his neck, and dropped him with a single blow.

He fought without mercy. For his life, for his men, for Sarah and Agnes – and for the hope that he might see Ana again. He leaped up on a cannon, feeling the heat of the barrel through his shoe, kicked a pirate in the face and then ran him through the belly as he stumbled back.

With a scream, a body thudded to the deck beside him. He looked up. More of his men were aboard now, and some had climbed the ratlines to dislodge the sharpshooters. They tore them from the rigging and hurled them down to their deaths.

The *grab* had not carried her full complement. Trusting to the number of his ships, Angria had spread his men thinly through the fleet – only enough to serve the guns. They had not expected to be boarded. Francis' men fought with unbridled fury, fired by their betrayal and the terrors they had suffered in the small boat. Soon, all the pirates were dead or driven into the water.

Francis looked down the deck and realized the ship was theirs. But they were still deep in the anchorage, with many of Angria's vessels still between them and the mouth of the bay.

'Cut the cable,' he ordered. It was the dark of the moon, and the spring tide was ebbing fast. It might yet carry the ship clear– if the pirates' cannons did not sink it first.

With a shock, he realized he was almost the most experienced sailor aboard. That did not speak much to their chances. But Merridew was with him, and he knew what was required. He showed the Marathas the anchor cable, and where to cut it. While they did that, Francis found the sheets and set men to hauling on them. The mainsail came loose. Merridew ran out onto the yard and overhauled the clew lines. Awkwardly, halt-ingly, the ship began to make headway.

Merridew slid down the backstay and landed, catlike on the deck. 'Might want to go below, sir.' He pointed to the line of *grabs* moored ahead. 'We've still to get past those to make open water.'

The bonfires had started to burn lower. The pirates on shore, unable to see clearly what was happening on the ship's deck, had held their fire for fear of hitting their own crew. Now, though, they would surely guess that the Marathas had taken her – and turn their fire on them.

Francis looked at the open hatch. 'I will not hide,' he said firmly. He looked to the *grab*'s bow. A square forecastle was built above it, open at the rear. Inside gleamed the long barrels of two nine-pounder cannons.

'Perhaps we can improve the odds.'

He picked out a dozen men whom he knew had crewed the siege guns, and sent them for'ard. The pirates had left plenty of powder and shot on deck. Working quickly, as Tom had drilled them, the men loaded the bowchasers and trained them on the stern of the ship ahead.

'Aim as low as you can,' Francis ordered. 'We'll rake her fore and aft.'

The ship shook as the guns roared out. To his delight, Francis saw the balls strike home through her stern, right in the line with the main deck. He knew, from being schooled by Tom and Aboli, that the balls would fly unimpeded down the length of her deck, cutting down any man in their way and leaving a bloody shambles.

'Reload,' he ordered. Most of the men could not speak English, but they understood the commands. They worked quickly, cleaning out the barrel, ramming home the new shot and hauling on the tackles to run out the gun again. The pirates, unused to such standards of gunnery, were not expecting another onslaught so quickly. They were now so close that Francis heard the screams coming from her gun deck.

Merridew had taken the wheel. Now, he altered course to bring them past the other ship. But rather than head for the clear channel to larboard, he made for the far side of the enemy *grab*. Francis nodded his approval. They could use Angria's ships to screen them from the castle's guns.

Even so, it was a dangerous course to steer. As they came level with the next *grab* in line, they passed so close that their yard arms clattered against each other. If the pirates had had their starboard guns ready, they could have broadsided Francis' ship at point blank range. But, as Francis had anticipated, all their guns were aimed at the clear channel on the other side. He saw the crews hauling on the tackles, moving the guns with handspikes.

'Let us see how they like this strong medicine,' he muttered. He found another grenado, lit it, and hurled it across the narrow gap onto the other boat. It landed on a coil of ropes and exploded. In an instant, the pirates forgot all thought of the guns, and raced to douse the blaze before it reached the casks of powder they had intemperately left on deck. One man poured a bucket of water over the fire, and was engulfed by a great sheet of flame that reared up from the burning oil.

A steady breeze blew off the land, funnelled through the narrow cove into something stronger. The *grab*, designed to manoeuvre in the lightest of winds, gathered speed. Now they had passed the last of the big ships, and were heading for open sea. A few cannons on shore opened up, but they did not trouble Francis. The guns in the castle could not depress low enough, while those across the bay were poorly aimed. None of the balls came near them.

He looked back, surveying the anchorage. They had sprung the trap, and made the pirates pay for their treachery. They had cut out one ship, and burned another, which had drifted among Angria's *gallivat*s, sinking or burning half a dozen more. But over half the pirate fleet still survived – and of the two hundred men who had rowed into the bay, only thirty or so were now escaping. It was a heavy price, and Francis felt the full weight of it on his shoulders.

He wondered what had happened to the boat he had left to guard their escape. He looked forward again, scanning the dark sea. That was where the attack had begun, he remembered: shots fired at the mouth of the bay.

He could not see the boat. But as he searched for it, he became aware of a thick dark line drawn across the sea. For a moment, his unwilling mind tried to believe it could be a shadow, or a trick of the waves. But that was a lie. He could not deny the evidence of his eyes: thick tree-trunks, fastened with chains, shutting off the whole mouth of the bay.

'They've closed the boom,' he cried.

The ship shuddered as Merridew put over the wheel.

'Hold your course,' said Francis wildly.

'But that'll take us straight into the boom,' protested Merridew.

'Then we will ram it.'

'It'll stave our bow. We'll sink.' They had both observed, reconnoitring earlier in the day, the pattern of ripples that spoke of vicious undercurrents where the bay met the open ocean. 'We'd be swept out to sea and drown.'

Hope died in Francis' breast as he realized the truth of what Merridew said. He thought they had escaped the trap; in fact, it had closed around them. Now their only choices were to smash their ship to pieces, or sit there and let the pirates blast them out of the water.

A cannon ball from the shore battery struck the bow. Angria's gunners were finding their range at last. Astern, a flotilla of *gallivats* swarmed after them, like sharks converging on a wounded whale.

Francis thought of Ana. He thought of Agnes and Sarah. Most of all, he thought of Tom, and how he had failed the Courtneys.

'What shall we do?'

Tom had never seen an army assemble as fast as Shahuji's. They swarmed from the camps, forming up in silent ranks on the slopes of the hill. He should not have been surprised. The Marathas were mountain warriors, men who slept with their swords in their hands and their spears at their sides.

Mohite, the *hubladar*, was there too, with the men who had followed him from Brinjoan. Tom was glad to have them. Mohite had put on a padded cotton cuirass, borrowed from the Marathas. His firelock was slung across his back, with the ammunition pouches on his belt next to the curved dagger. Most terrifyingly of all, he carried a mace, with a grip like a sword and a tip like an iron fist.

The Maratha warriors were passing small jars along the line. They dipped their fingers in, and daubed streaks across their faces.

'What are they doing?' wondered Tom.

'It is turmeric,' Mohite explained. He took the jar he was given, and drew three parallel yellow lines across his cheeks. 'It is sacred to the gods. By putting it on, we dedicate ourselves to them. Then we need have no fear of death, for the gods hold us in their hands.'

He handed Tom the jar. Tom scooped out the sticky yellow paste and copied the pattern Mohite had made. He offered a silent prayer to whichever god or gods held sway over that continent. He did not fear death – only failure. He could not leave Sarah, Agnes and Francis to die.

A heavy blow shook the earth under them. Tom flinched instinctively, fearing that the castle's defenders had spied their preparations and opened fire. But the walls on this side were silent and dark. All the battle was being waged down in the bay.

Three great war elephants paraded out between the men and halted at their head. Apart from their footfall, they made no sound. Tom marvelled at the animals' training, that they could keep so quiet.

Shahuji slid easily down from the lead elephant's back and came to Tom.

'Are you ready to lead the assault?'

Tom started. 'I thought you—'

Shahuji spread his hands. 'This is your battle. You asked for my army: I give it to you. If you mean to go through with this plan?'

'I must.'

'The breach in the walls is not low enough,' Shahuji warned. 'My gunners wanted another week at least to make it passable.'

'We can climb it,' Tom insisted.

Shahuji nodded. He gestured to the elephant he had dismounted.

'If that is your course, then here is your mount.'

Tom stared at the beast. There was no doubting it was magnificent, terrifying: a creature to strike fear into any enemy. But it made a vast, cumbersome target. Up on its back, he would be easy prey for every gunner and marksman in the castle.

Shahuji read his thoughts. 'The men need to know their commander is with them,' he said softly. 'If they cannot see you, they will fear you have given up the fight. And if you will not fight, why should they?'

More cannon fire sounded from down in the bay. Tom felt the eyes of the army watching him. He had no time to argue.

'It is safer than you think,' said Shahuji. 'A war elephant is different from a hunting elephant.'

The mahout made the beast squat, and Tom clambered on. At once, he saw what Shahuji had meant. The ornate *howdah* he had used on the tiger hunt was gone. In its place was an armoured box, sheathed with iron plates and with a falconet mounted on a swivel at the front.

Mohite clambered in behind him, while the mahout crouched in the front of the box. The elephant rose and began to move. Peering down, Tom saw the army surge forward around them. The men in the front rank were utterly naked. Their bodies were smeared with ashes, their hair torn and wild. They writhed and twisted, their dappled bodies like smoke in the night.

386

'Who are they?' he asked Mohite.

'*Ghosias*,' the *hubladar* answered. 'They are untouchables, devotees of Shiva the destroyer. Madmen who fear nothing.'

A howl rose in their throats: an inhuman wail that chilled the sweat on Tom's brow. The *ghosias* slapped their chests with the flats of their swords.

'Angria will hear us coming,' Tom fretted.

'You cannot stop them,' Mohite said. 'It has already begun.'

As they spoke, their advance had gathered pace, moving down the hill and towards the neck of land that led out to the promontory. The fires in the bay lit up the night sky, casting a ghoulish glow. From the elephant's back, Tom could look down into the anchorage and saw the battle raging. One of the big *grab*s had broken loose from its moorings and was drifting towards the sea. Another had caught fire. He could not see Francis' boats – though the water was strewn with wreckage and the bodies of drowning men.

The iron box rang like a bell as a musket ball struck the armour plating. Tom ducked, cursing himself. They were already in range. Angria's men were not sleeping. They had seen the Marathas approaching, and hurried to their defences. Now, they poured their fire across the little isthmus. Cannon balls tore through the Maratha ranks. Tom saw one of the *ghosias*, still capering like a berserker, plucked out of the air and smashed backwards into the men behind. His companions howled and ran forward.

The isthmus had become a killing ground. Men were dying all around Tom. Another cannon ball flew a few feet from the elephant's head. The beast twitched its ears, put down its head and lumbered forward. Musket balls struck it, but they did little harm. Tom knew from experience on the plains of Africa how even at close range, a ball might do little more than take the dust off the animal's hide.

But they stirred its temper. The enraged elephant charged

forward. The *howdah* bounced on its back like a small boat in a storm, shuddering with the impact of each massive step. The wind of their passage rushed past Tom's ears. The iron plating rang with the impact of other bullets. As Tom had feared, it made an easy target. The defenders knew where he must be. But the beast's size also offered protection. The Marathas flocked in behind the animal, using its bulk to shield them from the men on the walls. It reached the kalargi trees planted before the walls and crashed through them, leaving a splintered path in its wake.

The elephant slowed. Tom risked a glance above the rim of the box. They had come right up to the walls, though at terrible cost. Bodies lay strewn behind them all across the promontory.

The cannon had mostly fallen silent, but the musket fire was fiercer than ever. Now, the men on the walls were almost directly above the elephant. Tom leaped out and slid down the elephant's flanks. To his right, he saw the spikes protruding from the gate, long enough to deter even the proudest elephant. Ahead, a rubble slope rose towards the breach in the walls.

Tom's heart sank. From the watchtower on the hill, the breach had looked manageable. From the bottom, with musket balls flying all around, it looked like a mountain. He remembered Shahuji's warning – *my gunners wanted another week at least.*

But he could not doubt himself now. One whole section of wall had come down intact, sliding down and landing at the bottom of the slope as a makeshift barricade. He ran there and crouched behind it.

Men ran by. The *ghosias* had suffered terrible casualties approaching the walls, but they had not lost their will to fight. Catlike, they jumped onto the rubble and began hauling themselves up towards the breach.

Tom felt ashamed. He could not cower behind shelter, while other men risked their lives for his family. A desperate madness overcame him, some taint of the frenzy of the *ghosias* infecting his blood. He sprang out from behind the piece of wall and charged up the slope. Loose stones slipped away under his feet; musket fire crashed around him, but it was all drowned by the blood pounding in his ears. All that mattered was gaining the summit. He was almost there. One more stride up the treacherous slope and—

The rock he stood on gave way. It slipped down the slope in a shower of loose stones, sweeping his feet from under him. He fell hard, knocking the breath from his lungs and slid away. Dust and mortar filled his mouth.

But the *ghosias* had done their work. Carried on by their destroyer god, they had reached the top. Their success dismayed the defenders: and the rate of fire coming from the castle slowed. The *ghosias* capered triumphantly in the breach, bellowing their war cry.

All at once, a deeper sound obliterated it. It was the roar of cannons. Angria had known they would make for the breach. He had placed cannons behind it, loaded with grape shot and musket balls, ready to greet any attacker who fought his way to the top.

Tom, still sprawled on the slope below, saw the blast of the cannon like a flash of lightning behind the breach. He stared, sickened, as the men at the top disintegrated in an instant. A cloud of flesh and limbs rained down around him.

If I had not slipped, I would be one of them. But Tom had no time to be thankful for his escape. Now was the time to move, before the guns behind the wall were reloaded.

He found his sword, pushed himself to his feet and lunged up the slope. Leaping from rock to rock, too fast to let them pull him back, he charged.

A noise rose lower down the slope, a shout that began with a single voice and was rapidly taken up by others. '*Har! Har! Mahadev!*' The men behind him had been shocked to a standstill by the cannon blast. Now, they gained new hope. They followed him up, chanting the Maratha battle cry. Those who had lost their weapons scooped up rubble and pelted any defender who dared show his face. Others hurled their spears, threading the gaps between the battlements to strike down the pirates who lurked there.

Tom reached the top of the slope and stepped into the breach. Mohite followed a pace behind. A pirate came at them with a bayonet, but the *hubladar* swung his mace and crushed his skull like a ripe melon.

For a moment, the two men stood atop the broken wall, in the valley between two towers. They stared down into the courtyard, lit by the light of many torches and braziers. Tom licked his lips, and tasted the dry bitterness of the turmeric smeared over his face.

He raised his sword to the heavens in triumph, and bellowed out the battle cry with his men. '*Har! Har! Mahadev!*' *God is with us!*

They had breached the castle. Now he had to find Sarah and Agnes.

Far below, the sounds of battle carried down through the rock into the depths of the castle dungeon, thunderous groans and muffled roars magnified beyond recognition. Dust and pebbles slithered down the walls, shaken loose by the reverberations. It was like being in the belly of some monstrous leviathan.

Agnes and Sarah were alone. The guards had come earlier and taken Lydia away, as they did on so many evenings. The first time it happened, Agnes had stayed awake all night, imagining the things the pirates must be doing to her. But when Lydia returned, she shrugged off Agnes' concern. In fact, she seemed to be smiling. From this, and other brazen hints she dropped, Agnes deduced she had taken a lover among the pirates.

She did not condemn Lydia for it. They all did what they had to to survive. Agnes would never have done the same – but she had not entirely resigned herself to her fate. Sitting in the gloom, she worked at the lock of her manacles with a small iron nail. She had found it embedded in the rock, a remnant of some door or bracket that had once been fastened there. It had taken her a week, to pry it loose, cutting her nails to the quick and chaffing her fingertips bloody, working only when Lydia was away lest she betray them to her lover.

Now she had it. Lydia had gone, and so had the guards who usually manned the iron gate. At first she had wondered why; later, when the guns erupted, she guessed Angria had withdrawn them for the battle. That gave her efforts fresh urgency. She could not know that Tom and Francis were outside the walls, that even at that moment Tom was mounting the great war elephant. All she knew was that the castle was under attack.

She had been married to a soldier for twenty years. She understood what the invaders would do to two women, chained and helpless, if the castle fell.

Beside her, Sarah moaned and shifted her weight. She could no longer roll over. Her belly swelled out of her malnourished body, the skin stretched so tight Agnes feared it might burst open. The baby must be near its term. That gave Agnes added urgency: she did not dare think what sport the pirates would make with a baby born in their dungeon. With her numb, broken fingers, she worked the sliver of iron into the lock of the manacles. She had been doing this for over an hour, prying into the lock, probing for anything in the mechanism that would give. Occasionally, the nail seemed to snag something and hope caught in her chest. But each time, when she applied pressure, it lost its purchase and slid off without effect.

The rumbling coming through the rock seemed to grow deeper. Silt shivered off the walls. The battle was coming to its climax. Almost in despair, she jabbed the nail into the keyhole again. Blood from her torn fingers dribbled into the lock. Before, she had not dared apply too much force for fear of snapping the nail. Now, desperation made her careless. She leaned on the nail with all the force her thin arms could muster, driving it with the frustration of months of captivity.

The lock gave. The shackle sprang open and dropped off, so quickly it bruised her knee. She stared at it, dangling from her other arm, hardly able to comprehend her freedom. It was the first time in months she had seen her wrist. The skin was bruised black and raw, almost too tender to touch.

Unsteadily, she rose to her feet. Sarah was still asleep, and there was no point waking her yet. Agnes stole through the caves to the iron gate that barred the way to the stairs. Another lock – but this time there was a key, hanging from a hook in the wall at the bottom of the stairs. Summoned in haste to the castle's defence, the guards had overlooked it.

Agnes could not reach it. But she had the manacle, still dangling from her right wrist. She slid her arm out through the bars, then tossed the loose end of the manacle towards the hook like casting a fishing line.

It struck the wall, just below the hook, with a clang that echoed up the staircase. She tried again, and again the shackle missed.

By now, she felt sure someone must have heard it – but that only redoubled her determination. Concentrating as hard as she could, she fixed her gaze on the key and threw.

The shackle caught the key-ring and whipped it off the hook. It clattered to the ground. Using the shackle once more, Agnes dragged it across the floor until it was close enough for her to grab it. She put it in the lock – and the door opened.

Now to get Sarah out. But before she could return to their chamber, a wrenching cry rang out through the caverns. Her sister's voice. She ran back.

Sarah lay on the floor, curled into a ball, hugging her knees

392

against her distended belly. She breathed hard, trying to hold in a deep and wounding pain.

She could not. A rending sob of agony tore out of her. She tipped back her head, biting her lip until it bled.

Agnes knew what that sound portended. In Bombay, and later in Brinjoan, she had volunteered as an assistant with the surgeon when he tended women in childbirth. She had held their hands, and mopped their faces, and whispered encouragement in their ears. Sometimes, she had presented the happy mother with a newborn babe at the end of it. Other times, it had all been in vain.

All thoughts of escape were forgotten. She could not move Sarah now. She ripped Sarah's dress open, all the way from neck to hem, and spread it out to cover the filthy floor. Sarah writhed on the cloth. A sheen of sweat covered her naked skin, glowing in the dim light.

The screams came more often. Agnes counted the gaps between them. She knew from experience that the labour was advancing quickly. Sarah was not yet ready to push – but it would not be long now.

More cannon fire rumbled through the rocks. Then, near at hand, Agnes heard running footsteps approaching down the stairs.

'What shall we do?' Francis gazed between the boom ahead, and the flotilla of boats closing behind. He had no time to choose. The big *grab*s astern ran out their bow chasers. The boom rushed closer.

'We must put about,' Merridew shouted. 'Otherwise we will do their work for them and drown ourselves.'

'But then we will put ourselves back among the *grab*s. They will blast us to pieces.'

'Better to risk death than guarantee it.'

Francis stared wildly around. And as he did so, his gaze

caught the extremities of the boom. On one end, it was fastened to the small fort that guarded the far side of the bay. But on the other, it ran right up to the rocks at the foot of the castle. There, by the light of the bonfires, Francis saw a small jetty – and a gate leading in to the cliff.

'Alter course to larboard,' he ordered.

Merridew started turning the wheel before he finished speaking. But as the bow came around, Francis grabbed the wheel and pushed it back.

'We are not coming about,' he said. 'Steer for the rocks where the boom is fastened.'

'But we'll smash ourselves to bits.'

Francis gave a manic grin. He had thrown off the uncertainty that gripped him; he knew this was the only chance.

'We are going ashore.'

Their ship sailed across the mouth of the bay. Now she was beam on to the approaching fleet: a fat, unmissable target. Shots struck her sides, ripping her bulwarks to splinters. The pirates in the *gallivat*s, seeing they had her penned against the boom, increased the tempo of their oars. Angria would pay an extra bounty to the crew who were first aboard.

'What if we run aground before we reach the jetty?' Merridew asked. 'Tide's running out. We'd be as easy a prize as you could wish for.'

'Then we will have to swim for it.'

Merridew knuckled his forehead and ran to the rigging. Directing the men, he had them brace the yard around for their new heading. Though the sail was rent with many holes, the ship made more headway. Francis set the men to cutting away the broken wreckage that dragged in the water. He wanted every ounce of speed, to drive the ship as far up on the rocks as he could.

Now they were under attack from a different quarter. The pirates on the jetty had seen their approach and realized what

Francis intended. By the light of a fire, he saw them frantically levering one of their cannons with hand spikes, trying to bring it to bear. Others knelt and peppered them with fire from their matchlocks.

Francis ran forward to the bow chasers. Under cover of the high forecastle, they were well protected from the musket fire. He urged the crews on as they reloaded.

Crouching beside the big gun, he peered out through the gun port. The men on the jetty had manhandled their cannon into position, and were now desperately trying to load. It was like a duel played out in quarter-time, each side racing to get their shot off before the other.

The *grab* fired first. The guns belched fire and leaped back on their tackles. But the noise was lost in a greater roar as the *grab* hit the shore full on. Her shallow draft had allowed her to come so close, her bow smashed open and drove forward, higher and higher up on to the rocks. The men were thrown to the deck. Francis just missed having his leg crushed by a cannon as it rolled loose on the tilting deck.

'Up!' he shouted. 'Up and at them!'

The *grab*'s flat, open bow had been designed for boarding other vessels. Now, it made a clear ramp, projecting over the rocks all the way to the jetty. With Francis in the lead, the Marathas rushed over it. They leaped off the end, bellowing their war cry, and set about the defenders.

The bow chasers' last salvo had done its work. The pirate's cannon was upended, and its crew sprawled in their own blood. The attackers made short work of the remainder. Francis stabbed one of them through the heart, looked around, and realized there were no enemies left alive.

The jetty was theirs.

'What now?' said Merridew, wiping gore from his boarding axe. He pointed to the iron ring set in the rocks, where the end of the boom was fastened in place. 'Cut the boom?'

'It would do us little good. We have no ship left to make our escape.'

A musket ball struck the wall. Out on the water, he saw the pursuing flotilla of *gallivats* closing in. The lead boat had already moored up against the wreck. Her men spilled out onto the deck, using it as a bridge to gain the jetty.

There was nowhere to hide on the jetty – but a small door led into the cliff.

'Into the castle,' Francis shouted. He waited until the last of his men had come through, then followed them in, barring the door. Three musket balls thudded into the woodwork behind him.

A lamp burned in a sconce on the wall. He counted his men. A round dozen, of whom more than half were wounded, plus himself and Merridew. A small force for storming a garrison of a thousand men.

The door began to shake under the impact of heavy blows.

'That won't hold long,' Merridew warned.

Francis reloaded his pistol. 'They'll find a warm welcome awaiting them if they open it.'

'Mebbe there's another way.' Merridew cocked an ear. 'You hear that thunder up top? I reckon Mr Tom's launched an attack to draw the pirates off us. He'll be taking a terrible beating under those walls. If we could get up through the castle, open the gate, it could swing the balance.'

Francis glanced over his shoulder. A steep staircase led up through the rocks towards the castle. It was deserted. He presumed all the garrison had been drawn to the battle.

The door shook again. The tip of an axe blade burst through the timbers, withdrew, and came again. The hole grew wider.

'Then let us waste no time.'

Francis led his men up the stairs, pistol in hand. They had not gone far when he heard a mighty crash of the door giving way, and the shouts of many men pouring in. He doubled his pace, taking the worn stairs three at a time, flinging himself around every corner without thought for what might await him.

They came to a chamber where the passage forked. One set of stairs led down to the right, while another led on upwards.

Francis pointed up. 'This way. It must—'

A shrill scream sounded from down the lower steps. Francis paused.

'No time to dilly dally,' said Merridew urgently. From behind, they could hear their pursuers gaining quickly.

The scream came again – the excruciating sound of a woman in torment.

'Make for the gate,' Francis told Merridew. 'I will follow.'

Without waiting to explain, he broke away and ran down the right-hand steps. He could hardly find an excuse for leaving his men now. But Sarah and Agnes were somewhere in these dungeons, and he could not leave them to their fate.

At the bottom of the stairs, he found an iron gate. He stiffened. But the gate was unguarded, and the key was in the lock – on the inside. When he pulled, the gate opened without complaint.

The screaming had not stopped. It came at regular intervals, as if someone was twisting a hot knife deep in the victim's guts.

With his sword in one hand and his pistol in the other, Francis crept down the passage. He followed the sound, through a chain of rock chambers, until he came to a bend. The screams were so loud, here, they must be coming from the next cave. He pressed himself against the wall, steeled himself, then leaped out from his hiding place, brandishing his pistol.

He stopped in astonishment.

Sarah lay on her back, legs spread, presenting her whole body wide open to him. She was completely naked. Agnes knelt beside her, cradling her sister's head in her lap and murmuring encouragement. Sarah's eyes were open, but she did not register

Francis' arrival. Agnes saw the shadow fall across her, and looked up.

'Francis?' she said, amazed.

He ran to them and crouched beside her. Another paroxysm of pain wracked Sarah's body – longer than the last. Agnes wiped her brow.

'Is she—?' Francis blanched and averted his eyes as he took in Sarah's nakedness. 'What is happening? Have they tortured her?'

Even in their desperate plight, Agnes had to smile. 'She is having a baby, you ninny. And it will not be long now before it arrives.'

'A baby?' Francis echoed. 'But how—?'

'Do not fear: the pirates have not mistreated us *that* way. It will be Tom's child – your cousin – if it survives this night.'

Sarah's screams had given way to lower, sobbing breaths. Agnes lifted her shoulders and coaxed her up.

'Help me turn her over,' she said. 'It will be an easier passage for the child.'

Francis had witnessed foaling and lambing on the High Weald estate: he was not entirely ignorant of the mechanics of birth. But had not expected to turn midwife in the midst of a battle. He put down his weapons, and helped Agnes manoeuvre Sarah so that she crouched on all fours, panting hard.

Guns rumbled overhead. Agnes looked up. Belatedly, as if she had only just registered the unlikelihood of Francis' arrival, she said, 'Is that your doing? How did you come to be here? Have you taken the fort? Where is Tom?'

'In truth, I do not know what has happened,' Francis admitted. 'I led a cutting out expedition into Angria's harbour – but we were discovered. We escaped by forcing our way into the castle by the sea gate. I think Tom must have launched an assault on the walls above to draw the pirates' fire – but how he has fared, I cannot say.'

Sarah groaned. A different sound, lower and more purposeful

than her earlier screams, as if she were trying to shift a great weight. Agnes put her arm around her.

'The baby is coming.'

Christopher could not rest easy that night. Knowing the trap was set, waiting for the jaws to close: the uncertainty ate at his soul. He had told Angria about the proposed attack on the harbour, letting the pirate believe it had always been his intention to trick the enemy. He did not mention the pouch of diamonds he had obtained, safe in his room sewn into the lining of a belt; nor did he reveal anything of Tom Courtney. His revenge would be a private matter.

Christopher had wanted to lead the ambush in the anchorage, but Angria had forbidden it. The wily pirate feared treachery, that Christopher – having betrayed the Marathas – might yet make common cause with them. He had ordered Christopher to stay up in the castle. There, he paced the walls overlooking the cove, alone with his fears. What if Tom had recognized him? What if he had guessed Christopher's betrayal? What if they did not come? He leaned on the parapet, staring into the night, turning the Neptune sword in his hands. The *urumi* clenched tight around his waist. He thought of Lydia, waiting in his chambers. She would provide a welcome distraction. But there would be time for that later. Her charms would be all the sweeter when he could exult in his victory.

When the first fire went up, he knew the plan had worked triumphantly. From the walls, he saw the enemy boats caught deep in the anchorage, Angria's fleet closing around them. They would not escape from there.

And yet – they did not know they were beaten. He watched in amazement as one boat closed with one of the *grab*s, then boarded her. Somehow, the boarders got her underway, steering a course through the crowded bay. Despite the efforts of the pirate gunners, she was not sunk or dismasted. In fact, she managed to set some of the other ships on fire as she passed. She was getting away.

She could not escape. After the boats had entered the bay, Christopher's men had closed the boom. Even if the *grab* reached it, she would be pinned against it like a butterfly on a card.

But as he awaited her destruction, he became aware of a new sound intruding on the night. Shouts, wails and the jangle of weapons. The sound of an army mobilizing.

'What is happening?'

Angria's voice hissed out of the darkness. Christopher had not heard him come up. He spun about, but Angria was already on him. Without warning, he grabbed Christopher in both hands and swung him around, pushing him out over the edge of the rampart. He teetered there, with only Angria's grip to keep him from falling.

'Is this your doing?' Angria demanded. 'Was this whole stratagem a ruse to divide my forces and leave me open to my enemies?'

'No, lord,' Christopher pleaded. His toes scrabbled to keep their footing on the parapet. He did not dare look to see how far it was to fall. 'I do not even know—'

'The Marathas are coming. While our strength is concentrated in the harbour, they are coming at the walls.'

'I never dreamed they would attack. Our spies saw no sign that their army was preparing an assault by land.'

Angria looked in his eyes. Whatever he saw, it convinced him of Christopher's innocence. He hauled him in and let him slump against the battlements.

'Go to the eastern wall. You will take personal charge of the defence of the gate – and I will give an order that if any man sees you falter in your duty, he should cut you down that instant.'

Christopher ran along the rampart, and climbed the stairs to the top of the north-east tower. He could hardly believe what he saw. The entire promontory had become a sea of men, charging forward, while in their midst strode three mighty elephants. The castle's cannon had already carved bloody holes in the attackers' ranks, but they did not falter. Some of them seemed to be stark naked. Christopher wondered if the Marathas had put prisoners in the front line to soak up cannon fire.

'They are coming for the breach,' he realized.

All the men left in the castle were hurrying to the eastern ramparts. Christopher found one of the gun captains. 'Put two of your cannon at the foot of the breach. Load them with musket balls, grape shot, anything you can find. If our enemies reach the top, you will blast them off it like birds from a tree.'

He knew Tom Courtney must be behind this. He searched the darkness for him, trying to pick out his face in the flashes of muskets and cannons. Would he lead the attack? Or was he cunning enough to let other men die to achieve his ends?

The attackers were now so close that the castle batteries could not touch them. Christopher ordered the gunners to abandon their cannon, and join the marksmen on the walls. A furious storm of lead thundered down from the walls: he could not believe any man could survive it. Yet still they came. Through the smoke, he saw their pale bodies crawling up the slope, sheltering behind blocks of fallen masonry. However many the pirates picked off, more took their place.

He had to break them. 'Slacken your fire,' he said. 'Let them think they have won.'

The order was passed along the walls. The fusillade of musket fire eased off. Christopher raised the Neptune sword so the gunners down in the courtyard could see. The Marathas, sensing their chance, broke from cover and scrambled the few last yards to the top of the breach.

'Now!' bellowed Christopher. He brought down his sword. The guns in the courtyard blasted out a cloud of musket balls and partridge shot, cutting the invaders to ribbons.

The breach was emptied in an instant. The pirates cheered.

Sensing victory, they poured down off the walls to harry their broken opponents.

'Wait,' Christopher cried, but they did not hear him or heed him. Some of them discarded their muskets, drawing their swords for the close work of killing.

They assumed – as Christopher had – that the cannons would break the Marathas' will to fight. Yet as the smoke cleared, Christopher saw that the men further down the slope were not in full retreat. One of them had risen, was urging his men forward even as he clambered towards the breach. Other men came up beside him: some with pikes and axes, one with a huge mace which he wielded like some medieval knight.

The pirates were not expecting resistance. In their eagerness, they had left themselves exposed. Now the Marathas took advantage. They cut the pirates' legs from under them so they slipped down the loose stones. Those who had lost their weapons picked up pieces of rubble and dashed out their enemies' brains. The pirates fell back in confusion.

For the second time, the invaders gained the top of the breach. Again, Christopher waited for them to be torn apart by the cannons. But this time, the guns were empty: the gunners had been drawn into the fray and had not reloaded.

Christopher cursed. In the middle of the breach, sword raised in triumph, he saw a figure he knew must be Tom Courtney. He seized a firelock from the rampart and trained it on Tom's chest. Smoke drifted across the gap, obscuring his shot. When it cleared, Tom had gone.

He threw down the weapon in fury. All his plans were in disarray. He knew how the pirates fought. When they had the upper hand, they were invincible – but when the tide turned they lost all discipline. There would be no last ditch defence. Already, he could see the defenders fleeing across the courtyard, pursued by the Marathas who poured unhindered through the breach. The castle was lost.

A wave of loss and fury smote him. Tom Courtney had done this. Now, and at Brinjoan, and at every turn of his life from the very moment he was conceived, Tom Courtney had snatched away everything Christopher had ever wanted. He was his nemesis – his own natural father!

But even in defeat, he could make Tom's victory turn to ashes. He ran along the walls and let himself through the door into the keep.

The rapine had started even ahead of the invaders. In defeat, the pirates turned on each other: every man for himself, each taking what he could in hopes he might escape. They scoured the store rooms, and plundered anything they could carry.

Christopher glided through the chaos with relentless purpose. One or two of the pirates saw the sword in his hand and were tempted to take it, but they thought better of it when they saw the look on his face. The others were too busy looting to notice him.

The chaos faded behind him as he descended into the bowels of the castle. He quickened his pace – then stopped. He could hear footsteps approaching, not from above but from below. He pressed himself into an alcove, deeply shadowed and waited.

A dozen men ran past. Marathas, judging by their garb, led by an English sailor. For a second Christopher wondered if it was Tom – perhaps he had not been on the walls after all. Christopher's hand tightened on the hilt of the sword. He could have taken off the sailor's head simply by stretching out his arm.

'This way,' said the man, and Christopher relaxed. It was not Tom. He let them go, listening as their steps died away up towards the battle.

He continued down – to a small chamber where the path forked. But now he heard more footsteps coming, and here there was nowhere to hide. He raised his guard.

But these were men he knew. As they came into the lamp-light, he saw they were Angria's men, pirates he had sent to the ambush in the harbour.

They had not expected to find him there. 'Where are the hat-wearers?' they demanded. 'We followed them in through the sea gate when they tried to escape.'

'The castle has fallen,' Christopher told them brusquely. 'Our enemies are inside the walls.' He indicated two of the men. 'You and you, wait for me here. You others, go back to the water gate and prepare a boat for my escape. I will join you shortly.'

He hurried down the left-hand stair to the dungeon. He noted the open gate at the bottom, and paused. He could hear screams, the sound of a woman in immense pain. Had some of the pirates already come here to take their pleasure? But no: the screams were too regular. In between, he heard the murmur of soft, reassuring voices – a man and a woman's.

He unwound the *urumi* from his waist. Coiling it in his hand, he advanced stealthily down the passage until he reached that part of the cave from where the noises emanated. He peered around the corner.

A man and a woman knelt beside a second woman, who was crouched, naked, on all fours, gasping and moaning. None of them had seen Christopher arrive. He smiled. This would be his parting shot – his gift to Tom Courtney.

'Is the bitch going to whelp her pup?' he called.

The man turned, saw Christopher and sprang up. Exactly as Christopher had anticipated. The *urumi* blade hissed through the air and sliced open his leg. He dropped with a cry, rolling away in agony and clutching the wound. He tried to stand, but the leg gave way.

'Francis,' Agnes cried.

'Francis?' Christopher repeated. He had been about to run the boy through with the Neptune sword. Now he paused, hardly believing his luck. 'Francis Courtney?'

Francis spat a gob of blood from his mouth and nodded.

'I will enjoy making you watch what I do to your family.'

* * *

404

Tom leaped down the back slope of the breach, jumping across the lumps of rubble that had once been the castle wall. His sword was raised, but he hardly needed to use it. The defenders melted away in front of him, while behind him the Maratha army flooded in over the breach. The *ghosia* warriors were in an ecstasy of killing. They fought with the ferocity of demons, naked and wild. Those with weapons hacked their enemies to pieces; others simply tore them apart with their bare hands.

And somewhere in the carnage were Agnes and Sarah. Tom forced his way through the courtyard, Mohite beside him. A few pirates still fought on, pockets of resistance cut off from any escape. He avoided them, and made for the keep.

'Where do you suppose they keep their prisoners?' he shouted to Mohite.

Mohite shrugged. With a sudden burst of speed, he ran forward and grabbed one of the fleeing pirates by the shoulders. With a deft swipe of his foot, he dropped the man to the floor, pinned him down and put his knife to the man's throat. He shouted something in an Indian dialect.

The pirate stared at him, baffled, and then jabbered a reply. Mohite let him go and stood.

'The dungeon is in the caves beneath the castle. There is a stair in the north-east corner of the keep.'

They did not have to fight their way in. The mass of fleeing defenders swept them there effortlessly. No one paid them any attention. The pirates had lost all thought of fighting; they had turned to plunder, and Tom had nothing they wanted. At the foot of the tower, a stair dropped into the rock of the castle's foundations. Tom hurried down.

His hopes rose as they descended. The stairs felt unending, but none of the pirates, or the invaders, seemed to have reached these depths of the castle.

'We may yet be in time,' he said to Mohite.

But he had spoken too soon. They had come to the bottom of a flight of steps, into a small guard chamber where the passage divided. Looking ahead, wondering which stair to take, he did not see the two men in the shadows. They had heard Tom and Mohite coming, and hidden themselves either side of the door. As soon as Tom and Mohite were in the room, they lunged for them with their heavy, curved swords.

Whether it was some sound they made, or a disturbance in the air, or pure instinct, Tom sensed the attack coming a moment before it struck. He had no time to defend himself. He simply dropped to the floor, pulling Mohite down with him. The outstretched blades flew over their heads; the pirates, meeting no resistance, stumbled forward and collided with the men on the floor. Tom and Mohite threw them off, and dispatched them with two efficient blows.

Tom stared between the two doors, looking for any sign. *Which way?*

'You follow the right stair. I will search the left,' Tom decided.

They split up. Tom raced down the stairs, feeling the weight of every second that passed. Where had those two men in the guard chamber come from? Were there others? In the bitter frenzy of defeat, what might they have done to Sarah and Agnes?

An iron gate barred the bottom of the stairs. This must be the dungeon. Tom wondered if he should call Mohite back, but that would take precious time – and the gate was already open. From deeper in the caves, he heard a woman's scream, then a man's cry. All his fears rushed back at him. Abandoning caution, he ran along the passage until it opened into a wider chamber.

He took in the sight at a single glance. His wildest hopes, and his deepest fears, all made real at once. Sarah: naked, screaming, and covered in blood; Agnes, cowering back; Francis, lying against the wall clutching a deep wound in his leg. And standing over them all, with the Neptune sword in one hand

and the long, whip-blade in the other, the man who had betrayed them.

He had his back to Tom – but Agnes did not, and she could not hide the hope that flared in her eyes when she glimpsed his arrival. Before Tom could move, Christopher saw her reaction and turned, a ghastly grin spreading across his face.

'Tom Courtney,' he said in English. 'I had so hoped you would come to see this.'

Fury seized Tom. He hurled the sword like a javelin – the way he had once thrown the Neptune sword at Black Billy and pierced him through the heart. But the Maratha blade was heavier, lacking balance. The point dipped from its target; Christopher swatted it away with the hilt of the *urumi* and it clattered to the floor.

Now Tom was defenceless. Christopher advanced. The *urumi* blade slithered after him, rasping across the stones. The only other sound was Sarah, moaning.

'I can use this weapon like an artist with a paintbrush,' Christopher boasted. 'I will sever your limbs one by one, and when you are helpless I will make you watch as I butcher your wife and dash out your child's brains.'

Tom stared at him uncomprehendingly. 'Why? What have I ever done to you?'

'Do you not know? Can you not guess?' Christopher took another step forward. He pointed back to Sarah, on her knees with her hands pressed against the wall. The baby's head was starting to appear between her legs. Christopher saw the stricken look on Tom's face and laughed.

'There is nothing you would not do for that child, is there? You came to this impregnable castle and you tore down its walls simply to rescue it. So noble. So *heroic*.'

Still Tom did not understand.

'But you were not always so loyal. *Were you?*' He spat out the words. 'When you debauched my mother and fathered your

407

bastard, you could not be away fast enough. You abandoned me, and left your brother to cover my mother's shame.'

Christopher saw understanding dawn in Tom's face, horror and shame and fear for what he had done. In that moment, he knew everything Lydia had told him was true. He tensed his arm to swing the *urumi*, planning where the blow would fall. First, he would lick it around Tom's thigh and slice his hamstring. Then he could act at leisure.

'Who are you?' said Tom. His mouth had gone dry; the words came out as a whisper.

Christopher's eyes met his – the same eyes, like looking into a mirror.

'I am your son.'

He swung the *urumi*.

But something held him back. The *urumi* did not move. Francis had crawled forward and grabbed its tip, holding on with all his strength. His face was white. Blood spilled from between his fingers where they gripped the razor-sharp blade. But he did not release it.

With a cry of anger, Christopher let go the *urumi* and drew the Neptune sword. Perhaps that was best. He would finish Tom with the Courtney blade, and secure his rightful inheritance forever.

But in the time that Francis had distracted him, Agnes had sprung up. She ran to where Tom's sword had fallen and threw it to him. Christopher saw her: he swung at her with the Neptune sword, but she rolled away to the edge of the cave. Before he could strike again, Tom lunged forward. A hard stroke, heavy with pent-up rage; Christopher only just managed to parry it.

If he could get to Sarah, put the sword at her throat, Tom would be forced to surrender. But Francis had seen that danger. He picked himself off the floor and flung himself forward, putting himself between Christopher and Sarah.

Christopher could have disembowelled him with a flick of the sword. But that would have meant turning his back to Tom – and Tom was coming at him again. Their blades rang as he blocked Tom's attempt to get inside his guard.

Christopher was outnumbered. He launched a quick riposte, a flurry of well-practised strokes that drove Tom back, wheeling him around. Christopher still burned for revenge, but other dangers had begun to intrude. The castle had fallen – soon other men would find their way down here. He had to escape.

He had worked Tom around closer to Sarah. Now nothing stood between Christopher and the door. He went at Tom again: a series of precise, well-practised moves straight from the fencing manual. As he had predicted, Tom blocked them automatically – but as he readied himself for the final lunge, Christopher suddenly sprang back. Before Tom could react, Christopher spun on his heel and fled. Tom heard his footsteps disappear up the stairs.

Sarah cried out, a deep groan that rose to a powerful shriek. Tom ran to her.

With a belch of blood and fluid, the baby came out of her into Agnes' waiting hands.

'You have a son.'

The face was screwed up like an old man's, the eyes tight shut, the umbilical cord still connecting him with his mother. His skin was alarmingly blue.

'Is he . . . alive?' A hurricane of emotions wrenched Tom so hard he felt sick. A minute ago, he had been fighting for his life against a devil he had created; now he was reunited with Sarah, and a father as well. His thoughts pulled in so many directions he thought they must tear him apart.

Agnes gave the child a firm slap on the back. The baby coughed and spluttered. It half opened its eyes and fixed Tom with a drowsy, confused stare.

'Take him,' Agnes encouraged Tom. 'He is yours.'

She placed the babe in Tom's arms, though he hardly dared to hold it. The child was so tiny, he could barely feel the weight. Yet the moment Tom touched his son, he felt such a wave of love and responsibility as he had never felt before. Tears pricked his eyes. The storm of emotions that had roiled him died away, hushed in an instant by the serene peace in those innocent eyes.

But his work was not done. Quickly, he handed the baby into Sarah's waiting arms.

'Go,' said Sarah. The pain had left her all in an instant. She sat up, leaning against the wall, cradling the baby to her breast. Her hair was lank, her face covered in sweat and her legs smeared with blood. She was utterly naked, with the umbilical cord still snaking out of her. Yet she glowed with a light Tom had not seen before, an inner certainty as if some new part of her had come into being. Tom did not think he had ever seen her more beautiful.

'My place is with you and the baby,' Tom protested.

'We are safe,' said Sarah. 'But that monster still has the sword – and he would have killed us all with it. You, me – and *him*.' She hugged the baby tighter. It nuzzled her breast, its tiny lips searching for the nipple.

Someone was coming down the passage. Tom turned. He did not think Christopher would dare return, but there were many others in the castle. In the frenzy of pillage and destruction, every man was a possible enemy.

He relaxed as he saw Mohite round the corner, at the head of four men.

'We chased the pirates down to the water,' the *hubladar* reported. 'As we were returning, we met another on the stairs, but he ran away.' He frowned. 'I think it was the man who betrayed us. He carried the great golden sword.'

'Thank you.' Tom touched his shoulder. 'Wait here, and see that nothing happens to my . . .' He stumbled on his words as he saw the baby again, now contentedly sucking at Sarah's breast. 'My family.'

'Shall I send one of my men with you?'

Tom shook his head. 'I will do this alone.'

He ran back up to the castle keep. Automatically, he listened for men ahead, keeping the sword ready – but the greater part of his mind was occupied with a single thought: the baby, so small and helpless, like a feather in his arms.

I am a father.

You were a father before, the cruel voice in his head reminded him. He could hardly credit that the monster in the cave was his son. When he thought of what Christopher had intended to do to Sarah, to Agnes and the baby, his soul rebelled.

My father gave me no choice. When Hal Courtney discovered Tom's liaison with Caroline, and the hatred it had bred between Tom and Guy, he had taken Guy and Caroline off his ship immediately. He had arranged for them to take passage to Bombay, and arranged a position for Guy as secretary to Caroline's father. None of them had realized then that Caroline was pregnant; Tom had not even been allowed to say farewell.

Tom did not know it, but his father had deliberately kept it from him. When Caroline's father wrote to Hal to inform him of the child, he had torn up the letter and thrown it out of his cabin windows. He had only told Tom much later, when Dorian was lost and they were sailing back to England.

I should have married Caroline myself. But even as he thought it, he did not believe it. Then he would never have had the chance to marry Sarah. Probably, he would never have found Dorian. And now he would not have the son Sarah had given him.

Look at Francis, he told himself. Born of Black Billy's seed, raised by a wastrel stepfather: he had suffered every disadvantage, yet he was a true Courtney, willing to die for his family.

411

It was not birth that made a man. It was what he made of himself.

'Mr Courtney?'

Tom had reached the upper levels. He turned to the familiar voice, and saw Merridew standing in the tower doorway.

'Thank God you are alive,' he said. 'But how—?'

'Master Francis sent us up to open the gate. By the time we got there, you'd done the job for us. We looked for you and couldn't find you, so we was going back down to find Master Francis.'

'Go to him.' Mohite was with Sarah and the others, but Tom would feel happier with more men there to protect them. Then a thought struck him. 'Have you seen a man carrying a gilded sword come this way?'

Merridew shook his head. Tom glanced to the steps that spiralled up into the north-east tower of the keep. 'He must have gone up.'

He followed the stairs, twisting around in a tight climb. Narrow slit windows pierced the walls, and through them he caught glimpses down into the courtyard. Day was coming, and the battle was over. Shahuji's forces had opened the gates and begun to restore order. He saw the rajah mounted on one of the elephants, barking orders as his men rounded up prisoners. After the din of battle, all was eerily quiet in the blue, pre-dawn light.

He reached a door in the wall of the stairwell and paused, listening. He heard voices on the far side, a man and a woman's, talking urgently.

He kicked open the door and leaped in. The woman screamed and clutched her gown to her chest. She was naked, apparently in the act of dressing. Despite the outlandish circumstances, she seemed familiar to Tom; with more time, he might have recalled the name 'Lydia Foy'. But he forgot her in an instant, for standing by the window, strapping on a heavy belt, was Christopher.

412

Tom lunged for him. Lydia screamed. But Christopher, his reflexes schooled in the *kalari*, was faster. He snatched up the Neptune sword and leaped aside, bringing his blade down on Tom's and almost disarming him. Tom sprang back and took his guard.

Christopher feinted forward, then turned and ran for the stairs. He could not go down – if Tom caught him, a single kick might send him tumbling and break his neck. He went up. At the top of the steps, he heaved open the trap door that led on to the roof and climbed through. Before he could close it, Tom had followed him out.

They faced each other on the roof of the tower. Christopher bared his teeth. Tom was blocking the stair – and there was no other way down. This would be a fight to the finish.

'If you wanted to kill me, you should have made sure I was never born,' he spat. A storm raged inside him: conflicting thoughts of Guy's cruelties, his mother's distance, the men he had killed – and, above all else, the man confronting him. He did not know if he wanted to embrace him or run him through.

What is the third precept? asked a voice from his past.

Self control.

He made himself put aside his emotions, to feel nothing but the blade in his hand.

'I do not want to kill you,' said Tom. He meant it. In this high place, with the sun licking the horizon and the dawn breeze singing in his ears, he could feel the world being made afresh for a new day. 'Whatever you have done, if you are truly my son, I can forgive you.'

'Forgive me?' Christopher repeated in disbelief. 'You should be on your knees, begging *my* forgiveness. This is your doing. If you had not abandoned my mother . . .'

Emotion threatened him again; he forced it back.

'I did not even know Caroline was with child,' Tom protested.

413

'Because you did not care.' Christopher came at him with a flurry of sharp blows, driving Tom back towards the edge of the tower. 'You dipped your wick, and then you cast her aside, like a common dockside whore. *My mother!*'

'I had no choice.' Tom parried Christopher's strokes, every movement hindered by the ungainly weapon he was forced to use. Against it, the Neptune sword danced through the air.

'I am sorry,' Tom said, and he meant it from the bottom of his soul. From this high vantage, he could look out over the ocean and see how the threads of their lives had unspooled over decades, the myriad choices, chances and lies that had led them to this place. Surely, if fate had brought them together now, it was to a purpose.

'Why did you follow me here?' said Christoper. 'Why not let me escape?'

'For the sword,' said Tom, honestly.

Christopher tightened his grip. His face set hard with desire. 'It is mine.'

Tom stared at him. He stared at the gilded blade, and the great sapphire in the pommel gleaming in the sunrise. A perfect weapon. A legacy from his father, the honour of the Courtneys.

But what was a sword, against the love of his son?

'Keep it,' he said. 'If we can be reconciled, you are welcome to it.'

Christopher smiled. Tom felt a wave of relief and affection flood through him. Whatever Christopher had done, whatever evils had driven him to this point – Tom would find a way to forgive him.

He spread his arms wide. 'My son.'

'Father.'

Christopher let Tom take two paces towards him. Then he raised the sword and lunged.

That near to the roof edge, Tom had no room to retreat. But he was not entirely unprepared. He might have forgiven

Christopher, but he did not trust him. He had seen the malevolent light in Christopher's eyes, the twitch of the sword a second before it came up. He sidestepped the stroke, brought up his guard and parried the sword away to his right. The two weapons rang together, very loud in the quiet at the top of the tower. Christopher swept his sword back into position and attacked again. The blades clashed and locked together. Tom and Christopher pushed against each other, a pure trial of strength, neither able to disengage for fear of letting the other past his guard.

Suddenly, Christopher leaped back, hoping to unbalance Tom. Tom stumbled forward, and almost caught his foot on the trap door. He side-stepped the opening, staggered on and almost went over the edge of the tower. Christopher aimed a kick at him, but Tom's momentum took him out of range. He dropped to the ground, rolled to the side and sprang back onto his feet – just in time to defend himself against Christopher's next attack, a low thrust that almost caught his thigh.

The two men circled each other around the open hatch. Christopher attacked, Tom parried, but there was no heat in the exchanges. They were sparring, each waiting for the next real chance.

Or perhaps Christopher had another plan. He was twenty, and had barely fought at all that night; Tom was nearer to forty, and had been in the thick of battle for hours. The more Christopher slowed the engagement, letting him relax, the more the fire that sustained him cooled in his veins. Tom could feel his strength fading.

The realization made him angry. He launched another attack with renewed urgency, gripping the sword two-handed, forcing the energy back into his limbs as he hacked and chopped at Christopher.

But though his will was strong, his body was slow to obey. The harder he tried, the more clumsily his strokes landed. He was tiring. His breath came hard and ragged. Christopher pirouetted away from a lunge, knocked him back and gave a triumphant smile. He was letting Tom wear himself out. Then, like a cobra, he would strike.

But time was against Christopher. Down through the trap door, Tom heard shouts on the tower stairs. English voices – Francis, or Merridew, come to find him.

'Enough of this madness,' Tom called. 'You cannot win.'

Christopher gave him a look of pure malevolence. 'Perhaps. But I may yet have my revenge.'

'What will that gain you?'

Christopher stared at him with blank incomprehension. Then, with a roar of rage, he lunged – straight at Tom's heart. Tom brought down his sword, trying to deflect the stroke – but Christopher had moved so fast he was already inside Tom's guard.

The Neptune sword pierced Tom's left shoulder. At the same time, Tom's blow struck home. Not on Christopher's blade, where he had aimed it, but on the wrist of the hand that held it. The heavy sword, with the full power of Tom's shoulders behind it, cut through the sinews and the flesh, jointed the bones and came cleanly out the other side.

Christopher screamed. The Neptune sword clattered to the ground, with Christopher's hand still clasping it. Blood spewed from the severed stub of his forearm. Christopher stepped back, pressing his arm into his stomach in an attempt to staunch the bleeding.

Tom bled too, from his shoulder, but he knew the wound was not deep. He put one foot on the Neptune sword, lest even now Christopher try to reclaim it.

'It is over,' he said.

Christopher stood on the edge of the tower. The height made him dizzy; loss of blood made him faint. Far below, he saw the green sea surging around the rocks.

'Farewell, Father.'

At the last moment, Tom saw what he intended. He reached out to grab him, heedless of his own safety. But he was too late. Christopher stepped out of reach, into the air, and fell. Looking down, Tom saw him drop for what seemed an eternity, until he vanished into the water with the merest splash of white.

Tom stared down at the sea, waiting to see if Christopher would emerge. Could he have survived a fall from such a height? Or were there rocks below the surface that would have smashed his body to pulp?

He shuddered at the thought. The heat of battle had chilled in his veins. He felt no victory – only an enormous sense of loss.

My own son, he thought, *and I could not save you. Just as I could not save Billy.*

From the corner of his eye, he saw the gleam of the Neptune sword lying on the ground, with Christopher's lifeless fingers still wrapped around the hilt. Tom prised them off one by one, amazed how even in death the sinews fought him. The dead flesh made him want to vomit, a physical rebuke for what he had done. With a stab of revulsion, he hurled it off the edge of the tower.

He looked at the sword, gleaming in the morning, and almost threw it into the sea after Christopher. The glimmering sapphire seemed to mock him. Was it worth a man's life? His *son's* life?

But a new day had dawned, and a new life had begun. Looking out at the horizon, Tom remembered words he had once spoken with Sarah. 'What makes a man?' he had wondered, and Sarah had replied: 'From whatever he is made and whatever he learns, he will be his own man. And all you can do, Tom Courtney, is help him to find the right path to follow.'

Christopher had chosen his path, just as Billy had so many years ago. A family was a living, untamed thing, and like all living things it could turn on itself with savage ferocity. All Tom had done was protect himself.

He took the sword, and went down to his family.

Sarah and Agnes were still in the dungeon. They were free, after so many months of captivity, but Agnes did not think it safe to move Sarah lest it bring on more bleeding. Tom was anxious to find them fresh air and clean lodgings, but he saw the wisdom of staying put. Until the last pirates were scoured out of the castle, the dungeon was as safe a place as any.

Ana had joined them, unable to stay in Shahuji's camp a moment longer after the battle was won. She had brought food, bound up Francis' wounds, and given Sarah a salve to help heal her. Now she and Francis sat together, arms around each other, gazing in wonder at the child. From the looks on their faces, the strength of their embrace, Tom guessed it would not be long before he became a great uncle.

Oblivious to the life and death around him, the baby slept, still connected by his umbilical cord to the bloody mass of the afterbirth lying on the ground beside Agnes.

'Should we cut it?' Tom asked, uncertainly.

'We were waiting for you,' said Agnes.

Tom's hand went to the Neptune sword on his belt. It felt almost like sacrilege to use that noble blade in the business of childbirth – and to bring a lethal weapon so close to an innocent babe.

But the child was Tom's heir. The sword was the legacy of the Courtneys, and one day the tiny infant would grow up to wield it himself. Tom wiped the Neptune blade until the gilded steel shone flawlessly. Agnes took the slimy cord in both hands, and indicated where he should cut. The sharp edge sliced through it. Tom tied off the end, and kissed the baby on the forehead. What did his future hold? What sort of a man would he grow up to be?

All you can do is help him to find the right path to follow.

'What shall we call him?' he asked.

Sarah looked at Agnes, her sister who had nursed her so tenderly through her long, terrible pregnancy, unflinching and uncomplaining despite all the sorrows she had suffered herself.

'His name is James,' she said. 'In memory of Captain Hicks.'

Tears sprang in Agnes' eyes. Sarah leaned forward, to allow her sister a moment's privacy. She looked at the baby, with the umbilical stump still protruding from his tiny belly.

'Tom Courtney,' she said sleepily. 'Did you tie your son's cord with a rigging knot?'

The sentry at Bombay castle did not recognize the man who approached the gate. With his bald head, skin tanned deep brown, he might have been a high-caste Parsee, one of the agents who flocked to the Company's trade. But he was dressed as a European, with a ruby red coat of fine cloth, and white breeches that gleamed brilliant in the noon sun. One hand seemed to be drawn up inside the sleeve of his shirt; the other was clenched in a fist.

'His excellency the Governor is not receiving visitors,' the sentry warned.

'I have not come to see the Governor. I am here to visit my *father.*'

The sentry gaped. His face went pale. 'Master Christopher?'

'*Mister* Courtney.'

The sentry fumbled with the lock. 'Of course, sir. Only we thought . . .'

'You were wrong.'

Christopher was almost unrecognizable from the callow youth who had left the fortress almost two years earlier – let alone the battered, broken man who had dragged himself one-handed out of Tiracola bay. He strode across the courtyard and mounted the steps of the Governor's house with such confidence, the guard at the door only belatedly thought to challenge him. Ignoring him, and the shouts that followed, Christopher climbed the stairs to the top floor.

'Christopher Courtney,' he shouted to the uniformed guard outside Guy's office. 'Let me in to see my father, damn you, or I will have you tied to the triangle and flogged on the parade ground.'

The door opened. Christopher went through, into the airy space of Guy's office. Paint gleamed on the frames of freshly installed windows; the portrait of Sir Hal Courtney hung slightly askew, and there seemed to be a powder mark on the wainscoting where a pistol had been fired too close to it.

Guy, hearing the noise from the corridor, had started to rise from his chair. He stared at Christopher open-mouthed. Ink dribbled unheeded from his pen and pooled on the correspondence book lying open before him.

'Can it be . . . ?' he murmured to himself.

He collected himself. His jaw went firm and his eyes hardened. He gave a cold smile.

'The prodigal son returns. Hah! I suppose at least your mother will be pleased.'

Christopher nodded.

'Well?' barked Guy. 'What did you come back for? Expect me to kill the fatted calf, do you?'

'I do not need it. I am a rich man now.'

Chistopher opened his fist, showing a handful of bright, sparkling diamonds. Guy glanced at them and snorted.

'D'you mean to impress me with those gewgaws? You think you are rich? You do not know the meaning of wealth.'

'I am rich enough to marry Ruth.'

'Who?'

'Ruth. Corporal Reedy's daughter.'

Even then, it took a moment for Guy to understand. Then he tipped his head back, and laughed so heartily that the window panes shivered in their frames. 'Ruth Reedy? All this time, and you still remember that little trollop?'

'I am going to marry her.'

'I very much doubt it.'

Christopher rattled the diamonds in his hand like dice. 'I am a wealthy man, now. You cannot stop me.'

'I would not dream of stopping you,' said Guy ebulliently. 'You have my blessing. Only—' He broke off into laughter again. 'Your sweetheart is already married.'

Christopher felt as if the floor had dropped from under him. 'What?'

'She married not long after you ran off. A stevedore from the docks. She has a child now, too. I believe they are very happy. Though . . .' He pointed to the diamonds in Christopher's palm. 'She may regret her haste when she hears what she has lost.'

Christopher gazed at him in disbelief. This must be wrong. It was a lie, a cruel joke made purely from spite. Ruth would never have played him false.

But Guy's mirth was too real. Christopher looked into his father's eyes, and saw nothing but a cold, plain truth. Guy had won again.

In a fury, he hurled the diamonds across the room. They bounced and scattered off the walls, skittering across the polished floor into the farthest corners of the room. Even before they had come to rest, Christopher was making for the door. He could not breathe. He could not think. This moment of triumph he had anticipated so long, dashed from him once more by his father.

'Wait.'

For all Christopher had grown, Guy's command cut through the years and stopped him as surely as when he had been a boy. He turned. Guy had come out from around his desk and crossed the room towards him. They stood at arm's length, breathing hard, facing each other like a pair of boxers.

'I know you were fond of the girl,' said Guy. For once, he

421

seemed to be trying to make himself agreeable. 'But do not let her come between us again. You have sown your wild oats, and doubtless suffered a few scrapes along the way. Now come back to your family, where you belong.'

'I did not return to be some bluecoat boy, fetching and carrying. I am better than that.'

Guy studied him, and saw something that had not been there before: something adamant and fierce.

'Perhaps you are,' he mused. 'And I will give you the chance to prove it. I have received disquieting news that the Governor of Madras may not be entirely reliable – that he may have helped one of my gravest enemies. You might be the man to take his place.'

Christopher swallowed. The governorship of one of the Company's three great Presidencies would be an unprecedented honour for a man his age – a tremendous act of faith on Guy's part. Yet, he knew, it would irrevocably put him in Guy's debt. Everything he had sought to avoid.

'Can I rely on you?' said Guy.

The question hung between them. Christopher met his eyes, and thought of all the things he could say. *I know why you treated me as you did. I know why you cannot love me. I tried to avenge the hurt your brother did you.* Under his shirt cuff, the stump of his right arm throbbed with the memory.

Guy was still awaiting his answer. His fingers played with the button on his coat; he puffed his cheeks and blew out the air. He was anxious, Christopher realized. It actually mattered to him what Christopher did.

Tears pricked his eyes. He averted his face so Guy would not see. Guy thought he meant to leave. He reached out and grabbed Christopher's sleeve, unbalancing him. Christopher stumbled; the two men collided.

Christopher straightened. Father and son stood face to face, brown eyes and blue eyes inches apart.

'Can I rely on you?' Guy said again.

There were so many things Christopher could say, so many answers he might give, but what did any of them signify?

'Yes, Father,' he said.

He left Guy's office in such a daze that he did not register the woman waiting in the parlour – or notice the way she started at the sight of him. She rose from her cushioned chair and hurried to him, surreptitiously adjusting the neckline of her dress.

'Mr Courtney,' she called.

He squinted at her in surprise. A young woman, with a sharp face and full breasts pressing up out of her stays. For a moment, he did not see her clearly. With her hair tucked demurely under her bonnet, and the long sleeves of her dress hiding the shackle marks on her wrists, she was almost unrecognisable from the shameless lover he had known at Tiracola.

Then with a rush of horror he knew who she was. For the second time that afternoon, the bottom seemed to drop out of his world. She knew his secret. She would tell his father, and all the prospects that had opened in Guy's office would be snatched from him. Most likely, the Company would hang him for having consorted with Angria.

'Are we acquainted?' he said stiffly.

She beamed at him. 'I do not believe we have met – or else, so long ago I am sure you would not remember. My name is Lydia Foy.'

Christopher waited. Perhaps she would be willing to let him buy her silence.

'I heard a rumour you had returned to your father,' she said. 'I am certain the whole colony rejoices in your reconciliation.'

He eyed her warily. *What did she want?* He touched his coat, feeling the knife he kept tucked inside.

'Perhaps we should continue this discussion somewhere more private.'

'I am sure that will not be necessary,' she said. 'Neither of us has anything to hide. We are two respectable English people, are we not?'

He marvelled that she could speak with such serene innocence, giving not the least hint of their history together. *What was her game?*

'I heard you were captured by pirates,' he tried cautiously.

'I was freed.'

'It must have been a terrible ordeal.'

Her face darkened. 'Frightful. Although . . .' She gave a knowing smile. 'Not without its *excitements*. But I am sure you would agree that we should not dwell on what is past – not when the future holds such promise.'

Their eyes met – and a spark of understanding passed between them. Lydia reached forward and stroked his cheek.

'I do hope we shall soon become better acquainted.'

A hundred miles to the south, Tom stood on the quarterdeck of his new command and took in her unfamiliar lines. She was one of Angria's fleet, a *grab* that had survived Francis' night attack. Shahuji had given her to Tom, along with a crew of fishermen and Maratha volunteers, seasoned with the last survivors of the *Kestrel*'s crew. Merridew, promoted to Sailing Master, had declared himself satisfied.

'They'll get us to Cape Town,' he said. 'And wherever you choose to go after that.'

Above the bay, Shahuji's banner fluttered from the keep, announcing his victory to all passing ships. It had taken his men a week to root out all the treasure secreted about the castle, and some of it was still being loaded onto ox trains to be carried back to the palace at Satara. A goodly portion lay in the hold of Tom's ship, for Shahuji had been extravagant in his gratitude.

'It seems we have turned this voyage to our profit after all, Uncle,' said Francis, arm in arm with Ana.

'More than a profit,' answered Tom. He stared down at the infant in Sarah's arms, filled with such pride and love as he had never known. 'What we have found is . . . priceless.'

'You are sure we cannot persuade you to stay?' asked Francis.

He and Ana had chosen to remain in India, to rebuild Ana's family's business as factors. They meant to make their home in Cochin, a Dutch settlement where the English East India Company had little business. Mohite would go with them.

'Gather a good cargo for us,' Tom encouraged him. 'We will return after the next monsoon.'

'As long as you steer well away from the pirates.'

It was a real risk. Somehow, Angria had managed to escape the devastation of Tiracola. He had other forts and other ships; some day, he would no doubt venture out again to terrorize the Malabar coast. But for now, Tom hoped, he would remain ashore to lick his wounds.

'Will you make for the Laquedivas islands?' asked Ana. She looked well, her cheeks plump and her eyes bright. 'She has been letting out the waists of her dresses,' Sarah had confided to Tom two nights earlier. 'I think by the time we return young baby James may have a cousin to play with.' Tom thought he could already see the bump swelling in her belly.

'It is too late for that plan,' said Tom. 'We were supposed to rendezvous a year ago. Dorian will not have waited for us. We will sail for Cape Town, and hope to find him there.'

'God speed, Uncle,' said Francis. 'And thank you – for all you have done.'

Tom tousled his hair. 'A Courtney makes his own destiny.'

They all embraced, and said their farewells, and then embraced again. A boat took Francis and Ana ashore, while the *grab* weighed anchor and nosed out to sea. Tom watched approvingly as the new topmen raced aloft to set the sails. They had the makings of a fine crew.

Sarah came up beside him and linked her arm in his.

'I know what you are thinking, Tom Courtney.'

'What is that?'

'You are wondering where you might take this ship and her crew, and what profit you might turn, once we have recovered from this voyage.'

Tom shook his head. 'When we have disposed of our cargo, and settled our debts, we should still have a tidy sum remaining. I thought we might buy land in Cape Town, build a house for our family.'

'You were not meant to stay ashore,' said Sarah. 'After a few months, you would feel the call of the sea again.'

Tom thought of the baby, now asleep in the cot in their cabin, next to the hook where the Neptune sword hung. 'I believe things will be different, now.'

Sarah smiled, and nestled her head against his chest. They stood together at the rail, arm in arm, perfectly content. A rosy sunset spread across the western horizon. The ship sailed into it, while behind them the Malabar coast and the great continent of India receded into the gathering darkness. Tom thought of everything that had happened to them since they were thrown up on its shore so many months ago.

'I wonder if Dorian has had such adventures as we have,' he mused.

Sarah kissed his cheek. 'I am sure it will make quite a tale.'